Praise for Meg Benjamin's
Brand New Me

"Not only is this a well-written romance (which Benjamin always does), but the characters are hysterical... The plot twists and evil schemes will have the reader guessing all the way to the end."

~ *Romantic Times Book Reviews*

"Welcome back to Konigsburg, Texas. Won't you stay awhile? Catch up with familiar faces, and meet some new ones...If you enjoy a fiercely independent heroine who finally chooses her own destiny, a hero who would do anything for her, a small town full of unforgettable people, then plan your visit to Konigsburg. When you leave, you'll be smiling."

~ *Long and Short Reviews*

"This return to Konigsburg will have fans old and new cheering."

~ *Romantic Times On-Line Reviews*

"...this book was an engrossing read that just goes to show that even in the worst of situations, a woman can land the man of her dreams."

~ *The Romance Studio*

Look for these titles by
Meg Benjamin

Now Available:

Brand New Me

Meg Benjamin

To Mary Jo —
Hope you enjoy Tom + Deirdre
Meg Benjamin

SAMHAIN
PUBLISHING

Samhain Publishing, Ltd.
11821 Mason Montgomery Road, 4B
Cincinnati, OH 45249
www.samhainpublishing.com

Brand New Me
Copyright © 2011 by Meg Benjamin
Print ISBN: 978-1-60928-315-5
Digital ISBN: 978-1-60928-307-0

Editing by Lindsey Faber
Cover by Natalie Winters

First Samhain Publishing, Ltd. electronic publication: December 2010
First Samhain Publishing, Ltd. print publication: November 2011

Dedication

As usual, to my family, Bill, Josh and Molly, and Ben, as well as my terrific, supportive editor, Lindsey Faber. And to the legendary Texas singer/songwriter Steve Earle, whose wonderful song "Tom Ames' Prayer" is the source of my hero's name.

Chapter One

Tom Ames could never figure out the attraction of the Dew Drop Inn. It was dark. It was dirty. The beer on tap tasted like dishwater and the bottled stuff was overpriced. The barmaids looked like they ought to be performing community service, and they acted like they were.

Tom took a sip of his draft, holding back his grimace with an effort. Ingstrom, the owner, was watching him from the bar. No doubt he wondered why the owner of the Faro Tavern was in his place at five on a weekday. Maybe he thought Tom was trying to steal his trade secrets. Tom wondered briefly what trade secrets Ingstrom could lay claim to, besides the flattest beer he'd ever tasted.

The Faro, his bar, had this place beat by a mile. The draft beer was cold, and the bottled stuff included all the regulars plus some microbrews. The barmaids, if not exactly Hollywood material, were still better looking and better tempered than the two women working the bar at the Dew Drop. Now if Tom could only convince the citizens of Konigsburg, Texas, of those facts, maybe he could start doing the kind of business he wanted to do.

Not that the Faro was doing badly, particularly on the weekends when they had music in the beer garden outside. Tom was more than satisfied with the Faro's take. But the customers were still mostly tourists, out-of-towners. They were drawing young professionals from Austin and the weekend music fans from San Antonio. He wished he had more Konigsburgers drinking in the evening. Sooner or later the tourists always went home. The Konigsburgers stuck around.

Of course, the Konigsburgers all remembered what the Faro

had been like before Tom took over. The weekly fights. The scary customers who were more interested in doing some black market deals in the back than sipping cold beer out front. And they all remembered good ol' Kip Berenger, former owner and all-around shady character, now long gone.

Tom surveyed the customers at the Dew Drop, most of whom were locals. Of course, none of the tourists would put up with the place. But the Dew Drop had longevity. It had been around a lot longer than the Faro, or at least the Faro in its most recent incarnation. God only knew who the customers had been when the Faro had been a barbeque joint back in the eighties. Sometimes he thought the place still had a lingering mesquite smoke musk from that period. However, what little repute the place might have had once had gone missing when Berenger had taken over.

Arthur Craven, the head of the Konigsburg Merchants Association, sat at a table three or four feet from Tom. He'd joined the association after he bought the Faro, but he'd never been asked to do much. Maybe that was because Craven always stopped off at the Dew Drop on his way home from work. And Ingstrom, the Dew Drop's owner, had been a member of the association longer than Tom had.

The mayor, Horace Rankin, was sitting with his wife in a booth at the side. Rankin was a vet in his normal life, but these days he spent most of his time running the town. The previous mayor was under indictment for fraud, and Horace had a lot of mopping up to do. Drinking a beer at the Dew Drop might make that more palatable, but given the quality of the beer, Tom doubted it. He had a feeling Horace might appreciate some of the IPAs he was getting from Colorado.

The next booth held the Toleffsons, or two of them anyway. Tom squinted in the gloom, trying to identify which of the Toleffson brothers was sitting there tonight, given that they were all the same size—massive—and all had the same dark hair and eyes. He thought the one with his back to him was the County Attorney, Peter, and the other one was maybe the accountant, Lars. Lars Toleffson actually did Tom's books, and he was damn good at it. But in the darkness of the Dew Drop, it was hard to tell who was who.

The third man at the table was the dentist, Steve Kleinschmidt, the one everybody called Wonder, although Tom could never figure out why. He was smirking, as usual. Tom thought it was a miracle nobody had pushed some of Wonder's teeth down his throat by now, given the man's tendency to lethal sarcasm. Maybe that was why he'd gone into the dental business in the first place.

If Tom could only come up with some way to entice the Toleffsons to the Faro, he'd probably be able to siphon off at least some of the Dew Drop's business. Besides the County Attorney and the accountant, another Toleffson was Rankin's partner in the veterinary business and the fourth was the chief of police. Anywhere the Toleffsons congregated would be popular with a significant number of the citizens of Konigsburg. If he could build it, they would come.

Of course, uprooting the Toleffsons from the Dew Drop was the problem. They'd been sitting in that booth ever since the first one had moved to Konigsburg from Iowa. Getting them to change their habits would take something special. Something more than he had to offer at the moment.

Tom sighed. He could probably ask Chico Burnside or Clem Rodriguez for advice. He probably should do that—they were both Konigsburg natives, and they could help him figure out the town. But he knew in his heart he wouldn't. The Faro was his bar, his place. The first place he'd ever really had that was all his. He'd figure out a way to get the Konigsburgers to give it a try, and he'd do it on his own. His bar, his responsibility.

A barmaid approached his table through the gloom. She had on a violently turquoise T-shirt with the Dew Drop's logo, such as it was—a circle with something that was probably supposed to be a drop of liquid in the middle. For some reason it reminded Tom of post-nasal drip. Maybe it was the way the T-shirt stretched across the barmaid's significant rack. A nametag was placed low on the breast nearest his nose. *Ruby*, it said.

Tom did his best not to stare. Ruby's biceps looked almost as significant as her boobs.

"Ya want somethin' else?"

Actually, of course, he did want something else. Anything, as far as that went, instead of the watery beer in front of him. He shook his head. "Nope. Got to get going."

He started to slide out of his booth, but the barmaid didn't budge. If he kept sliding, he'd smash into her, something neither of them would probably enjoy. He dug into his pocket

9

and dropped a limp dollar bill on the table.

The barmaid lifted her upper lip in a sneer, but she moved fractionally to the side to let him out. He headed for the door.

"So long, Ames," Ingstrom called. "Come back any time."

Tom let his lips slide into a sour grin, but he didn't bother to answer. With any luck, he'd be able to stay out of the Dew Drop for most of the foreseeable future.

With any luck.

Big John Brandenburg was having one helluva good day. His technology branch, B-Tech, had landed yet another federal contract, this time writing and administering some software for the GSA. Big John could see years of subcontracts and maintenance work ahead. His energy consortium, KMB, was closing in on a contract to set up a wind-power farm in Eastern Europe. And even the small part of Brandenburg, Inc. that was still part of the oil business was flourishing. Life was good.

He tuned out the droning presentation from the accounting division—he'd already read the report, no need to endure the accountant's monotone—and studied the others at the board table. In particular, one other.

His daughter, Dee-Dee, was taking notes, her forehead puckering slightly as she wrote. As if she really was interested in what the accountant was saying. Oh, she probably had some kind of academic understanding of what was going on—she had that degree from that expensive business school, after all, and her grades had been high enough to get her into some kind of fancy-schmancy business honors association. But, as Big John knew only too well, what you learned in school only went so far. And thus far Dee-Dee hadn't shown she had much going for her as a businesswoman beyond the book learning he'd paid for.

Dee-Dee. His mouth twisted slightly. She'd told him a few weeks ago she didn't want to be called Dee-Dee anymore. He was supposed to call her Deirdre, for god's sake. Okay, it was her name, but hell, half the people she worked with wouldn't be able to pronounce it. Why he'd let Kathleen give her that name he'd never know.

His expression softened as it usually did whenever his thoughts turned to Kathleen. Deirdre looked more like her every day, with her black hair and dark blue eyes. Nobody on the Brandenburg side looked like that. She'd picked up some of the Brandenburg size, but not as much as her cousin Docia, thank the lord. There was something unnatural about women who were six feet tall, like Docia and her mother, Big John's sister Reba.

The accountant droned on, flipping to the next PowerPoint slide. Big John's gaze slid to the man across from Dee-Dee. Now there was somebody who looked just right at six-foot-whatever. Craig Dempsey. Former running back for the Dallas Cowboys, traded to Tampa Bay, injured in his final season, probably a sure thing for the Hall of Fame. He was one of Big John's smartest hires. Good publicity for the company, and somebody who knew the benefits of team play. He was shaping up nicely as a junior exec, and Big John made certain Dempsey was visible whenever Brandenburg, Inc. had something public to do. Dempsey had even had the original idea about the wind farms in Eastern Europe, which had surprised the hell out of Big John. He'd never thought the kid had that much imagination where business was concerned.

Dempsey wasn't watching the presentation—he was watching Dee-Dee. As well he should. He was currently Big John's leading candidate for son-in-law. Not that they'd ever discussed it in so many words, but Big John had seen the two of them together, and Dee-Dee didn't seem exactly averse to the idea. Once Big John managed to get the two of them married, it would take a weight off his mind. There'd be somebody to run Brandenburg, Inc. whenever Big John decided he was ready to retire. He didn't want the company to move out of the family, and he sure as hell couldn't pass it on to Dee-Dee. Nobody would accept a woman running the show, even if her name was Brandenburg. Dempsey would do nicely.

At the podium, the accountant was wrapping up. Dee-Dee flipped another page of the slide printouts, jotting down a note quickly as the last slide flashed onto the screen. Big John glanced at the printouts in front of Dempsey. So far as he could tell, he hadn't turned the pages or written anything. A tiny prickle of doubt edged through Big John's consciousness. He suppressed it ruthlessly. Dempsey had probably already looked at the report, just as Big John had done himself. Why take notes if you already understood the points being made?

Yeah, that was probably it.

The accountant cleared his throat and glanced at Big John expectantly. Hell, he must have asked if he had any questions, and Big John hadn't been listening enough to know.

At the other side of the table, Dee-Dee waved a hand. "Mr. Kaltenburg," she began in her soft voice.

The accountant didn't hear her at first, and then glanced her way with more annoyance than interest. Big John frowned. Dee-Dee might be a female, but she was a Brandenburg female. He cleared his throat and watched a flush spread across the accountant's face.

"Yes, ma'am." He turned toward Dee-Dee.

"I have some questions about your third quarter projections. If you'll go back to slide six..."

Big John sighed inwardly. This meeting had already stretched longer than he'd expected, but he supposed he needed to give Dee-Dee her chance to ask whatever was on her mind. He settled back in his chair.

Her questions took up another twenty minutes. Across from her, Dempsey was tapping his pencil on the table, his eyes glazed. Big John had to work to keep his own eyes open.

"If that's all?" Kaltenburg, the accountant, had an edge to his voice that Big John didn't like. On the other hand, the man probably didn't appreciate being questioned by some little girl, no matter how close she was to the boss.

"Just one more thing..." Dee-Dee began.

"I think that's enough." Big John managed to drown her out. Kaltenburg turned off his computer gratefully, while Dempsey tossed his pencil on the table as he stood.

Big John glanced at Dee-Dee. She still sat at the table, frowning down at her notes. Probably some hurt feelings there. Oh well, he'd apologize later. He picked up his folder as his administrative assistant scrambled to gather up his papers. The girl needed to get a life of her own, something outside the business. The sooner Dempsey got on the stick, the better.

Deirdre stayed in her seat until the boardroom was empty, giving an excellent imitation of someone reading through her notes one more time. In reality, the notes had blurred in front of her eyes long before the last man had stepped through the door.

If she'd had any doubts about what she needed to do, her father's ham-handedness in the meeting had firmed her resolve. She was apparently the only one who'd understood the shaky reasoning behind the accountant's projections, but she was also the only one her father would never listen to.

Because she was Dee-Dee. His little girl—emphasis on *girl*. Who would, apparently, never be allowed to play with the big boys.

She stood, smoothing the skirt of her St. John knit suit. The longer she waited to tell him, the harder it would be. She might as well get it over with now, before she really had anything serious invested in her role here. While he could still replace her easily.

At this point she had precious little invested anywhere. Eight months out of business school, and she still felt like she was spinning her wheels, at least professionally. She'd given it a shot—she really had. But so far, she hadn't made a dent in Brandenburg, Inc. and its solidly male superstructure. Part of it was her father, but part of it was her.

"Face it, Deirdre," she muttered, "you're not cut out for this kind of work."

Oh, she might do the job competently enough—and lord knew she was more competent than a lot of the people around her father, including that screw-off Craig Dempsey. But by now she knew the difference between competence and joy. And at Brandenburg, Inc., joy was definitely lacking, at least for her.

Normally, Deirdre refrained from trading on her relationship with her father at the office. Not that he'd ever noticed, but it made her feel slightly less dependent on him if she went through the same channels as everybody else. Now, however, she walked toward his office door without slowing down for his admin, Alanis, to announce her.

Her father looked up sharply as she opened the door, then let his face relax. "Hi, sweetheart. Sorry about cutting you off back there, but I didn't want the boys dozing off." He gave her a conspiratorial wink. "Bad for the image, you know."

She did know. The "boys" tuned her out, largely because her father did it first. "I've got something I need to discuss with you, Dad."

Her father waved a hand, grimacing. "No more about that

accounting right now. Kaltenburg will get it straightened out."

"No, this isn't about that." She took a breath, drawing her thoughts together. *Center yourself, Deirdre.* "Actually, I'm here to give you my two weeks' notice."

"Your...what?" Her father blinked at her, then let his mouth spread into a wide grin. "Goddamn! That boy should have told me!"

Deirdre had practiced her speech in front of a mirror. She'd brainstormed every possible response her father could make and the way she'd deal with each one. She had not, however, anticipated this. "What boy? Tell you what?"

"Dempsey. Why didn't he tell me you were getting married?"

"Married? To Craig Dempsey?" She managed to keep herself from snarling, but only just. "I'm not getting married to Craig Dempsey. I don't even like Craig Dempsey."

Her father's grin faded. "Then who *are* you marrying, Dee-Dee?"

Deirdre felt like shaking her head. How had this conversation managed to wander so far into La-La Land so quickly? "I'm not marrying anybody, Dad. Whatever gave you that idea?"

Her father looked genuinely confused. "Why else would you quit?"

Okay. She sighed. Now she was back on reasonably familiar ground. "Because I want to do something on my own. Something separate from Brandenburg, Inc."

Her father's eyes narrowed. "Has somebody made you an offer?"

"No. But I'm not really doing much for you here, nothing you couldn't find somebody else to do. And I'll be glad to work with whoever you bring in to replace me. I've been thinking about this for a while. Now just seemed like a good time to try it."

"Thinking about what? Just what are you going to be doing with your time, Dee-Dee?"

Deirdre took another deep breath. "I want to go into the restaurant business, to open a coffee roaster. I did that internship a few years ago with that coffee business in Austin. I've been interested in the industry ever since. So I decided now's the time to try it before I get too entrenched anywhere else."

"Coffee roasting." Her father's voice was flat. "You're going into the coffee roasting business."

"Yes, but not just roasting. I want to combine custom roasting with a coffee shop, sort of like Starbucks but with different blends and more distinctive roasts. I figure I'll start small, just a few tables, then work up to something larger once I'm established. Coffee's one of the fastest growing areas in food service."

"A coffee shop." Her father stared at her, eyes narrowing. "You'd go from a position as vice president of a multinational corporation to running a goddamn diner?" He pushed himself up from his chair, planting his fists on the desktop as he leaned forward. "Have you lost your mind? What the hell are you thinking, Deirdre?"

She stared at him blankly. She'd been ready for doubt, even for mockery. She hadn't anticipated rage. She frowned. "I'm thinking I need to be on my own, Dad. As I said, you don't really need me here. I don't seem to be doing much for the company, other than pointing out accounting errors. And actually, I think you might be happier with someone else doing my job." Probably somebody male, and preferably somebody with a professional sports background.

Her father straightened slowly, his jaw firming. She knew that look. It meant somebody was going to suffer. And this time that somebody was probably going to be her. "I won't pay for this, Deirdre."

She stiffened her spine. "No sir, I didn't expect you to. It's my business and I'll pay for it."

His mouth twisted slightly, as if he'd tasted something bitter. "So how did you expect to pay for it? I have approval on all your trust funds. And I won't approve any damn fool coffee shop. You've got a job here, and I expect you to do it."

Deirdre swallowed. She should have anticipated this particular move. *Three months. The funds revert to me in three months.* "I have my savings, Dad. And my portfolio. That should be enough to get me started."

"You can't sell any Brandenburg, Inc. stock without approval of the family, Deirdre." Her father's eyes bored through her. "Did you forget that? I won't approve it. And I'll make sure nobody else does either."

"Aunt Reba will," she blurted, and was immediately sorry she had.

Her father folded his arms across his chest. "Reba. Is that it? Did my fool sister put you up to this?"

She gritted her teeth. She knew from long experience that she wouldn't win any verbal battles with her father. "Nobody 'put me up to this', Dad. I told you. I've wanted to do this since college. And now seemed like the right time."

"All right then." Her father's voice sounded like a preacher threatening fire and brimstone. "Go ahead. Leave a job that most business majors would have killed to get. Go open your damn coffee shop. But you don't get a penny from me, not a penny, you understand? No cosigned loans, no stock approval, no credit. Go on out there and see how you do on your own, without any cushion from me."

Deirdre licked her lips. "I'm sorry you're upset, Dad."

"Upset?" For a moment, her father looked as if steam might issue from his ears. "You're making the mistake of your life. How the hell do you expect me to feel?"

Her pulse hammered in her ears. Her stomach roiled with a mixture of emotions—righteous anger with a soupçon of terror and maybe a touch of guilt. "I sort of hoped you'd feel proud of me."

"Proud of you?" Her father's mouth drew up into a sneer. "Think again."

She sighed. "Okay, I guess there's nothing more to talk about then. I have some vacation time coming. I'll take it over the next two weeks. As I said, if you want me to help train my replacement, I will."

Her father's face had turned the color of a nasty sunburn. "No. You don't get vacation time. I told you—you get nothing. I want you out of here now. You've got thirty minutes to clear out your desk. Security will escort you to the front door."

Deirdre's throat clenched so tightly she had a hard time breathing. "If that's what you want," she managed to murmur.

He said nothing, his eyes burning holes in her back as she left the room.

Outside the office she took a moment to catch her breath. Her heart hammered painfully. That particular conversation was going to hurt deep down to her toes as soon as she let it, but she didn't have time for that right now. "Thirty minutes," she muttered. "Well, thank god I believe in uncluttered desks."

Chapter Two

Deirdre cradled her cousin Docia's son, watching Docia make iced tea. The converted barn where she lived had a huge combination living-dining room, with bedrooms overhead. A shaft of sunlight fell across the scarlet and blue carpet on the planked pine floor, picking out the warm gold of the wood.

Docia had been her hero for as long as she could remember. Six feet tall, flaming red hair, outsized opinions to go along with her statuesque frame. Deirdre didn't think she'd ever seen Docia intimidated, afraid to say what she thought. She'd always done her best to follow her cousin's example, and she'd succeeded with everyone except her father. Of course, in a lot of ways, her father was the only one who counted.

She swallowed hard, trying to fight down the now familiar surge of panic in her gut. *It'll be all right, Deirdre. You can do this. You can.*

The baby in her arms gurgled, blowing a tiny bubble in her direction. She smiled down at his baby grin, ignoring her own churning stomach. "How'd you decide on Rolf? Is that a family name?"

Docia grimaced. "A Toleffson family name, and the alternative was Thor. I figured Rolf would at least give the kid a chance, although he'll probably get Muppet jokes. Or people who think it means Roll on the Floor Laughing."

"It's not spelled like that." She shifted Rolf to her other shoulder, noting the slightly wet patch he left behind. She stifled another clench in her chest, this one entirely practical. She only had two pairs of jeans and a couple of knit shirts, along with a single pair of khakis—not much for a job search in Konigsburg. Why the hell hadn't she spent some of her money on non-working clothes when she'd still had money to spend?

"Are you ready to tell me what's going on, Dee, or do you need another glass of tea?" Docia smiled down at her, but her eyes were speculative. "I'm really happy to have you here, but it's not like you to show up without any warning in a car full of power suits."

Another glass of tea would be welcome, but Deirdre knew she couldn't put explanations off forever. "Thanks for the tea, Dosh. I'm here because I quit my job with Brandenburg, Inc."

Docia raised an eyebrow. "Why?"

"Because I wanted to do something different." Deirdre blew out a quick breath, not meeting her cousin's gaze. "I want to open a custom coffee roaster with a coffee shop. Dad doesn't think much of the idea."

"But you had that internship with the coffee roaster in Austin. I remember. I stopped by and visited you once. And you were a barista too. You and Allie had all those conversations about free trade coffee the summer when you worked here."

Ironic that Docia remembered everything her father seemed to have forgotten. "Dad wants me to go on working for him, I guess. He's not too open to alternatives."

Docia grimaced. "No, he's not known for that. So does Uncle John know where you are right now, that you were coming up here to visit me?"

Deirdre shrugged. "I didn't tell him. I don't think he cares."

Docia leaned forward, resting her hand on Deirdre's knee. "Sweetie, of course he cares. He just lost his temper. When he's had a chance to cool down, he'll understand. You're all he's got."

"Maybe. I don't think he's going to cool down this time, though. Not for a while, anyway. I mean, he had security escort me out of the building after I quit, and when I got back to my apartment, they told me I had a day to clear out my things." Deirdre rubbed a hand against Rolf's warm back as he snuggled against her. It was oddly soothing.

Docia's eyes widened. "He evicted his own daughter?"

Deirdre shrugged. "Well, the apartment is owned by the company, after all, and I quit. So technically I wasn't entitled to it anymore."

"For god's sake, Dee, you're a major stockholder in that

company. So am I, for that matter."

"I was." She blew out a breath. "I mean, I still am. But my stock account is sort of in limbo at the moment. Daddy has control of it and he cut off my access."

Docia frowned. "But you've got other accounts, right? Savings? Credit cards?"

"The cards have been cancelled. And my savings accounts are frozen." Deirdre took another deep breath, trying to ease the tension in her shoulders. "I knew I should have taken Dad's name off those accounts after I graduated from college, opened new ones in my own name, but I never got around to doing it. And, of course, the trusts are blocked, but I expected that."

"But how can he freeze your savings accounts? It's your money, right?"

"It's my money, but it's in accounts he controls. I don't know how he managed to block them, but since he's a signatory on most of them, and since Brandenburg, Inc. is a major stock holder in the bank, he probably just pulled some strings."

Docia shook her head. "I think you need a good lawyer, Dee. And a good accountant. Believe me, I can set you up with both. The Toleffsons are a full-service family."

Deirdre shrugged. "It wouldn't help. No matter who I found, Dad would have better ones, and more of them. I just have to guts it out for three months until I hit twenty-five. That's when I come into the trusts. I don't think there's any way he could block that. They're part of Mama's will."

"But what will you live on until then?"

"Well—" Deirdre licked her lips, "—I've got an account here in Konigsburg. The money I earned that summer I worked as a barista, and some from the job in Austin."

"Your money from working for three months one summer? How far will that go?"

"Not far," Deirdre agreed. "I'll need to find a job here in town while I look for shop locations."

"Around here, in Konigsburg?" Docia gave her one of her dazzling smiles. "That's wonderful, Dee. And it's smart—you've already got family here, and friends."

Deirdre nodded. "Konigsburg was always my first choice for a location. There's no coffee roaster closer than Austin and lots of restaurants to buy custom blends. But I'll need to get a job before I can start working on the shop. You know, just temporarily." She managed to keep her smile bright. "I don't suppose you know anyone who needs some part-time help?"

Her cousin owned Kent's Hill Country Books. For a relatively small shop, it always seemed fairly busy. Deirdre was hoping they could use an extra clerk.

Docia shook her head, regretfully. "Bad timing. I just hired on a new clerk last week to help me and Janie at the shop. And Jess and I decided to hire a nanny together, so we don't need an au pair. She starts next week. If either of them doesn't work out, you'll be my first choice for a replacement, though."

Deirdre felt the same tightness in her chest she'd felt every day since she'd left Houston. *You'll be fine. You will.* It wasn't like she didn't have any alternatives. Really.

"Have you considered going down to San Antonio?" Docia asked. "Mama would give you a job at the foundation in a shot, and since she runs it, Uncle John wouldn't have any say."

Deirdre shook her head. "I need to stay here. I was hoping I could find a shop location and maybe start working on getting it in shape." Assuming she could find a landlord willing to give her a lease based on a windfall in three months.

Docia sighed. "Listen, Deirdre, I can't give you a job, but I can give you a place to stay. Cal's brother Erik just got married, and he and his wife have moved out of the upstairs apartment at the bookshop. I used to live there. So did Pete and Janie. You can stay there as long as you need to, rent free."

Deirdre licked her lips again. A truly independent woman would probably say no. A truly independent woman would be more concerned about making her own way in the world.

A truly independent woman wouldn't be scared shitless at the thought of being totally on her own, without funds, for the first time in her life. Deirdre blew out a breath she hadn't known she'd been holding. "Thanks, Docia. I appreciate it."

She patted Deirdre's hand. "That's okay, kid. Believe me. I've been where you are. I came up here on my own, too. And it was a pretty scary time."

Of course Docia's mama and daddy had never disowned her. If anything, from what Deirdre remembered, they'd wanted to help her more than she'd wanted them to help.

Baby Rolf whimpered slightly, and Deirdre eased her grip,

staring down at the baby's astonishing blue-black eyes. "He's so beautiful, Docia," she murmured.

Docia's grin could have lit the city of Konigsburg, with enough left over for Marble Falls. "He is, isn't he? Come to Mama, kid." She stretched her arms toward Rolf, who gave her a miraculous toothless smile.

Deirdre's chest clenched again, but at least this time it wasn't from fear.

Tom Ames watched the Steinbruner brothers shoot pool, badly. Pool was one of the games he'd learned to play well early on, since pool hustling had a longer and more honorable tradition than card sharping. He could do both, of course, and had when he needed to. Fortunately, now that he owned the Faro himself, his earlier professions made it easier to spot those who were trying to hustle his customers.

The Steinbruners could have been hustled by the average eight-year-old with good hand-eye coordination, but they were usually too broke to make hustling worthwhile. They'd been nursing their beers for over an hour now, close to the house record but typical.

The brothers were a holdover from the bad old days of the Faro. From what he'd managed to pick up listening to other old timers, Tom gathered they'd been better at fighting than at pool, which wasn't hard to believe. It had taken him a little while to convince them that the Faro's fighting days were through, but apparently they liked playing pool more than they liked bashing heads. At any rate, they'd become fixtures by now, even if they did manage to get by with no more than two beers in a night.

Tom leaned his elbows on the bar and watched one of them scratch for what seemed like the twentieth time. He wasn't sure which one it was—he had a hard time telling them apart. Probably Denny, since Harold and Billy Ray were even worse than he was.

Beside him, Nando Avrogado whistled through his teeth. "Maybe they could start betting on the one who makes the least number of points. That way they'd at least have some competition going."

"Probably make them start winning, given the well-known Steinbruner luck."

Nando grinned and sipped his beer. He was one of the few locals who frequented the Faro instead of the Dew Drop. Since he was one of the Konigsburg cops, he might have come around to keep an eye on things, but Tom didn't think so. Nando was currently off duty. No, his presence was more likely a tribute to Chico.

Tom glanced at the other side of the room where Chico Burnside sat dozing on his stool. His massive arms were folded across his chest. His legs were stretched out in front of him, far enough that anyone wanting to walk along that side of the room would have to make a slight detour. He wore a red bandana tied around his forehead to hold back his long black hair, and his arms were inscribed with a network of blue and red tattoos. Just looking at Chico was enough to make most drunks think twice about starting anything, which was sort of the point since Chico was the Faro's bouncer.

He was also a distant relation of Nando's, although Tom had never been able to pin down the exact degree of separation.

One of the Steinbruners hit the cue ball so violently it popped off the table, bouncing across the floor to rest against Chico's toe. One of them—Harold?—inched over in Chico's direction. He reached down for the ball, jostling Chico's foot in the process.

Chico's eyes slitted open enough to give the Steinbruner in question a lethal look. "Watch it," he rumbled.

Harold grinned and shrugged. "Sorry. Didn't mean to disturb your beauty sleep."

At the table, the other Steinbruners snickered.

Tom sighed, tossing his towel on the bar. "Crap." He strode quickly toward the opening at the end of the bar.

Chico's hands formed into fists at his sides. Harold had already turned away from him, heading back toward the table. Chico slid off his stool with an animal grace that would have shocked most patrons of the Faro if they'd ever paid attention. Tom, who'd seen Chico in action more than he liked to admit, wasn't shocked at all.

At the bar, Nando stood up from his stool.

"Hey," Tom called sharply.

Chico paused and turned in his direction, his shoulders tensing. The three Steinbruners gave him a cursory glance before they returned to their game.

Tom stepped next to the table. "You scratch that felt, Billy Ray, and you'll have to pay for the repairs."

Billy Ray blinked at him. "Aw, c'mon, Ames. It's just a game. We didn't do anything to the table."

"Maybe. But it's the only pool table I've got, and I don't want it gouged."

The Steinbruners all stared at him blankly, then slowly became aware of Chico standing at the side of the table. Denny cleared his throat. "Right. We'll be careful. No damages."

Tom watched them play for a few minutes longer, then walked back to Chico's stool. "Okay?"

He shrugged, slowly. "Just startled is all. I wouldn't have done anything to them, just reminded them about the rules. That Billy Ray's a disrespectful little shit, though."

Tom nodded. "Right." He picked up a few empty bottles from one of the tables and headed back toward the bar.

Nando had already relaxed, sipping his beer while he watched the Steinbruners rag each other.

Tom leaned back against the bar again. On the far side of the room, Sylvia was balancing a tray that was overloaded with beers. Tom tensed, ready to sprint to her side if they started to fall, but she managed to place them on the table. The customers at the next table were already waving empty bottles in her direction, and Sylvia turned toward them, glowering.

"You need a new barmaid," Nando commented.

Tom gave him a dry smile. "Maybe one of the Dew Drop barmaids is ready to move on."

Nando shook his head, grimacing. "You need a barmaid that would class up the place. Not a refugee from *Mystery Science Theater 3000*."

Tom collected the bottles Sylvia handed him, then supplied her with a new round. "He's right," she snapped, nodding in Nando's direction. "I can't do everything."

"Ah sweetheart, what you do, you do real well." Nando gave her his best killer smile.

Sylvia snarled and headed back to her tables.

"A new barmaid." Tom sighed. "Wonder if Docia Kent would consider applying."

Nando nodded. "Not a bad idea. Not Docia, of course," he

added hastily. "But maybe a Docia type."

"A six-foot redhead with a figure like Venus de Milo? There aren't many of that type available."

Nando grinned. "Just keep looking, Ames. If you build it, they will come."

Tom frowned. Coincidence that he'd been thinking the same thing? Maybe the universe was trying to tell him something.

Chapter Three

Deirdre bought a cup of coffee to go at a café a few blocks from her new apartment above the bookshop. The café was called the Coffee Corral, but the coffee wasn't one of its best features. At least, she hoped it wasn't. If it was, the food must be really awful. She wandered down the street, feeling the warm autumn sunshine on her face. This was the slow season in Konigsburg, assuming the place ever had a really slow season. No upcoming festivals, no school holidays to bring families up for the weekend, just the usual blue-haired retirees and shoppers clogging the sidewalks on Main.

She figured she could spend a couple of days checking out possible shop locations before she had to find some kind of temporary job. Once she had an idea of what was available, she could start sizing up the landlords, trying to decide how to convince them to give her a lease on spec, since she had next to no money for a down payment.

She took a deep breath, pushing away the familiar clenching in her chest. *You can do this. You're almost twenty-five years old. You have a degree from the McCombs School of Business. Docia can vouch for you with the Konigsburg landlords. You're not helpless.*

She felt helpless, though. It had always been so easy when she had money. And, of course, up to now she'd always had it. Having money was much easier than figuring out how to get it.

Which is why you're in this spot right now. You took the easy way.

Deirdre blew out a breath, squaring her shoulders. She wasn't taking the easy way any more. It was way past time to be a grown-up.

She strolled along Main, sipping the lousy coffee and studying the shop windows. This was the central part of town, the area with the most tourists and the greatest visibility. Also, of course, the area with the highest rent, and, probably, the fewest empty buildings. Not many landlords in this part of town would be interested in making a deal. She saw a couple of empty windows, but both spaces were wrong for what she wanted, more retail than food. She couldn't afford a place that needed lots of renovations. If the place she rented needed anything fixed, she'd have to do it on her own. At least at first.

Farther up Main, the shops thinned out. More restaurants and bars, interspersed with merchants who actually served the real citizens of Konigsburg rather than the tourists—insurance agencies, dry cleaners, a hardware store.

Deirdre glanced back down the street at the discreet sign for Brenner's restaurant. They'd be one of the first places where she'd try to sell her custom blends, the kind of restaurant where the customers would be willing to pay a little more for a premium cup of coffee. And the owners were friends of Docia's.

In front of her, another sign wasn't nearly as discreet as Brenner's. The Faro. Deirdre narrowed her eyes, trying to remember what she knew about the place. Live music on weekends. Beer garden out back. Limited food service, probably burgers, nachos, bar food. So not a potential customer.

She grimaced. Potential customers for a hypothetical coffee shop. Talk about putting the proverbial cart before the proverbial horse. She went back to scanning the storefronts. Maybe if she went one street over, back to the street where the Coffee Corral was located, she might find more affordable possibilities.

She glanced idly at the limestone block building that housed the Faro. And stopped.

Next door to the bar was a small, glass-fronted shop, the same aged limestone block construction and tin roof as the club. Maybe even part of the club once upon a time—they shared a common wall. She leaned forward, pressing her face against the glass so that she could see inside. It looked like a single room, fairly narrow, stretching back to a counter at the rear. She could dimly see a door in the back wall, probably to a storage area beyond.

The floor at the front looked like hardwood, although it also

27

looked like it hadn't been cleaned since the first Bush Administration. The walls between the built-in shelves were just as dingy. They'd need to be scrubbed, but she'd guess there was a good surface underneath.

Deirdre did a quick mental estimate of the floor space. Enough for four, maybe five tables with three or four chairs each.

Her chest clenched again. Her heart pounded in her ears. Perfect. Absolutely what she was looking for. Plus it just felt right.

This is the place. This is what I want.

Maybe she should go find Docia. Ask her what she knew about the Faro, particularly about the shop next door to the Faro. Maybe Docia knew the owner of the building. Maybe she could call him and...

Enough! This is your *project, Deirdre Ann.*

She licked her lips, squaring her shoulders again. *This is what I want.* The first step would be to locate the owner of the building. She'd see how things went after that.

Tom took a desultory swipe at the bar with his rag. It was clean, or as clean as he could get it without stripping it down to bare wood and starting over. He watched Bobby Sue take orders from the customers sprinkled around the lunch tables. Food service wasn't exactly their biggest source of revenue, but people liked Clem's burgers and enchiladas, and she was beginning to branch out into more interesting things, some soups and salads. They weren't making a lot of money off food yet, but the customer base was building.

Even with the widely spaced lunch tables, Bobby Sue was having trouble getting around. Tom figured her arthritis was acting up again. At her age she should probably be sitting with her feet up, knitting an afghan or something. Instead, here she was limping from table to table, writing orders on her green pad. Part of the reason she still worked the lunch crowd was her own aversion to what she called "idleness". The rest of it was most likely Bobby Sue's boy, Leon, who had a fondness for get-rich-quick schemes that quickly turned into get-poor-quick.

Oh well, better than a fondness for crystal meth and petty

theft, like Tom's long-lost brother Burton. Tom just hoped Burton had the good sense to stay lost.

Leon himself pushed open the kitchen door and headed toward the bar with a tray of glasses from the dishwasher. Tom had taken him on originally as a favor to Bobby Sue, but Leon wasn't all that bad. He could load the dishwasher at least, and sweep up. Besides, Tom sort of liked having people around who had a stake in the place, which Leon did, thanks to his mother.

Chico lounged in the doorway to the beer garden. They didn't need a bouncer with the lunch crowd, but he liked to carry the trays for Bobby Sue. And Tom got a kick out of seeing the tourists' reaction when he did.

"Excuse me?"

Tom stopped wiping. He wasn't sure he'd really heard anyone say anything, what with the jukebox blaring Reckless Kelly in the corner.

"Excuse me?" The voice was louder, but still faint.

He turned toward the other end of the bar, toward the most beautiful woman he'd ever seen.

Tall. Maybe five-ten or so. Hair the color of a moonless night, falling straight to her shoulders. Skin the pure white of marble, so that her faintly curving eyebrows stood out against it like parentheses. Full lips, dark pink.

And blue eyes. Sky blue. With a dark circle around the outer edge of the iris and lashes like dark smudges against her cheeks. He'd be willing to bet she wasn't wearing makeup. Everything was natural. If she ever put on mascara, she'd probably have to carry a stick to beat off the male population of Konigsburg.

Of course, now that he got a closer look, he realized she was dressed in some of the worst clothes he'd ever seen on such a glorious woman. At least he assumed she was glorious. Given the bagginess of her jeans and T-shirt it was hard to tell. Her clothes were so nondescript she might as well have been wearing bib overalls.

Lord have mercy!

"Excuse me?" she said for the third time, her voice becoming somewhat sharper.

Tom had the feeling she'd go on saying it, maybe getting a little more pissed, until he pulled himself together enough to answer her. He took a deep breath, dragging his scattered wits back into line. "Yes, ma'am."

"I was wondering...that is..."

She paused, licking her lips, and Tom felt a jolt of electricity straight to his groin. If she kept that up he'd be vaulting the bar in another five minutes. "Yes?" he said encouragingly.

"Do you happen to know who owns the shop next door, the one that's vacant?" It came out in a rush, as if she were trying to say the words before she lost her nerve.

"Yes ma'am, I do. That is, I own it." Shit, he sounded like a shy schoolboy himself all of a sudden. The brunette had a hell of an effect.

"Oh." She licked her lips again. "Well. I'd like to discuss leasing that shop. That is, if it's available. Is it available?"

Tom frowned. Not only was the shop available, he'd been trying to find a renter ever since Ken Ferguson had closed his T-shirt shop and taken off for parts unknown, owing a couple of months' rent and leaving him with a complete stock of cheesy T-shirts in his back room. "It's available."

"Oh, good." The brunette gave him a dazzling smile he felt all the way to the tips of his toes. Apparently keeping a poker face was not part of her negotiating style. "Maybe we could talk about it then." She reached a hand across the bar. "I'm Deirdre Brandenburg."

Tom nodded, taking her incredibly soft, warm hand in his. "Tom Ames." Reluctantly, he let go again.

She glanced quickly around the room. "Is there an office where we can discuss this, Mr. Ames?"

Tom watched Bobby Sue limp toward the kitchen. His only office at the Faro was a prep table near the walk-in refrigerator. Somehow he didn't think the brunette would be impressed, and Clem might drive them out with a meat cleaver if she was feeling feisty. He shook his head. "Sorry. I have to cover the bar."

He caught her glancing at the empty stools. Okay, so covering the bar didn't currently take a lot of effort. "Have a seat," he said quickly. "Can I get you something to drink? Maybe a soda?"

Deirdre Brandenburg shook her head as she slid onto a

barstool in front of him. "That's okay, I'm fine. About the shop, what kind of rent are you asking?"

Ferguson had been paying fifteen hundred a month, when he'd paid, but Tom hadn't had any nibbles yet at that price. And the shop had been empty now for a couple of months. They were too far up Main for a lot of tourist traffic. "A thousand a month. First and last month in advance."

"Oh." The brunette's forehead furrowed slightly as she chewed on her lower lip. "What's the square footage?"

Tom shrugged. "I don't know off the top of my head. I could look it up. It's a single room in front with a storage area at the back of the building. There's access to the delivery entrance for the Faro at back too."

"Could I get in to look at it? All I've been able to do so far is peek through the windows."

Tom sighed. A more trusting man would give her the key and let her look. But trusting men didn't usually own bars like the Faro. And if they did, they soon learned not to be so trusting. He himself had been born suspicious. "If you can wait a few minutes, I'll take you over there."

"Of course." The brunette turned as he signaled across the room. He watched her eyes widen in consternation as Chico lumbered toward them.

"Chico's the bouncer. His bark is usually worse than his bite," he explained. "Although not always."

Chico pulled out a barstool and sat. "What?"

"I need you to take over the bar for a few minutes while I show Ms. Brandenburg here what Ferguson's shop looks like inside."

Chico glanced at the brunette for the first time, narrowing his eyes slightly as he studied her. "Why?"

The brunette swallowed hard. Chico wasn't making much effort to be charming.

"I'd like to lease the shop," she murmured, her voice dropping again.

"What for?" Chico leaned back against the bar. "Crummy location. Lousy economy. What can you sell we don't already have more of than we need right now?"

Succinctly put. Tom leaned forward on his elbows.

"Coffee," the brunette muttered. She gave Chico a look of

mixed terror and defiance.

"We got coffee."

"Good coffee." Her voice sounded slightly more firm.

Chico shrugged. "We got good coffee."

Deirdre Brandenburg raised her chin. All of a sudden her eyes were flashing. "Not as good as mine," she snapped.

Chico grinned, slowly, which was a fairly terrifying sight in itself. He always reminded Tom of a smiling rhinoceros. "Well, then, you got something somebody's likely to buy." He turned to Tom. "I'll keep an eye on things. All they want is beer with their burgers, anyway."

"Right." Tom opened the gate at the end of the bar and motioned to the brunette to follow him.

Craig Dempsey was summoned to the big man's office at nine in the morning. He had a sneaky suspicion this had something to do with Dee-Dee, but he wasn't sure exactly what. Big John might have found out about Dee-Dee's breaking up with him, but he'd bet he hadn't. Dee-Dee wasn't the type to clue her father in on her love life. Or anything else, as far as that went.

Fortunately. Craig still had hopes of getting her to rethink the whole breaking up thing. He wasn't under any illusions about why Big John had hired him in the first place—it was the NFL-star shtick. Hire an athlete and pretend his accomplishments on the field somehow rubbed off on the company he worked for. Craig had no problem with that idea, as far as it went. His football career had opened most of the doors he needed to have opened. But marrying Dee-Dee Brandenburg would have made his position a lot more secure in the long run. And security was something he'd become very aware of over the past few months.

People seemed to think he'd come out of his years as a player with enough money to see him set for life. And he probably would have, if it hadn't been for that freakin' car dealership his brother Arnie talked him into. Or those weekends in Vegas. Who knew a few hands of poker could end up costing so much? His cards hadn't been that bad, all in all. He still had money left, but not enough to go on living the way he liked to live, at least not long term.

And Dee-Dee was nice enough. She cleaned up well when she put her mind to it. After all, he'd seen the body underneath those pricey suits.

So what if she sometimes seemed too smart for her own good? She hadn't been able to get any of her ideas across at Brandenburg, Inc. anyway, particularly when her daddy paid no attention to anything she said.

Craig paid attention. He had no problem with lifting ideas he'd heard Dee-Dee toss around. Her father never noticed they weren't his. And she didn't need the credit, anyway. She already had the money. Of course, when he'd lifted that last one, the one about the wind farms, she'd told him she didn't think they had a future together, which was as close as somebody that well-bred could come to telling him to go fuck himself. But she hadn't told her father, or at least she hadn't yet.

Craig frowned. Could that possibly be what this meeting was about?

The big guy didn't look happy, that was for sure. Big John stood around six-two, and was built like someone who'd once played football but hadn't kept it up. Craig hit the gym every morning, and he didn't have much patience with men who didn't, even billionaires. Big John could stand to lose at least fifty pounds and build up a little muscle in place of the fat.

But he was the boss, also the key to the immense wad of cash Craig could get access to once he reeled Dee-Dee back in. "What can I do for you, sir?" Craig gave him a practiced smile.

Big John turned bloodshot green eyes his direction. "Sit down, Dempsey. I've got a job for you."

Well, now, this was more like it. A job for him, possibly with a bonus at the end of it. Craig sat down opposite the big man's desk. "Glad to do what I can."

"Are you?" Big John ran a hand over his thinning reddish hair. "When did you last talk to my daughter?"

"To Dee-Dee?" A fairly stupid thing to say since Big John only had one daughter, but Craig needed time to think. "Maybe a week ago. Why?"

"Don't lie to me, Dempsey, I don't have time." Big John's expression turned bleak. "Do you know where she is?"

"The last I talked to her she was in her apartment. Isn't

that where she is now?"

"No, that's not where she is now. That's a company apartment. Only available to people working for Brandenburg, Inc."

"But..." Craig felt like he'd missed a step. *Dee-Dee's not working here?*

Big John narrowed his eyes. "You didn't know she was going to quit? She didn't tell you about it? What's going on, Dempsey? I thought you and my daughter were close."

"We were. That is, we are. We had a little...falling out...a couple of weeks ago. I was letting her cool off before I gave her a call."

He backpedaled furiously. Why the hell would she quit? Was she planning some kind of corporate take-over? Dee-Dee as ruthless corporate raider? *Nah.*

"Well, she's cool by now, believe me. She quit a couple of days ago. And now she's left Houston for god knows where."

Craig managed to conceal his confusion by staring down at the desk, pretending he was thinking. Dee-Dee going off on her own, away from Big John, made as much sense as Dee-Dee going off on a quick trip to Neptune. In his opinion, she didn't have the survival skills of the average eight-year-old. "We could have security run a trace on her credit cards if you need to locate her, sir. See where she used them last."

Big John cleared his throat. "She doesn't have any credit cards anymore."

Craig licked his lips. Clearly he was treading around the edges of a minefield here. "What about her bank accounts? They could check ATM withdrawals."

The big man's jaw tightened. He shook his head.

Well, damn. Craig cast around quickly, trying to think of something relevant that wouldn't make an already shitty situation turn lethal. "What about her friends? People she might call to ask for... People she might get together with."

Big John turned a burning gaze toward him. "You'd know her friends, wouldn't you? Who'd you two hang out with?"

His friends, of course. It hadn't occurred to him that she had any friends worth getting together with. Craig tried desperately to think of a few names and came up dry. "Nobody special. What about family?"

Big John blew out a breath. "There's my sister, Reba, down in San Antonio. She and Dee-Dee were close when she was a little girl. You might give her a call."

Craig made a quick note, wondering when he'd suddenly been placed in charge of this investigation. No matter. Not the best time to be asking the big guy any probing questions. "Anyone else?"

Big John shook his head. "No more Brandenburgs. And Kathleen's people are all in Ireland."

"All right, sir, so you want me to locate Dee-Dee. Do you want me to do anything else?"

Big John raised an eyebrow. "Such as?"

"Well, give her a message, maybe bring her back to Houston?"

The big man grimaced. "She won't come back. Says she's gone off to open a coffee shop. A coffee shop, goddamn it!" He brought his palm down on the desk with a smack. "A Brandenburg and she wants to be a goddamn waitress."

Craig blew out a quick breath. This situation was beyond weird, but he'd manage to find some way to make it work for him. "I'll find her, sir. And I'll let you know where she is, as soon as I know myself."

Big John gave him a weary nod. "You do that. And if you can think of any way to head her off before she ruins her life, you've got my permission to go for it."

"Yes sir. I'll remember that."

Craig managed to conceal his shit-eating grin until he was outside the office. Big John Brandenburg giving him carte blanche to do whatever he thought best. Oh, the next few days held all kinds of interesting possibilities.

Deirdre's heart was beating so fast she was afraid she might faint. The bouncer, Chico, was the biggest man she'd ever seen, including some of Craig Dempsey's old football buddies. He looked like one of the villains in biker movies, with his long black hair, his bandana, his moustache and goatee. She wasn't sure how she'd worked up the courage to talk back to him. Maybe because for a few moments he'd sounded like her father.

She shook her head. She needed to get hold of herself.

Even if this wasn't a world she was familiar with, she could still make it work. She was smart, she was experienced, and she wasn't going to take any more shit from anybody.

Oh yeah, as a mantra that really works well.

Ahead of her, the landlord, Tom Ames, was unlocking the door to the shop. She took a moment to study him. Maybe a little over six feet, but not husky. Lean, tough body. Close-cut blond hair. Blue eyes the color of ice.

That ice-blue gaze had seemed to bore straight through her when she'd asked about the rent. She had a feeling he was way ahead of her. Probably already knew what she was going to ask and knew how to turn her down.

One step at a time, Deirdre.

She moved inside the shop, blinking in the sudden dimness. Sunshine streamed in from the front window, and from the two side windows on the wall away from the Faro.

"The previous tenant left sort of...unexpectedly," Ames explained. "I didn't do much more than clear out the stock he left on the shelves."

Deirdre turned slowly, studying the room. The walls were in worse shape than she'd realized, with scuff marks and gouges. The concrete floor felt gritty beneath her feet. She turned toward the counter at the back. "Is that the storeroom behind the counter?"

Ames nodded. "I've got some of the previous owner's stock back there now, but I could clear it out. Maybe."

She stepped up to the door, peering through to the darker room beyond. There was a utility sink at the side. Several boxes were piled against the back wall. "Looks like a small space."

"It'll be larger without all the T-shirts."

"Does it have plumbing? Rest rooms?"

He shrugged. "The back room has water. There's a door through to the bar for rest rooms."

"Right." She turned back to him again. "It should work for me. And I like the location."

He frowned. "Next to a bar?"

"Away from the central retail area. I'm going to be roasting coffee beans. Some stores might not like the smell next door."

"Roasting coffee?" He raised an eyebrow.

"Right. Custom blends. Partly for restaurants, partly for

walk-ins."

He folded his arms across his chest, leaning back against the counter. "You've done this before?"

She nodded. "I worked for a specialty coffee shop in college and I interned with a coffee roaster for a year."

"And you've got the equipment you need?"

Okay, tricky. "I know what I need, and where to get it. I don't have it yet."

"References?"

Deirdre smiled. "Docia Toleffson is my cousin. She can vouch for me. So can my Aunt Reba. She runs a foundation in San Antonio."

"Okay." Ames pushed himself up from the counter. "Works for me. I'll have my accountant draw up the paperwork—he's Docia's brother-in-law, as a matter of fact. First and last month's rent in advance and you'll be good to go."

She took a breath, steadying herself. "Yes. About that."

"About what?"

"The rent. I can give you the first and last month in advance. But I can't give you more than that. Yet." She licked her lips. Even giving him the first and last month in advance would cut deeply into the little she had in the bank. Once she paid him, she'd have less than a thousand dollars to live on until she found a temporary job.

Ames leaned back against the counter again, frowning. "Yet?"

"I'm...I can't get access to my funds right now. For the next three months, in fact. But once I've found a job to tide me over, I can begin paying you on account. And, as I said, I can give you the two thousand up front."

Ames's frown looked even darker. "Look, Ms. Brandenburg..."

"I know it sounds awful," Deirdre blurted. "I mean, I wouldn't trust me either. But if you call Docia, she can tell you. I'm honestly good for it. And I'll start paying you as soon as I've found some kind of work."

The frown didn't disappear exactly, but he looked a little less dubious. "What kind of job are you looking for? What were you doing before you came here?"

She shrugged a little helplessly. Executive vice president of a Fortune 500 company. *Right. Which really explains why I only have two thousand dollars to pay you right now.* "I was doing office work. But right now I'm just looking for a job. I'm not fussy about what it is."

He stared down at his feet, then back up again. "Tell you what. I could use another waitress and barmaid. If you're interested. Pay's crappy, but the tips would be good. Probably. And you get lunch and dinner."

She licked her lips again. "I've never been a waitress. Or a barmaid. But I guess I could learn."

Ames stood up again. "I guess you could. It's not exactly rocket science." He extended his hand. "Deal, Ms. Brandenburg?"

Deirdre blew out another breath, then took his hand. "Deal, Mr. Ames."

Chapter Four

Craig Dempsey studied Reba Kent's office at the Brandenburg Foundation. Not as spacious as the big man's office at Brandenburg, Inc., but probably more appropriate for a non-profit, as the foundation was supposed to be. The building was a few blocks from the San Antonio River Walk, prime location if the foundation actually owned the place, and given how long they'd been in business he was willing to bet they did. Like everything else attached to the Brandenburg family, it reeked of money.

Kent's desk was some kind of old table, probably an antique or something. Craig's decorator could have told him, but he never paid much attention to stuff like that himself. If Reba Kent had the same tastes as her brother, Big John, it was probably not only an antique, but an expensive one.

Big John Brandenburg's sister was pretty big herself. Craig put her height at a little under six feet, although given the high-heeled shoes she was wearing, it wasn't easy to tell. She wasn't exactly fat, but she'd never make the cover of *Vogue,* either. Sturdy. That's how he would have described her if he was being diplomatic. She must have been a major babe at some point in her life.

Now she looked more like a society matron than a babe. Her suit was Texas class, bright blue with a diamond pin in the shape of a cactus on the lapel. Her hair was like a silvery platinum shell, with little feathery flips around her face, and she had one of those big grins that made people grin back. The look in her cornflower-blue eyes didn't match the grin, though. He couldn't decide if she was angry or wary, maybe some of both. Big John Brandenburg must be hell on wheels as a relative to inspire that kind of reaction long distance.

"You're looking for Dee-Dee?" she asked, fluttering her eyelashes discreetly. "Why? And how did my brother manage to lose track of his only child?"

"They had some kind of...falling out, as I understand it. Now Mr. Brandenburg would like to find her to apologize, but he doesn't know where she went. He thought perhaps she might have reached out to you."

In reality, of course, Big John would apologize when the demons went snowboarding in hell, but Craig didn't figure he needed to point that out.

"What sort of falling out did they have?" Mrs. Kent widened those cornflower eyes a little more, giving a really good imitation of innocence. He was impressed.

"I'm not clear on the details. Apparently it was some kind of business matter."

"How sad." She gave him a bland smile. "Family quarrels are always a shame. I'm sure John is devastated."

Actually, Craig was willing to bet she wasn't sure of that at all. But gamesmanship was apparently part of the Brandenburg genetic code. "Have you heard from your niece, Mrs. Kent? I'm sure it would relieve Mr. Brandenburg's mind to know she's been in touch."

"No doubt." She pushed a pencil around her desktop with her forefinger. "Unfortunately, I haven't talked to Dee-Dee in several weeks. I'm afraid I can't help you."

"I'm sorry to hear that." He gave her his best concerned expression. "Do you know anyone else she might contact?"

"Surely John knows her friends," she said in a bland voice. "Or perhaps you do."

"Me?" He raised an eyebrow.

"The last time I spoke to him, John implied you were interested in my niece, Mr. Dempsey. In fact, he implied that the two of you had some kind of...understanding. Something that was leading toward an engagement."

Craig didn't know whether to be flattered by Big John's confidence in his ability to pin Dee-Dee down or annoyed that he'd been the unwitting subject of a conversation with Reba Kent. "We've been dating, yes."

"Well, then, you must have met her friends. She must have

told you about the people who were close to her."

He managed not to grind his teeth. She was watching him all too intently. Why was it such a big deal that he didn't know Dee-Dee's friends? Hell, his friends were famous. Spending time with them was a big deal. Dee-Dee's family should be happy for her. And when they'd talked about her family, it was mainly Big John. He didn't remember her ever mentioning anybody else. Not that he'd ever asked. "She doesn't seem to have contacted anyone in Houston," he temporized, hoping to god it was true.

"And you've talked to the rest of her family?" Mrs. Kent's immaculately shaped eyebrow arched imperiously.

He licked his lips. "No, ma'am. Not yet. Can you suggest anyone I could contact?"

She seemed to weigh her answer for a moment before she shrugged. "I'll think about it. Why don't you call me back in a couple of days, and I'll let you know if anything has occurred to me."

Craig managed a thin smile. Clearly, this was the best he could get for now. "Thank you, Mrs. Kent. I'll do that."

Deirdre wrapped an apron around her waist, studying the patrons of the Faro apprehensively.

"Now, you'll need one of these little pads, too, only I don't have any extras. See if Tom can get you one. You need to write the orders down so Clem can see 'em. And you'll need a tray."

Bobby Sue Barksdale looked like she'd been born with a pad in her hand and a pencil tucked behind her ear. She wore running shoes, along with her navy knit slacks and button-down white shirt. Her graying blonde hair was permed into a tight frizz beneath a hairnet. Deirdre was fairly certain that Bobby Sue could write more orders in a minute than she herself could jot down in ten.

She felt like closing her eyes and doing some deep-breathing exercises, except that that would undoubtedly convince every customer in the place that she was a first-class nutcase. She could do this. She had a master's from the U of Texas, for Pete's sake. Like Ames said, it wasn't rocket science.

As if she'd summoned him, he appeared at her side, with a pencil and a small pad of paper. "Here. You take the tables on the side of the room toward the kitchen. Let Bobby Sue handle the ones toward the front window. More people sit over there. We'll start you out slow today. Write down the orders and take them into the kitchen. There's a rack there where you pin them so Clem can see what to plate up."

The room was divided down the middle by a lane that led to the outdoor beer garden entrance. Deirdre glanced at the four tables on the kitchen side. Two middle-aged women sat at one table, while a young man sat at another nursing a beer.

Ames nodded in the man's direction. "Don't know if he'll order food or not, but you can check on him." He patted her on the shoulder. "Go get 'em."

"But I haven't had time to look at the menu yet." She managed to keep her voice from squeaking in panic, but only just.

He shrugged as he headed back toward the bar. "Don't worry about it. All they order is burgers and enchiladas anyway."

Right. She took a deep breath and headed for the table with the two women. Both of them had water glasses and silverware. She realized suddenly she had no idea where to get those things herself. "Good afternoon. Can I take your order?" She forced her voice into a friendly tone. *Just us hospitality workers here, ma'am.*

The woman nearest gave her a shrewd look. She wore her bright red hair in an elaborately curled and teased style that might have been a wig, but apparently wasn't. "You're new. What's your name?"

Deirdre swallowed. "Deirdre. Deirdre Brandenburg."

The woman narrowed her eyes. "Brandenburg. Hmm. Any relation to Docia Toleffson's mama?"

"Yes, ma'am. She's my aunt."

The woman shook her head, her mouth flattening. "More Toleffsons. I swear, they're taking over the town."

Deirdre thought about pointing out she wasn't really a Toleffson, just a relative by marriage, but she let it go. She hated chatty waitresses herself. "Would y'all like to order now?"

The other woman gave her a sharp look from behind her cat's-eye glasses, then glanced back at the menu again. "No chicken salad?"

Deirdre suddenly wished, with a sinking heart, that she'd taken the time to check out the menu no matter what Ames had said. "I understand the burgers are very good, ma'am. And the enchiladas."

The woman shook her head. "I don't want a burger. Enchiladas give me gas."

Deirdre peered over her shoulder at the menu. "There's a club sandwich. And grilled cheese."

"Oh, all right," the woman said peevishly. "The club sandwich and iced tea."

Deirdre wrote the order as quickly as she could without it becoming totally illegible. "And you ma'am?" She turned to the woman with the sculptured hair.

"Rhonda," she said. "Rhonda Ruckelshaus. And I'll have the Faro burger. With fries."

Deirdre dutifully wrote the order on her pad. "And iced tea for you, too?"

"Coke. Diet."

Rhonda Ruckelshaus gave her a look that dared her to say anything. Deirdre tucked her pencil behind her ear. "I'll get those orders in right away."

She started toward the kitchen door, then paused at the table where the beer drinker sat. Might as well check on her way. "Did you want some food today, sir?"

The man glanced up at her, a little woozily, his mouth falling slightly open.

She upped the brightness of her smile. "Sir? May I take your order?"

The man blinked as if he was trying to focus. "'Scuse me?"

"Food. Did you want any food?" She was fairly certain that he'd had more than the single beer on his table, but maybe he'd had them elsewhere.

"Food. Yeah, okay." He blinked again, rapidly.

"What food do you want?" she said slowly. Maybe he needed time to kick his brain into gear.

"I don't...what's good? What should I have?" The man leaned forward slightly, peering up into her face.

"I'm new here myself. I understand the enchiladas are good."

"Enchiladas. Yeah. Sounds good. Bring me some

43

enchiladas." He leaned back in his chair, closing his eyes.

"Right. And something more to drink? Maybe some iced tea?" Coffee would probably be better, but she wasn't sure how far she could push him.

The man nodded. "'Nuther beer."

Deirdre started for the kitchen again. Behind her, she could hear a muttering of female voices. Apparently Rhonda Ruckleshaus and her friend were in conference.

She trotted to the hand-through window at the kitchen. The shoulder-high counter had a circular rack where two of Bobby Sue's green order sheets hung from clips. She tore off the order for the club sandwich, then the one for the burger and fries, attaching them to clips of her own. She was tearing off the enchilada order when a small, fierce female face peered up at her from the other side of the counter.

"Who the hell are you?"

Deirdre blinked. "I'm new," she stammered.

"No shit." The woman was maybe five feet tall. Deirdre was amazed she could see over the counter. Her dark hair was tucked haphazardly under a chef's beanie and she studied Deirdre with narrowed eyes that snapped like firecrackers. "Lemme see what you've got there." She pulled the two orders off the rack, quickly. "My god. You've got the neatest handwriting I've ever seen."

"Is that a problem?" She didn't think it would be, but with restaurants, who knew?

"No, ma'am. It took me a week to get to the point where I could decipher Bobby Sue, and I still have problems with her spelling. I'm Clem. Clemencia Rodriguez." She extended a hand across the counter for Deirdre to shake.

"Deirdre Brandenburg. Pleased to meet you."

Clem grinned at her. "Likewise. Now go back to your station. Chico will bring your food over when it's ready. Drinks are at the bar—just tell Tom what you want. Stick around for lunch after your shift is over and I'll fill you in on all you need to know."

Deirdre doubted that would be possible in under a week, but at least somebody had volunteered to try.

She stopped back at the bar. "The guy at the table near the kitchen wants another beer." She realized suddenly she hadn't checked to see what kind he was drinking. On well, maybe Tom knew already.

He glanced at the customer, eyes narrowing. "How soused is he?"

She looked back. "Slurring. Looks drowsy. How soused is that?"

"Too soused." He sighed, turning back toward the taps. He drew a glass of soda. "Tell him the bar's closed. Give him this. On the house."

Fortunately, the customer was also too soused to complain. He sipped the soda she handed him. When the enchiladas arrived, he dug into them happily enough.

By then, the lunch rush was pretty much over. Rhonda Ruckelshaus and friend left her a $1.50 tip, which was slightly over ten percent. Deirdre wondered if she'd done a bad job or if that was typical. She went to help clear away the plate and silverware from the table where the single man had been sitting and found a quarter next to the plate.

She sighed, dropping the quarter into her pocket as Chico piled dirty dishes on a tray. He gave her a dry grin. "Don't worry. Sometimes being drunk makes them tip bigger."

The kitchen door swung open, and the cook, Clemencia, walked into the room, untying her apron. "Did Tom give you any lunch?"

Deirdre shook her head. "I only waited on two tables."

"Doesn't matter. Food comes with the job. Besides, I've got leftovers to finish up. Come on."

Deirdre followed her back into the kitchen to a table toward the back. Chico carried the last tray of dirty dishes over to a sink where another man was rinsing them and stacking the dishwasher.

Clem pulled a pot from a burner. "Tortilla soup. Soup of the day, actually. Bobby Sue forgets to mention it half the time, which means we always have some left over." She ladled a bowlful for Deirdre and then sprinkled a handful of fried tortilla bits and avocado on the top. "Take a bite and tell me what you think."

Deirdre inhaled the scent of chicken broth and cilantro. Her stomach growled as she took the first bite. "This is really, really good," she muttered around her mouthful.

"Yes, it is," Clem agreed, ladling up her own bowl. "Now remember to mention the soup of the day tomorrow."

"I will." She slurped up another bite, tasting chicken and tomato, with bits of chili. Behind her, Chico dipped a bowl for himself and headed back out to the bar.

She took a longer look at the chef. Clem Rodriguez seemed to be around her age, maybe a little younger. She wore jeans and a faded Texas Tornadoes T-shirt under her apron, her dark hair clipped short under her chef's beanie. Her large dark eyes might have made her look demure if they hadn't glittered with intelligence. Deirdre watched her rapidly consume her soup, sipping from a large glass of iced tea as she did. "Do you do dinner, too?" she asked.

Clem shook her head. "Not yet. I've only been here six weeks or so. Tom says another few weeks and then we can try it, once we've built up the lunch traffic. Nighttime is mostly bar food right now—they can microwave most of it, so I don't need to stick around after I put it together." She pushed her empty bowl to the middle of the table. "Now tell me why you're waiting tables in a roadhouse. Not that Main qualifies as a road, but the Faro's as close to a roadhouse as Konigsburg comes. And frankly, you don't strike me as the roadhouse type."

Deirdre shrugged. "I needed a job. I'm trying to earn enough money to rent the place next door. Mr. Ames is going to lease it to me, but I've got some cash flow problems right now."

"The T-shirt shop?" Clem raised an eyebrow. "Doesn't strike me as a paying proposition."

"I want to turn it into a coffee roaster. With a few tables thrown in."

She leaned back in her chair. "Well, now, that's an interesting idea. You have any experience?"

Deirdre nodded, her mouth full of soup.

"Of course, waiting tables here isn't likely to make you a pile of money, even though you'll probably rake in more tips than poor old Bobby Sue."

"I have some other money, but I can't get at it for a couple of months." She pushed herself up from the table and walked to the stove. "I figure I can make enough here to keep Mr. Ames from renting to somebody else while I wait."

"Honey, 'Mr. Ames' hasn't been able to rent the place for

weeks. My guess is he'll wait no matter how little you can give him. And you'd better call him Tom, or everybody in the bar will start snickering at him and then he'll have to punch somebody. You have a place to stay yet?"

Deirdre nodded. "My cousin's letting me stay in her apartment." Of course, she currently had no furniture and only the basics in the kitchen. But she figured furniture could wait until she had enough to pay cash for her shop space.

"Well, then, I'd say you're on your way." Clem stood, wiping her hands on a dishtowel. "Now, come on with me and I'll show you everything Tom and Bobby Sue forgot to mention about how this place runs."

Docia had just put Rolf down for his nap when the phone rang. Not that the phone would have awakened him—like his father, once Rolf was out, he was out. Docia shook her head as she headed toward the kitchen. *Rolf. Geez. We might as well enroll him in therapy now.*

She checked the number and grimaced. "Hi, Mama. Rolf is fine, and I don't have time to bring him down to San Antonio this weekend. Anything else?"

Docia could almost hear her mother's pout. "Well, shoot. I've got the cutest outfit for him that I picked up at La Cantera yesterday."

"Bring it up the next time you come. He's not growing *that* fast." Although he did seem to be growing out of his clothes at a terrific rate, now that she thought about it.

"I'll do that, but to tell you the truth, that's not exactly why I called."

Docia sank into one of the kitchen chairs. A day when her mother didn't call just to talk about Rolf was pretty rare right now. "What's up?"

"I had an interesting visitor today. A Mr. Craig Dempsey. He said he works for your uncle."

"Uncle John?" She managed to keep her voice light, while her mind worked furiously. She hadn't told her mother anything about Deirdre yet because she wasn't entirely sure whose side she'd be on.

"He's looking for Dee-Dee. Apparently, she's disappeared.

Have you heard anything from her?"

Docia paused just long enough to let her mother know she was considering a lie.

"Oh please. Don't bother making something up. She's there, isn't she?"

She sighed. "Yes, ma'am. She came here a couple of days ago. I let her have the apartment since she wouldn't stay out here with us. You know Deirdre. She didn't want to be a bother."

"Is she all right? Dempsey said she and John had had a fight, hard as that is for me to believe. I can't picture Dee-Dee fighting with anyone, can you?"

"Maybe not Dee-Dee, but she's Deirdre now. And yes, I think she's finally found enough backbone to fight back with Uncle John. She's always been pretty good about taking care of herself with everybody else."

Her mother chuckled. "Well, good for her. John needs someone to stand up to him—it'll be good for both of them. But what's this Dee-Dee-Deirdre business?"

Docia poured herself a glass of iced tea. "She's changed, Mama. She wants people to call her Deirdre now. And she's here because she wants to go into business for herself—she wants to open some kind of coffee shop."

"Coffee shop?" Her mother sounded confused. "You mean like a Starbucks?"

"No, she wants to actually roast the coffee beans and sell custom blended coffee. She's got her business plan all worked out. It looked good to me, but I told her to show it to Lars."

Her mother snorted. "Deirdre doesn't need to get any accountant to look at her business plan, even an accountant as good as Lars. That child was always smart as a whip, and she graduated from McCombs with honors as I recall."

Docia nodded, then remembered her mother couldn't see her. "She did. And she is. But she's also never had to do much with her smarts. Uncle John always had her life planned out for her. And he never seemed to realize how smart she was, anyway."

"John didn't want to realize it." Her mother sighed. "He wanted a son. He never knew what to do with a daughter exactly."

"Well, he's found something to do with her now. He's pretty much disowned her. He cut off her credit cards and her accounts, even her savings accounts. And he threw her out of her apartment in Houston. All because she didn't want to work for him anymore."

"Oh my lord," her mother gasped. "No wonder John's feeling guilty. You tell that child to come down here right now. She can stay with me and I'll find her a job at the foundation. She doesn't know the first thing about being on her own."

"She doesn't want that, Mama. She really wants to make it on her own this time, with her own business."

"Dee-Dee—I mean Deirdre—wants to be on her own? Since when? She's always been the most cautious child I ever knew. And John wanted her that way. I was amazed when he let her go off to school by herself."

"I don't know what happened to her exactly, but she's trying to be independent. And I think we should back her up if we can. Which means not telling Uncle John she's up here, Mama. Please?"

Her mother sighed again. "You're right about that. He'd make things worse. Or he'd come down there and try to bully her back to Houston. I'm just worried about her, that's all."

"Me too." Docia sipped her tea. "But I'll keep an eye on her. Me and everybody else in the family. We won't let anything happen to her, I promise."

"All right." Her mother's voice warmed slightly. "Is she still as gorgeous as ever?"

"More. She's let her hair grow and it's down to her shoulders with a little natural wave. Even without makeup, which of course she doesn't wear because it never occurs to her to wear it, she's enough to stop traffic. And she's still got the worst fashion sense I ever saw. Nobody ever notices how gorgeous she is when she shows up in those baggy slacks."

"And she doesn't notice it either. Or understand what she could do with it. Thanks to my boneheaded brother who sent her to girls' schools all her life and never told her how beautiful she was." Her mother gave a disgusted snort. "This Dempsey character doesn't strike me as somebody who'd be much better about that. He seems too impressed with himself to be impressed with anybody else."

"Well, she's going to have to make it on her own now. No

more Armani suits and lunches at the Galleria."

"Oh my, she's a lamb among the wolves, Docia Mae."

Docia's lips curved up in a faint smile. "She may have been, once upon a time, Mama. Now I think the wolves had better get ready for a shock."

Chapter Five

Deirdre regarded the Faro's evening crowd a bit apprehensively. There were a lot more men than women, and the noise level had risen so high she could barely hear the music on the jukebox. The other barmaid, Sylvia, moved deftly between the tables, smiling at the customers. Chico loomed in a corner nearest the pool table. He didn't smile at the customers, but Deirdre figured that wasn't part of his job.

Tom Ames had been joined by another bartender, a small gray-haired man named Harry who seemed to spend most of his time drawing drafts and pouring the occasional glass of wine. Tom did the mixed drinks.

Deirdre fought back the tight sensation in her chest. *You can do this, Deirdre. You were an executive vice president.*

After she'd finished work that afternoon, Tom had suggested she wear something "a little more appropriate" to work the evening shift. Deirdre had no idea what clothes were appropriate for a barmaid, but she'd gone home to check through her wardrobe. The Escada pantsuit didn't strike her as an option, but the jeans she'd worn at noon apparently weren't good enough. She'd ended up in her sole pair of khakis and a knit shirt she'd bought for a corporate retreat. It looked more like something she should wear for a round of golf than something she'd wear to wait tables in a bar, but it was the only thing she had that might work.

Tom gave her a long look when she came in, then shrugged, leaning over the end of the bar where she stood out of everybody's way. "Ready to go?"

"I guess so. What do I do?"

He shrugged. "It's pretty straight. Take the orders. Bring

them to me or Harry. Pick up the drinks. Take them back to the table. Get the money."

Deirdre blinked at him. "What do I do with the money?"

He gave her a look that made her feel like a moron. Correction, *more* like a moron. "Bring it to me. Here. When you get a break." He turned back to open the cash register, reaching inside. "Here's a stack of ten singles to start with. For change—put it in your pocket. Keep your tips in your other pocket so they don't get confused."

She nodded, folding the money into the pocket of her khakis, then turned back to the room. *Just men. Nothing to be nervous about here. Just men.* She stiffened her spine and walked to the first table. "What can I get for you gentlemen?"

One of the men glanced at her, cupping a hand over his ear. "What?"

"What do you want to drink?" Deirdre felt like she was bellowing, but the rest of the table hadn't even turned her way yet.

"Hey," the first man called to his friends. "Doofus. What are you drinking?"

Two other heads swiveled back.

"What can I get for you?" Deirdre shouted.

"Shiner. Three drafts," the first man bawled out.

Deirdre turned on her heel and headed back to the bar. "Shiner. Three drafts," she yelled at Harry.

He poured them in record time, sliding them across the bar. Deirdre stared at them dumbly. She had no idea how she was supposed to pick them up.

"On the tray," Tom explained. He pushed the three steins together so that the handles formed a circle, then lifted them onto a metal tray. "If you get more than three or four, call Chico to help you."

Deirdre grabbed the tray and hoisted it to her shoulder—it was a lot heavier than it looked. She staggered back across the room, then plunked the steins into the middle of the table.

The three men looked up at her. One of them gave his buddy a quick grin. "I can't reach it, honey," he bawled. "Push it a little closer."

Deirdre frowned. He wouldn't have much trouble if he just leaned forward. Still, she was supposed to do her best even if this was a transparent attempt to look down the front of her shirt. Not that the front of her golf shirt was all that enticing. She leaned down slightly and shoved the beer in his direction.

The man's grin widened and then stopped abruptly. Deirdre had a sudden sense of someone at her side and looked up to find Chico glaring at the table.

The men looked away from her as the song ended on the jukebox. "That'll be six dollars," Deirdre said quickly in the relative silence.

The first man handed her a ten. Deirdre started to reach into her pocket, but he shook his head after glancing at Chico. "Keep it."

"Thanks." Deirdre moved on to the next table, vaguely aware of Chico in the background. She was glad he'd come over, but she needed to look out for herself if she was going to do this.

She went back to the bar to give Tom the ten, then pocketed the tip. Another table gestured at her, trying to get her attention. She had a feeling others were beginning to turn her way. *Oh well. The more tips you get, the closer you are to getting your shop.*

She pasted a smile on her face and headed for the next group of drinkers.

Tom watched his newest barmaid square her shoulders as if she were heading into battle. In a way, of course, she was. A battle against the assholes of the world. Unfortunately, it was a battle she wouldn't win, but then neither would anybody else.

Deirdre Brandenburg could eventually work out well, assuming that she got the hang of the job. Right now she looked at little like a refugee from prep school who'd stumbled into the bar by accident. He sighed. While she was dressed like that, most of the customers wouldn't give her a second glance. Hell, he even forgot what a knockout she was unless he was looking directly at her face.

On the other side of the room, Sylvia cast a few exasperated looks Deirdre's way, but given the amount of complaining she'd done about being the only full-time barmaid in the place, she didn't have any room to gripe. She wanted help, and now she'd gotten it, tentative and fumbling though it was at the moment. *Be careful what you wish for, Sylvia.*

Of course, that could also be good advice for him. He'd wanted a good-looking barmaid, and he'd gotten Audrey Hepburn, circa 1958. Not exactly what he'd been expecting. But the real question was, could Audrey Hepburn sell Shiner Bock?

He watched Deirdre slide nervously between the tables, apparently trying not to get trapped by groping hands. Of course, if anybody tried any serious groping, Chico would be on them in a split second. Still, he was amazed that someone so heartstoppingly beautiful was so unsure of herself. As if she had no idea what she looked like.

He blew out a quick sigh. At least a few more locals might come to the bar after the town heard his new waitress was related, although distantly, to the Toleffsons. And Deirdre didn't give any indication of being a pain in the ass. He'd known his share of knockouts, and they'd all been trouble on a stick. Deirdre Brandenburg didn't strike him as any kind of trouble at all. Except for the trouble she might cause if she ever showed up wearing something besides L.L. Bean.

"Two margaritas," Sylvia snapped.

He'd been so busy watching Deirdre he hadn't even noticed her walk up. *Oops.* He turned back to grab the tequila.

"Where'd you find her?" Sylvia's voice sounded particularly edgy tonight.

"She walked in today. Needed a job."

"She doesn't know what she's doing."

"She will." He placed the drinks on her tray.

"She doesn't belong here." Sylvia sounded almost envious, like she wished she didn't belong in the Faro either, all evidence to the contrary.

Tom sighed. "Sure she does. Just roll with it, Sylvia. She'll work out." He watched Sylvia flounce back across the room and profoundly hoped he was right.

Deirdre was at her shop by nine the next morning. *Her shop.* She paused to let the idiot grin fade away. She'd managed to get Tom Ames to give her the key the night before so that she could at least see what needed to be done. Now she stood in the middle of the room, fighting a mixture of elation and dismay.

The place was dirty. *Really* dirty. Dirtier than any place where she'd ever spent time before. The concrete floor was streaked with dust and some stains that looked like grease. The walls needed to be washed down and then repainted. The finish on the shelves was cracked and peeling. She walked slowly toward the back. The counter at the end of the room was at least in decent shape, although the surface needed a good cleaning.

She measured the space between the back wall and the counter carefully. The coffee maker could go here, although the roaster would need to go in the back storage room, along with the sacks of beans. Since the sink was on the other side of the wall, the plumbing connection should be easy. The cooler would go on the other side of the door, so that customers could see what they had for drinks besides coffee. Right now, she figured mineral water and maybe some artisan sodas. And iced tea for the traditionalists.

That was assuming, of course, that she could clean off at least a few layers of grime. Right now the health department would probably shut her down in about five seconds if she tried to serve anything edible. She turned back to the sack of cleaning supplies she'd picked up at the grocery store on her way there, hoping she'd gotten enough, at least to start.

An hour later, she'd managed to wash most of the surface dirt off the floor, although the stains looked like they'd need either a scraper or a steam cleaner. Deirdre bit her lip, wondering if Tom Ames would be interested in splitting the cost of renting one, assuming she could run it herself. She sighed. Probably not, since he'd let the shop get into this condition in the first place.

Someone knocked on the front door she had propped open, and Tom himself stepped inside. He wrinkled his nose. "Stinks in here."

She shrugged. "Ammonia. It's in the cleaner. That's why I've got the doors and windows open."

He glanced around the room, frowning. "Floor looks better. What do you want to do about the walls?"

"I'll get to them next. They'll need a good washing down and then some paint."

He nodded absently. "And the shelves?"

"They'll need to be stripped and repainted too." She swallowed. "Would you be willing to spring for the paint?"

He shrugged. "Sure. It's my place. Are you sure you can do all of this by yourself?"

Deirdre blew out a breath. "I've already figured out what I need. I can do it."

"If you think you can, go for it. Of course, I might need to raise the rent after you finish fixing the place up."

She stared at him until she saw the corners of his mouth edge up into a grin.

"Relax. I'm kidding."

"Good to know."

"You might want to go home and get cleaned up yourself. Lunch shift starts in less than an hour."

She glanced regretfully at the damp floor. One more pass might do it. On the other hand, she was currently too filthy to wait tables, even at the Faro. "I guess I'd better start bringing clean clothes with me when I come over here in the morning. Then I can just clean up in the back before I start work."

"Okay by me. See you later." He started toward the door.

"What should I do with those boxes in the back room?" she called after him.

He paused, frowning slightly. "Ferguson's T-shirts? I've been using them for bar rags. I guess you could use them for cleaning. They're not worth much more than that."

"Oh." She glanced back at the boxes piled in the storeroom. "They're all T-shirts? All those boxes?"

"Far as I know. Do what you want with them—like I say, they're not worth much." Tom headed back out the door.

Deirdre stood staring at the storeroom, with its leaning tower of T-shirts, then glanced at her watch. Unfortunately, Tom was right. She'd have to leave them until this afternoon, after the noon rush was over.

Craig Dempsey sat opposite Big John Brandenburg's desk, pretending he wasn't intimidated. Brandenburg's desk was an antique—heavy mahogany, burnished to the color of old honey, a good six feet across and a yard wide. Plenty of room for Big John himself and a message to anybody sitting on the other side.

Be impressed. Be very impressed.

Craig was. Money always impressed him, mainly because he knew how to spend it. He figured he'd be spending Big John's soon enough, right after he dragged Dee-Dee back where she belonged and got the requisite ring on her finger. Maybe he'd even get a desk like this one as a reward.

"So you talked to Reba," Brandenburg rumbled. "Did she know where Dee-Dee was?"

"She said no."

"You think she was lying?"

Now there was an interesting question. Unfortunately, it wasn't one he had a good answer for. "I don't think so," he said carefully. "She seemed surprised Dee-Dee was gone."

"Hell." Brandenburg stared down at the pile of papers in front of him. "She can't have gone too far. She doesn't have any money."

Craig thought of Dee-Dee trying to get by without money. Without her father's support. Without all the cushions she'd had most of her life. "No," he agreed. "She wouldn't be able to get too far away. Are there any other relatives she might call on?"

Big John gave him one of those looks that he'd grown to recognize. *Why don't you already know this? Weren't you almost engaged?* "We never spoke much about your family," he explained quickly. "It seemed to be a sensitive subject." He had no idea whether that was true, but it sounded like he cared.

Brandenburg shrugged. "Maybe so." He stared down at his desk again, his forehead creased in thought.

Craig wondered what he was supposed to do now, if anything. He wasn't a private detective, which was what the big man probably needed. He had no idea where else to look. Left to his own devices, he'd just wait for Dee-Dee to limp home on her own once she gave up in defeat. A defeated Dee-Dee would be a lot easier to bring around to his point of view anyway.

"Konigsburg," Brandenburg muttered.

"Excuse me?"

"Konigsburg." He glanced up at Craig. "It's where my fool niece ended up. Running a damn fool bookstore. Married some nobody and got herself a kid. Dee-Dee might head over there.

To see her cousin Docia."

"Konigsburg?"

"Hell, yes. Hill Country town. Don't tell me you never heard of it."

Of course, Craig had heard of it. Every Texan had heard of Konigsburg, and most of them had been there at least once. It was blue-hair central. His own grandmother had loved the place. She'd dragged him up there one summer to look for the over-decorated china figurines she collected. That was far from his favorite childhood memory. "Yes sir, I'm familiar with it. It just doesn't seem like the kind of place Dee-Dee would end up in."

"That's where she is, I'm sure of it." He brought his fist down on the desktop. "Goddamn it. Reba's got a house up there. I'll bet you anything, Dee-Dee's staying with her or that daughter of hers. She flat out lied to you, boy."

Craig studied his employer. The big man seemed a lot more pissed than the situation warranted. But he might be able to use that reaction to his advantage. "I didn't think she was lying, sir. But I've been wrong about women before." He shrugged, giving him a rueful little smile. Just one more man betrayed by female deviousness.

"You need to get up there."

"To Konigsburg?"

"Yes to Konigsburg. Get up there now."

Craig took a breath, trying to figure out how to be diplomatic. "What do you want me to do up there, sir?"

Brandenburg waved an impatient hand. "Find Dee-Dee, of course. Track her down. Tell her to stop being an idiot. Get her back here."

"And if she doesn't want to come?"

Brandenburg's face darkened. "She will. She's been out on her own for a while now. You can tell her she's got a job waiting in Houston. She'll be good and ready to come back by now."

Craig didn't comment on that. He figured even if Dee-Dee wasn't quite ready yet, he could always fix things so she would be. With Brandenburg money behind him, he'd find a way to bring her back to her senses. And, of course, back to him.

Deirdre managed not to groan as she sank into her chair at the back of the Faro. Two days of cleaning had shown her how little her yoga classes had prepared her for real physical labor. Every muscle in her body had its own particular ache. And now she had to go out to the bar and carry trays of beer steins for three or four hours.

Clem slid a ham sandwich in her direction before flopping down on the other side of the table. "You look like you've been dragged through a knothole. Are you sure it's a good idea to work both shifts and clean that shithole in between?"

Deirdre sighed. "Probably not. But I need to get the basic cleaning done so I can start painting. The place needs to be in shape before I can bring in equipment."

"You should ask Tom for advice on renovating. He brought this place back from the dead."

"How long has he owned the Faro?" Deirdre frowned. "I thought he'd been here for a long time."

"He's been here a couple of years. The owner before him ran the place into the ground, more or less. Tom put it back on the map and made it work. It's doing better now than it ever did before."

Deirdre glanced around the room, curiously. She hadn't really had time to take a good look at it until now, plus at night it was mostly too dark to see details. She didn't have a lot of experience with bars, but the Faro looked better than some she'd been in. Like a lot of Konigsburg, it had an old-timey feel. Limestone block walls, pegged pine floors, a carved mahogany bar that looked like it was part of the original fixtures. The pictures on the walls seemed to be antique too, sepia-tinted photographs and engravings, along with some mounted deer horns and a huge buffalo head at the end of the room.

Deirdre blinked. The buffalo was wearing hoop earrings.

Clem grinned. "That's Bruno. Part of the original fixtures. Tom added the earrings."

"Interesting sense of style."

Clem nodded. "He's got a feel for the place—that's what made me sign on with him. I had a catering business that wasn't going anywhere since I had to compete with people like Allie Maldonado and Brenner's restaurant. He hired me to make bar snacks for a while, and then he took me on full-time when he decided to try serving meals. Now we've got enough business to support you and Bobby Sue and Sylvia, with Marilyn on the weekends, along with Leon and Harry and Chico. Hell, he could probably use some more help. My guess is we'll be doing dinners within a month. Tom's making it work. It's his bar, and he cares about it."

Deirdre considered the unexpected phenomenon of Tom Ames as a successful entrepreneur. Well why not? Nobody ever expected her to have any business sense either. And yet she'd managed to keep a couple of her father's smaller divisions from going under.

Clem raised her eyebrows again. "You've never told me exactly how you ended up waiting tables here, you know. And don't tell me you're earning money for your coffee shop. We both know you won't earn enough here to open it, even with the good tips you could start pulling down eventually."

"I can always apply for a loan when the time comes." Deirdre took another bite of her sandwich and concentrated on chewing.

"Come on, give. Everything about you screams Smart Kid From the City, and if you're related to Docia, you're probably rich, too. What's going on, Deirdre? Where's the money?"

She sighed. "I have some money. I just can't get to it right now. My father and I had a...disagreement, and he's put a block on my funds. But that should be straightened out soon." At least she sincerely hoped it would. On the other hand, she wasn't too optimistic about it. "I'll use whatever I earn here to clean the place up, then I'll order equipment when I get access to my own money again."

"No offense, honey, but you need to use some of that money you're earning to fix yourself up, too."

Deirdre glanced down at her khakis. Okay, the knit shirt was looking a little wilted. She'd washed it out in her kitchen sink at night, so at least it was clean. It wasn't like she had a lot of choices in her closet, unless she started wearing her business suits. "What's wrong with what I've got on?"

"Nothing if you want to disappear into the woodwork, which, by the way, won't get you much in the way of tips. Plus you're beginning to look a little like a bag lady from River Oaks."

Deirdre frowned. "I can't afford a new wardrobe right now."

"Sure you can. Take tomorrow afternoon off from cleaning. We'll go over to Too Good To Be Threw, on Spicewood. They'll have stuff you can afford, I guarantee it."

"Shopping?" Deirdre felt like sighing. She really hated shopping. "I haven't done that for a while. I mean, I used to use a shopping service."

"You mean like a personal shopper? How does that work, anyway?"

"You tell them what you want, and they find it for you. Saves a lot of time. Besides, I'm no good at shopping."

Clem grinned. "Then it's a good thing I'm an expert. Think of me as your personal thrift store shopper."

Deirdre bit her lip, trying to fight back the sense of encroaching doom. She pictured her closet at Docia's apartment, the rows of sober business suits. Business suits she'd probably never need again, given that she was going into the coffee business. "Does this store buy clothes, too?"

"Sure. They're basically resale, so they take a lot of stuff on consignment, or Carolee can give you a flat payment." Clem took a gulp of her iced tea. "Why, you got some stuff to get rid of?"

"I might, now that I think about it. And then I could use the money to buy something that would be appropriate here."

Clem shook her head. "I shudder to think what that might be, but Too Good To Be Threw has a little of everything."

"Okay." Deirdre nodded decisively. "I'll take some time off tomorrow after the lunch shift."

"Good." Clem stood up again. "Time to set up the nachos so y'all can throw them in the microwave when you need to."

Deirdre pushed herself away from the table, thinking about her suits, her shoes, her matching bags. *A whole other life that I won't be needing anymore. At least with any luck I won't.* She rapped her knuckles lightly on the wooden table, then turned toward the bar to get change for the night.

Chapter Six

Craig drove his Suburban to Konigsburg, leaving his BMW at home. He figured it was best to be inconspicuous, at least at first, and the Suburban would definitely fit in better in the Hill Country. Dee-Dee should be glad to see him, given how long she'd been out there on her own by now, but he wasn't taking anything for granted. After all, he hadn't expected her to stay out this long in the first place.

He sauntered down Main, looking for a bookstore. Big John hadn't been able to give him the name of the place, just that his niece owned it and he'd know her when he saw her ("Six feet tall and orange hair. Never been one to hide her head under a basket either").

Kent's Hill Country Books looked like his best bet, given that the niece's maiden name had been Kent. He hadn't exactly decided what he'd say if he found Dee-Dee working there. It depended on how miserable she looked. Maybe she'd just let him bundle her up right then and there and take her home, which would really work out best for everyone concerned. He wouldn't remind her how dumb she'd been, either.

He didn't see Dee-Dee in the shop when he walked in, but he didn't see any six-foot redheads either. The woman behind the counter was small and dark-haired. He managed not to grind his teeth in frustration.

"Can I help you?" the brunette asked.

Craig gave her his best promoter's smile. "I'm looking for the owner."

The brunette smiled. "That's me. I'm one of them, anyway. Janie Toleffson."

Well, hell. This was going to be more complicated than he'd thought. "Actually, I'm trying to find Docia Kent. Is this her bookstore?" Big John hadn't been able to remember his niece's married name either.

Janie Toleffson's forehead furrowed slightly. "This is her store, but her name is Toleffson now, too. Are you a friend?"

"Not exactly." He upped the warmth of the smile. "We've never met. I need to ask her about someone—a common acquaintance."

The brunette's forehead didn't get any smoother. "I don't know when Docia will be here exactly. Perhaps you could leave a card with your number so that she could call you."

Craig figured he wouldn't hold his breath waiting for that call, but it was the best he could do at the moment. He handed the brunette a business card, with one more smile. "She can reach me at my cell number. I'll be in town for a few days."

Janie Toleffson glanced at the card, then looked more closely. "Brandenburg, Inc.?"

He nodded. "I work for Mrs. Toleffson's uncle."

Something flickered behind her eyes for a moment, almost too quickly for him to notice. But he had, and he had a good idea what it meant. She'd made the connection with Dee-Dee, and maybe she knew where Dee-Dee was.

The brunette smiled again. "I'll give this to Docia when she comes in."

"Thanks, I appreciate it."

Craig left the store with a spring in his step. He might or might not hear back from Docia Kent Toleffson, but he'd learned something even more important. He was reasonably certain now that the old man had been right—Dee-Dee was somewhere in Konigsburg. Which made her a hell of a lot easier to find.

Deirdre wasn't exactly sure what to make of Too Good To Be Threw, but then she'd never been to a vintage clothing store before. She wasn't even sure what made something vintage instead of just used.

Clem introduced her to Carolee Guttenberg, the owner, and Deirdre brought in a half dozen of her suits. She figured she might need to keep something to wear to the bank when she applied for the loan she was more and more certain she was going to need, but she also figured she wouldn't be wearing most of them any time soon.

Carolee held them up, narrowing her eyes slightly, then blew out a quick breath. "Good quality. Very good. The labels alone should bring in a nice price. You're sure you want to get rid of these?"

"I don't need them anymore. Do you think they'll sell?"

Carolee grinned. "Lord above, they'll sell in a split second to the right person. Some yuppie from Austin's going to find this stuff and think she's hit the mother lode. That's if I don't grab them myself first. You want to leave them on consignment or take a payment now?"

"I'll take a payment this time—I need to buy some things for myself. I may have some more for consignment later."

Carolee grinned again. "Any time, sweetie."

Deirdre tucked the money from the suits into her purse, then headed toward the back of the store.

Clem had already started flipping through a rack. "Okay, grab a few of these and try them on. Let's see what fits."

Deirdre narrowed her eyes. "Jeans? I've got jeans."

Clem shook her head. "I've seen your jeans. They look like boyfriend pants, and not in a good way either. We're trying to come up with a look that will improve your tips at the Faro, not one that'll scare the customers away."

Deirdre thought about protesting. Then again, she'd bought her jeans for comfort, not fashion. They were what she'd worn to laze around her apartment on the weekend. Maybe comfort wasn't as important at the Faro.

Clem pulled a couple of pairs of jeans off the rack and handed them to her. "Try these on first. That way we can get an idea of fit."

Deirdre stepped into the minuscule dressing room at the back, pulling off her sandals. The jeans were so old the fabric felt like suede. She pulled them on, zipped them up, and stepped out to look at herself in the mirror. "These look nice."

Clem shook her head. "Wrong size. Try these."

Deirdre squinted at her reflection. The jeans looked fine to her, but Clem was her personal shopper this time around. And she needed those tips.

She stepped back into the dressing room and pulled on the next pair. These were a lot harder to zip. She took a breath, pulled up the zipper, and stepped out again, panting.

Clem narrowed her eyes, studying her in the mirror. "We're getting there. Maybe a half size more." She handed her another hanger. "Try these."

This time, Deirdre had to ease the jeans over her hips bit by bit, unfolding them gradually until they reached slightly below her waist. It took two tries to get the waistband closed. She worried about the strength of the zipper. Taking a few shallow breaths, she stepped out of the dressing room again, telling herself she didn't really see spots dancing in front of her eyes.

Clem broke into a grin. "That's it."

"But I can't breathe," Deirdre gasped.

"They'll loosen up a little as you wear them. Besides, breathing's overrated."

Deirdre gritted her teeth. "Not by those who do it regularly. Anyway, I can't bend over in these. How am I supposed to serve drinks?"

"Try bending your knees."

She bent slightly. She could swear the fabric groaned behind her.

"See? You can bend down like that. And besides, once they get molded to you, you'll be able to bend over too if you want."

"I don't know, Clem."

"Carolee?" Clem called. "Come back here and look at her, will you?"

Carolee peeked over a clothes rack, then broke into a grin. "Oh my. You're gonna wear those to wait tables? You'll start a riot. Everybody in town will be down there."

"I rest my case." Clem handed her another pair of jeans. "Try these, too. Boot cut Levis."

After a half hour, Deirdre had three pairs of jeans and a stitch in her side from holding her breath. "I guess they'll be okay. But I need to buy some blouses to go with them. I don't have anything besides that knit shirt I've been wearing all week." Obviously, the tailored silks she had for her suits wouldn't exactly work for the Faro, although they'd be a sort of interesting look with the jeans.

Clem shook her head. "No blouses. T-shirts. Preferably in juvenile sizes." She headed toward a table at the side of the shop. "Check these out. Vintage concert shirts. You can load up on country and heavy metal."

Deirdre picked up a shirt and then set it down again quickly. "My lord! Did you see how much these cost?"

"They're vintage. I told you. Collectibles."

"I don't think I can afford vintage. And I need something for wearing, not collecting. Can't I just get something new?"

Clem frowned. "I guess you could go for some of that sequin crap like the stuff Carolee has up front, but they're sort of obvious. And that's what Sylvia wears. You need your own look."

"Well, I can't afford this look." Deirdre picked up another shirt, then paused. "Wait. You want T-shirts? I've got T-shirts. And they won't cost a thing."

Clem's frown didn't lighten. "What T-shirts? Something you brought with you? You'll want to clear it with me first, believe me."

Deirdre shook her head. "The ones in the back room at the shop. Tom said he didn't have any use for them. There's got to be something in there that will fit."

"As long as they're not something your grandmother would wear, I guess they'll work."

Deirdre's grandmother had never worn anything that hadn't come from Neiman-Marcus or New York City, but she figured that wasn't something she needed to share just then. "Believe me, they won't be."

"Okay." Clem rubbed her hands together. "Now let's talk jewelry."

Considering that it was a weeknight, business was surprisingly brisk that evening. Tom did a quick head count—two or three empty tables, and a couple of groups of six. He checked his watch. Deirdre was a few minutes late, which didn't seem like her. But Tom figured she was entitled to the occasional messed-up day, as long as she didn't make a habit of it. Besides, she'd stayed late with the lunch shift today.

Fortunately, Sylvia was on time for once. And making sure

everybody knew it. "Where is that Deirdre, anyway? I can't take care of all these tables by myself."

"She'll be here. Have Chico carry the drinks over for you."

Sylvia pouted in his general direction before flouncing back to her tables, giving her hips an extra flip in his direction. Tom made a show of not noticing. He hadn't taken Sylvia up on any of her earlier implied offers, and he wasn't interested in starting now. He mixed a couple of whiskey sours and checked his watch again.

"I'm here," Deirdre panted behind him. "I'm sorry. I got held up."

Tom turned toward her and froze, staring.

Her jeans were like a second skin that fit better than most people's first one did. Her bright red T-shirt looked to be maybe a half-size too small—it hugged the curves of her breasts lovingly. She'd pulled her long black hair up in a topknot, but a few strands lapped against her neck and the golden hoops at her ears. And her lips were pinker than usual, as if she'd been chewing on them.

She was, without doubt, the hottest woman he'd seen within the last month. Possibly year. Possibly decade.

Tom squinted at the black printing across her chest. "Liddy Brenner Festival 2007?" Somehow he managed to keep his voice from shaking.

"It was one of the ones in the back room at the shop. I hope you don't mind." Deirdre chewed her lip for a moment and Tom felt all the blood leave his brain, heading south.

"That's okay," he croaked. "Use them any way you want."

"All right. Could I get some change?"

Tom went on staring at her, trying to get his brain back in gear again. "Change?"

"My ten dollars in singles?" Deirdre's brow furrowed. "Are you feeling okay?"

He closed his eyes for a moment. "Never better. Ten dollars, coming up." He turned hurriedly toward the cash register. Anything to get away from staring at the honky-tonk vision in front of the bar. She'd probably have to slug him in another minute or so.

When he turned back again, Deirdre gave him a dazzling smile that had his groin throbbing. "Thanks."

She started to tuck the money into her jeans pocket, then paused, sliding her fingers in slowly so that she could work the dollar bills under the skin-tight fabric.

Amazing. He hadn't thought it was still possible for him to get this hard this fast.

Deirdre gave him another bright smile then and headed for her first table.

Tom blew out a breath as he watched her. Something told him it was going to be a very interesting night.

The first table she walked by stared after her, mesmerized. One kid's jaw actually dropped in disbelief. Finally, one of them raised a hand. "Miss," he called. "Ma'am?" His voice sounded as if it was on the verge of cracking, although Tom had already carded them and knew the kid was at least twenty-one.

Deirdre turned back to him, raising one of those parenthesis eyebrows of hers. "Yes? Can I get you something?"

The kid stared at her, his face flushing in the dim light of the bar. "Yes, yeah," he stammered. "Beer. I'll have beer."

"What kind of beer?"

"A...draft." The boy winced, probably because somebody had kicked him under the table.

One of the other boys leaned across the table, waving a bill at Deirdre. "A pitcher. Bring us another pitcher, sweetheart."

Tom saw Deirdre narrow her eyes. She was so far out of the kid's league he should be getting the bends, but Tom had to admire his *cojones.*

"A pitcher it is." She leaned forward slightly, snatching the bill from his hand, then turned back toward the bar, her hips giving a natural swing that looked like the move Sylvia had been trying unsuccessfully to perfect.

The boys stared after her, spellbound. One of them clasped both hands across his heart, flopping them to imitate a beat. The others broke into desperate snickers.

Deirdre flicked an annoyed glanced over her shoulder without breaking stride. A couple of the boys looked like they might faint.

Dear lord in heaven. Tom only hoped they'd all get through the evening without any visible scars.

Deirdre had felt breathless with excitement, to say nothing of the jeans, when she'd finally made it to the Faro. She'd had to dig through a stack of T-shirts before she found one Clem approved of, but when she pulled it on, Clem nodded slowly, grinning. "Oh boy. I'd almost like to stick around tonight to watch, but I think I'll leave you to it. Have fun."

She had. At least for the first hour or so. Sylvia had cast a few annoyed glances in her direction, but Deirdre had been too busy to pay much attention. All of a sudden, everybody in her station needed something. Beer. Nachos. Pitchers. Margaritas. Even a couple of glasses of wine. They'd kept her hopping back and forth between the tables, so busy that Chico had started following her with a tray of drinks.

Actually, she figured Chico was following her for reasons other than carrying her tray. The more raucous tables quieted down noticeably when he walked by.

However, the first fight of the evening actually didn't involve her at all. A couple of the guys at the pool table got into an argument that graduated to shoving. She'd seen them before, and Harry had called them the Steinbruner brothers. At the moment, they weren't being very brotherly. Chico stepped up beside them and the two subsided into snarls.

Deirdre stood at the side of the room, watching with wide eyes. She'd never really seen a bar fight before, although she'd sat through her share of yelling at Brandenburg, Inc.

"Miss," somebody brayed from the other side of the room. Deirdre took a deep, calming breath and walked briskly toward the table—four more boys who looked barely legal. She knew Tom checked IDs, but she hoped he recognized fakes. She'd never noticed how many young guys they had in the Faro before.

"What can I get for you gentlemen?" She gave them the smile she'd begun using, spreading her lips to show just the right amount of teeth. She'd practiced in the mirror a few times after watching Sylvia. It didn't exactly feel natural, but it seemed to do the trick.

"Depends, honey." One of the boys leaned forward with what he probably thought was a sexy smile. "What have you got?"

The easiest way to deal with juvenile jerks seemed to be to take them literally. "We have Shiner, Lone Star, and Bud on tap. A lot of bottled imports—some new microbrews. And mixed drinks. Would you like to order something?" She delivered the speech without smiling, since smiling seemed to bring out the worst in kids like him for some reason.

"Yeah." The boy leaned sat back in his chair, his gaze traveling up and down her body. "Bring me another one of these. A Bud." He shook his beer stein in her direction. "You can take this back, too."

Deirdre stood still. She'd have to lean across the table to get the stein, and she had a feeling that wouldn't be pleasant. On the other hand, this was her job. She blew out another breath and stretched her hand toward him. As she leaned down, one of the other boys reached up and squeezed her breast.

She straightened abruptly, staring at him in shock. "You...jerk," she blurted.

The other boys guffawed, high-fiving the groper.

"Out." A male voice sounded over her shoulder. Deirdre turned, expecting to see Chico. Instead, Tom Ames stood behind her. All of a sudden, he seemed a lot taller than the six-feet-something she'd originally estimated. His blue eyes were glacial. He held a sawed-off pool cue in one hand.

"Aw, man," one of the boys began, "we were just..."

"I know what you were just. Pay your tab and get out. Now."

Another of the boys struggled to his feet, knocking over his chair in the process. "You can't throw us out of here. We didn't do anything."

"You groped my waitress. And you're shit-faced, or close enough to be dangerous. I want you out of my place."

The boy took a staggering step in Tom's direction, and then stopped as Chico stepped up to the other side of the table. "You heard what the man said."

"Deirdre?" Tom half turned in her direction. "What do they owe?"

She shook her head. "Nothing. They're paid up."

Chico's mouth slid into a grin that didn't reach any other part of his face. "Except for the tip."

"Tip?" The first boy stared at him open-mouthed. "You have got to be kidding me."

Chico's biceps flexed, sending a ripple through his tattoos. "Give the lady her tip, jerk-off. You need to pay her for the insult."

Tom frowned. Deirdre had a feeling he hadn't planned on going quite this far. Chico folded his arms across his massive chest, studying the boy in front of him. He seemed to be considering weak spots.

The boy reached into his pocket and tossed a wad of singles on the table. "Here you go...Deirdre." Somehow, he made her name sound like an obscenity. "Come on, let's get out of here. Place is a shithole anyway."

Chico frowned. For a moment, Deirdre was afraid he'd take a swing at the kid on general principles.

Tom shook his head slightly. "Just go."

The boys headed for the door, rolling their shoulders and trying for macho. From the far side of the room, somebody gave a particularly moist raspberry. One of the boys paused in the doorway, his hand clenching. Then his buddies grabbed his arm and pulled him outside.

Deirdre exhaled slowly. She stuffed the tip in her left pocket, then began piling dirty glasses onto her tray, praying that nobody would say anything to her. The noise level seemed to increase again, everyone talking to fill in the silence left by the boys' exit.

"Are you okay?" Tom brushed the table with a rag, grabbing the empty pitcher.

"Of course," Deirdre mumbled. She wasn't exactly okay, but she needed to be. And she needed everybody to leave her alone until she got it together again. *Guts up, Deirdre.*

Tom took the tray out of her hands and walked back toward the bar. Deirdre pressed her lips together hard to keep them from trembling. Then she headed to the next table.

For the rest of the evening she worked on autopilot. Part of her desperately wished Clem were there, if only to tell her this was supposed to happen and that she hadn't screwed up somehow. Across the room, Sylvia moved with the kind of no-nonsense stride that Deirdre wished she could develop. Maybe she had do-me jeans, but she didn't yet have the follow-through to go with them. She should probably just go back to the khakis and knit shirts. They felt safe, even if she didn't get anywhere near the tips she was getting with this outfit.

But the tips were the point. The more tips she made, the closer she was to getting the shop ready to go.

She reminded herself to smile, although she'd never felt less like it in her life. She remembered how she'd felt when she'd walked into the Faro that evening. Strong. Powerful. Sexy.

Well, maybe not sexy. Deirdre closed her eyes for a moment. *Yes, damn it, sexy!* She, who'd never been known to turn anybody's head, had been really sexy. Clem had grinned at her on her way out of the kitchen, muttering, "Go get 'em, tiger."

And then somehow she'd managed to screw everything up. She blew out a breath as she wiped off an empty table. Oh well, tomorrow was another day.

Maybe she'd go back to her old jeans again. Built for comfort, not for speed. The bills waded in her pocket pressed hard against her thigh as she leaned over. Lots of bills. Probably twice as many as she'd made before.

She stood up again and tossed her towel back on the tray. *Guts up, Deirdre.* Maybe she'd give the new jeans one more night.

Chapter Seven

Tom watched Deirdre work the room. Her spine was ramrod straight, and it looked like she was making a major effort to keep her hips from swinging. Not that it made much difference. She was still the sexiest thing in the Faro, although the competition was admittedly slim.

He'd had a feeling something was going to happen when he'd seen her come in, but he'd figured it would be a couple of those young fools fighting over her. His fault. He should have anticipated some asshole getting grabby.

Now Deirdre was trying to act like she was still wearing her khaki camouflage. *Not gonna happen, babe. Not in those jeans.*

As the evening wound down, Tom found he really wanted to punch somebody, preferably one of the jerks who'd been sitting at her table. At least the guys who were left in the room were treating her like the rare jewel she was. Although the fact that Chico was sitting in the doorway to the beer garden regarding everyone with his one-wrong-step-and-I-flatten-you expression probably helped. Tom only hoped they were also rewarding her heavily for the privilege of watching her walk across the room. Sylvia sent a fairly smug smile Deirdre's way every once in a while, as if she'd somehow gotten what she deserved.

Tom knew she hadn't.

Nando Avrogado showed up around ten on his way home from work. Tom served him his usual Negro Modelo.

"Heard you had some excitement tonight."

"A little. Why? Were they talking about it at the Spur?" The Silver Spur was Tom's major competitor. He figured the morons who'd groped Deirdre had headed there rather than driving back to Austin or San Antonio or wherever the hell they'd come from.

"Some talk, yeah. Tolly Berenger called me to pick up a couple of drunks who were trying to start a fight. Said they'd started drinking here, but you kicked them out. Is that right?"

Tom shrugged. "They deserved it."

"Yeah, I'd guess they did. And now they get to wake up to Chief Toleffson in the morning. That should scare the idiocy out of them for a while. He hates drunks."

Erik Toleffson, the Konigsburg Chief of Police, was indeed one of the scariest individuals Tom had ever met, closely followed by the police dispatcher, Helen Kretschmer. Between the two of them, he figured they'd put the fear of god into the punks.

He knew exactly when Nando caught sight of Deirdre—that quick intake of breath followed by a shit-eating grin. "Oh my, my, my. So that's what the fight was all about."

Tom didn't want to analyze the quick spurt of irritation he felt. Hell, Nando already had more women than he knew what to do with. "You've seen her before. She's a nice woman. They were assholes. Case closed."

Nando raised a questioning eyebrow. "I saw her, but I can't say I really *saw* her until now. You involved?"

"I'm her boss." Already he regretted opening his mouth.

"Yeah, right." Nando turned back to watch as Deirdre set her tray on the bar.

"I need two margaritas." Her voice had dropped down to murmur range again—like she was trying to melt into the wallpaper. Tom felt like sighing.

He turned to the blender, wishing he had a mirror over the bar so he could keep track of Nando. Maybe he'd consider installing one. If Deirdre stuck around, he'd probably need to keep a closer eye on the main room.

If Deirdre stuck around. He ignored the slight clenching in his gut. *Not your problem, boyo. You've got enough on your plate running the place.*

Deirdre was still waiting patiently when he returned with her margaritas. Beside her, Nando was watching the rest of the room. Tom couldn't tell if that was strategy or if he really didn't have any interest in her.

Right. The idea of Nando Avrogado having no interest in the hottest woman in Konigsburg was about as likely as Nando Avrogado believing in the tooth fairy. Tom went back to wiping the bar so he wouldn't have to take part in any further conversations about his barmaid.

Nando left after he'd finished his beer, and the other customers finally thinned out around midnight when it was clear that nobody else was going to get into a fight. Tom wasn't sorry to see them go for once. The testosterone level in the room had stayed at critical for most of the evening, and he'd been afraid Chico might bash a few heads just to make a point.

Sylvia flounced by, dropping her tray on the bar. "I came early. Let Deirdre clean up."

Tom gritted his teeth but let it pass. He wanted her out of the room anyway. Actually, he wanted everybody out of the room except for Deirdre. He didn't like the stiff way she was holding herself, as if she were afraid of walking the wrong way.

He wanted that hip swing back.

Finally, the room was empty. Harry closed down his end of the bar, and Chico looked like he'd fallen asleep on his stool near the outside door. Tom picked up a tray and began loading glasses beside Deirdre. "How's it going?"

She glanced at him, her eyes bleak. "Okay. I'll clear the rest of the tables. Do you need me to sweep?"

Tom shook his head. "Leon'll do it when he cleans tomorrow." He took the tray of glasses out of her hands. "Come sit down."

Deirdre's forehead furrowed, but she followed him.

Tom rounded the bar, taking down a couple of clean glasses. "I'm having a beer. What can I get for you?"

Deirdre's forehead smoothed slightly. "A Lone Star, I guess."

Tom pulled two drafts and then motioned her to a stool across from him. "Quite a night."

She nodded, sipping her beer, her gaze glued to the floor.

"Look..." Tom began, wishing for once that he was better at talking than playing poker. "This wasn't exactly a normal night. I've never seen those guys before, but we get assholes here pretty regularly. You don't want to take it personally."

Deirdre took another swallow of beer. "I guess not. I just...maybe I shouldn't dress like this. Maybe I gave them the wrong idea."

Tom felt like groaning. "You're dressed exactly right for the Faro. Don't let those idiots make you back down. It was their problem, not yours."

"I don't want to start trouble."

"You're not starting trouble. You're working as a barmaid, and you're doing a great job. You can dress any way you want to. If those guys have a problem with it, they can go drink at the Silver Spur."

Deirdre gave him a tiny smile, just the slightest lift at the corners of her mouth. "So you're okay with this? The jeans and the T-shirt and...everything?"

Tom licked his lips. "Totally. Don't change a thing. Well—" he paused, "—you might want to change the T-shirt every day or so. God knows we've got enough of them."

"Okay." Deirdre took a final swallow of her beer, sliding off her bar stool. "I'll check into it tomorrow. I guess I'll go on home now. Thanks for the beer."

Tom frowned. "You're walking?"

"Sure—it's only a few blocks."

"It's after midnight. You shouldn't walk around by yourself. Even in Konigsburg." Especially when she was now established as the hottest cowgirl in town. Tom wiped his hands on a bar towel and then stepped around the end of the bar, nodding at Chico. "I'll be back in fifteen minutes or so. Just walking Deirdre home."

Deirdre looked like she might protest again, so Tom took her arm and headed for the door. "Where do you live. Up Main?"

For a moment he thought she wouldn't answer, then she shrugged. "I'm staying in the apartment above Docia's bookshop. The entrance is on Spicewood."

Tom didn't think he'd ever been in Docia Toleffson's bookshop, but he had a general idea of where it was. He headed back up Main. The air was still warm, even at midnight, with the scent of petunias wafting from the half whiskey barrels set up in front of the shops. He kept his hand on Deirdre's elbow, guiding her from one pool of light to the next, the dark velvet night enveloping them. Contrary to his expectations, the street seemed deserted.

"So where'd you find the jeans? They weren't in Ferguson's

stock were they?"

Deirdre shook her head. "Clem took me shopping at a place called Too Good To Be Threw. They had a lot of stuff."

Tom made a mental pledge to raise Clem's salary yet again. "Good for Clem. Did you count up your tips yet?" He navigated them around a folding sign in front of Brenner's restaurant.

"Nope. But I know I made more than I've made the last two nights. Maybe now I can start pricing stuff for the shop."

"Let me know when you're ready to paint." Tom wasn't sure how he was going to do it, but he figured he'd find a way to do some of the painting himself.

"Probably next week." Deirdre turned at the corner of Spicewood.

He tried to think of some not-entirely-transparent way of keeping the conversation going. All of a sudden, he wanted to see the inside of Deirdre's borrowed apartment. "So Docia Toleffson's your cousin. Lars Toleffson does the books for the Faro. I guess he's her brother-in-law." He winced. That sounded even lamer than he'd expected.

"Right." She began fumbling for her keys. "There are four brothers, you know. Docia's married to Cal. I think the other two are in politics somehow."

"Erik's the chief of police," Tom supplied. "The other one is Pete. I think he's one of the county attorneys." He took the key from her hand and unlocked the door. Inside, a flight of stairs led up to a darkened hallway overhead. "You should leave the light on when you go out in the evening."

"I do, usually. I was rushing tonight." She sounded slightly annoyed.

He figured his chances of being invited inside were not improving. He started up the stairs in front of her. "Where's the light switch?"

"To the left of the door upstairs." She trailed up the stairs behind him dutifully.

He felt his way along the wall until his fingers brushed the switch. The hall was marginally brighter. "Better than nothing, I guess. Not much candlepower, though."

Deirdre stepped around him. "It's not that much of a threat. The only way somebody can get in here is through the street door, which is always locked, or the bookshop, which locks up at six." She took the key from his hand and unlocked the apartment door. "Do you want to come in and check under the bed?"

Tom ignored the sarcasm and stepped into the room, then stopped, staring. The apartment was empty.

In the living room he saw two plastic lawn chairs. So far as he could tell, the dining room didn't have any furniture at all. He took two steps farther inside. The kitchen had a vintage Formica table with bent aluminum legs. Through the partially open bedroom door, he saw a sleeping bag and an air mattress on the floor.

It was the sleeping bag that got to him. "What the hell, Deirdre?"

"Docia and the other people who lived here took most of the furniture when they moved. I don't have anything of my own."

He surveyed the room again, shaking his head. "Okay, we've got some spare furniture in the storeroom at the Faro. We'll go through it tomorrow. I'll have Chico carry some of it over here for you."

"Oh, I couldn't..."

"Take what you need, damn it," he snapped. "You shouldn't be sleeping on the floor."

Her mouth compressed to a thin line. "You have a bed in the storeroom?"

"No, actually." He rubbed the back of his neck. "Look, suppose I give you an advance on your salary. You could at least get a mattress or something."

"I need to put all my money into the shop. I can think about furniture once I get it launched."

He gritted his teeth to keep from growling at her. "Come on, it wouldn't take more than a couple hundred bucks or so. And you'd be off the floor."

She shook her head stiffly, her mouth back to a thin line.

He rubbed the back of his neck again, harder. "Deirdre, what's going on here? You're not some bag lady. You're a smart woman, for Christ's sake. What are you doing sleeping on the goddamn floor?"

For a moment he thought she'd tell him to go to hell, although very politely, as usual. Then she blew out a breath. "I'm having a disagreement with my family. Right now I don't have access to my money. I do have some funds, though, and when I can get to them, I'll be able to pay for everything. Until then—" she shrugged, "—I'm roughing it. Urban campout."

"Okay." He turned toward the front door, and then back again. "But you're still going through the storeroom tomorrow for furniture." And he swore to god he'd find a way to get her a bed. Even if he had to put her in his.

"Right." Deirdre sighed. "More vintage. Good night, Tom."

She didn't exactly push him out the door, but he went. At least the sight of the sleeping bag counteracted his visions of her in a negligee. The idea of putting her into his bed was torture enough.

Craig might have wasted a lot more time looking for Dee-Dee if it hadn't been for the concierge at his hotel. She was, it turned out, a football fan. A *real* football fan. One of those football fans who memorized team rosters for every year, possibly as far back as the Cowboys had been in existence. Which meant she recognized Craig, which, in turn, meant that she was eager to help him. Very eager.

Easy enough to get her to sit down for a cup of coffee in the hotel breakfast room. Easy enough to get her to give him all the details he needed. Like any good concierge she kept up with everything going on in Konigsburg. And in her case, that meant knowing what was going on with the people in town as well as the cultural scene.

There were, it turned out, four Toleffson brothers. One was married to Docia Kent. Another was married to the woman in the bookshop. The two others held no interest for him and he promptly forgot them. The concierge knew about Docia Toleffson's mother, Reba Brandenburg Kent, but hadn't seen her in town recently. The Kent family home, it seemed, was back in the hills somewhere. Right now nobody was in residence except the caretaker and his staff, one of whom was the concierge's niece.

As for visitors at Docia Toleffson's house, the concierge just laughed. Those particular Toleffsons lived in a converted barn with their baby son and assorted pets. While it was vaguely possible that somebody might be staying with them, she was pretty sure nobody was. Her cousin's neighbor's youngest girl was Docia's babysitter, and she hadn't mentioned anything about that.

Craig poured her another cup of coffee and asked about newcomers. But about them, the concierge was less help. A new Target was being built outside Marble Falls, and some of the labor force lived in town. She'd heard a new furniture store was opening on West, but she hadn't seen it yet and didn't know who'd be running it. When he asked about new girls, she gave him a narrow-eyed look that almost made him apologize for thinking about other women.

She took a sip of coffee, then shrugged. "We've always got people moving through, you know—temporary help at the restaurants and the gift stores. Nobody keeps track of them."

Craig managed not to grind his teeth. "I'm just looking for an old friend. Somebody said she might have moved up here from Houston."

"What's her name? Maybe I've heard of her." The concierge raised an eyebrow.

"Dee-Dee," Craig supplied, carefully leaving off the Brandenburg. He didn't want people making too many connections before he'd had a chance to spirit Dee-Dee back to Houston.

The concierge shook her head. "Nobody named Dee-Dee around that I know of. Except—" her lips quirked up in a slightly nasty smile, "—that new barmaid at the Faro. She sounds like somebody who might be named Dee-Dee." She gave Craig a slightly guilty look. "No offense to your friend."

"None taken." Craig switched to his promoter's smile. "A new barmaid?"

"Started a fight last night, from what I hear. Had some of the college kids beating each other up over her. Of course, the Faro's a rough place. Used to be, anyway, Tom Ames has cleaned it up some."

Craig nodded, still smiling. The mental image of Dee-Dee Brandenburg as a barmaid was so ridiculous it almost made him laugh out loud. He wondered if she could wait tables in those dark suits she usually wore. They didn't look like they'd stand much wear and tear. Neither did Dee-Dee, if it came to that. On the other hand, this was the only lead he'd managed to dig up in three days of searching.

"Well maybe I'll check out the Faro then. But Dee-Dee's not

really the barmaid type."

The concierge shrugged. "She's the only new girl I've heard of around here. You could always try Johnson City, I guess. I don't know the people over there." She made it sound like you needed a passport to get there.

"Thanks for all your help anyway." Craig laid a twenty-dollar bill on the table, then headed for the door, never noticing the concierge's flat-eyed stare at his back.

Clem wasn't upset about what had happened in the bar the night before. If anything, she seemed to be elated. "It's all over town," she whooped when Deirdre took her seat at the kitchen table after lunch. "The place should be full tonight. Everybody'll want to see what you look like. Did you know two of the guys Tom threw out of here ended up in jail? Nando Avrogado hauled them out of the Silver Spur. Helen Kretschmer said they were frat boys from Austin."

Deirdre stared down at her chicken salad sandwich, wondering where her appetite had gone. "Terrific."

"Oh buck up." Clem grinned. "It doesn't hurt to be a little notorious in this town. It gives you a leg up over the competition. I'll bet Sylvia is gnashing her teeth at this very moment. Besides, you're helping Tom, and that's a good thing."

"Helping him?" Deirdre raised an eyebrow. "How exactly does this help him? Doesn't it make the place look bad?"

"It's a bar, honey. A roadhouse, like I said. Fights come with the territory. And anything that gets people in the door helps us, particularly if they're local. We can't depend on the tourists forever. We need to get people from town coming in. Somebody besides the Steinbruners. We need regulars."

"How will coming down here to stare at me turn them into 'regulars'?"

"Like I said, you're getting them in the door. After that, it's up to Tom. And me. And everybody else. The food and drinks are better here than the Silver Spur, and god knows everything about the place is better than the Dew Drop Inn. All we need to do is convince some of the locals that they don't need to stay loyal to Ingstrom or Tolly Berenger. Then we've got our base. They'll bring in others."

"I see." Deirdre forced herself to take a bite of her sandwich. "So I'm a door buster special. Sort of like a cheap widescreen TV."

Clem's grin widened. "Not a bad comparison. Come on, Deirdre, it's kind of a compliment if you look at it in the right way. You're the girl they were fighting over at the Faro. I mean, have you ever had men fighting over you before?"

Deirdre paused, chewing. Now that she thought about it, having men fight over her was definitely a novel experience. "That's an interesting approach."

"Right. Those guys were the assholes, not you. Anybody who sees you will know that. And believe me, a lot of people will want to see you. Plus now the word is out, nobody's going to try anything. Not that they'd try anything normally. Not with Chico around."

"Actually, Tom's the one who threw them out."

Clem blinked. "Tom? That's interesting. Usually he leaves the policing to Chico. He's too busy behind the bar. How did he know what happened?"

Deirdre shrugged. "I don't know exactly. Maybe he was watching. But right after that guy...grabbed me, he was there with a pool cue in his hand, telling them to get out."

There was a moment of silence as Clem stared down at the table. "Tom came to your rescue? I have no idea what that means." She looked back up at her, frowning.

Deirdre felt a quick flutter in her chest, a feeling she really didn't want to analyze too much. "Are you and Tom...? I didn't know. Honest. And there's nothing going on between us. I mean he walked me home, but that was just because it was dark."

Clem stared at her, eyes widening. Then her lips spread in another grin. "He walked you home? Tom walked you home? Oh man." She shook her head, chuckling.

"Clem, look, I'm sorry. I didn't mean..."

She raised a hand, still chuckling. "Forget it. And FYI, I play for the other team. Plus I'm in a committed relationship."

"You play for the other team? I don't understand."

Clem shrugged. "My partner's name is Lucinda, Deirdre. That team."

Now it was Deirdre's turn to blink. "Oh. Oh! Well, good. I mean you're not...involved with Tom, I guess." Her cheeks suddenly felt much too warm. "I mean...not that I have any interest in who he's involved with. Not that I have any right to have any interest in..." She stammered to a halt, cheeks flaming. "Crud," she muttered.

Clem was grinning again. Widely. "It's okay, trust me. Tom could definitely do worse than getting involved with you. He's been dodging Sylvia for the past couple of months, and she's done everything except send smoke signals. Right now he's spending all his time on the bar anyway. He's always seemed to be too busy to have any outside interests. Of course, you're not exactly *outside*, are you?"

"But I don't...I can't..." Deirdre paused, drawing in a deep breath. "I'm not trying to get together with Tom. He's a really nice guy. But I've got enough complications in my life right now." Not to mention the fact that he'd shown no interest in getting together with her.

Clem narrowed her eyes. "You've got somebody else? Why isn't he here helping you? What does he think about your father cutting you off?"

"No." She shook her head. "There's nobody else. Nobody at all." There never had been, now that she thought about it, given that Craig Dempsey's interest had been less in her than in what she could do for him.

"Well then. You're unattached and so is Tom. Sounds ideal to me. Now we need to find you the right T-shirt for tonight. Something cute, but not slutty, if you know what I mean. Let's check through a few more of those boxes Ferguson left next door."

Deirdre closed her eyes, but managed not to pound her head on the table. She had a feeling it wouldn't do any good anyway.

Chapter Eight

Craig couldn't decide whether to visit the Faro that night or not. He still thought the idea of Dee-Dee Brandenburg serving as a barmaid was ludicrous. On the other hand, he hadn't had any luck in locating her anywhere else in town. Docia Toleffson hadn't bothered to call him back, and none of his other leads had panned out. Either Dee-Dee had gotten wind of his presence in Konigsburg and was hiding out, or he wasn't looking in the right places. Since he refused to consider the first possibility, he was stuck with the second one.

It was Friday night, and he figured he might have to jostle through a few tourists to get a look at the barmaids at the Faro, but the crowd turned out to be a lot bigger than he'd anticipated.

The place was packed with customers, mostly men but some couples around the edges of the room. All the tables were full, and bodies were packed two deep around the bar. The jukebox in the background was almost drowned out beneath the noise of voices. Craig wedged himself against the bar, grabbing a beer from the harried bartender. Another man was working the other end, but Craig couldn't quite see him. He glanced around the room, trying to find the barmaids.

The one on the far side was definitely not Dee-Dee. Her blonde hair fell straight down to her shoulders as if she'd been ironing it regularly. Her T-shirt sparkled with sequins above low-slung jeans that managed to show both her navel ring and a significant amount of untoned abdomen. Except for her running shoes, she looked like a standard-issue floozy, and he figured the shoes were a concession to the amount of time she probably spent on her feet.

She looked like she might spend a fair amount of time on her back, too, but he didn't figure that was any of his business. At least not at the moment.

He scanned the room again, looking for other barmaids. He saw a few women customers scattered around the room, but no one else. Then the line of men at the bar seemed to shift, moving back ever so slightly, and he saw her.

The other barmaid was a knockout. Her lush figure was outlined in worn jeans and a white T-shirt. Her hair was pulled up in a loose ponytail on the top of her head, with tendrils floating down in the humid air as she moved across the room. Large golden hoops dangled from her ears. Craig swore he could hear a collective sigh from all the men at the bar as she leaned forward to speak to the bartender at the other end.

He said something back and she nodded, then turned to head back to her tables. And for the first time he got a good look at her face.

Damn. Goddamn. Goddamn it all to hell!

Craig fought back the quick surge of white rage in his gut when he recognized her. He'd dated Dee-Dee Brandenburg for almost six months, give or take. She'd never worn anything like that around him. He knew, of course, that her figure was good. He'd seen her mostly naked. But she'd never given him so much as a hint that the woman prowling across the Faro right now was lurking somewhere beneath the sober dark suits she wore to the office. She'd never pulled her hair up like that. She'd never worn earrings like that. She'd never worn jeans like that. Hell, he didn't think Dee-Dee Brandenburg had even owned a pair of jeans.

But clearly she did now. Craig wanted to put his fist through the bar. He wanted to shake Dee-Dee until her teeth rattled. If she'd only looked like that when he'd dated her, he'd have put more effort into the whole relationship. A woman who looked like that would have been someone he could have enjoyed taking to parties with his old teammates. The Dee-Dee he'd known was so reserved it had been embarrassing. Getting her to talk to anybody besides the wives had been more trouble than it was worth. If it hadn't been for Big John's money and power and the things they could provide to a future son-in-law, Craig had often thought he'd have thrown in the towel long before they'd actually parted company.

And, of course, any woman who looked like that would have been a tiger in bed. The Dee-Dee he'd known had been more like a timid housecat. A woman who looked like that would be someone worth coming home to. The Dee-Dee he'd known, the old Dee-Dee...

He took a deep breath. No use going there. It wasn't like it had been any great love affair between them anyway. But it had been a useful love affair until Dee-Dee had screwed it up. Now, seeing what she'd been able to do for herself since she'd flounced out of her daddy's office, he had something to work for, another reason to get things back on track again, beyond the obvious reason of keeping Big John happy.

As she headed back toward the side of the room with her tray of beers held high, Craig watched the men at the tables lean back slightly to let her pass. Nobody made a move in her direction, even by accident. It was the politest bar he'd ever been in, nobody even trying to cop a feel as she slipped by. Then Craig caught sight of the man leaning against the wall near the pool tables.

He was the size of a small bull. Massive biceps like hams stretched the sleeves of his black T-shirt. His long dark hair was pulled back in a tail and he had a bandana wound around his head. A thin black moustache curved around the ends of his mouth, with a small soul patch in the middle of his lower lip. At first, he looked as if he were drowsing, but only if you didn't look too close. Craig did. The man was watching Dee-Dee, or rather he was watching the men around her. Every once in a while, somebody would glance his way, but his slightly bored expression never changed.

Craig had known tackles like that. They were very painful men to be around. If the bull served as Dee-Dee's bodyguard, it meant there'd be no chance of talking to her tonight, at least not without a lot of fancy footwork. He sighed and drained his beer. There'd be other chances. Now that he knew where to start.

Deirdre had to admit that being the center of attention wasn't as bad as she'd expected. After twenty-four years on the sidelines, only earning her father's notice when he found something to criticize, she actually enjoyed having people watch her. At least sometimes. Of course, the fact that nobody did anything more than watch had something to do with it. And the fact that both Chico and Tom were guarding her had a lot more to do with it. Still, after the first half hour she had a spring in her step, even though her arms ached from carrying her tray.

The last customer trailed out at one, and Tom motioned her to a barstool, drawing her a Shiner. "We had a good night."

"Busy, anyway. Is this what Fridays are like usually?"

He shrugged. "Hard to say. Maybe a little bigger crowd than we're used to. Saturdays are still our best nights."

She sipped her beer, enjoying the relative quiet. "Why's that?"

"Musicians. Tomorrow night we've got a roots rock combo from Arlington."

She gazed around the room. "In here?"

"No. Outside in the beer garden. You may want to come a little early so you can get set up."

"Set up?"

"I want you to take the garden. Sylvia can handle the main room, along with Marilyn. She comes in on weekends, although we may start needing her on weeknights too if this keeps up."

Deirdre felt the familiar clenching sensation in her chest. "You want me to handle the garden alone?"

"Well, no. You'll have the band and Chico and hopefully some customers." He gave her the grin she'd come to recognize as his *Trust me* look.

"But I don't...I mean, I've never..."

"You'll be fine. There aren't as many tables out in the garden, And Chico will be around to make sure nobody pulls any funny stuff. And you get to hear the music. I'll take the bar outside, and Harry can handle the traffic in here."

She started to object again, then paused. She was going to be paid to walk around an outdoor café on a warm Texas night and listen to music. How was this a bad thing? "Okay, it sounds like fun."

He shook his head. "It's still work, but it has its points." He gave her a lazy grin.

His eyes were the color of a hot summer sky. His short golden hair was mussed from his fingers. The lines around his eyes and mouth should have made him look old or tired. They didn't. Deirdre felt the clenching sensation again, but this time it wasn't in her chest.

Okay, enough. More than enough. No way was she getting involved with her boss, no matter what Clem said. She pushed her glass back across the bar. "Thanks for the beer. I guess I'll head home."

He tossed the bar rag back on the counter behind him. "Okay. Let's go."

"You don't need to do this."

"And you don't need to tell me that every time I do. Come on, it's late."

A slight breeze ruffled the leaves of the live oaks as they strolled up Main. "What will you do if it rains? You can't stay out in the beer garden, can you?" she asked.

"It won't. But if it does, we move the band inside where the pool tables are. Gets a little noisy, but it's Saturday night in Konigsburg—nobody notices. Except the Steinbruners since the pool table will be gone."

"Okay." Friday night in Konigsburg looked pretty sedate, all in all. Most of the downtown windows were dark behind the street lights. "Are you from here?" she asked on impulse.

"From Konigsburg?" He shook his head. "Not hardly. I'm from Missouri. I've only been in Texas for a few years."

"Where were you before Konigsburg?"

"Dallas." Something about the way he said it told her the subject wasn't open to further discussion.

"Oh." She rummaged through her small stock of polite conversation, trying to think of something to say. "I'm from Houston."

He nodded, as if that information were a little too obvious to be worth comment.

"How did you end up here?"

"Process of elimination." He turned up Spicewood. "I wanted to settle down and open a bar. Konigsburg seemed promising. How about you?"

"I used to stay here with my aunt and uncle in the summers. It's a place that had happy memories for me. Plus they need a coffee roaster, according to my research."

Tom narrowed his eyes at her. "You did the marketing research?"

"Sure." Deirdre shrugged. "It's what I do. Or anyway what I used to do." Back when her father had been willing to indulge her illusion that she was performing some necessary function at Brandenburg, Inc. "Did you think I'd hired someone else?"

"I guess I figured you just came up here and decided to open a coffee roaster. It's the kind of thing people do around Konigsburg all the time."

"That's not a great way to go about it. You wouldn't want to open up a store that nobody needs."

He gave her another of those lazy grins. "I wouldn't. A lot of other people do, though. Like old Ken Ferguson and his several hundred T-shirts."

"Well at least we're getting some good out of them. I mean, I am, anyway."

"Oh I am, too. Believe me."

Tom's grin turned faintly sultry, and Deirdre felt her ears grow warm. She pulled her key out of her purse and fitted it into the lock of the outside door. "I'd better go up. Thanks for seeing me home. Again. You know you really don't need..."

"Good night, Deirdre." Tom grinned one last time, then turned and walked back up Spicewood toward Main.

The Friday night Toleffson poker game was running long. Long enough that Jess and Lars had already taken off with their kids in tow, and Docia was feeling vaguely guilty about not heading home with Rolf. Shouldn't they gather up the baby and go to bed? She watched her husband lay down his hand, chortling.

Janie raised an eyebrow. "You want to go to sleep? I can put you in the same room with Rolf if you want. There's a double bed in there. You could stay overnight with us and go home in the morning."

Pete and Janie lived in a house that had once been a bed and breakfast. It came equipped with more bedrooms than any normal couple could ever use.

"Maybe they'll quit after this hand." Docia stifled a yawn.

Morgan, Erik's wife, settled a little lower on the couch. "Not going to happen, Docia, trust me. Pete's down by five dollars and Erik's down by two. They'll never let Cal quit now."

"Oh well, I should take advantage of the company. You guys are about the only people I get to talk to these days besides Rolf's sitter and Jess when she brings Jack over in the morning. The rest of the time it's just customers."

Janie reached for her Diet Coke. "Did you ever call that guy back who was in the shop a couple of days ago?"

"You mean Mr. Craig Dempsey?" Docia shook her head. "I checked with Mama. He's the same one who talked to her. He's after Deirdre, and I'll be damned if I'll help Uncle John clean up his mess."

Morgan frowned. "He's after your cousin? Shouldn't you tell Erik about this?"

The three of them turned automatically to stare at Erik's craggy profile frowning at the cards on the table. He wasn't wearing his uniform, but he might as well have been—he looked like a cop no matter what he wore.

Docia shook her head. "He's not stalking her or anything like that. He works for my uncle. My guess is Uncle John just wants to see if she's ready to come home yet."

"Do you think she is?"

"Nope." Docia grinned. "I think she's having a great time, although she may not be willing to admit it. Did I tell you she got a job waiting tables at the Faro? Mind you, this is the woman with an MBA from the McCombs School of Business."

Morgan's eyes widened. "Oh my lord, the new barmaid at the Faro. She's that girl. The one who started the riot."

"Riot?" Janie shook her head. "What riot? I didn't hear about any riot at the Faro."

"Well maybe it wasn't exactly a riot. More like a ruckus. I got it secondhand from Esteban Avrogado at the winery, who got it from his brother Nando. Some guys got grabby with her and Tom Ames threw them out of the place. Then Nando ended up throwing them in jail when they got rowdy at the Silver Spur."

"Deirdre?" Docia managed to keep her voice down, barely. "Some guys tried to grope my cousin? The most sedate girl in Konigsburg? Besides, she's not a barmaid, she's a waitress."

"She's probably both," Janie mused. "The Faro serves more booze than food, although I guess they've got a pretty good cook now from what I hear."

"And your cousin may be sedate, but she's developing quite a following. Nando says she's a knockout."

Docia sighed. "She is that. Always has been. But she's never really believed it, so far as I can tell. And she's always dressed like somebody from the IRS, so nobody else noticed it either. This is so far out of character for her I wonder if we've got her confused with somebody else."

"Maybe working at the Faro will change her style." Janie passed the pizza box around again. Docia ignored her conscience and took another slice.

"Maybe working for Tom Ames will change her style." Morgan's eyes took on a faraway look. "A man of mystery who's a dead ringer for Steve McQueen. Sounds like the ideal job to me."

Docia managed to catch the piece of pepperoni that threatened to slide off her slice. "What's so mysterious about him? Other than how he's managed to stay unattached after two years here. And I always thought he looked more like Daniel Craig than Steve McQueen."

"According to Nando, nobody knows exactly how he got the Faro in the first place. It wasn't even on the market, so far as anybody knew. Then all of a sudden here's Tom Ames with the deed, taking over."

"I remember that. Nobody knew Kip Berenger was even thinking of selling the Faro, even though he was running it into the ground."

"Kip Berenger?" Morgan raised an eyebrow. "Related to Tolly? The guy who owns the Silver Spur?"

"His cousin. From what I hear, Tolly was really pissed, too. The Faro wasn't supposed to be any competition to the Silver Spur, and as long as Kip was in charge it wasn't."

"You can say that again." Janie licked cheese off her fingers. "Nobody went to the Faro unless they wanted to drink or fight. Or both. It's really changed since Tom Ames took it over. But nobody knows where the money came from to get him started."

"Does it matter?" Docia stifled another yawn. "The old Faro was a dump as I recall. Ames has turned the new one into a pretty nice place. Allie says his cook is a real up-and-comer."

"It doesn't matter, really. It's just fun gossip." Morgan

pushed herself to her feet. "Erik, whether you're winning or losing, it's time to go home."

Pete sighed, tossing his cards on the table. "This is what comes of allowing wives to come to poker night."

"'Allowing' wives to come?" One corner of Erik's mouth edged up. "I don't know about you, Pete, but there's no question of 'allowing' at our house."

"Everyone is welcome to stay over." Janie's voice had a slightly acid quality. "We have loads of room. More than usual, in fact, since Pete's going to be sleeping on the couch." She headed toward the kitchen.

"Aw, Janie, come on. It was just a joke. A lousy, insensitive, sexist one. One that I already regret. Truce?" Pete trotted after her, grimacing.

"Come on, chief." Morgan smiled down at Erik. "Let's go home."

Erik pushed himself up from the poker table, his smile spreading. "Let's do that." He put his arm around her shoulders, guiding her gently toward the front door.

"Newlyweds." Cal sighed. "Suddenly I feel a hundred years old."

"C'mon, gramps." Docia grinned up at him. "Let's grab the Rolfman and get ourselves down the road to the barn."

Chapter Nine

Deirdre walked up Main, headed for the apartment and a quick shower. She'd spent the morning washing walls, and if she walked into the Faro in her current condition, she'd probably send customers running for the exit, let alone trying to wait tables there. She was also wearing her old comfortable jeans rather than her new uncomfortable ones, and she figured Clem or even Tom would make her go home and change even if she didn't do it herself.

She paused for a moment, thinking. She hadn't even known Tom Ames a month ago, but now he'd become *Tom*. She hadn't owned a pair of tight jeans a month ago. She hadn't known how to heft a tray loaded with beers a month ago. She hadn't been on her way to realizing the dream she'd nursed for three years a month ago.

Times change. People change.

She found herself grinning. *Not bad, girl. Not bad at all.*

"Deirdre?"

She recognized Docia's voice even as she kicked herself for not hurrying along a little faster. She really didn't have time for an extended conversation. Not if she was going to wash her hair, too. She forced a smile and turned back toward the bookstore. "Hi, Docia."

"Hey." Docia narrowed her eyes. "I thought you were waiting tables. The Faro must be rougher than I remembered."

Deirdre glanced down at her dusty clothes and shook her head. "I've been working on the shop. And I need to get cleaned up for the lunch crowd."

"Okay, let me walk with you." Docia gave her a dazzling smile that did nothing to convince Deirdre she wasn't being grilled. "How's everything going?"

"Oh fine. I'm making some good tips. I should have enough to put a down payment on some stock soon." She walked briskly toward the apartment door, hoping Docia would drop back.

Of course, since Docia was a few inches taller, her stride was more than long enough to keep up. "So you're working lunch?"

"And the evenings. That's when I get the best tips."

"I didn't know they did dinner at the Faro."

Deirdre stopped at the door, turning back to look at her cousin and trying to keep the belligerence out of her voice. "Okay, Docia, I'm a barmaid, not a waitress. Is that a problem?"

Docia at least had manners enough to blush. "Of course not, Dee. I just didn't realize you were doing it. Morgan said you had some trouble the other night."

"It was nothing. Tom took care of it. It was over in a couple of minutes." She pushed the door open and headed up the stairs.

Docia trailed after her. "Tom?"

"He's my boss. He's also a nice guy. He gave me a job when I had no experience and he's letting me have the shop more or less on spec." She held open the apartment door a little reluctantly and then immediately felt guilty. Docia was letting her live rent-free in a prime apartment. She was entitled to ask whatever she wanted.

Docia stepped inside, and stopped, her jaw dropping. "Dee, what happened to your furniture?"

Deirdre shrugged. "I don't have any. The furniture I had in the condo in Houston belonged to Brandenburg, Inc."

"But surely you had some at Uncle John's house—your own bed at least. And I'll bet Aunt Kathleen meant for you to have her breakfront and her dining room table. They came from her side of the family, as I recall. Irish workmanship and beautiful."

Deirdre's lips tightened as she fought back a grimace. "Somehow, I didn't feel like asking Daddy to send them to me."

"But..." Docia sank into one of the plastic lawn chairs Deirdre had been able to scrounge from the dollar store. "You don't have anywhere to sit."

"I've got those." Deirdre gestured toward the chairs. "And I'm hardly ever here anyway. I'm either working at the Faro or working at the shop. I'll worry about furniture later."

Docia's eyes narrowed. "What are you sleeping on?"

"My sleeping bag. And an air mattress. It's okay."

Docia pushed herself up and headed for the bedroom. "It's not okay, Deirdre. Not by a long shot. We've got some extra furniture and so do the rest of the Toleffsons. To say nothing of Mama's big barn of a place in San Antonio. We can outfit you."

"No, Docia, honestly." Deirdre wasn't sure why she was fighting off this sudden attack of generosity. But she didn't want to keep taking things from Docia and Aunt Reba, to keep being rescued. She started after Docia only to turn back as the doorbell sounded from the street door downstairs. "Just a minute," she called down the staircase.

Two delivery men stood on the sidewalk outside her door. The truck parked behind them on the street had *Hempleman's Discount Furniture* painted on the side. "You Deirdre Brandenburg?" one of the men asked.

Deirdre nodded. "I didn't order anything, though."

The delivery man shrugged. "I don't know anything about that. We got a delivery here. All paid up." He handed her a clipboard with an order sheet. "You sign here after we take it upstairs for you." He turned toward the truck where his assistant had already opened the back and pushed down a ramp.

"Take what?" Deirdre frowned down at the page, trying to make sense of it.

"The mattress." The two delivery men began easing a large innerspring mattress down the ramp toward the street.

Deirdre stared. "But I didn't order any mattress."

"Somebody did. And paid for it too. Check the address—it's supposed to be delivered here."

"But..." Deirdre stammered.

"Take it upstairs. I'll show you where."

Docia's voice made Deirdre jump. She glanced down at the paper again, then trailed after the two delivery men as they wrestled the mattress up the stairs to the apartment.

Docia led the parade through the front door. Inside, she tossed Deirdre's sleeping bag and air mattress into the hall, then pointed the men into her bedroom. "Where do you want the head, Dee?"

Deirdre gestured mutely toward the end of the room opposite the windows, and the delivery men pushed the mattress against the wall. One of them pulled a pen out of his pocket. "You need to sign for this down here." He pointed toward the corner of the page.

"But I didn't order it," she said again, trying to keep her voice from rising in frustration.

"Look, lady, it's all paid for. The delivery address is this place. I'd say you've got yourself a mattress. Just sign it, okay? We got other places to go."

Sighing, she scribbled her signature in the corner, then took her copy of the sheet from the delivery men as they headed back out the door.

Docia peered over her shoulder. "So who sent you a very nice present?"

"I don't know. I don't suppose it was you?"

She shook her head. "If I'd known you were sleeping in a freakin' sleeping bag, it might have been, but I didn't get a chance. I'll find you some sheets for this thing, though. Looks like it's king-size. Who else knew about your furniture? Or lack thereof."

Deirdre sighed. "Nobody. I haven't had anyone in here." She stopped suddenly, remembering just who had been inside her apartment in the last week. "Oh."

"Oh what?"

"Nothing," she muttered, suddenly wishing Docia would go back to work.

"C'mon, Dee, give. Who's been in here?"

Deirdre licked her lips. *Oh well.* "Tom walks me home every night. I've told him he doesn't need to, but he says I shouldn't be walking around Konigsburg by myself that late."

"He's got that right." Docia's lips spread in a slow grin. "Oh my. Are you telling me Tom Ames has seen your bedroom?"

"He just came in the apartment the first time to make sure..." Deirdre paused. *To make sure of what? That no mad rapists were hiding under your sleeping bag?*

"Yes, well." Docia was still grinning. "You be sure and thank him when you see him. That's a very nice mattress."

Deirdre's jaw tightened. "Oh I will. I most definitely will."

Tom knew he was in trouble the minute Deirdre walked into the Faro. Not that she looked angry. In fact, she looked amazing—but he'd come to expect that from her after a week. She had another of Ferguson's T-shirts, this one black and white, advertising Rustler's Roost, a particularly disreputable biker bar outside the city limits. Realistically, he shouldn't have been happy to see her wearing a shirt that advertised somebody else's bar, but the idea of Deirdre's bosom advertising a biker bar was too weirdly funny to mess with. Plus the black set off her milky skin and dark hair, giving her more of that Audrey Hepburn vibe. Only now she looked a little more like a young Elizabeth Taylor.

When the lunch traffic had thinned down a little, she stalked up to the bar, dropping her tray in front of him. "Did you buy me a mattress?"

Tom blinked. He hadn't really expected her to make the connection so quickly. Wouldn't it have been more logical to assume that her cousin or her other rich relatives had sprung for a mattress? He leaned forward, placing his elbows on the bar. "You needed one."

"I would have bought one eventually. I can't accept a mattress from you, for heaven's sake." Her cheeks turned a lush, pale rose.

"Why not?"

"Because..." she sputtered, then stared down at the bar, her lips a thin line. "You know why I can't."

He shrugged. "The store won't take it back now. Technically it's used. It would be against the health code, so you'd just be wasting my money." Actually, of course, he wasn't sure about that, but it didn't matter. He was slowly beginning to enjoy himself. Even sputtering, Deirdre was better looking than any woman he'd ever met.

"I'll pay you back then," she snapped. "Take it out of my salary."

"Deirdre..."

"I mean it, Tom!" She huffed out a breath that fluffed the tendrils on her forehead. Her indigo eyes were flashing. "I insist."

He sighed. "Okay. I'll take out five bucks a week. How's that?"

"How long will it take to pay off?"

At that rate, probably around a year and a half. But Tom saw no reason to tell her that. "Six months."

She narrowed her eyes. "You only paid a hundred and twenty dollars?"

He shrugged again. "It's a discount furniture store." Which, of course, didn't exactly answer her question and avoided an outright lie.

She gave him a look that told him she knew exactly what he was doing, but didn't know exactly how to stop him. "Thank you," she said between gritted teeth.

"You're welcome. Stick around after your shift this afternoon and we can go through the furniture in the storeroom."

For a moment, he thought she'd say no, but finally she shrugged. "All right. But that's the extent of it, okay? No more helping me."

"I won't send you any more furniture without talking about it first, but I'm not promising not to help you if you need it."

Deirdre gave him another annoyed look, but then turned, grabbing her tray, and headed toward the kitchen to pick up her orders.

Tom managed not to grin after her, but it was a near thing. Across the room, Chico watched him with narrowed eyes. Okay, it probably wasn't the smartest thing he'd ever done, but it was still fun. And he could afford a new mattress now and then.

The beer garden was full by seven thirty that evening. Deirdre didn't know if that was the effect of the band or the nice weather or the phase of the moon. All she knew for sure was that she was a very busy barmaid all of a sudden.

She was almost late getting there because Tom had insisted on sending her a table and chairs from the storeroom that Leon and Chico had carried up to the apartment for her. She had to admit that it made her dining room less barren, but giving Chico a tour of the place and then finding beers for both of them had definitely slowed her down.

Most people in the garden ordered beer and nachos, with the occasional chips and salsa or popcorn, along with the occasional margarita. Unlike the people in the inner room, the beer garden customers were mostly couples or mixed groups. College kids up from Austin or College Station, hikers from the state park, biking baby boomers up for a weekend ride in the Hill Country. For once, she didn't feel under observation all the time.

Tom poured drinks at a small built-in bar at the side, while Chico lounged at the street entrance, checking IDs on everyone who came in. The band was okay—not the kind of music she usually listened to, but fun. Couples whirled around the small dance floor periodically, laughing as the warm breezes blew through the live oaks.

Deirdre tried to remember if she'd ever gone to an outdoor show before. Actually, she hadn't been to that many indoor shows either. Men like Craig Dempsey didn't go to music shows that much. They went for the owner's boxes at sports arenas instead. She watched one of the couples slide across the floor, eyes locked on each other, and bit her lip. She'd had dancing lessons when she'd been at school, but since it was a girls' school, they'd had to practice with each other. She was better at leading than following. And then at the school dances, most of the boys had had other things in mind besides dancing. She wished now she'd tried a little harder. The couples looked like they were having fun.

Tom placed two margaritas on her tray with a snap, bringing her back to the job at hand. He cocked an eyebrow. "Everything okay out there?"

"Great." Deirdre smiled in his general direction and hoisted the tray to her shoulder. Dancing could wait. Right now she needed to make some tips. After all, she'd be down by five dollars on her salary this week. She pressed her lips together to avoid a grin. It might not have been quite proper for Tom Ames to give her a mattress, but she wasn't all that upset that he had. He was just fun to spar with.

As the evening went on, the crush intensified. Some people pulled out chairs from inside to listen to the music. Sylvia served the crowd nearest the door, as well as part of her normal station, and complained to Tom about it in a low voice. Marilyn, the weekend barmaid, took care of the rest of the inner room. Deirdre trotted between the outside tables, picking up glasses and taking orders and trying to stay out of the way of the dancers as they spread around the open space. The band had shifted to a lot of fast stuff, including the occasional two-step, that had at least half the crowd on its feet.

Suddenly the lead guitarist played a slow descending scale. The keyboardist did a riff on his accordion. The singer grasped the microphone. "Okay," he yelled, "everybody grab somebody you want to rub crotches with. Time for some *'Volver'*."

Deirdre stopped, clutching her tray to her chest. In her opinion, *"Volver, Volver"* was the sexiest song in the world, even if she couldn't understand more than half the words. One of her roommates had translated it for her in high school. All she could really remember was the chorus: "To return, to return, to return to your arms again." She turned toward the stage as the band began to play the slow, pounding beat.

The singer leaned forward, crooning, *"Este amor apasionado..."* He sounded a lot more like Jon Dee Graham than Vicente Fernandez, but Deirdre didn't care. Neither did the crowd. They roared their approval, then began moving to the slow beat. She turned to watch. The dancers moved unhurriedly across the floor, laughing and dipping to the beat. A couple of them were dancing so close Deirdre was half afraid they might set the place on fire. She began to sway along with the music, half-closing her eyes and humming along.

Someone pulled on her tray, and she looked over her shoulder to see Tom, smiling at her. He set her tray on the bar counter, then placed his hand at her waist, nudging her gently out onto the dance floor.

Deirdre's stomach immediately clenched itself into a knot. *Dance? Here? Now? In front of everybody?* Tom grasped her other hand in his, the arm around her waist pulling her closer. His thigh brushed against hers and she rested her hand on his arm, feeling the hard muscle of his biceps beneath her fingertips.

"*Y volver, volver, volver...*" the singer growled.

Tom turned them in a slow curve, his feet moving hers. Deirdre swayed against him as the drumbeat sounded behind them. Suddenly, she was resting her cheek against his, feeling the slight prickle of his beard against her skin. They turned again, and she drew back a little, wishing that her heart weren't thumping quite so loudly. She only hoped Tom didn't hear it above the sound of the music.

"*Y volver, volver, volver...*" The whole band was singing now, along with at least half of the audience.

Tom maneuvered her expertly around a swaying couple, his hand moving down slightly to the side of her hip. She could feel the warmth of his palm against her skin where her T-shirt had pulled up.

Every inch of her body was suddenly sweltering, infected by the heat of his hand. Deirdre felt a clenching deep in her body that had nothing to do with nervousness and everything to do with how close his body was to hers as they made one more turn across the dance floor.

She closed her eyes. *Oh god, oh god, oh god.* This really wasn't supposed to happen. At least not like this. Not with him. Not right now.

"*...volver, volver, volver,*" the singer finished, and Tom dipped her low over his arm, leaning down over her so that their bodies were almost horizontal and touching again. The accordion and the guitars played the final chords through a chorus of yells from the crowd.

He brought her upright again slowly in the midst of the noise and applause. She felt her face growing warm. What should she say? What could she say after something like that? She felt like she'd just engaged in some kind of sex act in front of a large crowd of beer drinkers. And she wasn't even embarrassed—just sort of stunned.

Tom's teeth flashed white against his sun-warmed skin. "Thanks for the dance. Now go sell some beer." He tapped her lightly on the shoulder, and she turned, numbly, to pick up her tray again.

At a nearby table, a woman raised her hand and gave her a tiny wave. Deirdre squinted. *Oh lord. Of course. The one night I didn't want anyone I know to be here.* She walked over toward the table, picking up some empty glasses on the way to give her time to catch her breath. "Hi, Janie, how are you?"

"Great, Dee. This is terrific. I've never been to the beer garden at the Faro before. Actually, I've never been here before at all."

Janie Toleffson grinned up at her. Her soft lilac tank top set

101

off the olive tone of her skin, and her dark eyes sparkled. She had the kind of haircut that probably only needed a quick brush to put it back in line. Deirdre thought wistfully how nice it would be to have hair that didn't have to be hauled off her neck every morning. Maybe when she got some money ahead she'd actually get her hair cut.

She wondered if Tom Ames liked short hair.

"Dee?" Janie was frowning slightly, and Deirdre realized she'd missed something.

"I'm sorry, I didn't hear."

"Do you do this every Saturday at the Faro?" Janie bellowed over the surging noise of the crowd.

"Oh. I don't know. This is the first one I've worked." Deirdre glanced around the beer garden at the full tables. "I think we do it most weeks during the summer and fall. Until it cools off, anyway."

Beside Janie, her husband Pete studied the beer garden with a lot less enthusiasm. Deirdre wondered if he danced. Probably not, given that every dancer in the place had been on their feet during "*Volver, Volver*" and she hadn't seen him there.

"Are you the only waitress out here?" he said.

Deirdre nodded. "Which means I'd better get back to it. Nice to see you." She turned away quickly and headed toward a table where a couple of men were waving at her. Pete Toleffson must be very good at his job as a county attorney. He made her feel guilty, and she hadn't even been doing anything.

Other than dirty dancing with Tom Ames, of course. But she doubted Pete Toleffson could arrest her for that. And, in truth, she didn't care if he did.

Janie gave Pete a narrow-eyed look "Will you relax? Everybody's having a great time. Nobody looks like they're getting ready to take a swing at anybody else. You're off duty, for heaven's sake."

Pete shook his head. "Erik says this place used to be the toughest bar in town. Hard to believe it's been transformed overnight."

"It did used to be the toughest spot in town, but it clearly isn't anymore." Janie grinned again as she surveyed the room.

"I can't believe what Tom Ames has done with this place. It's really nice."

Pete glanced toward the street entrance where the massive bouncer was watching the crowd with narrowed eyes. "Ames may not be the only reason the crowd is staying in line."

Janie followed his stare, and then shrugged. "That's just Chico. He looks scary, but he's a great guy."

"You know him?"

"Sure. He was a few years ahead of me in high school, but he was a star on the football team. He went into one of those special military branches, SEALs or Rangers or something. I don't remember what exactly. Then he was a pro wrestler. Then he came back here."

Pete frowned. "You know a lot about him."

"It's a small town, Pete. I know a lot about everybody. We should try to get Erik and Morgan to come here with us sometime. And maybe Cal and Docia, too. Even Lars and Jess— looks like they've got a play area over under that live oak."

"Yeah. Somehow I doubt Ames would be all that delighted to have the chief of police sitting in his beer garden on a Friday night."

Janie thumped him on the arm. "Quit being a grouch. We're here to support Dee."

Pete glanced across the room, rubbing his arm absently. "She looks like she's enjoying herself. So does Ames. So do all the tables of guys who've come in to watch her tonight. I'll bet the ones inside are pissed."

Janie watched as Deirdre gracefully dodged around a live oak to reach a table in the corner. "She really is lovely, isn't she?

Pete nodded slowly. "Yep. Way above class for most of these kids. But they can come in here and look. And Ames can do more than that, judging from the way they were dancing."

"I don't think Dee sees it that way."

"Come on, Janie, don't tell me I'm a romantic. There's something going on there."

Janie shrugged. "Maybe. But I'll bet it's not what Tom Ames thought it would be when he hired her."

"What do you think he was after?"

"Maybe just another waitress. Who knew she cleaned up

this well?"

"I don't know, babe. One look at that face, and you'd have to be an idiot not to know she'd turn out to be a knockout in the right outfit."

Janie grinned again, reveling in the warm evening air. No matter what Pete said, she'd find a way to get the family in here, if only so that they could get a look at Dee being a certified knockout. She glanced around the room, taking in all the tables full of men watching Dee swing by with her tray. Oh, definitely a Konigsburg legend in the making.

Everyone seemed to be having a good time except for one man at the far side. He sat glowering in Dee's general direction. Janie frowned, trying to remember where she'd seen him before. Sandy hair. Broad shoulders. He should have been smiling—for some reason she thought of him with a smile.

She blinked. Craig Dempsey. Watching Dee and glaring. The sight sent a slight shiver down her spine, particularly since Dee didn't seem to realize he was there.

Janie made a mental note. Dee might not have realized it before, but she'd definitely hear about it by tomorrow if Janie had anything to say about it. She turned back to Pete. "C'mon, stud. Let's dance!"

Chapter Ten

A large part of the Saturday-night crowd stayed both inside and outside the Faro until the official closing time of two in the morning. Tom and Chico circulated among the remaining diehards, moving them relentlessly toward the door, while Deirdre and the other barmaids cleaned off tables and stacked glasses for Leon to run through the dishwasher. The empty bottles were tossed back into the cardboard cases, ready for recycling. All in all, it looked like a very successful night, at least as far as Deirdre could tell.

Part of her wanted to slip out the door before Tom noticed and head back to her apartment. After that dance, she wasn't sure what she could say to him. More seriously, she wasn't sure she could casually walk down the street beside him as if nothing had happened.

Apparently, from his point of view, nothing had. He was still acting the same way he always did, joking with Harry and Chico, listening to Sylvia's complaints with a certain glazed patience, bagging up the most visible trash so that the restaurant could open at noon tomorrow, even though Leon didn't come in until Sunday afternoon. For him, it seemed to have been a quick turn around the dance floor and then back to business. Nothing special.

Deirdre, on the other hand, felt as if her world had tipped on its axis. She wasn't sure how long it would take her to return to an even keel, but she knew she wasn't there yet. And walking anywhere alone with Tom Ames wasn't likely to make that equalizing any easier. Finally, she leaned behind the bar and retrieved her purse, hoping she could get to the door while he was stacking chairs.

He was at her side in an instant. "Hang on a minute. I'm almost through."

She thought about telling him she could walk herself home, as she'd told him every night, hoping this time he'd take her at her word. But she figured it was probably a lost cause. At this point telling him not to bother was more a formality than anything else.

Guts up, Deirdre. Time to put on your big girl panties.

"I'm walking Deirdre home," he called to Chico, then started toward the door.

She caught a quick look at Sylvia's face. Her eyes and mouth had narrowed as if she'd just tasted an unripe persimmon.

"Why don't you or Chico walk Sylvia home?" she asked.

Tom blinked at her, then he shrugged. "She drives to work. I think she lives closer to Johnson City. Chico keeps an eye on the parking lot."

Deirdre's face felt warm in the darkness. Geez, shouldn't she be too old to blush now? "Oh."

Somewhere in the distance, the muffled roar of a motorcycle rumbled out of town, probably heading off toward one of the campgrounds back in the hills. Other than that, Main seemed more silent than usual, with everything closed down except a distant Stop and Go. Briefly, Deirdre pictured the streets outside her condo in Houston. She didn't think she'd ever seen them empty, even at two a.m. *Different world, Deirdre.*

Tom grinned lazily as they strolled up the street. "Another good night," he mused, finally.

"Did we have more people than usual, or is that what you expected?"

"We've been building the audience for a while now, but this was the first weekend where we really had a sell-out, or close to it anyway. How'd you like the band?"

"They were very..." She searched for the word. "Eclectic, I guess."

He chuckled. "They do a lot of different stuff. Classic bar band. Whatever the crowd's looking for, they can deliver. At least they had the people up on the dance floor most of the night. Kept them thirsty."

She nodded, trying to think of something—anything—to say

that didn't involve "*Volver*". "You're a good dancer," she blurted. Apparently, her brain and her mouth weren't currently on speaking terms.

He grinned down at her. "So are you."

"No I'm not." She blew out a breath. "I don't really dance much. I never had the time. Or I didn't. Maybe now I will." She was once again profoundly grateful for the darkness that hid the fact that her face was flaming. Clearly, this was her night for idiocy.

"I hope so."

She knew he was still smiling. She could hear it in his voice. Fortunately for both her sanity and her dignity, the door to her apartment was just ahead. "Well," she murmured as she dug in her purse for her key, "thanks again."

Tom took the key from her fingers and unlocked the door for her, then turned back. He stood between her and the open door, but she suddenly had no desire to ask him to move. She stared up at his face in the dim light. As he turned, the reflection from the streetlights caught tiny flecks of gold in his hair. He reached out slowly, smoothing an errant lock of her hair back behind her ear.

Almost without thinking, Deirdre shifted up on her toes, leaning toward him and ignoring the frenzied alarm bells clanging in her brain. Maybe it was time she tried making the first move for a change. Just because she'd never done it before didn't mean she couldn't do it now. She remembered the feel of his hand on her hip when they danced, the warmth that had spread across her body. *Just a taste. Just a touch. Nothing serious.*

Her lips touched his, lightly, gently, almost as if she were afraid he might run.

She leaned closer, into the heat of his body. Running didn't seem to be on his mind at the moment. She moved the tip of her tongue along his lower lip, tasting salt and warmth. He reminded her faintly of potato chips, and she felt almost like giggling. Her *bête noire*. She'd never been able to resist potato chips.

Her hands moved without her willing them, resting on his chest, her palms rubbing across the smooth fabric of his T-shirt, feeling the slight jut of his nipples underneath.

And then his arms locked around her waist, pulling her

tighter against him. His mouth opened against hers and she answered him, sucking on his tongue as he pushed against her lips. Her head was spinning, and she wondered if she should take a breath. But she knew the spinning had nothing to do with breathing and everything to do with the heat that spread slowly from the point where their bodies met, the swell of his arousal and the throb of her own.

He angled his head, taking the kiss deeper, and she followed him, winding her arms around his neck now, pressing herself against him, feeling the heat and pressure and excitement building deep inside as she moved closer still. As she moved her hands up the back of his neck, feeling the prickle of short hair against her palms. As she pressed her body against his, shoulder to knee, her breasts flat against his chest. As she...

Oh my god. What am I doing?

Deirdre pulled back, her body screaming. She managed to draw in one breath, then another, almost panting as she stared up into Tom Ames's ice-blue eyes. He was frowning down at her, maybe trying to figure out what the hell she had in mind.

She only wished she knew.

"Okay?" he asked, raising an eyebrow.

She didn't trust herself to be able to come up with a coherent sentence. She nodded, managing at the last minute to close her mouth so that she didn't look like a complete moron.

"Is there a problem I need to know about?"

She shook her head, slowly. *Don't mind me, boss. Just your average doofus.* She took another breath, closing her eyes, trying to steady herself. "Wow," she whispered finally. "Just...wow."

When she looked up, Tom was grinning, and she wanted to sink into the ground where she stood. She needed to escape through the door to her apartment, where she could properly dissolve into a pool of humiliation. If only she could make it up the stairs without tripping over her own feet and flopping onto the floor.

He put his hand on her shoulder. "Wait."

She took another breath and stared back at him, trying not to grimace. *Yes, we're all in agreement. I am a complete moron. Can I go now?*

"Wow is right," he said softly. He touched her cheek with his fingertips, running his index finger down the slope of her nose.

She stared up at his ice-blue eyes again. *If he kisses me now, what will I do? If I ask him up, what will we do? Do I have the* cojones *to find out?*

He rested his index finger on her lower lip for a moment, then leaned down and gave her one last, swift kiss, brushing his lips gently across her own. "Good night, Deirdre. See you at lunchtime."

He closed the door, and she stood in the darkened hallway, staring after him through the door glass as he moved through the pools of light, heading back toward Main, then merging into the shadows at the corner. "But I don't work Sundays," she murmured after he'd gone too far to hear.

He probably shouldn't have kissed her back. If he'd been thinking at all, he wouldn't have. Except, of course, that when she'd looked up at him with those indigo eyes, then leaned into him, touching those lush lips to his, all coherent thought had immediately deserted his brain.

Well, not all thought. But everything he could act upon.

He'd been varying degrees of hard ever since he'd danced with her. Which was the first stupid thing he'd done that evening. He still didn't know exactly why he'd walked out from behind the bar in the middle of the busiest part of the evening. She'd been standing there at the side of the garden, alone, clutching her tray to her chest, and all of a sudden he only wanted to hold her. The dance floor provided the perfect excuse.

By the time they were done, every cell in his body had been on fire. It was all he could do to keep from kissing her right there at the end of "*Volver, Volver*" as she bent back over his arm. But that really would have caused no end of trouble, particularly when Janie and Pete Toleffson were sitting at a side table, watching. He still wasn't sure how Deirdre fit into the extended Toleffson family, but he didn't particularly want to find out by having the chief of police and the county attorney arrive on his doorstep.

Not to mention the problems this relationship could cause with Sylvia, Chico and Clem. He paused outside the window of

Siemen's Mens Wear. Actually, Chico and Clem most likely wouldn't give a damn, although Chico would probably feel duty bound to threaten his life if Deirdre got hurt.

Sylvia, on the other hand, would raise holy hell. She was already close to it, complaining constantly about the size of her station, the length of her shift and the decline in her tips since Deirdre had come on board. He sighed. Sylvia might be a royal pain in the ass, but she was also good at her job, and replacing her would be a bigger pain than keeping her. Maybe he could hire Marilyn on for more hours so that Sylvia wouldn't have to cover so many tables. The increased evening traffic Deirdre brought in could probably pay for more help.

Already Deirdre Brandenburg was costing him money, and they hadn't even gone out yet. They had, however, shared one hell of a kiss.

Tom rubbed his jaw, ambling back up the street toward the Faro. Calling what he had with Deirdre a *relationship* was really straining the definition, but he was damned if he knew what else to call it. He wanted her. She seemed to want him. Why the hell was the whole thing so complicated? At this point in most of his previous relationships he would already have been in her bed, particularly considering he'd paid for it.

But not this time. And he knew better than to push it. One soul-shaking kiss, and she'd been ready to run upstairs and hide. Hell, for all he knew she'd been ready to head back to Houston. She looked sort of like the squirrels who came to nibble corn in his backyard every morning—really grateful for the treat, but ready to head back up into the highest branches if he so much as set foot out the door.

He foresaw a lot more aching evenings in his future until he finally figured out what exactly Deirdre Brandenburg was looking for in a man. Or more specifically, what she was looking for in him.

Chapter Eleven

Craig Dempsey sat in a gas station café down the street from the Faro and nursed his coffee. It was some of the lousiest coffee he'd ever tasted, so nursing it involved the occasional sip and grimace, but the café was the only place open on this end of Main at ten on a Sunday morning. The lousy coffee actually seemed to be the ideal accompaniment for the stale Danish that was the other half of his breakfast. Mornings in Konigsburg sucked.

Particularly this morning, which had started with an eight a.m. call from Big John Brandenburg. Craig had managed to keep his head from exploding when the phone rang, but it wasn't easy. After the Faro the night before, he'd gone on to a couple of other bars, downing enough boilermakers to half-quench the fire that had started in his gut when he'd watched Dee-Dee dancing with a friggin' bartender. Just another in a long line of things that showed how far down the slope she was slipping. Eight a.m. was definitely not his wake-up time of choice.

"Dempsey?" Big John barked. "What the hell is going on up there? You find my daughter or not?"

Craig put one hand on the top of his head to keep it from flying off. "Yes sir, I found her yesterday. She's here working as a waitress. I'll talk to her soon."

"A waitress? Dee-Dee? Bullshit! And what the hell do you mean 'soon'? Why didn't you talk to her yesterday if you found out where she was?"

Craig's headache spread rapidly from his forehead to the back of his eyeballs. "About that. What is it you want me to say to her, exactly?"

"Tell her to get her ass back to Houston. I told you that already."

Craig massaged his forehead. If his brain hadn't been on the point of melting, he'd probably be handling this better. On the other hand, there were times when it was best to just face Big John head on. "Why should she do that?"

There was a long pause on the other end of the line. He had a feeling that possibility had never occurred to the big man before.

"She's been there on her own for a few weeks now." Brandenburg's voice sounded less gritty, as if he was actually thinking for once instead of issuing orders from his ass. "She should be good and ready to come home. Why wouldn't she be?"

Craig's forehead gave another quick throb. Death would be preferable. Actually getting off the phone with Brandenburg would be ideal. Then he could swallow the bottle of aspirin he obviously needed. "She should be, particularly when you think about the kind of blue collar job she's working. But you know how women are. Her pride and all."

The silence was longer this time. Maybe Big John was actually considering the possibility that somebody somewhere wouldn't hop to his bidding immediately. Craig hoped it was giving him heartburn.

"All right, use your best judgment," Big John rumbled finally. "I'm giving you free rein here. Offer her whatever it takes. Tell her she gets her job back. I'll unfreeze her accounts. Everything goes back the way it was. That should be enough to do it. I'm leaving for Europe this week. I want this settled now. Take care of it, Dempsey."

"Yes sir." Craig sighed. "I'll do that." He'd managed to dress and shower then, after slurping down a handful of aspirin. Then he'd headed to downtown Konigsburg to take care of everything. Of course, he should have realized nobody would be around the Faro yet. The freakin' bar didn't close until two in the morning.

He took another sip of coffee—the bitterness actually seemed appropriate this time. Last night had almost made him throw in the towel. It was bad enough having to sit through a hick country band playing two-steps for the yahoos. But he'd also had to watch Dee-Dee, his fiancée-in-all-but-name, bumping and grinding around the garden with some guy in jeans and a T-shirt whose monthly salary was probably equal to what Craig dropped for a dinner at La Mistral. That was wrong on so many levels, he couldn't even count them all.

Dee-Dee was part of his Master Plan, his post-football career. Marriage to one of the richest women in Texas and a suitable corporate position where he didn't have to do much beyond occasional grip-and-grins—that was how things were supposed to work out. And he'd be damned if he'd let Dee-Dee wander off and spoil everything.

It was time to put an end to this farce. Time to reel Dee-Dee in, take her back where she belonged. He was thoroughly sick of Konigsburg and his role as Big John's personal investigator. He wanted to be back in Houston, back in his office, back in the restaurants and clubs where they knew him well enough to give him the best table in the house. He'd go to the Faro today and tell her it was over, that her father was ready to take her back, that it was time for her to grow up and do what she was supposed to do—hold down a high-paying job at Brandenburg, Inc. and marry Craig, preferably in that order.

There wasn't much chance she wouldn't come, but if she got pissy about it, he'd offer her something she couldn't refuse—a new office, say. Or a diamond the size of a Super Bowl ring. He grimaced. Maybe he'd even give her credit for that wind farm idea, although that probably wouldn't be necessary. The unfrozen accounts alone should do it. That Dee-Dee could be living happily on a waitress's salary didn't seem likely.

Craig did another sip and wince. He still didn't know where she lived, which made this meeting that much more difficult. The Faro was his only lead, and it didn't open until noon. Sitting in this godawful café drinking godawful coffee for two hours wasn't much of a plan, but it was the best he'd been able to come up with so far. Who knew how early she came to work?

Still, no matter when she showed up, he needed to catch her on the street, before she went into the bar. He didn't much like the idea of confronting that bouncer if she decided to play hard to get.

Craig pinched the bridge of his nose, sighing. This was all supposed to have been so simple. Find Dee-Dee. Tell her Big John wanted her back in Houston. Accept her hysterical gratitude for being rescued from this shit-hole. Now here he was, stuck in Konigsburg, only marginally closer to getting her back home and getting Big John off his back.

Across the street, somebody was unlocking a shop next door to the Faro. Craig took that as a hopeful sign. Maybe other people on this end of Main were going to show up early, including the staff at the Faro. He squinted at the person opening the shop, then sat up straighter in his chair.

It was Dee-Dee. Dressed like the old Dee-Dee. Or sort of like her, anyway. The jeans she had on now were loose and baggy, just like she used to wear, although the T-shirt, in a shade of purple so bright it made Craig's teeth ache, outlined her breasts in a way the old Dee-Dee would never have considered.

Not that Craig was necessarily opposed to it. Maybe when he got her safely back to Houston, they could explore some new clothing options. He had a few lingerie recommendations he'd be glad to make.

He dropped a couple of dollar bills on the table and headed for the door of the café, studiously ignoring the poisonous look the waitress gave him. If she wanted a better tip, she should get a job in a place where the food didn't cause instant heartburn. Hell, she should move to Houston like a sensible person.

Deirdre unlocked the back door to the shop. She was already running behind since Cal Toleffson had showed up at her door at nine with his brother Lars and a large walnut dresser and headboard sent by Docia from god only knew where. She should have told them no, but they'd already lugged it up the block and she didn't have the heart to make them take it back. Of course, that meant they had to wrestle it up the stairs, which was probably even more work.

She started to carry in the cans of primer she'd left stacked outside next to her car. The guy at the hardware store had recommended seven, but she'd gotten eight just to be sure—she could always return the last one if she didn't need it. And besides, Tom would reimburse her for paint. He'd already said so.

Tom. Deirdre resolutely pushed any and all thoughts of Tom Ames to a back corner of her mind where they wouldn't get in her way. What had and hadn't happened last night was *not* going to obsess her today, not if she had anything to say about it.

Of course, she'd eventually have to face Tom himself, and she had no idea how she was going to do that. *Wow. Right, Deirdre, such an amazingly intelligent thing to say about being kissed.*

She blew out a quick breath. Not going to think about it. Absolutely not. Painting. That's what we're doing today. Painting. She dragged the last can of paint to the storeroom, along with the sack of brushes and rollers. The boxes of T-shirts were still sort of in the way, although she'd managed to shove them to the side. Maybe she'd ask Chico to help her stack them later.

"Dee-Dee?"

Deirdre jumped violently, clamping her hand to her chest. She must have left the front door open, but she hadn't heard anyone come in. Maybe it had happened while she was storing the primer. She turned to see a large male body silhouetted against the sunlight streaming through the front windows. A very familiar large male body.

"Craig?" she gasped. "What are you doing in here? You startled me."

He didn't look good, she noted. His eyes were sort of pink around the edges, as if he hadn't been getting enough sleep, and his hair was more greasy than groomed. He was wearing the same knit golf shirt and khakis that he always wore on the weekends, but this time they seemed wilted, as if he'd been wearing them for a while. All in all, he didn't look much like a rising junior executive in a Fortune 500 company.

"What are you doing here?" she repeated.

"I...uh...came to help you out," he stammered, blinking. He glanced around the empty shop for the first time. "What are you doing in here, anyway? Don't tell me you're doing janitorial work, too."

Deirdre frowned. None of this made any particular sense. "Help me out? What do you mean? Help me here in the shop?"

"No. Not exactly. I mean..." He paused. He looked like he was trying to regroup. "Look, I need to talk to you. Let me take you somewhere for brunch."

Brunch. *Right.* Once upon a time she'd had a couple of hours available to be bored out of her skull on Sundays, but those days were long gone now. She shook her head. "Sorry. I can't lose any time this morning—I've got work to do here. This is my day off, and I need to get some things finished while I can."

Craig's forehead furrowed. "If this is your day off, then what are you doing here?"

"I'm trying to finish cleaning the walls so I can start slapping on the primer. This is the only day I've got to work on it full-time."

"Work on...what?" His eyes looked slightly dazed.

She took a deep breath. Maybe if she slowed down he could catch up. "This is my shop, Craig. Or it will be when I get it cleaned up and renovated. I'm going to open the coffee roaster I told you about."

"Coffee roaster?" He stared around the room. "Here?"

"Well, yeah. I mean, it needs to be cleaned up. But I'm working on that. I'm hoping I can start putting in equipment next month. Furniture, at least. I'll have to wait on the roaster itself."

"Next month." He was frowning again, as if the conversation had slipped away from him when he wasn't looking. "You're going to open a coffee roaster? Here? Next month? Why?"

She gritted her teeth. How many times had she told him about what she wanted to do with her life? How many times had she mentioned her plans, how much she wanted to open a roaster in the Hill Country? Not enough times, apparently, for the information to have stuck in his mind.

He took a deep breath, squaring his shoulders. And then he gave her one of those smiles she'd once found so dazzling. His promotional smile. Unfortunately, his eyes didn't smile along with it. "The coffee roaster can go on hold, sweetheart. Maybe you can try something in Houston later on. I'm here to bring you back home. I know you and your father had a blow-up, but he regrets it. He wants you to come back."

Deirdre's chest clenched hard, although she wasn't sure why exactly. "He wants me to come back," she repeated.

Craig nodded. "Look, Dee-Dee, he's sorry. He's going to make it up to you. You don't have to stay here in this...place." He waved a hand at the shop, his voice dropping to the kind of tone he usually used when he discussed the current Dallas front four. "You can have your job back. And your apartment."

The clenching in her chest was rapidly replaced by a burning sensation. She recognized the emotion, although it wasn't something she'd allowed herself to feel too much in the past. *Rage.* She was, she realized with some surprise, thoroughly pissed at Craig Dempsey and at her father. And it felt, well, good. Surprisingly good, in fact.

"This place is *my* place, Craig," she snapped. "I'm not going anywhere."

"Your place?" He stared around the room again, incredulously. "You own this?"

She shook her head. "I'm leasing. It belongs to Tom Ames, the man who owns the Faro. But the shop is my idea. And I'm doing the work to get it into shape. I've waited a long time to do this, and now that I've started, I'm not going to quit until I've finally done what I want to do." She pulled a paint roller out of the sack on the counter. "Maybe I'll make it, maybe I won't. But at least I'll have tried."

Craig had that pole-axed look again, although she didn't think she'd said anything that would be particularly confusing to anyone who was actually listening. "Tell my father I said thanks but I'll pass. Or he can hear it straight from me if he wants to get in touch with me in person."

"Thanks but you'll pass?" It might be her imagination, but his face seemed to be a little grayer all of a sudden.

Deirdre felt another quick shot of fury-inspired adrenaline. "Look, Craig, I'm happy here. This place is perfect for what I want. And I've wanted it for a long time, although nobody seemed to notice what I wanted back in Houston. So I guess you can head back home, and report to my father. Sorry you wasted a trip."

She began sorting through the bag of brushes again, looking for the extension wand for the paint roller. Maybe if she ignored him long enough, he'd take the hint and get out of her sight.

Unfortunately, Craig had never been much for hints. "Dee-Dee..." he began through clenched teeth.

"And it's not Dee-Dee anymore." She screwed the paint roller onto the extension with several fierce twists. "It's Deirdre. I think I mentioned that to you back in Houston."

117

He stared at her for a long moment, as if he were weighing exactly how serious she was. She could have told him. Very.

"Okay...Deirdre." He almost spat the word, which at least made her look at him more closely. His face wasn't gray anymore. In fact, it had turned a red that reminded her of little boys holding their breath. "Listen to me. Your father has gone to a lot of trouble to find you. You owe him the courtesy of discussing this with him in person. I'll call him this afternoon. He can send a car for you if you don't want to drive yourself back to town."

She frowned slightly. He'd raised an interesting point. *You owe him.* Even more interestingly, she didn't feel the usual pinch of guilt that those words should have inspired. "Actually, now that I think about it, I don't think I do owe him much of anything." She leaned back against the counter, studying him. "Daddy's the one who decided I had to leave, and he's the one who cut off my access to funds that actually belong to me. I'm not asking him for anything here. Not now. Not his money, and certainly not his approval."

Craig opened his mouth to say something, and then frowned, as if whatever he'd been going to say didn't seem relevant all of a sudden. She could almost see the questions he was considering and rejecting.

She shrugged. "I don't really know what Daddy and I would talk about right now. I told him what I wanted to do and why, but he wasn't interested at the time. I guess you can tell him he's welcome to come down after I open the shop in a couple of months. I'll send him an invitation. And I'll be sure to make him a good cup of coffee." The corners of her mouth edged up in a faint grin. She was, she realized, enjoying herself.

Craig stared at her blankly. "Dee-Dee...Deirdre, he's worried about you. You need to talk to him."

"No." Her jaw tightened again. She'd already wasted a lot of good painting time on this conversation. "If he wants to talk to me, he knows where to find me. That is, he will after you tell him once you get back. Now good-bye, Craig."

She walked over and opened the front door without looking at him. She was fairly sure he'd be watching her with fire in his eyes, but she was also fairly sure she didn't care. She stood holding the door open as she glanced back at him.

It took him a moment to accept that she really was

throwing him out. She could see the moment when the penny finally dropped. The look he gave her then moved from annoyed to faintly murderous. Deirdre felt the first stirrings of unease feathering along her backbone.

"You haven't heard the last of this...Dee-Dee," he growled. "Your father's not going to be happy. And you know when he's unhappy, he tends to lash out at the things that are pissing him off."

Deirdre sighed. Already this conversation had gone on way beyond where it should have ended. "My father's never been a particularly happy man, Craig. You should know that by now. And that doesn't change the fact that I'm opening a coffee roaster here in downtown Konigsburg. And there's nothing either of you can do to stop me."

Her lips tightened as she stared back at him, a knot of tension forming in her gut. She'd never seen him looking quite that angry before. If worse came to worst, she could always call next door for Chico.

Then Craig pushed by her, stepping outside the shop onto the street. He paused for a moment, looking back, as if he had one more devastating remark that he chose not to deliver. He shook his head and stomped off toward the central part of town.

She exhaled slowly. For someone who'd just won a major victory, she felt a little unsteady. On the other hand, she'd managed for once not to cave in to her father or to his hirelings. That alone should have been worth some mild celebration.

She walked back into the shop, wishing she had something better than a lukewarm Diet Coke to toast herself with.

Craig marched up Main Street as if he had somewhere to go. Actually, of course, he did. Houston. But he had a feeling Big John wouldn't be delighted to see him until he had the runaway daughter tucked into his back seat.

Deirdre. The name alone left a bitter taste in his mouth. She was Dee-Dee, goddamn it. Big John's puffball daughter. His once-and-future fiancée. Key to the Good Life. Where the hell did she get off telling him no? Sure he'd mentioned the possibility she might do that to Big John, but he'd never actually believed it would happen.

She thought she was going to turn that piece-of-crap hole-in-the-wall into a coffee roaster? A coffee roaster she'd manage herself? Shitfire. The woman had enough money to have her coffee flown in daily from Timbuktu if she wanted. Why the hell was she playing around with some half-assed business she knew nothing about?

Something pricked at the back of his mind. Something about Dee-Dee and coffee. He couldn't exactly remember what it was, but now that he thought about it, maybe she'd said something once about working in some coffee shop someplace. Hell, it was probably behind the counter at Starbucks or something. She must think being a part-time barista was enough to qualify her to own the place. Typical rich airhead.

Part of him wanted to let her go ahead. The place would go under, and she'd slink back to Houston with her tail between her legs, at which point Big John could give her a position in the mailroom and Craig could dry her tears. But there was always the thousand-to-one chance that she might succeed.

Actually, the odds were a little better than that, if he was realistic. Dee-Dee had a decent track record on her ideas. He'd stolen enough of them to know they usually worked.

Which meant he needed to head this one off before it got too far. He paused at an open space that turned out to be the city park. Some families sat at the park tables, parceling out fried chicken to the kids. A couple of old men played checkers on one of the benches. Craig plopped down on a seat in the central gazebo to do some thinking.

If Dee-Dee actually succeeded with her shop, she'd be a lot less susceptible to pressure, from him or from Big John. Getting her back to Houston, back to her father and back to her carefully planned future with Craig, would be a lot more difficult if she had a life somewhere else.

The answer to that was simple—she couldn't have that life. Not even slightly.

He pondered his options. Technically, he should probably notify Big John before he did anything. But the big man had told him to use his own judgment. And he'd basically given him carte blanche to do whatever he thought best, so the first thing he needed to do was find a way to head Dee-Dee's plans into the dirt. After that, he'd find a way to make her life here in blue-hair central a lot less pleasant than it was at the moment.

He took a deep breath, pushing down the tight knot of resentment that still burned in his gut. Before he did anything else, he needed to work on a quick scheme to wipe that confident little smile off Dee-Dee's face. The smile she'd had the audacity to try on him. Nobody smiled at him like that and got away with it, not even a wayward almost-fiancée.

Craig's mouth spread into his own taut little grin. Once he'd taken care of that smile, the rest should fall into place without much trouble. Once Dee-Dee was truly down and out, she'd be a lot easier to deal with. And then he could get them both out of this shithole and back to the big time where he unquestionably belonged.

Chapter Twelve

All during the lunch hour, Tom had to fight the impulse to go next door and see how Deirdre was doing. Actually it was more like a compulsion than an impulse. Chico had headed over to her shop once it was clear that the lunch crowd was made up strictly of elderly tourists and young couples who didn't need his policing. He'd gone to see if she needed any help, and he hadn't come back. Which meant she was probably painting. Which meant she could use another pair of hands. Only Tom's hands were currently occupied drawing beers and pouring the occasional glass of wine.

Clem grinned at him when he headed to the kitchen for a quick sandwich before the next round of orders. "Heard you had a big night last night."

He froze with his ham and cheese halfway to his mouth. What exactly had Deirdre told her friends?

Clem's expression faded to something more like curiosity. "The band, boss. I'm talking about the band. Chico said it was really rocking."

The band. Right. He took a quick breath. "Yeah, they were real good. Big crowd." He wolfed another two bites of sandwich, hoping he could finish eating and get away before Clem could ask anything else.

The curiosity hadn't faded from her eyes. If anything, she looked more interested. "What else happened? More fights? Visits from the cops?"

He shook his head, swallowing a last large bite. "The only cop I saw was Nando, and that was just long enough to have a beer. Oh well, gotta get back to the bar now."

He dived through the door before Clem could think of

anything else to ask, but he saw her sardonic grin as he went.

By two, the lunch crowd had departed, such as it was. The Faro didn't really compete with the Sunday brunches the big restaurants served, and the drinkers wouldn't start trickling in until later. He helped Bobby Sue clean up the tables, hauling dirty dishes to the kitchen where Leon was loading the dishwasher.

Clem sat at the kitchen table, resting her feet on a chair as she took a bite of a bacon burger. "So you danced with Deirdre? To '*Volver, Volver*'?"

Tom stared at her. So far as he knew, nobody except Bobby Sue had gone into the kitchen since his own ignominious exit. Clem must be plugged into information sources far superior to his own.

She grinned more widely, nodding toward the open back door where Chico leaned as he drained a glass of iced tea.

"Just a dance," he muttered, trying for studied nonchalance. "Nothing big."

"To '*Volver, Volver*'? No such thing as 'just a dance', *jefe*." Clem took another massive bite of her burger. "Damn, I'm good."

He grabbed at the escape he saw glimmering on the horizon. "Yeah, you're very good. We need to talk about a dinner menu sometime. Particularly on the weekends. As long as the weather holds we could sell a lot of burgers and sausage out in the beer garden on Saturday nights. Maybe set up a grill."

"Got that right. Why should the Silver Spur have all the fun?"

"Why don't you work up a sample menu? Stuff we could handle with the staff we've got right now.

"I'll do that." Clem's eyes danced. "Nice diversionary tactic, by the way."

Tom stepped back into the main room as a single customer approached the bar. He was a big man. Not as big as Chico, of course, but few men were. This one looked like he'd been an athlete in his prime—broad, muscular shoulders and heavy arms. Tom guessed the guy had played football at some point in his life, but he'd already begun to go a little soft around the middle. The clothes looked expensive, but they also looked like they'd been lived in for a while. Judging from his bloodshot brown eyes and slightly pallid face, Tom would bet he was also nursing one hell of a hangover.

The man turned toward him as he approached the bar, his narrowed eyes giving him a quick assessment and then dismissing him. "Afternoon." He glanced around the room. "I need to talk to the owner. Is he here?"

Tom shrugged. The guy didn't exactly look like a salesman, but who knew? "I'm the owner. What can I do for you?"

The man's eyes widened slightly in surprise as he looked back at him. Something about his expression was vaguely hostile, but since Tom had never seen him before in his life, he figured he wasn't reading it right. After a moment, he reached a beefy hand across the bar. "Craig Dempsey."

Tom shook his hand, managing to avoid the crush grip Dempsey tried to use. "Tom Ames. What can I do for you, Mr. Dempsey?"

"I heard you own the place next door too. Is that right?"

"Yeah. It's all one building."

"I'm interested in leasing it. The shop, that is." Dempsey pushed his lips into one of the phonier smiles Tom had ever encountered. "Good location."

Tom managed not to look as incredulous as he felt. In fact, the shop was in one of the lousier locations in town. At the wrong end of Main, next door to a previously notorious bar. Deirdre might be able to make something out of it because she was determined and because she knew her market. Somehow, Craig Dempsey didn't strike him as similarly gifted. "It's not available. Sorry."

Dempsey's eyebrows went up in an exaggerated version of surprise. "It's not for rent?"

"Already rented. The place is being renovated."

"So you've got a contract and all?"

Something about his tone rankled, as if he already knew the answers to his own questions and was much too pleased about it. Tom unloaded some glasses from the rack Leon had just placed behind him. "We've reached an agreement, yeah."

"Well, Mr. Ames, I can guarantee you I'd be willing to pay a lot more than whatever rent you've agreed on with the current occupant. You'd definitely come out ahead on this deal, believe me."

Dempsey leaned an elbow on the bar. His expression was so elaborately casual that Tom immediately assumed he was lying about something even if he was telling the truth about the money.

"Sorry. Like I said, I've already rented the place." He stacked a few more glasses, deliberately not looking at Dempsey.

"You ever heard of Big John Brandenburg, Ames? Brandenburg, Inc.?"

A drip of ice coursed down Tom's spine. At least they were finally getting to the point, even though that point seemed a lot more dangerous to Deirdre than he'd figured before. "No. Can't say that I have." He gave Dempsey a tight smile. "He from around here?"

"No." He narrowed his eyes again. "Houston."

"That could explain it, then. Why I haven't heard of him." He went back to stacking glasses. He couldn't see any reason to make Dempsey's job easier.

"Look, Ames, let's quit screwing around here. Dee-Dee Brandenburg is renting your shop. Her father is Big John Brandenburg. More money than god and a couple of his angels. He wants her out of here and back in Houston where she belongs. He'll rent the shop from you for whatever price you want."

Tom turned to stare at him. *Deirdre? More money than god?* Fortunately, his years as a gambler had taught him how to keep a straight face no matter what he was thinking. "Okay, first of all, I don't know anybody named Dee-Dee. I'm renting the shop to Deirdre Brandenburg. She's been working her ass off getting it into shape. Why the hell should I screw her over because her father wants her to go back to Houston? Doesn't look like she's interested in going right now herself."

Dempsey's jaw tightened. There was no suggestion of a smile anymore. "If you do it my way, everybody wins. You cancel her lease, she goes home, her father's satisfied, you get a lot of money. Everybody's happy."

"Except Deirdre."

Dempsey shrugged, glancing at his watch. "She'll get over it. In fact, her father would also appreciate it if you found yourself a new barmaid. Believe me, Big John Brandenburg can be a very generous friend. And you don't need the kind of

125

trouble here that Dee-Dee Brandenburg could cause you."

For a long moment, Tom considered how satisfying it would be to plant his fist in the middle of Dempsey's doughy face. A broken nose might give him a little character. On the other hand, given Dempsey's personal sliminess, Tom doubted even a complete body cast could do that. "Let me get this straight, Dempsey. I'm supposed to fire Deirdre. Then I'm supposed to cancel her lease on the shop. All because, according to you, her rich daddy wants her to go back home and you'll make it worth my while."

Dempsey shrugged again. "That's it. Straightforward enough, I'd say. Big John Brandenburg's a good man to have on your side. And he'll definitely be on your side after you do this. You won't be sorry, believe me."

Tom closed his fist around his bar rag, largely to keep from closing it around Dempsey's throat. "No. I promised the shop to Deirdre, and she's doing a good job waiting tables here. I keep my promises. Plus I don't fire people just because somebody else wants me to."

Dempsey stared at him, his expression blank. Then he sighed. "Suit yourself. If you change your mind within the next forty-eight hours, I'm staying at the Woodrose Inn."

"After forty-eight hours, you leave?" Tom tried to keep the hopeful tone out of his voice.

Dempsey gave him a wintry smile. "After forty-eight hours, the offer expires. And believe me, when it does, you'll wish you'd taken it."

He turned and stalked out the door. Tom watched him go, wishing once again that he'd simply decked the bastard when he had the chance.

Deirdre stood in the doorway, studying her shop. *Her shop.* She fought down the little bubble of elation that formed in her chest. She was still a long way from being ready to open. But she'd come a long way already.

The paper overalls she'd worn to paint had made her sweat. Her hair, stuffed into an oversized painter's cap that kept sliding down her forehead, itched. She was dirty, paint-smudged, and she probably smelled, but she didn't give a damn. The shop—*her* shop—was shaping up nicely.

Chico pushed the roller across the ceiling one more time, covering the final strip of dingy gray with white primer. Deirdre figured she'd let it dry for the rest of the afternoon before she pulled the tarps off the floor. She'd paint the shelves and floor next week.

She squinted up at the shadowed ceiling. Maybe when she got a little money ahead, she'd install pressed tin. It would fit with the architecture and the room had probably had a tin ceiling once upon a time. For now, the primer would have to be enough. It was so far up nobody could see it clearly anyway.

She heard a step behind her and turned to see Tom walking up the sidewalk from the Faro. He paused in the doorway beside her, whistling. "Wow. Hard to believe a coat of paint could make that much difference."

Deirdre licked her lips. It was the first time she'd seen him since last night. Thanks to Craig's visit this morning, she hadn't really thought about that kiss for the past couple of hours. Until now. Suddenly she felt as if she'd swallowed a flock of luna moths.

"It's just primer. I've got a nice creamy brown picked out for the walls, sort of mocha. And then the floor and the shelves will be chocolate. Kind of a theme. You know, chocolate and coffee." She was babbling, but it was better than standing there tongue-tied, which seemed to be her other option.

Tom reached down and pushed her cap off her forehead, freeing a lock of hair as he did. "Looks great so far."

Deirdre wasn't sure how he could tell, given that he was looking at her instead of the room.

"Hey man," Chico called from the stepladder in the corner. "Put on some overalls and grab a roller. We still got half a wall to do."

Tom grabbed a set of overalls from the back room, pulling them over his jeans and T-shirt. "Glad to oblige."

Deirdre took another breath and told her hammering heart to calm down. She had to work with the man, and that meant trying to get back on something approaching a normal footing. She grabbed her own brush and went back to painting the strip of wall that ran along the top of the baseboards.

A couple of hours later they were more or less done. The

paint smell was so strong that Deirdre retreated to the back room. She thought about opening some windows, but then decided against it. Open windows would be an invitation for someone to try a little breaking and entering. Potential burglars couldn't get into the Faro from the shop, but they might not know that.

Chico pulled off the coveralls he was using. They didn't snap across his chest, and they left significant parts of his arms and legs uncovered, but he didn't seem worried about it. He tossed them in the corner. "When you want to put the paint over the primer?"

"This week sometime—after the primer dries. I might be able to get part of a wall done between the lunch and dinner shifts, or before lunch if I get up early enough."

Chico snorted. "I'll help you out in the afternoon. No getting up early, though."

"Thanks. I really appreciate it."

But he was already gone, striding out the back door toward the door to the kitchen.

Leaving her alone in the shop with Tom.

"Come on," he said. "Let me buy you dinner. Someplace better than here."

"Dinner?" Deirdre blinked at him. "Don't you have to tend bar?"

"Not on Sunday. No customers to speak of. Harry covers it. He's got Mondays off." He tossed the coverall next to Chico's. "Where did you get these? Did they come with the paint?"

"Sort of. Mrs. Grandview over at the hardware store let me have them for a couple of bucks. She said nobody wanted them because they tore too easily."

Tom's eyes drifted toward Chico's overall which was already splitting at every visible seam. "I can see her point. Dinner?"

Deirdre glanced down at her hands. "I'm really filthy."

Tom gave her a long, assessing look, long enough to make her toes curl. "So come next door and wash up. We can go over to the Coffee Corral. Believe me, Al Brosius won't care how you look."

Washing up in the kitchen of the Faro wasn't the easiest thing she'd ever done, particularly since she had a feeling Leon was checking her for wet T-shirt cling. Fortunately for her peace of mind, she'd managed to clean her face and hands without slopping too much on the rest of her body. Deirdre had a feeling her hair looked as if it had been jammed under a cap all afternoon, but she also had a feeling that sticking her head under the kitchen faucet would not be the best way to deal with the problem. Particularly since it would probably result in just the kind of view Leon was hoping for.

Tom gave Leon a narrow-eyed glance as he came into the kitchen. "You can take off. Looks like the dishes are all done now. Go sweep the main room."

Leon gave her one more look, maybe hoping she'd doused herself since the last time he'd looked at her five seconds before, and then headed out the kitchen door.

"Here. I raided some more of Ferguson's stock. Figured we could both use something that didn't smell like sweat and paint." Tom tossed her a T-shirt then pulled his own T-shirt over his head and dropped it on the floor at his feet.

Deirdre took a deep breath and told herself to calm down. She'd seen a man's naked chest before. Craig had displayed his every chance he got.

But somehow Craig's chest hadn't been so...nice. Tom's muscles were hard and flat, not bulging like Craig's, as if they'd been inflated shortly before he entered the room. His skin was slightly pale, but still warm, dusted with fine golden hair. He wore a silver medal on a chain around his neck that nestled in the center of his chest, catching the light.

Tom pulled on the clean T-shirt, and she almost groaned in disappointment.

Get a grip, Deirdre. She picked up the dark blue T-shirt from the prep table where he'd dropped it. On the front, two obese referees seemed involved in a fight to the death. "Fourteenth Annual Labor Day Soccer Tournament and Beer Fest," the letters read. Deirdre sighed. She'd seen worse—in fact, she'd worn worse within the last week. "I'll change and meet you out front."

Tom stood where he was for a moment, then grinned. "Yes ma'am. I'll give you some space." He turned and walked back through the swinging door, out into the main room again.

Deirdre stared down at the T-shirt, telling herself she wasn't disappointed in the least.

Chapter Thirteen

Tom glanced around the Coffee Corral, trying to assess the amount of business they were doing on a Sunday night. Good, but not spectacular. People who came to the Corral were usually local. It wasn't on Main and it served neither goat cheese nor pork rinds, which put it sort of in the middle of the road for Konigsburg. The owner and cook, Al Brosius, raised an eyebrow when he saw Tom and Deirdre heading for the counter to place their orders. "Scoping out the competition, Ames?"

"Looking to get fed, Al." Tom gave him an easy smile. Al wasn't as much of a tight-ass as Tolly Berenger at the Silver Spur, but he still had his reasons for not wanting Tom to move into the Konigsburg restaurant trade. "Besides, the Faro and the Corral draw different crowds. Believe me, you don't want my frat boys."

Al shook his head. "Nah, but I'd take a few of your blue-hairs. Send me the overflow next time, okay?"

"You got it." He turned to Deirdre. "What'll you have?"

She was chewing on that delectable lower lip again as she studied the menu posted above the counter. Tom carefully studied the menu himself so he wouldn't watch her. Getting a hard-on in the middle of the Coffee Corral was not on his agenda.

"I guess I'd like the Corral Burger with fries." She gave Al one of those smiles of hers, simultaneously innocent and sultry. "Could I get a salad, too?"

Al grinned back at her, his dark eyes much friendlier than they'd been when he'd looked at Tom. "A beautiful woman who eats. Will wonders never cease?"

Deirdre's cheeks turned a faint pink. "I'm really hungry.

And it smells wonderful in here." She gazed up at Al from beneath her lush dark lashes, the naughty librarian sprung to life.

Tom studied Al's menu for all he was worth. Apparently, Deirdre's lower lip wasn't the only thing that sent his body into overdrive.

After he'd placed his own order for fried catfish and coleslaw, Tom guided her to a booth near the back. He didn't think they'd run into anybody they knew at the Corral, but he had no idea where Dempsey was hanging out when he wasn't making threats at the Faro. And he wanted some time for a personal conversation.

All afternoon he'd been trying to figure out how much to tell her, and how to phrase it. *Guess what? Your billionaire daddy wants me to fire you and throw you out of the shop* was accurate but wasn't likely to earn him any points for sensitivity. Still, however he phrased it, he knew he needed to tell her something about what was going on—to at least warn her about what her father was apparently planning. Who knew what else the old man might have in mind?

Dempsey's parting shot still echoed in his mind. *You'll wish you'd taken it.* Even allowing for the fact that Dempsey was a self-dramatizing asshole, he didn't much like the sound of that. Particularly since he figured Deirdre had a good chance of being hurt in the fallout of whatever dumbshit thing Dempsey was planning to do, probably on her father's orders.

She nibbled on a leaf from the salad Al had handed her before they'd left the counter. "Would you like some of this? It's really good." A drop of oil glistened on her pouty lower lip.

Jesus, would you just forget the freakin' lower lip?

"That's okay. Have at it." Tom stared down at his iced tea. "I met a friend of yours this afternoon."

Deirdre half-raised her gaze to his as she bit down on a tomato. "Who was that?"

"Said his name was Craig Dempsey."

Her forehead furrowed in what looked like real confusion. "Craig? Why would Craig come to see you?"

"So he is a friend?" Tom hated to admit it, but he'd been sort of hoping she'd stare at him blankly, and the whole thing would turn out to be a hoax.

Deirdre shrugged. "Not a friend really. More like a business associate. A former business associate, that is. What did he want?"

"It's more what he didn't want." Tom sighed, looking up into those indigo eyes again. "He wanted to steal the lease for the shop out from under you, to rent the shop for himself. Or rather he wanted to do that for your father."

"My father." Deirdre lowered her fork slowly to her plate.

"That's what he said." All of a sudden, he wished he'd waited until after they'd finished dinner. He had a feeling she might not be eating much more.

"Did you..." She paused, staring down at her salad. "When he asked, did you—"

"It's your shop. I'm not going to rent it to somebody else when you've put all that work into it. I wouldn't do that to you."

She closed her eyes, briefly, blowing out a breath. "Sorry. For a moment there, I thought you might have given him what he asked for. Believe me, he would have paid you. Probably a lot."

"It's not about the money." Tom managed a faint grin. "Well, not entirely. The Faro's doing okay, and you're doing a good job, Deirdre. I'll help you out if I can."

"Thank you."

Those indigo pools had him again. If he didn't find something else to talk about, ASAP, he'd end up saying something not only stupid but possibly dangerous to his health, given that the Toleffsons seemed to be taking a personal interest in Deirdre's future. "What's your father like?"

She speared another cherry tomato, grimacing. "He's a businessman. A very successful one. He's used to running things. And people."

"What about your mom?"

"My mom died when I was eleven. Cancer."

"So your father raised you?"

"More or less." She sighed, running her fork through a pool of dressing in the bottom of her salad bowl. "Mostly less. I spent most of my time after Mom died in boarding school. In the summer I went to camp, and sometimes I got to stay with my Aunt Reba and Uncle Billy here in Konigsburg. Docia too. I saw Daddy every month or so when he was in town. And we'd spend the holidays together."

"Not exactly hands-on."

She shook her head. "It wasn't so bad. He let me know what he expected, and then he left me alone. Sort of."

"Sort of?"

"Well, I didn't always get to make my own decisions. Like I wanted to major in art history for a while at college, and he told me flat out it was a waste of time and money, and that he wouldn't pay for it. So I ended up majoring in business."

Tom frowned. "Did you want to major in business?"

"Not at first." She moved her fork back and forth in the dressing again, carving a small zigzag. "Once I got into it, I enjoyed it, though. And I was really good at it. I ended up going on for my MBA."

"That must have pleased him."

"You'd think so, wouldn't you?" Her mouth twisted slightly. "I guess it really did—at some level anyway. But he told me classroom learning was nothing compared to real life. And then he gave me a job."

"So he helped you out." He felt like he was tiptoeing through a china shop. Blindfolded.

"In a sense, yes. He didn't really pay any attention to what I had to say, though, once I was working there. He had all these other people who'd worked for him forever, so I guess he felt like he didn't need to. My opinion wasn't worth much compared to theirs. And he wanted me to marry Craig."

His gut clenched. "You were going to marry Craig?"

"I think Craig thought so. I'm pretty sure Daddy did." Her eyes took on a faraway glint.

"What about you?"

She shook her head slowly. "Not so much."

Tom exhaled. "And that's why you left?"

Deirdre shook her head again, her mouth tight. "It's complicated."

Before he could ask her to uncomplicate it for him, Al's wife, Carol, arrived with a tray full of food. She gave Tom a narrow-eyed look. "Clem's cooking not good enough for you?"

"Clem's off in the evenings. And I like Al's catfish." He lifted his platter of fish and fries off her tray, while she placed a huge bowl of coleslaw alongside it.

Carol smiled at Deirdre. "You're Docia's cousin, right? The one from Houston who's waiting tables for this shifty-eyed character? I'm Carol Brosius. Pleased to have you here."

Deirdre's smile made him ready to forgive Carol for the "shifty-eyed" comment. "I'm Deirdre. It's good to be here."

"So are you really happy being Tom's barmaid? Because we could use another waitress, you know." Carol gave him a quick grin to let him know she was kidding. Sort of.

"I wouldn't think of it."

"Ah well, never hurts to ask." Carol glanced around the table with a practiced eye. "Okay. I'll bring you some more tea in a minute. Let me know if you need anything else."

Tom stared after her, reminding himself that sending Deirdre to wait tables at the Coffee Corral wouldn't make her any less vulnerable to her father and her erstwhile boyfriend. He speared a piece of catfish off his plate and took a quick bite.

Deirdre picked up a French fry and dragged it through some of the leftover salad dressing. "So what about your family?"

He regarded her warily. "What about them?"

"Where did you grow up? Brothers and sisters at home? Parents still living? That kind of thing."

He bit through a hush-puppy, trying to decide how much to share. The Ames family legacy. Not the kind of thing he usually talked about. And obviously a long way from her life among the Texas billionaires. "I'm from Kansas City. The 'burbs on the Missouri side. My dad took off when I was in grade school. My mom raised us, only she worked waiting tables at Jack's Stacks, so she wasn't home that much. We moved around a lot—apartments mostly. I've got an older brother and a younger sister. I haven't seen either of them in five or six years. In Burton's case, largely by choice. In Minnie's case, probably because we didn't have much to say to each other."

"And your mom?"

"Living in Florida last I heard. She got remarried a few years ago and moved down there."

Deirdre's forehead was furrowed. "She didn't keep in touch with you?"

Tom sighed, feeling faintly defensive. Hell, it wasn't like his life was all that unusual. Just sort of...basic. "Look Deirdre, not all families keep tabs on each other. We had a tough time growing up. My mom did the best she could, but I don't think she was all that happy to be stuck with a three kids and no child support. She kept us clothed and fed and at school, but that was about it. The three of us grew up and got out, and so did she."

"But it sounds sort of...bleak."

He shook his head, his jaw tightening. "It wasn't that bad. Taught me some important stuff."

"Such as?"

"Such as not expecting anybody to give me anything. Learning to depend on myself. Thanks to my family, I learned to take care of myself and not look for somebody else to rescue me."

"Still..." She looked like she'd like to say more, but after a moment she concentrated on her burger instead.

Tom's shoulders began to relax. Talking about his family wasn't his favorite occupation, but at least those discussions never lasted long, given that there wasn't much to say. At least she didn't act like she was horrified to be spending time with a Midwestern redneck. He speared another good-sized bite of catfish.

"So how did you end up with the Faro?"

Well, hell. He put down his fork. "If I said it was complicated, would you let it go?"

Deirdre shook her head. "I'll tell you why my stuff is complicated if you'll tell me about yours."

He chewed on his catfish for a moment, thinking. But there was no polite way to put it. Might as well let her know how much distance there was between them from the start. "Okay, here's the thing. I'm not a college grad. When I finished high school, I didn't have the money or the inclination. And my trade skills out of high school were pretty much limited to road construction, which didn't strike me as much of a life."

He paused. Judging from the line currently marring Deirdre's perfect forehead, he had her attention at least. But she didn't seem too dismayed. Yet. "So I tried the army for a few years, but that didn't exactly do it for me either. On the other hand, I picked up a hell of a skill set."

"Doing what?" The line was more pronounced now. He

figured she'd made the leap to mercenary soldier. Or maybe armed robbery.

He blew out a breath. "Poker. Actually, cards in general. But poker's the most profitable game, so it's the one I played most."

The line disappeared as Deirdre's eyes widened. "You won the Faro in a poker game?"

"Pretty much. Up in Dallas. Kip Berenger was in to me for a lot of money. He asked if I'd be interested in the Faro instead. Frankly it wasn't worth as much as he'd lost, but I was ready to move on anyway. And I always liked the idea of my own bar."

"You lived in Dallas."

"I stayed there. Hotels, mostly."

"But where did you..." The frown was back. "Didn't you have a home anywhere?"

Tom gave her a tight smile. "Not really. I've never had a home until Konigsburg. Never owned any property, that is." *No, sweetheart, I'm definitely not a dues-paying member of the middle class.*

Deirdre shook her head slowly. "So all the stuff you've done at the Faro was from your poker winnings?"

He shrugged. "Yeah, that and the money I saved from the army. I didn't have any other use for it. And now the place is paying its way. On average, I figure we're pulling in about as much as the Silver Spur most nights."

"Clem says you're going to start serving dinner."

"Thinking about it. We need to attract the locals, too, and food helps. So does the music."

"You've done really well. Congratulations."

Tom blinked. She seemed sincere. The billionaire MBA, late of the Houston Brandenburgs, congratulating the poker-playing saloon owner on his business sense. Only in America.

She started to take another bite of her burger, but he shook his head. "Nope, you don't get out of this. Your turn to uncomplicate the story. Why did you leave your father's company?"

Deirdre set her hamburger back on her plate as the line appeared in her forehead again. "It's sort of hard to explain. Not the part about my leaving—Dad threw me out, basically. But the part about why I told him I didn't want to work for him anymore."

"Wait." He held up his hand, his jaw tight. "He threw you out? Literally?"

She shrugged. "I was living in a company apartment, and he said since I wasn't going to work for the company anymore, I didn't get the apartment. Plus I'd been sort of an idiot because I'd never gotten around to establishing my own credit cards and bank accounts. His name was on everything as a holdover from when I was in college, and he basically blocked me from getting hold of any of my money. Including all the savings I had from my salary." She gave him a wan smile. "You'd never guess I had an MBA, would you?"

Tom bit back all his immediate responses, which pretty much amounted to *son of a bitch!* "You probably just didn't expect your father to cheat you out of your own cash. I'd guess that's more par for the course in my neighborhood than yours."

"It's just..." She stared down at her burger for a long moment. "He never seemed to listen to me when I was there. If I wanted to get something done, I'd have to tell him two or three times before he'd pay attention. And by then sometimes somebody else would have heard what I was trying to do and stolen the idea." Her jaw tightened. "That happened more than once, to tell you the truth. With people I should have been able to trust. It taught me who my friends were."

"So you figured he wouldn't care if you wanted to leave and open a coffee roaster in Konigsburg?"

Deirdre nodded slowly. "That's exactly what I figured. Why would he care? I wasn't doing anything special for him—any number of young MBAs could have taken my place. And it didn't seem to matter to him whether I was there or not."

"Maybe he just wanted you to stay with his company. Maybe he had plans for your future."

She sighed. "Probably he did. Of course, he never bothered to share those plans with me. I could have saved him a lot of grief if he had."

"You always planned on doing this?"

"Yeah." She picked up another French fry. "I figured I'd give my dad a couple of years and then strike out on my own. I mean, it wasn't like he was going to pass Brandenburg, Inc. down to me or anything."

"He wasn't?" Tom frowned. He thought that's what people in the Brandenburgs' tax bracket always did.

Deirdre shook her head. "He already had his succession figured out. Plus we both knew I wouldn't be good at it—I'm not big on big. The idea of running a major corporation gives me hives. Maybe he thought I'd stick around in some honorary post."

"Not what you wanted to do."

"Not even slightly. I actually told him a couple of times that I was interested in getting into the coffee business. I guess it didn't sink in."

Or he hadn't heard. Or he hadn't wanted to. Deirdre stared down at her dinner plate, munching on a fry. She'd eaten maybe half of her hamburger, and now she was drawing patterns in the ketchup.

Tom really wanted that desolate look out of her eyes. He wanted it out now. "Want to see where I live?"

She glanced up at him. "I don't know. Do I? Is it memorable?"

"Not particularly, but I've got a friend you might like."

"You live with a friend?"

"I do indeed." He waved across the room to Carol. "What do you say we get the rest of this boxed up to go."

He knew at least one thing that should put a smile on her face, assuming he wasn't totally out of practice. At any rate, it would definitely put a smile on his.

Chapter Fourteen

Tom's house really wasn't much to look at, Deirdre conceded. She estimated it was from the teens or twenties, early twentieth century anyway. Shotgun layout with one room opening into another in a straight line. It was painted white with black trim, set back from the street by a small yard enclosed with a wooden fence and an iron gate.

The front yard was shadowed by a huge cottonwood that had dropped its cotton in dense mats on the street. The breeze kicked up clouds of fibers, as if someone were shaking a feather pillow somewhere.

"Messy," he acknowledged. "I spend half my summers raking up that muck." Deirdre followed him up the creaking front porch steps to the door, where he pushed his key in the lock.

The living room was cool and dark, the light of the setting sun reflected through the side windows. He stepped inside and turned on a lamp. From somewhere nearby, she heard an odd scratching sound, like insects running across a wall. She glanced around the room with a quick shiver.

One corner had its own light. As she moved closer, Deirdre realized it was actually a cabinet, only not exactly. The walls were made of plywood on three sides. The front was something transparent—glass or Plexiglas. She could see a couple of shelves inside, with what looked like tree limbs propped against them. Ivy hung around the edges and bright lights illuminated the sides.

Tom stepped beside her. "So this is who I wanted you to meet. The friend I live with."

She shivered again. "I don't see anybody."

"She's hiding." He stepped closer to the cabinet. "Come on Doris, come out and meet the nice lady."

More scratching sounded from the upper part of the cabinet. Then a large lizard emerged from the shelter of the shelves. Her body looked like it was covered in tiny polka dots that Deirdre assumed were scales. Her head was a deep green that shaded off down her body into moss and brown, ending with a long striped tail. Small spikes ran down the edge of her spine from head to tail. Her long toes were tipped in curving claws, the origin of the scratching sound as she edged carefully down the branch that angled closest to the door.

She licked her lips. She had no intention of getting any closer. In fact, she wondered if she could possibly move back a bit without being insulting.

He turned toward her, grinning slightly. "Don't worry. She's not free range. She stays in here most of the time, although I give her a shoulder ride every now and then."

The lizard, Doris, raised her head, setting her wattles trembling, and regarded him with black peppercorn eyes. For a moment, Deirdre thought she looked almost affectionate. Probably projection.

"Have you had her a long time?"

He shrugged. "A few months. A customer owned her—she belonged to his girlfriend who took off and left her. He was getting ready to take her out and let her loose someplace in the hills. That struck me as a really lousy idea for everybody involved, especially Doris, so I said I'd take her off his hands."

"Did you build her...enclosure?"

He grinned again. "It's a cage. And no, she came with it. Don't know if the girlfriend built it or if she inherited it like I did."

Deirdre inched closer. Doris stayed on her branch, watching her carefully, as if she'd head back up to the shelves in an instant if Deirdre started to pose a threat. "What does she eat?"

"Iguana chow."

Deirdre narrowed her eyes.

"Iguanas are herbivores. She gets alfalfa and other greens, like kale. And she's very big on nopal. Probably reminds her of home."

"Cheaper than a carnivore."

"Yeah, the most expensive thing about her is temperature control. She can't get too cold or too warm, which pretty much means she has to live inside, at least in Texas." He gestured toward the lights. "Those help. And there's a heater."

"And she's a female?"

He shrugged. "Haven't a clue. Supposedly males have bigger pores on their rear thighs, but I didn't particularly want to hoist Doris up to find out."

"So you just decided she was a she?"

"Hey, I've got a fifty percent chance of being right."

Deirdre was standing beside him now. Doris really wasn't that big once you got used to her. Maybe three or four feet in all. And the emerald green on her head was really pretty. "Do you ever pet her?"

"Nope. I think she considers me a sort of soft, warm tree limb. And tree limbs don't scratch your ears, at least not deliberately. Right now I need to give her fresh water."

He opened the catch on the cage door as Doris's long tongue flicked out and back. Deirdre fought the impulse to back up again—she really was a nice-looking iguana overall. Of course, she had no idea what a bad-looking iguana would be like.

Tom took the water bowl out of the cage and headed toward what she assumed was the kitchen. Doris descended to the cage floor, using her curved claws to hang onto her branch. They looked very sharp.

"Nice Doris," Deirdre muttered.

"She doesn't bite. Well, she could, but she hasn't. And if she really is female, she's less likely to. Males can get aggressive in mating season, but females just sit back and wait for males to come to them." Tom set the water bowl back in the cage.

"When's mating season?" As soon as she'd said it, Deirdre wished she hadn't, but there was, of course, no backing up now.

He grinned again. "I'd love to give you a smartass answer, but I won't. It varies from iguana to iguana, which is to say I'm not sure."

She blew out a breath and gazed around the rest of the room. A leather couch was pushed against one wall, with a couple of Mission-style chairs sitting next to a woven rug. A large steamer trunk strewn with magazines and a coffee cup sat in the middle of the room, a sort of rough-and-ready coffee table. "Nice furniture. Where did you get it? Or did you bring it with you?"

He shrugged. "Most of it came from the antique and second-hand stores downtown. I sold them some stuff I didn't want from the Faro, and they gave me a break on prices for the chairs and the trunk. And I picked up the rug from Elsa's weaving shop down on Main—West Texas wool. The couch I had when I lived in Vegas."

Deirdre managed not to blink. Of course he'd lived in Las Vegas. Where else? "I need some furniture myself. Or I will when I finally get enough cash to start living again. You can tell me where to go."

Tom glanced at her as if he were considering pursuing the comment about her cash flow problems, but then he let it go. "Most shops in town have good stuff, and they'll give you a fair deal if you're willing to bargain. Some are a little weird, though. I'd avoid Milam Broadus, for example."

"Which one is he?"

"The Republic of Texas store on Spicewood. He deals in Texana. He's also nuts, but that may go with the territory." His teeth flashed white against his skin in the dimming light.

She took a careful breath, avoiding that ice-blue gaze. "I probably can't afford Texana. I'm sort of into comfort anyway."

His grin turned slightly sour. "Which is why you were sleeping on a sleeping bag?"

"Well, I'm not anymore. It's a great mattress. You should try it sometime." Deirdre's face promptly heated to fever temperature. *Oh very subtle. Why don't you come up and see me sometime, handsome?*

"Would you like something to drink?" He turned away from her, maybe to let her have some time to recover. "I've got a bottle of red wine the distributor swore was first rate, as opposed to the jug stuff we're stocking at the Faro."

"Yes, please." She managed to say it without stammering, which she took as a major advance. She watched Tom uncork the wine, his movements with the corkscrew smooth and sure. "Why don't we stock any Texas wine? Morgan Barrett's got some really nice stuff at her winery. She's married to one of Docia's in-laws."

He turned back, handing her a glass. "She's married to the chief of police, as a matter of fact, and her winery does make good wine. If the Faro starts serving dinner, I'll probably stock more individual bottles. Right now, we only get orders for single glasses, usually women who don't like beer. The place isn't exactly a wine bar yet."

Deirdre sipped, tasting smoky flavor and deep fruit. "This is really good. I'd drink it."

"You already are." His grin was back as he sat down beside her on the couch. "Like I say, once I get a dinner menu set up, I'll see about expanding the wine list. Of course, that's if Clem comes up with something besides burgers. Burgers work better with beer."

Deirdre couldn't think of anything to say to that. The moment of silence fell between them like a drop of clear water.

He sipped his wine slowly. "So. Were you engaged to Dempsey, or just 'engaged to be engaged', or what?"

She stared down at her wine, mainly to avoid looking at him. There was something sort of unnerving about those blue eyes, that slow grin. "We didn't have anything formal. He may have thought we were more involved than we really were. Plus my father wanted me to be involved with him."

"Why?" One golden eyebrow arched.

"Because it made a lot of sense from a business point of view. And it would have looked great in the annual report." She managed a dry smile. "I'm being sarcastic, but hiring Craig was always more a PR strategy than a business decision. He used to play for the Cowboys. I guess he was sort of famous—a lot of people recognize him, anyway."

Tom's forehead furrowed. "I didn't. But I'm more a Chiefs fan."

"He's sort of got that famous-person attitude. He expects people to recognize him. He must have been unhappy when you didn't."

"I don't think he was considering me as a potential fan." Now it was Tom's turn to look away. She wondered what exactly he was trying not to tell her.

"Anyway, we dated for a while, and Daddy kept inviting him to dinners and other stuff. He acted like Craig was part of the family."

"But you didn't think so?"

She shook her head. "We didn't have anything in common. And then it got sort of...bad." She paused, trying to think how to explain it.

Tom's jaw hardened. "Did he hurt you?"

"No. Nothing like that. He stole from me. I told him some ideas I'd had and he passed them on to my father as his own. Daddy loved them. Of course, he might not have felt the same way if he'd known they were mine." Her father had shown a distinct lack of interest in most of her proposals up to that point.

He set his wineglass down on the steamer trunk. "That was shitty. Did he have any explanation?"

"He said we'd discussed them, 'brainstormed' them. So what he'd proposed wasn't really mine. It was his idea that had grown out of my idea. Except that it *was* my idea—exactly the idea I'd told him about. We didn't have any kind of formal relationship—we'd just been dating for a few months. So I stopped going out with him. I'm not sure Daddy even noticed." Her father seldom noticed things that didn't fit into his idea of what was supposed to happen. If he went on not noticing for a while, sometimes things might go back to the way he wanted them to be.

"So old Craig gets credit for being smarter than he is, and your father gets to go on believing he'll have an NFL star on the family team." Tom grimaced. "Sweet."

She swallowed a larger sip of wine. "It's my own fault. If I'd stood up for myself and stopped being such a pushover, Craig wouldn't have gotten away with it."

Tom reached over and took the glass out of her hands, gently, setting it on the trunk in front of her. "Listen to me. The only one who's responsible for Craig Dempsey being an asshole is Craig Dempsey. You didn't force him to steal your ideas. You didn't tell your father to believe in him. It sounds like you got stuck in between a couple of men who weren't paying any attention to anything except what they wanted themselves. That's not your fault."

"No, but..." She paused. All of a sudden what he was saying made a lot of sense. "Damn. You know...that's true. And I came up here to get away from that. Good for me."

"You got that right. Good for you."

His slow grin started a tightening somewhere around her stomach. *Come on, Deirdre, that's definitely not your stomach!* She took a breath, trying to calm her fluttering nerves. Just sex. No big deal.

Oh yeah. And you really believe that, right?

He reached for her, tracing the line of her cheekbone with his index finger. She tried to think of something to say, something bright and sophisticated, something that would maybe make the butterflies in her stomach stop fighting each other. "You...have a nice house."

Deirdre closed her eyes so she wouldn't have to see him grin. *Such an idiot!*

"You have a nice mouth. It's been driving me crazy all night."

His hand moved to cup her cheek pulling her gently toward him. His mouth against hers felt soft and warm. She opened to him, tasting him, smelling the mixed scents of sweat and soap that marked him.

Oh god, oh god, oh god. We're going to do this. And I'm so not ready!

He could taste the wine on her lips, faintly woody and dark. Her body seemed to vibrate with nerves under his palms as he moved closer. He had a feeling if he made one wrong move, she'd be out the door and down the walk.

Of course, that meant he had to figure out what a wrong move was and then manage not to make it.

He slipped his hand along her side, feeling the stretched cotton of her T-shirt. The T-shirt he'd given her earlier in the evening. The T-shirt he planned to remove within the next five minutes or so. Carefully, he slid his tongue deeper into her mouth, tasting her again, that faint sense of spice and heat that seemed to go along with her.

He pulled back for a moment, resting his forehead on hers. "Deirdre..."

Her hands moved lightly across his chest, sliding up toward his shoulders, leaving smooth trails of heat where they touched. Then she tilted her head, bringing her lips against his again.

A pulse began to beat at the back of his brain. *Now, now,*

now. So easy. Move forward, push down, find the edge of the shirt, pull up, taste, touch, have.

Something dry and scratchy pressed against his elbow.

Tom jerked upright. "What the hell?"

Doris gazed up at him from the floor beside the couch, black eyes alight. *Well, hi there!*

Beneath him on the couch, Deirdre gasped and then scrunched as far away from Doris as she could.

Tom closed his eyes. Clearly the fates had it in for him. On the other hand, he really didn't want to do this on his couch anyway. He slipped to the floor, then crouched down beside Doris, sliding both hands underneath her body, careful not to come down from above, which might frighten her. The iguana's tongue flicked out and back and he tried to remember if that was one of the warning signs of an incipient bite. He didn't think getting sutured in the emergency room would be a romantic highlight of the evening.

He lifted Doris carefully, then carried her back to the cage. The door was slightly ajar, no doubt his fault because he'd been concentrating on herding Deirdre toward the couch rather than seeing that the cage door was shut securely. He placed Doris inside and clicked the latch closed.

Deirdre gazed after him. Her dark hair was tousled around her face in waves, her indigo eyes were wide, her full lips swollen with his kisses. Even with Doris's untimely interruption, he still felt luckier than he'd ever been before, even when he'd had a winning night at the casinos. The billionaire's daughter hooking up with the vagabond gambler. *Yeah, that's real likely.*

He blew out a breath. Likely or not, it was going to happen. "Come on. Let's go somewhere more private."

Deirdre grinned at him, her lips moving lazily. "Maybe Doris thinks it's mating season."

"Maybe she does. But I don't necessarily want to share the experience with her right now." He extended his hand. After a moment, she reached up and took it, allowing him to pull her to her feet and then lead her toward the bedroom.

For one of the few times in his life, Tom felt like thanking the US Army for turning him into a compulsive bed maker. One less thing to worry about. He didn't bother flicking on the light.

Instead, he pulled Deirdre into his arms again, reaching behind her to shut the door.

Her lips ran a quick whispering line down the side of his throat. Her tongue flicked across his collarbone, and he was instantly hard—no, *harder*—his chest clenching tight. He grabbed the edge of her T-shirt to avoid grabbing her, pulling it up and over her shoulders.

She wore a white cotton bra. Not exactly rich-girl variety. He might have expected satin and lace, but cotton seemed more like Deirdre's style. He leaned down to take her nipple in his mouth, sucking through the thin fabric to feel the areole dimple. She moaned faintly, her fingers twisting in his hair. He slid his hands underneath the fabric, pushing the bra up until he cupped her breasts, feeling their perfect weight against his palms. He sucked the other nipple, blowing slightly against the puckered surface until she pulled at his hair again. Then he unfastened her bra and threw it beside the bed.

Her eyes were pools, wide, dark, shining in the depths. She leaned forward, pressing her mouth desperately to his, her hands cradling his face, her tongue thrusting deep.

Tom moved against her, his fingers searching for the button on her jeans. In another minute he'd be tearing them off, regardless of niceties like unzipping, which might be fun for the moment but might piss her off in the long run. Not that he thought Deirdre would notice right now.

She was pulling desperately at his zipper. He moved her hands away, a little afraid of the damage the zipper could do if it came down as quickly as she wanted it to. "Slow down, babe," he whispered. "Just a little." He pushed her jeans off her hips, then pulled her down beside him on the bed, kicking his own jeans off at the side.

"The spread," Deirdre whispered. "Shouldn't we take it off?"

Tom hoped she couldn't see his shit-eating grin too clearly. "I'm not worried about laundry right now." He pulled back to look at her.

She wore a single strip of white at her crotch, maybe cotton but gratifyingly brief. Her body was a slender thread of darkness against his bed, her contours caught by the moonlight. Long legs, curving torso, breasts... Tom closed his eyes for a moment. Perfect breasts, perfect girl. Maybe too perfect for him. Definitely lucky.

Deirdre stretched her arms toward him, her lips curving in a slow, sensuous smile that set his lower body on fire. Good thing he wasn't expected to do any major thinking right now, given that no blood remained in his brain.

He slid his hands down her sides again, feeling the warm silk of her skin beneath his palms, then he lowered his mouth to her throat, running his tongue along a line to her earlobe and pulling it between his teeth as she sucked in a breath. Her hips rubbed against him urgently, as she moaned again.

"Tom," she gasped. "Ah, Tom."

He pulled back to look at her again, still smelling the faint scent of jasmine that cloaked her hair. Dark eyes, dark hair, full lips opened for a quick glimpse of white teeth. "Tom," she murmured again.

"What?"

White teeth flashed again in the darkness. "You really need to get naked."

Deirdre wondered how she could possibly feel so excited and so terrified at the same time. Surely one emotion should cancel out the other. She was trying very hard not to think about how limited her experience was, how likely she was to disappoint him.

Tom jerked off his jockey shorts and she marveled once again at his wonderful rightness. Shoulders broad but not too broad. Hard, sculpted muscles on his chest, not blown up to something out of a body-building magazine. The swath of golden hair over the dark brown disks of his nipples. So perfect. So…right. The jut of his arousal from the dark nest of hair between his legs made her feel weak, then warm. Then aching.

He knelt again over her body, running his hands along her flanks, then parting her legs gently. His lips grazed her inner thigh and she almost came off the bed. "Oh, god."

"Okay?"

She nodded quickly. She couldn't have said anything to save her soul.

He bent over her again, his fingers tightening on her thighs, his tongue sliding along the delicate skin at the top.

Deirdre concentrated on breathing. She wasn't sure she'd remember to do it if she didn't.

She felt warm breath on her sensitive skin, and then his mouth, rubbing the soft cotton of her panties against her mons. *Oh damn!* Why hadn't she taken them off when she'd had the chance?

His tongue pressed insistently against her, rubbing hard. She felt the moist heat of his mouth, the fine texture of the cotton burning her skin. "Please," she whispered, straining toward the elastic at the top. "Please, let me…"

He paid no attention, his tongue repeating the relentless pressure, lapping against her. She could feel the tension building, spreading, her thighs beginning to tremble. "Please," she whispered one more time, but she wasn't sure what she was asking for anymore.

She felt lips and teeth again, and then she was breaking, shattering, her body jerking against him. Her breath whooshed from her lungs, and she clutched at his arms. "Oh my," she gasped. "Oh my god."

He leaned away from her for a moment and she heard the sound of a drawer opening. She reached down and jerked off her panties, her fingers shaking, then reached for the foil packet in his fingers. "Let me. Please."

In the darkness, his eyes were icy fire, his lips turning up again in a slow grin. "Have at it, babe."

She took the packet from him, then ran her hands down his shaft, feeling the smooth skin over hard muscle, her hands tightening as she slid up, then down again. Above her she heard him catch his breath in a gasp.

"You're supposed to be putting that thing on," he gasped.

"I am," she whispered. "Just very slowly."

She shook the condom loose, unrolling it over him, listening to his sharp intake of breath. She cupped him with one hand, while the other ran up and down again, tightening at the head. His eyes narrowed while he sucked in another breath. She leaned upward, cupping him with both hands, running her tongue in a line down his abdomen.

And then his hands were on her shoulders, pushing her flat. He balanced above her for a moment, his fingers spreading her, testing her wetness, sliding in for a moment. She felt him pressing against her, entering her, opening her wide. She grabbed hold of his shoulders, wrapping her legs around his waist as he began to move. Her eyes closed as her head fell back.

"Stay with me," he rasped. "Don't you dare go away."

Deirdre's eyes popped open, and she stared up at him. "I won't," she breathed, moving her body against his. "I can't."

"Good."

The rhythm of his thrusts increased, pushing her again and again, higher and higher. She felt the heat growing in her abdomen, the tension spiraling through her, driving her. "Oh, Tom," she cried, and then came undone, her body moving in ways that seemed completely out of her control.

Everything was out of control. Not that she minded.

Above her, Tom reached his own climax, his body jerking spasmodically against her, thrusting deep inside in a way that set off a new round of rolling climaxes in her core. By now, she was beyond saying anything, even moaning. She wrapped her arms around his shoulders and hung on, waiting for the moment she'd touch earth again.

She heard his breath sighing against her ear, his lips running almost absently up the length of her throat. "Oh, babe," he whispered. "Babe. So good"

Deirdre closed her eyes now, holding him tight against her. The world spun away again, and she let her legs fall back against the sheet, her muscles gone now to mush. One last thought flitted through her brain before she shut down completely.

If I ever see Craig Dempsey again, I am so flipping him the bird!

Chapter Fifteen

Tom awoke to cool air against his back. He squinted at the other side of the bed, but he already knew what he'd find. Deirdre wasn't next to him, where she should have been. He'd been having a very enjoyable dream, featuring her, strawberries, and some unique ways of eating dessert. Then he heard a woman humming, and although it wasn't part of his dream, reality suddenly seemed to have a lot going for it.

He grabbed his jeans from the floor and pulled them on, zipping as he walked. With any luck he could catch her before she left. With really good luck, he could convince her to come back to bed for a couple of hours or so. That dream had given him some really interesting ideas he wanted to explore.

He followed the smell of coffee to the kitchen, then stopped. Deirdre was, unfortunately, fully dressed and busily slicing toast. She was also...dazzling. Her dark hair was loose around her shoulders, still slightly damp from her shower. The blue T-shirt from yesterday clung lovingly to her curves. Even her everyday loose jeans seemed to emphasize the slim roundness of her hips and the length of her legs.

Tom leaned back against the doorway to keep from pulling her into his arms. Maybe he should get a sense of how she was feeling about him before he starting talking about encores. "Morning."

She turned toward him, glowing. No makeup. Didn't matter. He'd never seen a more beautiful woman, certainly not in his own kitchen.

"Good morning. I made coffee—I hope that's okay."

He nodded, trying to pull his thoughts together. "Sure. Help yourself."

"You don't have much in the way of food, but I found some bread for toast."

Tom shrugged. "I mostly eat at the Faro. Clem cooks better than I can."

"Breakfast?"

"Don't eat it, usually. Just coffee."

Deirdre wrinkled her nose slightly. "Your coffee needs some help, too. I think it's stale."

"Stale?" Tom frowned. "I didn't know coffee could get stale."

"How long have you had this bag?"

He narrowed his eyes, trying to remember when he'd bought the thing. "A few months? I know I got it after the Fourth of July."

She shook her head. "If you're going to keep it for a while, you need to put it in a cool place. And you'd be better off with beans instead of ground—they keep longer because they don't lose their essential oils so quickly."

"I don't have a coffee grinder."

She gave him another heart-stopping smile. "I'll sell you one as soon as I get my stock for the shop. In fact, I'll give you one as a thank-you gift."

His mouth edged into a grin. "Thanking me for what?"

He watched her face turn a delectable shade of pink. Even embarrassed she looked better than most people did normally.

"To thank you for all you've done. Giving me the shop on spec, springing for the paint, giving me a job, keeping Craig from buying me out. That kind of thank you."

"You're welcome." He was grinning more widely now. He couldn't help it—something about her just made him want to grin whenever he saw her.

"Would you like some toast?"

He pushed himself away from the doorway, moving toward her carefully. She had a certain flight-risk look. "I'd like you. Preferably in bed, but we can try it on the kitchen table if you want."

She stared down at the piece of bread in her hand. "Oh."

"Is that a yes?" he asked hopefully.

She looked up at him again, her mouth moving into a slow grin of her own. "Can you guarantee we'll get some food somewhere along the way?"

He'd have guaranteed her anything at that point, including a gem-encrusted coffeepot if she wanted one. "Absolutely."

"Then lead the way."

For a moment, he almost considered the kitchen table. All he'd have to do would be to clear off the stack of *Konigsburg Herald-Zeitung*'s at the side. But it looked a little hard, and maybe a little cold. And besides, his dream hadn't included dodging salt and pepper shakers. He extended his hand to her. "Come on, babe. I don't think the boss will mind if you're a couple of hours late this morning."

For the next few days, Deirdre kept expecting Craig to show up again. She wasn't sure what she'd say, when and if he did. She was fairly sure that thumbing her nose and singing "Nyah, nyah, nyah" wasn't an adult thing to do, so she'd just keep it to herself.

It didn't matter anyway because Craig didn't appear. Deirdre didn't know if that was bad or good, but she'd opt for good, given her choice. Thinking about Craig wasn't high on her to-do list at the moment anyway.

Tom was.

He didn't seem to care whether people found out about them or not, but Deirdre discovered that she did. She figured Sylvia wouldn't be happy, and Chico and Bobby Sue might not be all that pleased either. She didn't want to throw off the smooth working relationship they all had.

Well, her working relationship with Sylvia wasn't exactly smooth, but Deirdre could sort of work around her if she had to.

But keeping her connection with Tom quiet wasn't easy. Even the brush of his shoulder against hers when she leaned back against the bar was enough to start a mild bonfire low down in her body.

She did her best not to be obvious about the way he made her feel, but her best wasn't good enough for Clem.

"You did it!" she crowed when Deirdre walked into the kitchen on Monday afternoon. "You and Tom. Together. Hot damn!"

Deirdre made a damping motion with her hand. "Keep your

voice down. I don't know what you mean, anyway."

"Oh, don't even try to deny it." Clem's grin lit up her face. "Any idiot can see what's going on just by looking at the two of you. Way to go!"

"I don't..." Deirdre blew out a breath. "Look, I'd rather not have this get out. Sylvia would be really mad, and I don't know how Bobby Sue would feel about it."

Clem waved an impatient hand. "Don't worry about Sylvia. She's always mad about something, and she was never going to get together with Tom anyway. This will just free up her attention to go after somebody else. Believe me, Bobby Sue won't care. As long as your relationship doesn't get in her way, and it won't. Of course, it may have some effect on the lunch trade."

"The lunch trade? Why?"

"Because all the women who come here to stare at Tom's ass and fantasize won't be able to do that anymore. Or they'll have to work harder. Oh man, Rhonda Ruckelshaus is going to really reduce your tips."

Deirdre blew out a breath "If it's a choice between Rhonda's seventy-five cents and Tom, I'll take Tom, believe me." She felt a giggle bubbling up from somewhere deep inside. *Giggling. Geez.* She hadn't giggled since she was a teenager—and she wasn't sure she'd done it much then either. She really wasn't the giggling type. Or she never had been before.

Clem threw back her head and guffawed. "Absolutely, honey. Glad to see you've got your priorities straight."

Chico seemed to take her and Tom in stride, although Deirdre had to admit it was hard to tell since his expression didn't usually change all that much. Still, he helped her spread the first coat of paint on the walls without being asked, and he seemed not to notice when Tom brought her one of Clem's sandwiches and a glass of tea, then kissed her quickly just before her shift began.

"Come over tonight," Tom whispered to her that night while she waited for Harry to fill her order.

"Can't," she murmured. "I've got to finish the walls tomorrow. Why don't you come over to my place Saturday night after we finish here. I'll fix you supper."

"And breakfast?"

Deirdre's heart gave a mighty thump. "That too."

She had a feeling spending her nights in Tom's bed as he clearly wanted her to do wouldn't leave her with much stamina for the following days. She had just enough of her old determination left to keep to her schedule.

On the other hand, spending the nights alone in her own bed didn't result in a lot of sleep either. Once she was there, thoughts of Tom kept her awake, and dreams of Tom weren't particularly restful.

By Thursday night, she was beginning to think about the weekend, and how they'd spend it. On Saturday, they'd be at her apartment. They needed to try out his mattress. And besides, Deirdre could guarantee that her coffee would be more drinkable. And they could stay there Sunday morning since not much happened at the Faro on Sunday. A long, lazy morning in bed before the lunch crowd. Deirdre stood at the bar, trying not to look at Tom. She felt like fanning herself.

Her reverie was interrupted by the crash of a chair hitting the floor and two angry male voices coming from the main room. Turning, she saw two unfamiliar men, both largish although not in Chico's class. They were standing on opposite sides of a table, yelling. As she watched, one of them stepped around and began to shove the other backward in swift, sharp movements.

Chico headed across the bar, moving very fast but not fast enough. Something flew through the air, and she heard breaking glass, along with other angry voices from the nearby tables. Two more men jumped to their feet, yelling obscenities through the beer that dripped from their faces.

Suddenly, Tom was pulling her backward. "Get behind the bar," he barked. And then he was running toward the knot of struggling men that had grown larger in the seconds since she'd looked away.

Deirdre knelt behind the bar, peeking around the end. She could see Sylvia, crouched beside a table on the far side of the room. More glass smashed against the floor, and she heard someone nearby roar in disapproval. And then Tom and Chico began wading into the crowd from opposite sides. Chico picked men out of his way like stones in his path, pushing them to the side or sometimes flinging them in the general direction of the floor. Tom grabbed shoulders and pushed men apart, yelling.

"Break it up, goddamn it, knock it off. Get the fuck out of my bar."

Several men stumbled backward, away from the table. A few staggered toward the door, but she didn't think they included the ones who'd started the fight. Behind the bar, Harry clutched Tom's cut-off pool cue to repel anybody who headed their way. Chico was still tossing bodies around, but Deirdre saw the door to the beer garden open and close as some of the combatants headed out the back way.

After a few more minutes, the fight seemed to collapse. Men who hadn't been involved now moved cautiously toward the door, although a couple of them had resumed their seats at the tables. She wondered how many were sneaking out with unpaid bar bills. The room suddenly seemed a lot emptier than it had been before the first chair had hit the floor.

Tom pushed a chair upright at the table in the center of the room where the fight had started, then turned back toward where Leon hovered just outside the kitchen door. "Get a broom," he snapped. His voice sounded slightly husky. He glanced back toward the bar and Deirdre saw his face for the first time. His mouth was set in a thin line, and his shoulders rose and fell with his breath. He had a reddening bruise close to one eye and a slight cut over his eyebrow, but otherwise he seemed unhurt. He was also furious.

She stood slowly, releasing the beer bottle she'd held clenched in one fist. She didn't exactly know what she would have done with it, but it had felt good to at least have something she could throw. "Are you okay?"

Tom nodded brusquely, then turned away again, jerking chairs upright and kicking beer bottles out from under his feet. Deirdre leaned down to pick them up.

"Leave it," he growled. "That's Leon's job."

Leon looked as if he disagreed, but he also looked like he wasn't going to argue with Tom right then. Deirdre thought that was probably a smart move. She started to clear off the empty tables, picking up glasses and the occasional bottle that hadn't been thrown.

Tom turned toward Chico. "Who were they?"

Chico shook his head, rubbing his hand across his shoulder. "Damn if I know. Not local."

"Didn't look like frat boys."

"No, too old. Tourists maybe."

"Not tourists." Tom took the push broom out of Leon's hands and began sweeping up glass with quick, angry strokes. "I don't know who they were or where they were from, but they weren't here for fun. Unless you're into busting up bars."

Chico shrugged. "Could be that's what they were after. Some people get off on it. And this place used to have that kind of fight every other night."

"It doesn't any more." Tom paused for a moment, his hands flexing on the broom. "You see them again, you let me know, okay?"

"Sure." Chico rubbed his shoulder again, stretching his neck.

"You're hurt," Sylvia said.

Deirdre stopped gathering glasses and looked around. Sylvia was standing next to Chico, chewing on her lip. Her mascara was smeared around her eyes, as if she'd been rubbing them. For once she looked exactly like what she was, a very tired waitress on the far side of thirty. "You're hurt," she repeated.

Chico stared down at her, then shrugged again, grimacing as he did. "Asshole hit me with a bottle. Aiming for my head. Got it on my shoulder instead."

"Sit down," Sylvia ordered. "Let me see." She pushed the slightly bemused Chico into a chair, sort of like a toy poodle herding an elephant, then she pulled up the back of his shirt. "You've got a bruise the size of a saucer back here. Let me get you some ice."

She stalked purposefully toward the kitchen door, while Chico stared after her.

Deirdre glanced at the tables in Sylvia's end of the room. The last customers were standing up and dropping bills on the table. Apparently, the Faro was closing early this evening.

Except, of course, for the Steinbruners, who'd resumed their pool game as if nothing had happened. The dry click of the pool balls was oddly soothing.

"What the hell? Linklatter said you had a fight." Nando Avrogado stepped through the doorway, surveying the room. "Who was it?"

Tom shrugged, leaning on his broom. "Not much to it. Over

in ten minutes or so. No casualties, or none who cared to stick around." His voice sounded more normal now, Deirdre realized—less like a man who wanted to throw a few punches of his own.

Nando nodded slowly, narrowing his eyes at the broken glass. "Who started it?"

"Strangers." Tom went back to sweeping. "Never saw them before. Here's hoping I never do again."

"What was it about?"

Tom looked at Chico again. "What did they say when the whole thing started? Did you hear?"

He shook his head. "First thing I knew they were yelling like they were gonna tear each other apart. Didn't do it, though." He flexed his arm again, rubbing his shoulder.

"I noticed that. They yelled at each other, but once the action got going, they went after the other guys instead."

"Weird kind of fight."

"You got that right."

Deirdre carried her tray of bottles into the kitchen. She stood for a moment next to the stack of cases in the corner, putting the bottles into their slots. Her hands had begun to tremble, but she ignored it. Everybody else was acting as if the fight hadn't been anything to get upset about. She should do the same thing—be a grown-up. She took a deep breath and blew it out, but it didn't really help. The adrenaline that had raced through her body was gone now, and she felt jittery and cold.

Behind her, the kitchen door swished open. "Deirdre?" Tom said. "Are you all right?"

"Sure." She bit her lip. Hard. It wouldn't do to start sniffling when everybody else was treating this like a routine evening.

He stepped beside her, draping his arm across her shoulders. "It's okay. You don't need to do the stiff-upper-lip thing with me. I know that wasn't anything you're used to."

She turned against him, pressing her face against his shoulder. "I'm not a wimp. Honest. I've just never seen a fight like that close up before."

He rubbed a circle on her back, slowly, warming her chilled skin. "It's okay. We're all a little shook up. Usually there's more warning than that when something's getting ready to blow. But it was just a fight. No big deal."

"What are you going to do?" Deirdre leaned back to look at him.

Tom shrugged. "Clean up. Close up. It's all over now. Everybody's gone home. Except for the Steinbruners, of course."

"But..." She frowned. "Isn't there any way you can find out who those men were? Have Nando chase them down? Don't you want to know?"

He grimaced. "More trouble than it's worth, babe. Bar fights are bar fights. If they come in here again, I'll throw them out. But chances are they'll stay away now. It was a one-time thing."

Deirdre nodded, trying to believe it. And trying to ignore the faint uneasiness that danced up her spine. Everything would be all right. She was being idiotic to worry. But still... She shivered again.

Tom brushed a finger across her eyebrow. "Okay?"

"Sure." She nodded. "I'll help you clean up."

"Clean-up's all done. Come have a drink with me." He grinned at her, but above his smile, his blue eyes were bleak.

He doesn't believe it either. She dropped the last bottle into the rack. "Okay. But then I'm going home to bed."

"C'mon, babe. Leave something open to negotiation." His hand dropped to the small of her back, pushing her gently toward the door back into the bar.

Deirdre felt the warmth from his palm spread through her body, brushing away the faint echoes of concern that still lingered at the back of her mind. She leaned her head against his shoulder, letting the warmth flow through her. Everything would be all right. Even if they both thought something strange was going on.

Right, Deirdre. And ignoring your instincts has worked so well up to now.

Chapter Sixteen

Friday morning after the fight, Deirdre decided to take a day off from painting. Not that it wasn't going well, what with half the crew at the Faro wielding the occasional roller. But she was tired of smelling paint and dust and scuffing through tarps. And she still felt faintly uneasy about what had happened the night before.

Just a fight. Nothing to worry about. But somehow she didn't quite buy that.

She decided to look for tables and chairs more as a kind of scouting mission than serious shopping. After all, she wouldn't be able to buy anything until she either earned a lot more tips or was able to get her hands on some of her trust fund. Docia had offered her the services of her brother-in-law, Lars Toleffson, who was apparently a very good accountant. Unfortunately, Deirdre was pretty sure her father's accountants would have him for breakfast, no matter how good he was. Daddy's accountants hadn't gotten their jobs by paying a lot of attention to ethical niceties. Lars was supposedly taking a look at her finances, but Deirdre wasn't optimistic about getting more money any time soon.

She wandered up and down a few side streets, checking the used furniture stores. The antique stores were largely off limits, since even with haggling there was no way she could afford their stuff. Most of them seemed to specialize in Victorian Heavy anyway, with tables for twenty that would have taken up all the room in the shop before she even thought about chairs.

Still, there were enough used furniture stores to provide her with a lot of possibilities, most of them bad. Metal patio tables so flimsy the average five-year-old could probably flip them over. Vintage kitchen tables that looked like they needed serious paint stripping. She even found a couple of laminated plastic tables with vinyl-covered chairs that would have been perfect if she'd wanted to open a fifties diner knock-off.

Deirdre sighed. She might have to go with the bentwood chairs and wooden café tables she'd found in a discount catalog, even though she suspected they'd fall apart within a couple of months. Using them would also make it tough to convince people to stick around for a second cup of coffee since their rear ends would be numb after fifteen minutes.

She wandered up another side street, giving the shop windows a desultory glance. Another candle store, one that sold what looked like cast-iron lawn ornaments, another candy shop—Konigsburg seemed to specialize in sugar shock. She stopped, peering into the next window on the block. From the street, the room looked too crowded to move around in. She could see rows of dark, lumpish shapes, a couple of dusty coat racks, what seemed to be a marble washstand. She stepped back so that she could read the sign in the window—The Republic of Texas. She frowned. Somebody had mentioned this store to her, but she couldn't remember who. It was worth a look anyway. At least the stuff might be in her price range. She pushed the door open and walked in, hearing the tinkle of the shop bell.

The inside didn't look much better than it had from the street. The space was divided into a series of narrow rows, marked by huge breakfronts and armoires, along with some battered chests of drawers. Deirdre inched down one aisle, peering toward the end. From what she could see, most of the stuff seemed to date from the forties and fifties and featured dark wood laminates, which didn't exactly bode well for funky café tables and chairs.

A figure appeared at the far end of the row, but the room was so dim she had trouble seeing him clearly. "Hello?" she called.

"What do you want?" the man growled.

Somehow Deirdre managed not to jump. Customer service must not be a big feature here. "I'm looking for café tables and chairs. Metal if you have them, but wood might also work, depending on the style."

The man moved toward her, his eyes narrowing. He looked

a little like the kind of actor who specialized in serial killers—very tall, very thin, sharp cheekbones jutting at the sides of his face, deep-set, burning eyes. She half-expected him to cackle and rub his hands together.

"Over there." He motioned with his head, his eyes never leaving her face.

Deirdre turned quickly and edged through a small gap between a couple of pine dressers. Behind a particularly ornate walnut armoire, she saw three metal café tables. The legs were bent in graceful curves, gathering to a single circle underneath the beveled glass tops, then flaring out to spread in three-legged stands. The four metal chairs had curling designs on the backs to echo their striped circular seats. They looked like they'd been part of an ice cream parlor set, maybe for something like *Meet Me In St. Louis*. Surely nobody made café tables that looked that perfect, at least not anymore.

Of course, they'd need to be stripped and repainted. And the striped seats would need to be reupholstered, given the tufts of cotton batting she could see drifting through the worn spots. Maybe Tom would let her use the yard behind the Faro so that she could do them all at once. She glanced at the price tag and managed not to gasp. "Any more chairs to go with these?"

Mr. Serial Killer shook his head, his dark eyes still burning. Deirdre swore she could hear the soundtrack for *Deliverance* tinkling in the background.

She drew herself up, squaring her shoulders. "What can you do for me if I take all three, along with the four chairs?"

He shrugged, pursing his lips. "Maybe could come down fifty."

Right. "I'll give you three hundred for the lot."

"Three hundred?" He smiled derisively, showing widely spaced picket-fence teeth. "I might take eight."

"I'm sure you would." She managed a faintly derisive smile of her own. "Four hundred. They need to be refinished and the chairs need to be reupholstered."

"Six. And you haul them off. That's my last offer."

Deirdre managed not to choke. She didn't even have four hundred dollars, let alone six. Maybe she could borrow the money from Docia, or float a loan at the Konigsburg bank. "Can

I leave a deposit while I find out when I can get them hauled away?"

Serial killer narrowed his eyes again. "Twenty percent. And if you don't pick them up, you forfeit."

"Right." She dug into her purse, pulling out the crisp twenties she'd gotten from the bank this morning. The hundred and twenty would take care of her spending for the week, but she could always get her meals at the Faro. If she were being practical, she should probably be saving her money for the roaster, but who knew when she'd find tables and chairs like this again?

She handed Mr. Serial Killer the money. He jerked his head, motioning for her to follow him.

Amazingly enough, the far end of the room seemed to be an actual antique store. Glass cases surrounded a battered desk against the back wall. Deirdre glanced at the contents—lots of guns, something that looked like a cannon ball, some ancient bottles with corroded tops.

Above the desk on the back wall, she saw a bumper sticker that looked like the Texas flag with the word *Secede* emblazoned across it.

Oh well, it wouldn't be Texas without a few nuts hanging from the trees.

Mr. Serial Killer pulled open the desk drawer and rummaged through the contents until he found a battered notebook.

"What's your name?" he snapped.

"Brandenburg. Deirdre Brandenburg."

Suddenly, his eyes were burning again. Deirdre tried not to look self-conscious. Maybe he knew Aunt Reba or Docia.

"Address?"

"You can reach me at the Faro. I work there." *And I have a couple of very capable bodyguards at my back.*

He studied her for a moment, then scrawled something in his notebook. "I'll hold 'em for a week. No longer." He handed her a piece of paper with a couple of scrawled sentences— apparently her receipt.

"I'll get them from you before then, Mr...." Deirdre licked her lips. "I'm sorry, I didn't get your name."

"Broadus." His lips stretched to show the picket fence once

again. "Milam Broadus. This is my store."

Deirdre blinked at him. Suddenly she remembered exactly where she'd heard about the shop before. Tom. And he'd told her Milam Broadus was crazy. Well, judging from the whole serial killer thing, not to mention the bumper sticker, she could see his point.

Tom had been in a bad mood since he'd woke up that morning. Hell, truth be told he'd been in a bad mood before he woke up—since he'd watched Deirdre scamper up the stairs to her apartment. He should have stayed with her, only she hadn't exactly asked for his company. He should have asked her to stay with him, only she hadn't looked like she was interested. Mainly she'd looked shaken up, like maybe she was reconsidering her association with the Faro—and him. Maybe she'd finally realized just how far apart their worlds really were.

For the twentieth time that day Tom cursed the good ol' boys who had tried to break up his bar. Not only had they driven out his customers, they were affecting his sex life.

And that he would not tolerate.

He checked the bill from his liquor supplier against the case of bottles one more time, trying to find the bottle of Triple Sec that was supposed to be there.

Three years. Three fucking years. And not a fight. It had taken him around a month after he'd won the Faro from Berenger to convince Berenger's customers that beating each other up would not be part of the evening's entertainment. Hiring Chico had helped since only a maniac would start a fight when Chico was involved.

Or at least that had always been true before. Last night's combatants hadn't seemed as impressed with Chico as they should have been.

He'd barred some of Berenger's old customers permanently and warned others like the Steinbruner brothers to clean up their act. Thanks to Chico, with some minor help from Leon and Harry, he'd managed to kick the bar into shape. Even the frat boys knew better now than to start a fight in Tom's place.

So who the hell were the idiots who didn't know better? And how the hell had they managed to get away clean last night?

Tom heard the door open as he bent over to stow the new bottles of bourbon and tequila on the shelves beneath the bar. He straightened, ready to tell a potential customer that they weren't open until eleven, until he recognized the figure in the doorway.

Erik Toleffson. Chief of the Konigsburg Police Department. Tom blew out a breath and leaned his elbows on the bar. "Morning, Chief. What's new?"

Toleffson strolled across the room without a lot of hurry. All the Toleffson brothers were built like redwoods, including the one who was Tom's accountant. But sometimes the chief looked more like a stone support pillar. Tom was by no means a small man, but next to the Toleffsons, even tall men sometimes looked like elves.

"Morning, Ames. Heard you had some excitement last night." Toleffson eased onto a barstool, removing his Stetson and placing it on the bar.

Might as well cut to the chase. "We had a fight. Not much to it. Some broken glass and a few bruises. Didn't last more than a few minutes."

Toleffson nodded slowly. "That's what Nando said. Any idea what started it?"

Tom shrugged. "Somebody pissed somebody off. Lot of yelling, but nothing specific."

"Tourists or locals?"

"Not locals. Chico didn't recognize them, and neither did I."

"Tourists then."

Tom rubbed the back of his neck. He'd love to lay the whole thing off on a bunch of idiot tourists, but he didn't think he could. "Not exactly. Too old to be frat boys, and they didn't look like the type who'd visit Konigsburg for the scenery."

Toleffson watched him steadily. "Interesting. That's also what Nando said. Which leads to the question of what they were doing here at the Faro."

"Drinking?" Tom said hopefully.

"That too." Toleffson's half-smile faded. "You pissed off anybody around here lately, Ames?"

Tom felt the same prickling at the back of his neck he'd felt the night before. "A few, I guess. The usual."

"Anybody specific?"

For a moment, Tom considered telling him about Craig Dempsey and the threat from Deirdre's father. But Toleffson was Docia's brother-in-law, which made him kin to Deirdre in that roundabout way people were related in Konigsburg. It wasn't that he thought Toleffson would be on Brandenburg's side, but he wasn't exactly sure what the family would think. Maybe they'd decide he wasn't good enough for her, which was possibly true. Or maybe they'd think he was a dangerous man for her to be around, which was possibly even more true.

Plus the thought that Craig Dempsey might be engineering his downfall felt too paranoid to be taken seriously.

He shrugged. "Nobody offhand. I might have stepped on some toes I wasn't aware of, I guess."

Toleffson sighed. "Here's the thing, Ames. I know nobody much gave a damn about the Faro in the old days—about the kind of fights that went on here. When Brody was chief, he was too busy stealing the city blind, and Olema wasn't around long enough to take much interest in anything except deer hunting. But I figure I'm in for the long haul, and I'm not happy having a bar in town where there's trouble."

Tom stiffened. He and Toleffson had never had any disagreements before. In fact, he'd once considered hiring him as a bouncer back when Toleffson had been a part-time officer. Being on Toleffson's shit list would not be pleasant, and he wasn't going to end up there if he could help it. "I'm not planning on the Faro being a bar that has trouble. This is the first fight we've had in a couple of years. As far as I'm concerned, it'll be the last."

"I figured as much. Just wanted to touch base." Toleffson pushed himself to his feet, picking up his hat from the bar. "You got somebody playing in your beer garden tonight?"

"Yeah, it's usually Saturdays, but I managed to book Frankie Belasco. The guy who does the Wine and Food Festival every year."

Toleffson grinned, settling his Stetson on his head. "Frankie, huh? Morgan and I might stop by. Got a soft spot in my heart for old Belasco."

Tom nodded a little warily. "Glad to have you, Chief." Having the chief of police in the beer garden might put a bit of a damper on things. On the other hand, pulling in the Toleffsons could do a lot toward making the Faro look respectable to the local population, and maybe offset last night.

Toleffson strolled toward the door as Chico entered. The two of them together were sort of like a giant sunspot, blocking all the light from the window for a moment. Chico nodded in Toleffson's direction, then stood back to let him pass. For a moment, Tom thought he saw Toleffson smile, but then he was gone.

Frankie Belasco's band was the biggest act Tom had booked yet, which meant he was the also the most expensive. Which meant a cover charge.

Tom stationed Leon at the front door, with Chico at the beer garden entrance where trouble was most likely to break out, assuming trouble decided to come by that evening. He watched the crowd carefully, looking for faces from the previous night, but none of the fighters showed up so far as he could tell.

He should have been counting the house, seeing if they'd made back Frankie's upfront money. Instead, he ended up counting Toleffsons.

They all seemed to be in the beer garden, although there were so many Toleffsons in town by now, it wasn't always easy to keep them straight. Deirdre's cousin Docia was there with her husband, Cal, the vet. Janie Dupree and her husband, Pete, were there again, along with Lars, Tom's accountant, and his wife, Jess.

Around nine, just before Frankie was ready to take the stage, Chief Toleffson arrived with his wife Morgan, whose family had a part-ownership in one of the wineries outside town. Toleffson didn't drink, as everybody in town knew by then, but his wife did. Tom wondered if she'd want wine, and if she did, whether she'd settle for the rotgut he'd been serving the lunch crowd. He really needed to start classing up the joint a little more.

Deirdre waited on them, moving swiftly between tables despite the obstacles presented by long Toleffson legs. Tom had wondered if she'd feel strange waiting on tables in front of her family, but it didn't seem to bother her. Her face had that ethereal glow it took on when she was happy, as if she'd only just stepped down to earth temporarily, and would be heading back up to a nearby cloud any minute now.

Tom considered requesting *"Volver"*, but he decided to let Frankie do his thing. He wasn't sure how the Toleffsons would react to Deirdre dirty dancing with the bartender anyway.

Belasco wore a fedora pushed forward onto his forehead and dark glasses, his silver ponytail bobbing in time to the music. He had the crowd on their feet within the first five minutes. His fingers danced over the keys of his accordion, coaxing out a combination of Tejano and Cajun, the spicy mix of Third Coast music.

At the outdoor bar, Tom loaded beers for Deirdre and Marilyn, along with the occasional mixed drink and even one or two glasses of wine, although he noticed few of the patrons took a second glass. Definitely time to move up. Chief Toleffson's wife drank Coke, while the chief stuck with Dr. Pepper in between dances. Tom couldn't say any of the Toleffsons were all that graceful when they danced, but they made up for it with enthusiasm, and their wives were apparently a very tolerant bunch.

Frankie watched them for a while, grinning as he goosed his accordion, then leaned to the microphone again. "I remember some of this crowd," he said, "from the last Wine and Food Festival. First time my music ever made a woman go into labor. Here's a little something in your honor."

Docia Toleffson blushed bright pink in the beer garden lights, burying her face against her husband's shoulder.

"Jolie Blonde, ma chere 'tit fille," Frankie crooned.

The Toleffson table whooped with laughter, applauding lustily as Cal and Docia waltzed with the crowd.

Deirdre stepped up to the bar. "Dos Equis and three Coronas."

Tom piled the bottles on her tray, then watched her deliver them to a nearby table. When she came back, he slipped around the bar, pulling her into his arms. Deirdre slid her hands around his neck, laughing as they circled the small area near Chico's seat at the door. He watched them with drowsy eyes.

"Jolie Blonde..." Frankie sang.

Tom twirled her around again, feeling buoyed along by the music and the warm evening air. Maybe a quick visit to his house was called for. They could still go to Deirdre's place tomorrow night.

Frankie swung into the last chorus, and Deirdre pushed away from him gently. "Got to make my rounds at the tables, boss. I need the tips." She smiled at him, her eyes like stars in the light of the hanging lanterns.

Tom returned to his place behind the bar, watching her thread her way among the crowd. As he looked up, he was suddenly aware of several people staring his way. The Toleffson table seemed to have transferred their interest from Docia and Cal to him and Deirdre. And now to him alone.

Tom turned quickly to the margarita mixer, dipping a glass into the salt rimmer. When he looked up again, the Toleffsons seemed to have gone back to watching other people on the dance floor. He breathed a quick sigh of relief.

All the Toleffsons except one, that is. Docia Kent Toleffson was watching him with narrowed eyes, her forehead slightly furrowed until Deirdre handed her a bottle of beer. Docia glanced at her cousin and then back at him one more time, her lips spreading in a slow grin.

Well, hell.

Deirdre made one last check on her side of the beer garden. Belasco seemed to be wrapping up, which meant maybe one last round before the crowd began to drift away. She leaned over Cal Toleffson's shoulder, placing his Dos Equis on the table in front of him.

Docia looked up at her, smiling. "You look like you've been doing that most of your life."

Deirdre shrugged. "It's not exactly rocket science. You get used to it pretty quickly."

Docia's grin widened. "I don't know, kid, the Deirdre Brandenburg I knew a year ago might not have been able to do this nearly as well as you're doing now."

Deirdre frowned slightly. Was that a compliment?

Docia didn't seem to notice. "Seems like ages since we've had a chance to talk. How about having lunch tomorrow?"

"Sorry—I work lunch on Saturdays. Maybe some other time."

"Breakfast, then." Docia gave her a level look. "We need to touch base."

Deirdre took a deep breath. After all, she needed to ask Docia about a loan for the tables. Now would be as good a time as any. "Okay, sounds good. What time?"

"How about eight? We can meet at Sweet Thing and have some of Allie's scones." Her lips spread in a slow grin as her eyes flicked to Tom. "Unless that's too early."

Deirdre grinned back. "It's fine with me. I'm not the one with a baby at home."

Docia's grin turned wry. "Yeah, well, I've given up sleeping for the time being. See you at eight, cuz."

Chapter Seventeen

The last stragglers wandered out of the Faro at 2:00 a.m., which was the official closing time, although most nights people cleared out earlier. Frankie Belasco had apparently infected the crowd with his own shit-kicking attitude, and nobody wanted to leave.

Tom didn't much want to leave either, unless it was with Deirdre. He watched her now, piling beer bottles on her tray to carry them to the kitchen. How could anybody look that good while hefting a tray full of empties above her shoulder? It defied logic.

Leon leaned back against the kitchen door to open it for her and was rewarded with a lesser version of that dazzling smile that made Tom's pulse rate raise by five. He tried for a moment to remember what she'd looked like when she'd first walked into the Faro. A mouse. With a will of iron. But even then, he'd known there was a knockout underneath. Now he only had to figure out a way to hustle that knockout over to his place, *hustle* being the operative word.

Back from the kitchen, Deirdre climbed onto a barstool beside him, resting her elbows on the bar as she surveyed the main room. "I think that's everything. The beer garden still needs to be picked up around the edges, but Leon said he'd do it tomorrow."

Tom grimaced. "Since that's his job, he'd better."

She reached up to run her fingertip along the edge of his ear. "Don't be a grouch. This was a great evening, and you know it. I've never seen so many people in here. We must have made a mint!"

He wasn't sure he'd ever heard her refer to the Faro that

way before. *We.* Like she was part of it. He stared down at the bar rag clutched in his hand, trying to decide how he felt about that. First and foremost, the Faro was his place. But maybe he could share a little. "We did okay. Frankie takes a big cut, but he brings in the crowds."

"He does that." She pushed herself up, slowly, stretching her arms above her head. "I guess it's time for me to go home."

"You sure you want to? Doris misses you. Maybe you should drop by and reassure her." He managed not to groan. At least she didn't roll her eyes at him.

She turned, her lips curving up slightly at the ends. "Doris misses me? I didn't think we'd gotten to know each other that well. I only met her last Sunday."

"Oh yeah, definitely." He tossed the bar rag beside the sink. "She's really sensitive. For a lizard. Almost burst into tears when I came home without you the other night."

The curve of her smile increased. "Well, I wouldn't want Doris to suffer."

He nodded. "You really wouldn't want that. Might make her grumpy."

"All right then." Her voice dropped into the sultry range. "Let's go see Doris."

Tom blinked at her. Since when had she developed that smoldering look? Since when had she turned into a temptress? Since when had he gotten so lucky?

Only a fool asked questions like those. And whatever else he may have been, he definitely didn't consider himself a fool. Lucky maybe, and certainly not deserving of anybody like Deirdre. But not a fool. "Let's do that," he said. Sliding his arm around her shoulders, he headed for the door.

The only way Deirdre managed to get to Sweet Thing by eight the next morning was to leave Tom's house at seven. He hadn't wanted her to go, and she hadn't particularly wanted to either. But she had a feeling if she didn't make it to breakfast, Docia might come looking for her, probably in the least convenient places.

She slouched back to the apartment for a quick shower and a change of clothes before she headed for the café. Docia would definitely notice if she wore the same T-shirt and jeans. She considered putting on her old khakis with one of her decorous knit shirts, but she couldn't bring herself to do it.

They weren't who she was anymore. And she liked who she was now.

When Deirdre walked in, Allie Maldonado was working the main counter in Sweet Thing, selling scones and muffins and pastries to a long line of customers. She nodded toward the back patio when she saw Deirdre. "She's out there. I've already got you set up with coffee."

Docia was sitting under a live oak, leaning back in an Adirondack chair with her eyes closed. For a moment, Deirdre felt slightly guilty—Docia should probably be sleeping at home, looking after her baby. Then she reminded herself it was Docia who'd set up this meeting, and besides she had just as much reason to be sleepy. Maybe more. She slid into the chair beside her cousin, yawning. "Morning."

Docia opened one eye. "I guess it is. Whose crazy idea was this, anyway?"

"That would be you." Deirdre poured a cup of coffee for herself from the pot on the table. There was also a plate of golden scones, probably peach. If she had to get up this early, at least she got to eat something wonderful to make up for it. She picked up one and bit off a corner.

"So." Docia sighed. "How are things?"

Deirdre nibbled on her scone. "Gee, Dosh, if that's all you want to know, you could have asked me last night so both of us could still be asleep. Things are fine."

Docia nodded absently. "You like working at the Faro?"

"Sure. It's easy. And the tips are good."

"And Tom Ames?"

Deirdre kept her gaze on her plate. "He's good too."

"As a boss, you mean?"

"Of course. What else would I be talking about?" She ventured a quick glance at her cousin.

Docia was grinning widely.

"Oh for Pete's sake." Deirdre sighed, picking up her coffee cup. "I'm almost twenty-five, Docia. It's not like he's my first boyfriend."

"True. Of course, given your age, we were all concerned

173

that you'd be an old maid. The family had almost despaired of you." She was still grinning.

Deirdre gritted her teeth. "You may not be all that wrong as far as Daddy is concerned. I'm sure he was beginning to wonder."

Docia's grin faded. "Have you heard from him?"

She shook her head. "I didn't expect to. He's probably waiting for me to call him." Or waiting for Craig to call him. After he'd reeled her in and sent her back to Houston.

"He won't stay mad, Dee. You mean too much to him."

"Let's not talk about him. It's his problem, not mine. And I don't have much to say about it anymore."

Docia blinked at her. "That's very...mature of you."

"You mean I wouldn't have said that a couple of months ago." Deirdre shrugged. "What can I say? Being on your own makes a difference. I know what I want now. And I'm going after it."

"Dee, you've always been a strong woman. You just didn't have to show it too often."

"I don't know how much I'm showing it now. But when it's sink or swim, you learn how to paddle." She took another quick swallow of coffee. *Time for a change of subject.* "So why was everybody laughing about Frankie singing *Jolie Blonde* last night?"

Docia's face turned bright pink at the memory. "Last year at the Wine and Food Festival I was still pregnant. My water broke when Cal and I were dancing to *Jolie Blonde*."

"And they were all there when it happened—all the Toleffsons?" Deirdre didn't know whether to be amused or appalled. Some of both, actually.

"Oh yeah. And they all came to the hospital with me, except for Jess because she had to look after the kids. Then they brought her and the kids along later, after Rolf was born. You never do things alone when you're part of the Toleffson family. Which has its good and bad points."

Deirdre smiled, thinking how nice it would be to be part of a large family group. The Brandenburgs didn't quite have the same heft. And besides, the only time she saw most of them was at weddings and funerals.

"Erik likes Tom Ames." Docia munched on a golden scone.

"So does Lars. I don't think Cal really knows him. They all say he's sort of mysterious, though."

Deirdre frowned. So they were heading back into her business again. "Mysterious how?"

"Well, nobody knows how he came to have the Faro, for one thing. I mean, one day Kip Berenger owned it and nobody knew he wanted to sell. And then all of a sudden Tom Ames was in charge. And nobody knows where he was before he took over the Faro or what he was doing. Or even where he was from originally. He's not local, but that's about all anyone knows about him."

Deirdre opened her mouth to fill in the blanks, and then closed it again. She didn't know for sure how Tom would feel about sharing his history with Konigsburg. And it was his history to share, not hers. "He doesn't seem mysterious to me. He's a nice guy."

Docia grinned again. "That's good, sweetie. That's all that matters, I guess." She took another swallow of coffee, closing her eyes in the morning sunshine. "So you're settling in, working on your shop, earning big tips. Did you finally buy some furniture, or do I have to start ransacking attics?"

Deirdre licked her lips. The perfect opening, assuming she had the *cojones* to take it. "Um...about that. About furniture, I mean."

Docia cocked an eyebrow. "What about it?"

"Well. I found the perfect set of tables and chairs for the shop. And I was wondering if maybe you'd be willing to cosign a loan with me. I mean, I wouldn't ask, but I'm afraid he might sell them to somebody else, and I don't have the money right now. But I will. Have the money, I mean." She heard her voice trail off into nothing. Whatever happened to her ability to negotiate multi-million-dollar deals? Maybe it was different when you needed the money personally.

Docia's forehead furrowed. "How much money are we talking about here?"

She took a breath. "Six hundred dollars. Well, four hundred eighty, actually, because I gave him a twenty percent deposit."

Docia stared at her, her forehead even more furrowed than before. "Four hundred eighty dollars."

"I know it's a lot." Deirdre sighed. "Maybe I'll ask for three hundred and get the rest from my tips."

"Dee, for god's sake," Docia snapped. "I can *give* you four hundred eighty dollars. You don't need to go to a bank for that. Hell, I can give you six hundred. For that matter, Mama would be glad to front you however much you need to open your shop right now. You're her only niece and she's worried sick about you. Why are you nickel and diming yourself like this?"

Deirdre stared down at her hands again. "I know it sounds crazy, but I don't know how to explain it. It's just...I want the shop to be mine. I want to do it for myself. And that means not taking help from the family for once. I spent most of my life letting Daddy have his way about everything. Well, now I want my way. And I want to show that I can do it on my own." She met Docia's gaze slowly. "Like I say, maybe that sounds loony, but it's just the way it has to be."

Docia's smile was rueful. "It doesn't sound loony, sweetheart. It sounds familiar. When I came to Konigsburg I'd just lost eighty grand in a lousy investment orchestrated by my ex-fiancé. I didn't want to talk to anybody in my family about anything—didn't want to hear them say *I told you so,* I guess. So I came up here and I opened the bookstore on my own. Invested a lot of my own money, got a loan from the bank, hired Janie, all of it. I felt just the way you feel now—I wanted it to be mine. Mama and Daddy kept trying to give me money, and I kept turning it down."

She leaned back in her chair, resting her coffee cup on the arm. "It wasn't easy. I spent a lot of time kicking myself for not asking for help. But now I'm glad I did it my way. And I've let Janie buy in as my partner, so it's not even exclusively mine anymore. But the thing is, Dee, I had some money to begin with." She took another small sip of her coffee. "I didn't dip into my trust funds, so it wasn't a huge amount, but it was enough so that I could do most of the renovations on the shop without having to get a loan. I could wait to go to the bank until I had a business plan and could show them what I was going to do, what kind of inventory I was going to stock. And it didn't hurt that the bankers thought Daddy would back me up if I didn't make it on my own."

Deirdre licked her lips. "I've got a lot of the shop renovations done now, Dosh. I've cleaned the place out and painted the walls and ceiling, although I've still got to finish the storeroom. I'll enamel the shelves over the next couple of weeks. Then in a few more weeks I'll be eligible to draw on the trust funds Mama set up, and I can get the coffee roaster and the stock for the shop. If I could just get these tables now…"

Docia shook her head. "No, Dee. I won't cosign any loan for tables at the bank. That would be a piss poor financial decision on your part. You may need to go to the bank later on for a business loan."

Deirdre felt as if her chest had gone hollow. She licked her lips again.

"I will, however, give you the six hundred as a personal loan. I'll even let you write up a note if you insist. I'd prefer to give you the stupid six hundred outright and be done with it, but if you want it to be a loan, it'll be a loan."

Deirdre closed her eyes for a moment, feeling her heart begin to beat again. "Thanks, Dosh."

"No problem. Who has these tables you need to get?"

"His name is Milam Broadus. He's got a store down on C Street."

"Oh god," Docia groaned. "Crazy Broadus. Are you sure you can't get these tables anywhere else?"

Deirdre shook her head. "They're perfect, and he's selling them for way less than they're worth, although they need a lot of work."

"Better you than me, kid." Docia covered her hand with her own. "I know you don't want people giving you things, but I wish you'd let us help you a little more now and then."

"You can come to the Faro." Deirdre gave her the best smile she could manage. "Come dance in the beer garden like you did last night. That'll help me a lot. The more people, the better the tips. And the Toleffsons seem to draw the crowds."

Docia grinned at her. "Oh I think we can probably manage that. It's a tough job, I know, but believe me, the Toleffsons can do it!"

The band on Saturday night wasn't as famous as Frankie Belasco, and the crowds weren't as big. But nobody threw any punches and the dance floor stayed full, so Tom figured they were ahead.

Clem stayed later than usual, trying out a new combination of bar food—sliders with chipotle sauce, quesadillas with slices of peach and brie, seafood nachos with shrimp and crabmeat along with two kinds of cheese and her own salsa.

Tom was pretty sure this qualified as bar food only if the bar in question was in Las Vegas, but he was willing to give Clem her head. He figured the Faro was working its way up to a dinner menu, slowly but surely. And Clem definitely helped with the classing up part of things.

With no cover charge to collect, Chico was back to watching the dance floor, his arms folded across his massive chest. Tom hadn't asked him if he'd gotten over the bruises from the fight. He figured Chico might take that as an insult. Midway through the evening, Sylvia appeared at his side with a bottle of Topo Chico. Tom restrained himself from pointing out that she was supposed to be covering the main room, watching Chico take the bottle from her fingers with a half smile.

Well, that's an interesting development. He wasn't sure whether a romance between Sylvia and Chico would screw things up personnel-wise or not, but it seemed harmless enough.

Deirdre moved through it all like a moonbeam. He was no longer bothered by this weird impulse toward poetic similes whenever he was around her—it seemed to be part of the territory. His main problem at the moment was keeping his mind on his work and not fixating on her and memories of last night, as well as plans about what he wanted to do after everybody finally went home.

At one point he glanced up and saw Chico and Sylvia moving in a sort of ponderous two-step around the edge of the crowd. He shook his head—things seemed to get a little weirder every day, but business was booming.

The crowd had thinned out by one o'clock, and the band began packing up at one-thirty. Tom yawned. The only compensation for keeping the insane hours he had at the Faro was the chance to catch some extra sleep in the morning before heading in for the lunch crowd. But he hadn't been able to sleep that morning after Deirdre left. The bed had seemed too empty.

He blew out a breath. Obviously, he was heading into very dangerous territory, the kind of country you only entered if you were really sure of your guide. He wasn't sure of much anymore, except that he wanted Deirdre in his bed as often as he could convince her to go there.

She perched at the bar next to him, watching him transfer the last bunch of glasses from the dishwasher rack Leon had brought out from the kitchen to the shelves behind the bar. "Are you almost done here?" she said brightly.

He blinked at her. She sounded much peppier than she should have, given how little sleep she'd gotten the night before. "Pretty much." He opened the gate at the end of the bar and stepped through. "Did you take a nap or something? You look a lot more awake than you should be."

She laughed, the sound moving over his skin like the brush of her fingertips. *Goddamn poetry.*

"Can you help me move some tables tomorrow? I found just the right ones, and I need to pick them up from the store."

He shrugged. "Sure. We can take the truck." He opened the door, holding his arm high so that she could duck through. Her hair brushed his arm, sending faint shivers through his muscles.

Okay, enough already. She's hot. I get it.

Main stretched before them, illuminated dimly by the mercury lights on the corners. The night heat seemed to shimmer around them. From somewhere on the far side, he thought he heard an owl, hooting softly.

"I love this time of night," Deirdre murmured. "I never used to be out this late—always in bed by midnight at the latest. I never knew what I was missing. It's so quiet. But not exactly. You know what I mean?"

Tom shrugged. "Yeah, it's a Konigsburg special. You wouldn't see it or hear it this way in a city like Houston."

"I believe it. I'm so glad I'm here." She glanced up at him, her smile glowing.

"I glad you're here too," he murmured, his voice suddenly thick in his throat.

They rounded the corner to her apartment door. He wondered if she remembered inviting him for Saturday night. She hadn't said anything about it. Suddenly, he wanted nothing more in life than to follow her up the stairs to her empty apartment.

Deirdre unlocked the door, then smiled up at him again. "Come up?"

He nodded, unsure of his voice. He watched her move up the stairs ahead of him, her beautiful behind swaying in her "do-me" jeans, her sneakers whispering on the treads. He figured he'd be using every ounce of willpower he had to keep from jumping her as soon as they were in the door to the apartment.

She stepped inside ahead of him, clicking the light switch at the side of the door. "I still don't have much in the way of furniture. Sorry."

"That's okay." All they really needed was a mattress. Which he'd already supplied. Lucky him.

She tossed her purse on one of the chairs and then turned back to him. "Well..."

His mouth inched up into a grin. "Well...now."

She ran her tongue quickly around her lips, which managed to send a new jolt of heat to his loins. "Would you like something to drink?"

He shook his head, running his fingers along the neckline of her T-shirt.

She swallowed hard. "Maybe...I don't know if I have anything to eat except cereal."

He stepped forward. "I'm not hungry. Not that way, anyway." His hands slid to her shoulders almost automatically, as if that was where they were supposed to be, and then he brought his mouth down on hers, trying not to push too hard and failing as he did.

She gave a little moan beneath him, maybe of protest. He pulled back to look at her, and got another moan, this one definitely of protest. She stretched her arms to circle his neck, pulling him down to her mouth again.

"Ah, Deirdre," he whispered, sliding his lips to her throat. "You make me crazy."

One slender leg wound around his hips, and he felt the edge of her teeth moving over his earlobe. "No, I don't. I make you happy."

"Oh yeah, babe, you do that too," he muttered against her collarbone, dipping his tongue into the hollow at the base of her throat.

She buried her fingers in his hair, then pulled his head up gently, licking the tip of his nose, then running her tongue along his lower lip. "What I want," she whispered. "What I really want is to get out of the living room and into the bedroom. There's no place to sit down out here."

Tom leaned down and scooped her into his arms, heading down the hall to his right as she giggled. "Your wish is my command, lady. Particularly if it happens to be my wish too."

Deirdre lay back against her mattress—the mattress Tom had so thoughtfully provided. She was beginning to think he hadn't been entirely altruistic in that respect. His hands brushed down her legs, pushing them apart gently as he ran his tongue along the delicate skin at the joining of thigh and hip. She sighed, feeling the gathering of heat at her core. Not wanting to rush him exactly but still...wanting.

Warm breath brushed against her center, and her back arched in pleasure. *Too much, too much.* If she started this high, where could she go?

She felt his thumbs parting her folds, opening her, and then his mouth against sensitive flesh. "Oh Tom," she gasped. "Oh god. So good."

"Just starting," he whispered. "I want you to feel it, sweetheart. Just feel."

His tongue swept over her and she dug her heels into the mattress. She should be touching him, making him happy too, but her hands were too busy gripping the sheets beside her. "So good," she murmured.

His tongue plunged deep, and then back to her clit again as he slid a finger inside her. She groaned, digging her heels in deeper. She should be...but she wasn't. She lay still again, letting him take her where he wanted.

"Tom," she breathed. "Ah, Tom."

"Let go," he said. "Just let go, sweetheart."

And she did. The pleasure washed over her in a wave, taking her down, spinning her beneath him. She wondered for one hazy moment if she'd ever felt this with anyone before, but it was pretty much a rhetorical question. She knew she hadn't.

Tom stroked her thighs softly. "Ah, babe, I love watching

you. But I love being inside you a lot more."

She raised her head to look at him. "Then come in. I want you. Hurry."

He reached beside the bed, pulling open the foil packet almost in a single motion. "I'll do my best," he gasped.

She fought the urge to giggle. So *not appropriate*. And then she didn't feel like giggling anymore. He was pushing inside, opening her, making her his.

Making her his? Where had that archaic thought come from? She reached up and pulled his head down, fastening her mouth to his as his hips pounded against her. She pushed her tongue against his, echoing his thrusts into her body. *Oh god, oh god, oh god.*

"Ah, Deirdre, holy shit." His voice broke on the last word and he was plunging hard, hips flat, body straining.

"Deirdre," he whispered. "My Deirdre."

Her eyes popped open and she stared up at him, but his face was in shadow, pressed against her shoulder. *My Deirdre?* It probably didn't mean anything. Probably just the emotion of the moment.

But still. *My Deirdre.*

Her lips curved up in a faint grin as she pulled the sheet over their bodies, snuggling close against him.

Chapter Eighteen

Craig Dempsey was not a happy man. He'd spent a great weekend in Austin, free from both the irritations of Konigsburg and the demands of Big John. He'd even found a pick-up game of Texas Hold 'Em, and he hadn't lost much. Or anyway, not as much as usual.

And then he'd returned to Shitsburg after three days of blessed relief and discovered that nothing had worked out the way it was supposed to. He'd left simple instructions that should have been carried out without any screw-ups. Instead he'd gotten nothing for his money. Or, more specifically, Big John's money. He was both hungover and seriously pissed.

"So tell me again, Hardesty, why couldn't you do what you were paid to do? It's not like it was all that difficult."

"You'd be surprised, Mr. Dempsey." Hardesty sliced off a large piece of chorizo and scrambled eggs, shoveling it into his mouth in one simple motion. "Breaking up a place ain't as easy as it sounds."

He was a reasonably large man—not as large as Craig himself or Ames, from what Craig remembered of him. But large enough to get a decent bar fight going, particularly since he'd had ample help, judging from the money he'd spent hiring it. In the unforgiving light of morning, Craig upped his estimate of the man's age—maybe late forties. And the shape of his nose showed he'd been in a more fights than the one on Thursday. He'd also seemed reasonably bright at first, although Craig was beginning to have a few doubts on that score.

He pinched the bridge of his nose, trying to coax the headache away from his eyes. At least the coffee in this coffee shop was better than the poison at the place across from the

Faro. "Doesn't seem that hard to me. You start a fight, you break up some tables, throw something through the windows. What's the problem?"

"The problem, Mr. Dempsey, is that this ain't a movie." Hardesty picked up his coffee, sipping as he explained. "Chairs don't break all that easy unless they're the breakaway kind, and you can't throw something through a window if you've got a bunch of people standing in the way. More likely to hit a person than the glass, which might get you into some nasty assault charges. Cops take those serious enough to follow up."

He shoveled another bite into his mouth. Craig felt vaguely queasy just watching him. "So you had a fight, but the place still opened the next day? That doesn't strike me as the kind of fight I paid you for."

Hardesty leaned back in his chair, his eyes narrowing. "You also didn't mention the bouncer they got there. Fucker's a human mountain. And the owner's not that small himself. Man could get seriously messed up fighting people like that."

Craig shrugged, pulling out a pair of sunglasses. The light in the coffee shop seemed a lot brighter than it should be. Next time he'd look for a table away from the windows. "So? Take them out first. I shouldn't have to tell you your business, Hardesty. If the bouncer's a problem, make sure he can't do anything to stop you."

Hardesty's fork stilled. "Are you asking me to kill somebody, Mr. Dempsey? That's not my usual kind of business. I'd have to think about that."

Craig settled the sunglasses more firmly on his nose. This conversation was becoming irritating. "Hell no, I'm not telling you to kill somebody. What kind of idiot do you think I am? I'm telling you to put the bouncer and Ames out of commission early in the fight. Hit 'em over the head with a bottle or something. Whatever you usually do."

"Right. Hitting someone over the head with a bottle is likely to give them a concussion. Or worse. So at the very least, you're asking me to send these men to the hospital. Which gets us back into the whole assault charges problem."

"Jesus, Hardesty! All I'm asking you to do is break up the goddamn bar. Put it out of business. That's what I paid you for. You're saying you can't do it?" Craig took a savage bite of his own scrambled eggs, then immediately wished he hadn't. His stomach gave a slight lurch, just to remind him that food was perhaps not the best idea.

Hardesty shook his head. "I'm saying it's gone beyond just breaking the place up. Ames and his bouncer won't let that happen without taking out a lot of my guys. And if you want us to put people out of commission, that's a different deal. More likely to bring some serious law into it. Be more expensive." He wiped his napkin across his lips, as if he was hiding a smile.

Craig gritted his teeth. "Don't even try it, Hardesty. You screw around with me, and it'll get back to the people who recommended you in the first place." Namely, Craig's bookie and his assorted friends. Craig couldn't guarantee they'd go after Hardesty, but he figured they might not be averse to a little kneecapping, just to keep in practice.

Hardesty's smile disappeared. "Okay, I'll see if I can line up some more men. But it's gonna be more money regardless, Mr. Dempsey, because this is another fight. I can't send the same guys in, at least not at first—Ames or his bouncer are likely to recognize them. But you'll get what you want this time, or you'll get your money back."

Craig nodded, hoping his head wouldn't fall off as he did. "Fair enough."

Hardesty stood up, tossing his napkin onto the table. "One more thing to keep in mind, Mr. Dempsey. Just FYI. This town has one of the toughest police chiefs in the Hill Country—name of Toleffson. If he finds out what we've done, we're all toast. And if that ain't enough, the County Sheriff is Ozzie Friesenhahn. Between the two of them, they'd have your liver for breakfast if they got word about what you're up to here."

Craig's stomach gave another heave. Liver for breakfast didn't exactly excite him. "The only way they'll find out is if you don't keep your mouth shut, Hardesty."

"Right. Well, I ain't the only one who needs to keep quiet. I'll be in touch. You have a nice day, Mr. Dempsey." Hardesty turned on his heel and headed out the café door.

Craig stared down at his plate and tried to quiet his suddenly roiling insides. One way or another, Dee-Dee was going to pay for all the trouble she was putting him through. A large, media-heavy wedding would be a good start.

Deirdre had nothing in her cupboards except cereal and coffee, with milk in her refrigerator. Tom wasn't too impressed by her taste in cereal since it looked a lot like the stuff he put in his bird feeder, but her coffee was out of sight.

Nor surprising, of course, but sort of reassuring. After two cups he took her back to bed for a rematch. If all her coffee had the same effect, Tom figured she'd be a rich woman by the end of her first month in business.

Of course, she already was a rich woman. At least technically.

Tom told himself he didn't care, and for the most part he didn't. Whatever money Deirdre might come into eventually, she didn't have much now, judging from the still-sparse appearance of her apartment.

But he knew he'd have to think about it eventually—the very great distance between a bar owner and a billionaire's daughter. Once her father came to his senses and begged her forgiveness, Tom might well have to step aside. All the more reason to enjoy what they had right now.

"Let me take you out for brunch," he said when they'd finally, reluctantly, gotten up for good.

"What about the Faro?"

"I gave everybody the day off. We don't get enough Sunday customers to justify keeping the place open, and it's been a rough week. I'll open up tonight for the bar crowd."

Deirdre frowned slightly, as if she were remembering some of the elements of that rough week, but then she smiled. "Okay. We can go to Allie Maldonado's restaurant. And then you can take me over to pick up the tables."

Sweet Thing, Allie Maldonado's bakery and café, was almost as packed with tourists as the Faro was on a good night. Allie, small and round in her flour-speckled chef's coat and chili-emblazoned pants, waved at Deirdre as they came in the door.

"You just missed Pete and Janie. They finished breakfast about five minutes ago."

"Oh, too bad." Deirdre managed to sound as if she really meant it, although he was pretty sure she preferred what they'd been doing to having lunch with the Assistant County Attorney and his wife, even if he was a Toleffson.

"Do you know Tom Ames?" Deirdre asked.

Allie turned bright brown eyes in his direction. He had a feeling he was getting a thorough, albeit fast, once-over. "I've heard your name. You're the guy at the Faro. You've got a new cook, right?"

Tom nodded. "Clem Rodriguez. She does lunch."

"I hear she's good. I'll have to stop by sometime and see."

Tom bowed slightly. "Please. We'll be glad to have you—on me."

Allie's grin widened. "Thanks. Now I'll definitely check it out."

Deirdre managed to polish off three sausage kolaches before Tom had finished his eggs and bacon. He wasn't really surprised—after all, they'd both had quite a workout. He grinned to himself and bit into a superlative buttermilk biscuit. "Where's the store with your tables?"

"On C Street. Republic of Texas."

Tom frowned. "Milam Broadus? He's..."

"Crazy, yes I know. You and Docia both told me, and I didn't think he was wrapped too tight either." Deirdre peeked up at him from beneath those lush lashes. "He had the right tables, though. And I couldn't find anything like them anywhere else. Plus he's selling them for way under what they're worth."

Tom shook his head. "You realize any money you pay him will go to finance more lunacy."

"It's Texas, Tom, lunacy is our birthright." She plucked a slice of bacon off his plate. "Besides, I'm just buying tables from him. I'm not signing on to lead the charge on the state house."

"Okay, but I'm glad I'm going with you. I'm not happy about you going into Broadus's place by yourself."

Deirdre frowned slightly. "To tell you the truth, I'm glad you'll be there too. He's a little, well, weird."

"Weird is putting it mildly. The son of a bitch is demented." Tom sighed. "Okay, let's go get your tables, assuming Broadus is open on Sunday. With him, you never know. Maybe he needed to go picket the capitol."

"He'll be there," Deirdre said flatly. "I owe him money."

Deirdre studied the front of the Republic of Texas, fingering the money in her pocket. Docia had given her the six hundred out of her cash from the bookstore since they both figured Broadus wouldn't take a check in any form.

She was relieved that Tom was at her back. Broadus's store still looked like a maze of dark furniture, with a fortress of solitude at the center. Maybe he'd planned it that way. Maybe people who bought antique guns from him didn't like being seen from the street.

"Cheery little place," Tom muttered. "Just what every aspiring tyrant needs."

"What?"

"A den of iniquity."

Deirdre snickered, then promptly froze. Milam Broadus was standing in the doorway, watching them with narrowed eyes.

She cleared her throat and gave him a decorous smile. "Good afternoon, Mr. Broadus. I came to pick up the tables and chairs."

Broadus's eyes stayed narrow. "You got the four hundred eighty you owe me?"

"Yes sir." Deirdre carefully avoided looking at Tom. She had the feeling he wouldn't be pleased.

Broadus turned without speaking again and marched into his shop. Beside her, Tom made a noise that sounded a lot like a snarl.

She patted his arm. "Be nice. I need those tables. And it shouldn't take long."

"Freakin' maniac," he fumed. "I thought those guys all treated women like fragile blossom."

"Probably not barmaids."

Tom gave her a narrow-eyed look of his own but followed her through the maze of armoires and breakfronts until they reached Broadus's desk. Deirdre pulled five hundred-dollar bills out of her pocket. "If I could get change, please? I don't have exactly four hundred and eighty."

Broadus pulled a battered wallet out of his back pocket and tossed her a greasy twenty.

"And could I also have a receipt?" She gave him the smile that had worked in the past with head waiters who'd tried to put her in a corner.

Broadus rummaged through his desk until he found the

original note he'd written with her name, then scrawled *Paid* across it. "Here."

Tom peered at the paper, then back at Broadus. "No sales tax?"

Broadus's face turned dull pink. "Who're you anyway? You work for them pricks up in Austin?"

Tom folded his arms across his chest. "Tom Ames. I own the Faro."

"A honky-tonk," Broadus spat. "I suppose you pay the revenuers when they come by your place."

"Yep." The corners of Tom's mouth tightened. "I like having the fires put out in town and having a cop on the beat. Not to mention getting the roads repaired after the spring floods. Figure I ought to help pay for it since I benefit from it."

Broadus's eyes were burning. "You pay for traitors to suck the blood of patriots."

"So far as I know, that hasn't come up at the City Council meetings lately."

Deirdre sighed. *Enough.* "We'll just take those tables and chairs, Mr. Broadus. Do you have a loading dock?"

Broadus was still engaged in a staring match with Tom, but it didn't seem to be going anywhere. He turned back to her, his mouth a thin line. "No dock. Take 'em out the back door."

"Right. Come on, Tom, I need you." She grabbed hold of his arm, towing him through the store. "Don't bait him," she murmured. "Just help me get my stuff out of here."

"Sorry." He sighed. "That asshole just pushes my buttons. Show me where the tables are and I'll become your beast of burden."

It took them a half hour or so to edge all three tables out of the furniture maze and place them in the back of the truck. The chairs were wedged in the corners, with one behind Tom's seat.

"I can walk back," she offered. "It's not that far."

She saw Tom glance back at the window. Broadus watched them from the shadows, like a warm-blooded gargoyle.

"Don't think so. It's not far to drive, either."

She slid in, fastening her seat belt as he started the engine. "Where do you know Broadus from? He doesn't seem to know you."

"He's too wrapped up in his own little conspiracy world to

notice anybody else, unless you present some kind of threat. Or opportunity. Believe it or not, he's a member of the Konigsburg Merchants Association, although whenever he shows up, he tries to make sure the Q and A ends up being about the evils of the guv'mint."

"He really does push your buttons, doesn't he?"

Tom grimaced as he pulled out onto the street. "Medicaid paid for a lot of the medical care that got me through childhood whenever my mom could get around to taking me to the clinic, and the US Army paid for a lot of the life experience I got after that. Far as I'm concerned, the evils of the guv'mint are vastly overrated."

Deirdre frowned slightly, thinking about the kind of reply her father would probably give to that statement. On the other hand, her father wasn't here to help her haul some tables to her new shop, and his idea of connecting with her was to send Craig Dempsey to drive her out of business. By now, the value she placed on her father's opinions was just about nil.

Craig Dempsey watched Dee-Dee and Ames drive away in the truck, feeling the now-familiar burning in his gut. Of course, Big John Brandenburg would never let somebody like Ames get his foot in the door at Brandenburg, Inc., but it still rubbed Craig raw to see it. Dee-Dee was supposed to be sitting in his BMW, not Ames's piece-of-crap Ford pickup. What a waste of potential! And time.

On impulse he walked into the shop they'd come from, although it didn't look like the place had much he'd be interested in. Still, with a name like Republic of Texas, there was always the off chance that the owner was a Cowboys fan, willing to exchange information for an autograph.

A man stood at the front window staring after Ames's truck. From his expression, Craig guessed he wasn't any more impressed with Ames than Craig was himself. Although the guy didn't look like he had much room to feel superior, given his shaggy hair and general lack of personal hygiene. Craig doubted those teeth had seen a dentist since the nineties, if then.

The man narrowed his eyes. "You want something?"

"Just looking. This your place?"

He nodded once, still regarding Craig as if he were a potential sneak thief.

"Just noticed a friend of mine in here," he said easily. "Little brunette. Maybe you know her—Dee-Dee Brandenburg. She one of your customers?"

The owner looked like he might have spat on the floor if he weren't standing in his own place. "Bought a couple of tables and chairs off me. If she's your friend, what's she doing with the pissant Ames?"

Craig's jaw tightened. "Ames is just after her money. She'll figure it out."

"Her money?" The owner raised an eyebrow.

"Her old man's money. Big John Brandenburg's got enough to buy and sell Ames ten times over. My guess is he will when he finds out Dee-Dee's been hanging out with him."

"John Brandenburg?"

Something about the man's voice made Craig take a closer look. His eyes seemed a lot brighter all of a sudden. But given that the guy was probably a typical Konigsburg moron, Craig didn't give him credit for much in the way of brainpower. He probably needed things spelled out for him.

"John Brandenburg," he said impatiently. "Brandenburg, Inc. Girl's been spoiled rotten by her daddy. He'll have something to say about what she's up to now. Probably pay Ames off and take her back home to Houston with him, one way or another." That was, of course, if Craig didn't pry her loose himself, which he was planning to do as soon as Hardesty could get his ducks in a row.

The owner turned back to the window again, his eyes narrowing. "I imagine so," he muttered. "We'll have to give him something to think about, then."

Craig stared at him. Clearly the man had at least one screw loose, and possibly more. He turned and headed back toward the door.

The owner didn't seem to notice when he left.

Sunday night was as quiet as usual. Chico sat propped on his stool across the room, watching the Steinbruners play a fairly inept game of pool through half-closed eyes. Now and again, Sylvia sat beside him. They didn't seem to talk much, but Tom thought Chico's expression might actually have moved closer to a smile when she was there.

In between pouring drafts and mixing the occasional margarita, he watched Deirdre move gracefully between the tables. She didn't usually work Sundays, but Marilyn had asked for the night off, and Deirdre volunteered to fill in. He did his best not to think about their activities for the past couple of nights since that led to a general lack of attention to his job. The tourists regarded her with awe, while the small but steadily increasing number of locals sat back to enjoy the view.

When she came to the bar with an order, she looked up at him through those wondrous lashes again, and he suddenly felt short of breath.

"Two margaritas on the rocks and a scotch straight up," she said, then blinked at him. "Is everything okay?"

Tom realized he was staring at her. Probably not the smartest thing to do. "Sure," he said and turned back to fix the drinks.

His hands had a slight tremble all of a sudden, and his heart was racing. He wondered briefly if he might be having a heart attack. *Not that kind of heart attack, moron!* He poured the scotch, then set the glasses on her tray, managing not to meet her eyes until the last moment.

"Thanks." She gave him a smile that set off another small heart episode.

Tom watched her walk away, telling himself this was nothing to get excited about. He'd been involved with women before. This was just the initial hormone rush that would settle down soon. *Right. Keep telling yourself that, moron.*

"Man, you got it bad. I can see all the signs."

Tom glanced at Nando, who'd taken a seat at the bar while he was fixated on Deirdre. *So nice to have an audience!*

"You drinking? Or does that interfere with your advice sideline?"

Nando shook his head. "I'm on duty. Wouldn't say no to a soda, though."

Tom filled a glass with cola from the bar, then set it in front of him. "What's up?"

"Not much. Real quiet. Had some news about that little

ruckus you had the other night, though."

Tom's shoulders tensed. He rubbed a hand across the back of his neck. "What did you hear?"

"At least one of the boys was hired. He got picked up in Johnson City on a DUI, then started talking to the cop who brought him in. Of course, he was plastered, but the Johnson City guy said it sounded possible."

"Hired by who?"

Nando shrugged. "Somebody from out of town, I guess. The drunk didn't know him. Just took his money."

Tom rubbed harder. "I figured as much. But if I don't know who's hiring them, I can't do much to stop it."

Nando raised an eyebrow. "You got any guesses?"

"Maybe." Tom shrugged. "Not anything I'm ready to talk about."

"Well, watch your back. There could be more coming." Nando took a sip of his cola. "Plus you've got Margaret Hastings with a hair up her ass now."

Tom frowned. "Margaret Hastings? Hell, I don't even know her except by sight. She's the one with all the angels, right?"

Nando nodded. "Got that Angels Unaware shop back on the other end of Main."

"So what's she pissed off about? I don't buy enough angels?"

"She's a teetotaler, one of those who thinks everybody else should be too. And that all places that sell demon rum should be shut down."

Tom felt a drip of ice down his spine. "So one fight and she wants to close me down? Hell, the old Faro had a fight every week."

"And Margaret Hastings did her best to get them closed. Kip had his liquor license suspended a couple of times because of her. Best watch your back there too."

Tom blew out a breath. On the whole, he'd rather face the barroom brawlers than Margaret Hastings. "Any other good news?"

"Nope. That's about it." Nando turned to survey the room again, grinning when he saw Sylvia rest a hand on Chico's knee. "I better take myself off. Looks like cupid's running amok around here. I need to steer clear."

Tom gave him a slightly forced smile and went back to watching Deirdre. Even if he had the feeling doom was approaching, at least he could enjoy the view until it did.

Chapter Nineteen

Monday night was usually slow, although they seemed to have a few more people than usual this Monday. It was hard to tell what was *usual* at this time of year, though—they were still drawing tourists even though the summer rush was over.

Deirdre thought she could see tension in Tom's shoulders, but it might just be exhaustion. They really should cool it on work nights. Even though they'd gotten away at midnight last night rather than two, they'd still stayed up an extra hour or so. Of course, *staying up* had been the whole point.

Deirdre smiled, turning toward Tom again. He was talking to Harry and Chico, his face half hidden by Chico's massive back. But she could see the chill in his expression, and the tension in the way he held himself.

She shivered as a ribbon of anxiety snaked across her own shoulders. Something was up. Something he hadn't mentioned to her. *He didn't want to worry you.* That should have made her feel better. It didn't.

She took another order for beers from a group of four men, who might be frat boys but didn't exactly look the part. Maybe the Faro was beginning to pull in more people from around town—she recognized a few faces scattered among the other tables. A couple of locals were playing pool with the Steinbruners at the end of the room, the click of the balls serving as a kind of counterpoint to their voices.

Deirdre did another quick survey of the room. Nothing seemed out of place. But she thought she could feel something now. A strain vibrating through the air, just below the surface. She moved her shoulders uneasily, then told herself, again, to knock it off.

It was Monday night, for god's sake. Nobody seemed to stand out. Nothing weird was happening. She put her tray on the bar. "Two Buds, Dos Equis, Lone Star."

"Drafts or bottles?"

"Bottles. And a bucket." She leaned against the bar, watching Tom pull bottles out of the cooler then lodge them in the tin bucket of ice. "Slow night."

"About usual for Monday." His gaze darted around the room before it settled on her again. "Any problems?"

She shook her head, then took a breath. "Are you expecting some?"

"Not necessarily."

"Is everything okay?"

He looked at her directly then, ice-blue eyes sharp. "Sure. Everything's terrific."

Sylvia stepped up beside her with her own order, and Deirdre turned back toward the tables. The prickle of unease played across her shoulders again. Something was up, and Tom wasn't sharing.

After she'd placed the bucket of beer in the center of the table and collected the money, she drew back to study the customers again. Mostly men, but that was usually the case except when they had a band. Mostly young. Or youngish. Mostly... She sighed. She hadn't really paid much attention to the crowds before, truth be told. She didn't exactly know what she was looking for. If she wasn't sure what *normal* was, she couldn't really tell what *abnormal* was either.

Chico leaned next to the beer garden door, looking deceptively sleepy. Deirdre could see him checking out the tables just as she had been, only he probably knew what constituted a problem. He stayed in place, his arms folded, but his eyes were sharp, like Tom's.

"Waitress?"

She turned toward the voice. Another table, this one closer to the pool tables. Two men. Twenties. Jeans and T-shirts. Accent sounded like East Texas. Was that supposed to be ominous?

"Can we get a bucket like that?" He gestured toward the bucket of beers she'd placed on the table nearer the door.

"Sure. Are you ready for more?"

The man raised a questioning eyebrow at his friend, then nodded. "Yeah. Bring us two Coronas."

Deirdre headed back toward the bar again. Behind her, somebody near the pool table whooped in triumph, but she managed not to jump. Maybe the atmosphere was getting to her more than she wanted to admit.

She gave Tom her order and turned back to consider the room again. Men talking and laughing. The smell of beer and cigarette smoke mingled with sweat, the noise of the pool game and men's voices layered over the distant sound of the jukebox. Deirdre sighed. For the life of her, she couldn't see anything that didn't look like every other night at the Faro.

The door to the beer garden swung open and Chico half-turned toward the men walking in. As Deirdre watched, a fist smashed into his face.

Almost simultaneously, one of the men at her table stood up and swung the bucket of beer by its handle, bashing it against the back of Chico's head. Chico's knees seemed to fold beneath him as he sank to the floor. Across the room, Sylvia screamed. And then chaos erupted all around them.

Tom leaped over the bar, yelling Chico's name. From the corner of her eye, Deirdre saw Harry grab the sawed-off pool cue, swinging it toward a pair of men who ran toward him from the front of the room.

Bottles exploded on the floor and the hanging light over the pool table shattered when a thrown bottle connected. One of the Steinbruners yelled, but she couldn't tell whether it was from fear or outrage. She heard the crash of tables overturning, and something splintered on the far side of the room.

She whirled back to where Tom was wading through the crowd toward Chico's prone body, pushing men out of his way and landing a few punches when they didn't want to move fast enough. Deirdre grabbed a bottle of Dos Equis and her tray and started after him.

Behind her, she heard splintering glass and Harry's shout. Across the room, Sylvia pushed men out of her way as she stumbled toward Chico. The Faro was a whirlwind of sound and movement, bodies sprawling into her path, flailing arms that she pushed away from her face.

And then suddenly, everything seemed to focus on a single point—a man from her table was raising a bottle behind Tom's

197

head, ready to bash it into the back of his skull.

Deirdre threw herself forward and hit the man in the face with her tray. He blinked at her, shaking his head as if his ears were ringing. Without thinking, she whacked him on the side of his head with the beer bottle, then watched him slump against the table. When she turned back, Tom had reached Chico's side.

"What the hell are you doing?" he shouted at her. "Get back!"

Deirdre didn't answer, largely because another man beside her had picked up an empty beer bottle and was headed toward Tom. She tossed the Dos Equis bottle in Tom's general direction, then hit the new combatant across the back of his head with her tray. One of the Steinbruners grabbed the front of his shirt and threw him against the wall, so that his head bounced. Deirdre stared at him, watching his eyes flutter before he sagged.

"Deirdre," Tom yelled, "goddamn it. Get over here!"

She pushed her way through the last couple of men, then braced her back to the wall beside Sylvia. "How's Chico?"

"They knocked him out, those bastards." Her voice sounded choked.

Deirdre glanced at her tear-stained cheeks. "We'll take care of him." Another crash echoed from across the room and Deirdre glanced back at the bar.

Harry crouched in front of the sink, wielding the pool cue like a baseball bat. At the other end of the bar, Leon swung his push-broom at shoulder level, jabbing at faces.

Deirdre heard a thump on her other side and watched the Steinbruner brothers toss fighters out of their way. They seemed remarkably cheerful about it.

Tom had grabbed one of the pool cues off the floor and was using it like a lance to drive people away from Chico. "Go out to the garden," he yelled. "Call Nando. Now!" He grabbed hold of her shoulder, pushing her outside.

Deirdre stumbled to a table at the side, fumbling for her cell phone, then punched in 911. A woman's voice answered. "Konigsburg police. You got an emergency?"

"I'm at the Faro," Deirdre panted. "There's a fight. A bad fight. Chico Burnside's been hurt. Send us some help. Please.

Hurry."

"Wait," the woman barked. Deirdre heard voices in the background, and then she was back again. "I need your name. Tell me what's going on right now."

Deirdre managed not to roll her eyes. "My name is Deirdre Brandenburg, and what's going on right now is a fight, which means a bunch of men are punching each other and trying to smash up the bar. Now I'm going back inside. They need me." She snapped the phone closed and pushed it into her pocket, then jerked the door open.

At least the situation didn't look any worse than it had before. Several people had already left by the front door, and the ones who remained were concentrated around the pool table and the bar. Sylvia knelt beside Chico, holding his head in her lap. Tom had carved out an empty space in front of them, and was using his cue to help the Steinbruners, who still seemed to be enjoying themselves way too much as they threw a couple of men to the floor. Across the room, Harry and Leon pushed men back from the bar, but a lot of bottles had been smashed. The smell of spilled alcohol bit at her nostrils.

Suddenly, she felt Tom's hand on her shoulder. "Down!" he yelled, a moment before glass shattered to her left. Something heavy struck her back. Deirdre squinted over her left shoulder. The plate glass window at the front of the bar lay in shards, glass covering the tables and the floor.

The front door slammed open, and Nando Avrogado pushed his way inside. "Police," he shouted. "Everybody freeze where you are!"

For a moment, everyone seemed to pause, and then men were stampeding for the beer garden exit, pushing Deirdre aside in the rush. Sylvia threw herself across Chico's body to protect him, and Tom reached into the running crowd to pull one of the men out, shoving him back against the wall. "Not you, asshole."

The man aimed a desperate punch at Tom's jaw that landed on his shoulder. Tom grunted in pain and then threw the man across the pool table, shoving the handle of the cue under his chin. "Don't you fucking move. I'd love to take your head off."

Nando yelled at someone outside, probably another cop, and then stepped back into the room, pausing to take in the general carnage.

Harry and Leon slumped against the bar. The mirror behind them looked cracked and the floor in front was littered with broken bottles. Two of the Steinbruner brothers had dropped into chairs at the side, mopping their foreheads with the tails of their T-shirts. Sylvia was huddled against the wall, still cradling Chico's head.

And Tom held the last man flat on the pool table, the cue jammed so tight beneath his chin he was gurgling. Deirdre had a feeling Tom was only holding himself back from more serious assault by a thread.

Nando stepped up beside him, laying his hand on his arm. "Okay, Ames, I'll take it from here."

Tom blinked at him for a moment, then stepped back, reluctantly moving the cue away from the man's chin. "This is the SOB who started it. He hit Chico with a beer bucket."

Nando nodded, staring down at the man on the pool table. "Anybody call for an aid car?"

"I did," Sylvia whispered.

"Good. Should be here in a couple of minutes, then. How about the rest of you? Anybody else hurt?"

Tom glanced around the room, his gaze coming to rest on Deirdre. "Are you okay?"

She nodded. "I think so."

"Looks like we're all right, then."

Another policeman entered from the beer garden. "I couldn't keep up with them, but Ham had a couple in his sights. He may be able to bring another one down."

"Thanks, Curtis." Nando jerked his head at Tom's captive, now hunched over the pool table. "Put the cuffs on this one and take him down to the station. I'll be there as soon as I get this sorted out."

As the second cop was leaving with his prisoner, the aid car arrived, which meant several minutes spent helping the groggy Chico into the back. Sylvia was adamant about going with him, and no one felt like arguing with her, given that Chico never let go of her hand. Nando had a quick conversation with the Steinbruners while Chico was being taken care of, then sent them on their way.

Finally, Nando pulled up a chair and sat, resting one booted foot on the end of the pool table. "Okay, boys and girls, let's hear it. What happened here? Who were these guys?"

Tom shook his head. "Damned if I know. I never saw any of them before." He turned to Harry. "You recognize any of them?"

"No, sir. They weren't from around here. Not unless they all got here within the last two weeks or so."

"How many were there?" Nando asked.

"About twenty," Leon said. "Maybe more."

Tom shook his head. "Nine or ten. But after they took Chico down that was enough."

Nando had pulled out a small notebook and pen. "What started the fight?"

Tom's jaw tightened. "They hit Chico, that's what started it."

"Were they arguing?"

Tom frowned. "I didn't see it."

"No." Deirdre sighed. "They came through the door from the garden and one of them punched him as soon as they walked in. Then a man at one of my tables hit him on the back of his head with a beer bucket."

Nando winced, writing a quick note. "Sounds like they wanted to take him down."

"Sounds like." A muscle danced in Tom's jaw.

"So then what?"

"So then they started busting up the place."

"They didn't try to take out anyone else?"

Tom shook his head. "Nope."

"Yes they did." Deirdre swallowed as Nando turned to look at her. Her palms felt wet, her shoulders were trembling. *Reaction.* Only she couldn't afford that right now. "Another one of the men who were at my table tried to hit Tom with a bottle when his back was turned."

"What happened?"

She swallowed again. Why was her throat so tight all of a sudden? "I hit him with my tray and with a beer bottle. Then the Steinbruner brothers finished him off. He must have gotten away, though. I didn't see him after that."

Tom was staring at her blankly. "You did what? Jesus, Deirdre!"

"It worked," she said flatly. "That's all that matters."

Tom looked like he was going to disagree, but Nando cut him off. "So they took out Chico, and they tried to take you out too. And then they busted up the joint. Sounds about right."

Tom squinted at him. "Right for what?"

"Right for somebody who wanted to put you out of business. What do you think—did they make it?"

Deirdre stared around the room for the first time since Chico and the others had left. The bar was a small disaster, at least half of the liquor destroyed, the mirror cracked, the cooler door hanging from its hinges. In the room itself, most of the tables were standing but a few tottered dangerously, legs broken. More chairs lay in pieces. And the glass from the front window covered a third of the room.

Nando raised an eyebrow. "You check the beer garden yet?"

Tom pushed himself to his feet slowly, as if his body hurt. He opened the door and gazed out the back. "Shit."

"Yeah. Looks like they took out some of the tables and chairs before they came in the door. How about the outside bar?"

"Broken up. Maybe totaled. I'll check it tomorrow, in daylight."

He slumped back into a chair near the door. Deirdre felt a pain in her chest every time she looked at him. Wasn't this the point at which Mickey and Judy were supposed to hop up and start a dance number? Something about being down but now out? Right now they both looked about as out as she could ever remember looking.

"You got any insurance, *vato?*" Nando's voice was surprisingly gentle.

Tom nodded. "Some. Not enough, probably. And it'll take time to get everything put back together."

"Well, if we figure out who's behind this, you can always sue 'em." Nando leveled his Stetson on his head again. "Which is what I'm going to do right now—figure it out, that is. I'll let you know if that asshole you caught gives me any names."

"Thanks. I guess I'll go to the hospital and check on Chico after we board up the window."

"I'll go with you." Deirdre stood up and then put a hand on the pool table. Her knees suddenly felt shaky.

Tom turned back toward her, his eyes bleak. "You should go home and get some rest."

She bit her lip. "I'll go with you. Wherever." It was as close as she could get to a declaration, under the circumstances.

Tom and Harry located some sheets of plywood in the back of Deirdre's shop and nailed them across the window in front. It wasn't completely covered, but it was probably enough to discourage anyone from coming in. "Not that there's much left worth stealing," Tom muttered.

While they were still hammering, Clem arrived, wearing jeans and a T-shirt, her hair in spikes. "What the hell?" She turned to Deirdre. "Helen Kretschmer called me from the police station. What happened? Who did this?"

Deirdre pushed a broom through the shards of glass, concentrating on neat piles. "We were attacked. We don't know yet who did it. They've got a man in custody, maybe two. Nando said he'd try to get some answers."

"Holy shit. Did they touch my kitchen?" Clem trotted across the room, detouring around broken bottles.

Deirdre followed her. "They didn't seem interested in it, but I couldn't see that side of the room."

Clem flung the kitchen door open, then sighed in relief. "It's okay. I don't think anyone was in here except Leon."

Deirdre stared around the kitchen, then leaned her head against the doorjamb. Suddenly, she felt like crying. "Good. I'm glad they missed something." She closed her eyes, fighting back the clenching in her throat.

Clem rested a hand on her arm. "Is Chico really hurt? How bad is he?"

"We don't know yet. I'm going over to the hospital with Tom as soon as they finish boarding up the window. Sylvia's over there with him."

"I'll come too." Clem peered into the mirror over the sink, brushing through her hair with her fingers. "Damn. I look punk." She turned back again to Deirdre. "Okay, toots, who do you think did this?"

Deirdre shook her head, her throat so tight she was afraid she might choke. "I don't know. I told you."

"But your best guess would be...?"

She closed her eyes. "I don't know." But the more she thought about it, the more she thought she did. She just wasn't ready to face the answer yet.

Chapter Twenty

Tom stared down at the beer in his hand. The beer he hadn't touched in fifteen minutes. He should drink the goddamn beer. He should go home, get some sleep, leave all of this until tomorrow. He should definitely get Deirdre to stop sweeping.

He wasn't sure why she was doing it. It seemed to make her feel better. He could hear the slight scratching of the broom across the floor, along with the occasional tinkle of glass as she pushed the debris into heaps.

He stared down at his beer again, willing himself to take a sip.

Chico had a concussion. Sylvia was going to stay at the hospital until they threw her out, which he figured would be any minute now given her frequent bouts of hysterics. Harry and Leon had already left when he and Deirdre got back. Clem said she'd be back for lunch, even though they probably wouldn't be able to open.

And Deirdre was sweeping.

He studied her pale face, her hands clenched tight around the broom handle. Probably not healthy. He should be worried about her, but somehow he didn't have the energy to worry about anything else on top of the Faro right now.

He'd probably managed to fulfill all her family's worst expectations about his not being worthy of her, to say nothing of his tendency to put her at risk.

He sighed. "Deirdre?"

She glanced at him, reaching down to toss a larger piece of broken bottle onto the pile. "What?"

"Leave it. I'll start the clean-up tomorrow."

"I'm almost..."

"Leave it!" Tom snapped, then winced. He didn't want to start taking out his frustrations on people who were trying to help, particularly not on Deirdre who had apparently saved his worthless hide from a concussion like Chico's, which would probably have led to the complete destruction of the Faro.

He gazed around the room again, charting the rubble. His bar. His place. His wreck. At least he still had a pool table and a kitchen. Now he had to figure out how to put the rest of it back together again.

Deirdre slid into the chair opposite, her face pale in the dim light. She licked her lips, and amazingly enough, he felt a slight jolt of heat. Maybe he wasn't as dead as he thought he was. Or as dead as he felt.

She took a deep breath. "Tom, I'm so sorry."

He shrugged. "For what? You didn't do this."

"No, but you think my father did, don't you?" Her eyes were fathomless, dark pools of pain. "That he ordered it."

A muscle spasmed in his jaw. "I don't know who did it."

"Did Craig threaten you when he was here before? Something you didn't mention at the time?"

Tom sighed. The hell with it. She was too smart to be lied to. "He said if I didn't take his offer, I'd regret it. This is probably what he was talking about."

"Which means my father was responsible for this." She gazed around the room again, then closed her eyes. "I'm sorry."

"Not your fault. You didn't do it. I'm a big boy, Deirdre. I can take care of myself. And I make my own decisions. You didn't talk me into this."

She rubbed a hand across the back of her neck. "Can we go home now?"

"Sure. I'll walk you."

"And stay?"

"I don't..." He blew out a breath. Too many things to think about. Too many things to take care of. "I should probably stay here. Make sure nobody comes back."

"Right." Deirdre's lips firmed. "They missed the kitchen, didn't they? Maybe they'll swing by again and take another shot."

"Deirdre…"

She waved a hand at him. "It's okay. We both need to get some sleep. We've got lots of work to do tomorrow."

Tom looked around the wreckage of the Faro, feeling the numbness gather in his chest again. *Not we. Me. My place, my problem.* "Lots of work."

Deirdre considered calling her father as soon as she got home. Let him see how he liked being awakened at two in the morning by an outraged daughter. But she wanted this to stop, and further pissing off her father was probably not the best way to go about it.

She managed to drag herself out of bed at seven to call his cell, but he didn't answer. "Dad," she said when she heard the beep of his voice mail, "it's me. We have to talk about this situation. Please call me as soon as you get this message."

After breakfast, she dialed his office line. He usually got in early, assuming he was there and not sitting somewhere in the vicinity of Konigsburg, gloating.

Her father's assistant, Alanis, answered the phone. If she was surprised to hear from Deirdre after a several-week absence, she didn't show it. "Your father's not here, Miss Brandenburg. He's in Europe—Slovenia this week."

Slovenia. Well, as an alibi it was unique. "What day will he be back?"

"On Friday, assuming he doesn't change his plans. He'd originally planned to be back last week, but apparently the negotiations have been more difficult than he anticipated."

And then perhaps he'd also decided it was best to be out of the country when his plans finally clicked into place. For a moment, she wondered if he'd even considered that she might be in the Faro when his goons showed up to break the place to splinters.

"Shall I ask him to call you when he returns?"

Deirdre squared her shoulders. "Yes, Alanis, thank you."

Plan B was to find Craig, who had to be hiding out somewhere in Konigsburg. Although getting her father to call everything off would be easier. Putting Craig on notice before she approached Nando or Erik Toleffson might be enough to keep the goons from coming back for another shot at the Faro. But when she looked at her watch, she decided to put that step off, at least for the moment. She had more important concerns, namely Tom. She ate a quick breakfast, then headed back to the bar.

As she'd anticipated, he was there, hammering some of the tables back into shape, the ones that weren't smashed or missing legs. As she hadn't anticipated, Clem and Marilyn and Bobby Sue were there too, sweeping up glass. Harry was behind the bar, doing inventory. The door to the beer garden swung open and Leon entered, carrying a full trash bag.

"Where do you want the bags?" he asked.

"Put it out back with the others." Tom shrugged. "Pick-up's tomorrow."

"Lot of broken stuff out there."

Tom's shoulders stiffened. "Just clean it up, Leon."

Deirdre leaned into the kitchen and grabbed another broom. Lucky they had so many. She closed her eyes for a moment, gathering herself together, then walked back in. "What do you need done?"

Tom glanced at her, then shrugged again. "Clean-up mostly. Then I can start figuring out what comes next. Insurance adjuster should be here sometime this afternoon. I want to have a preliminary run-down by then."

"We need this room cleared by lunchtime," Clem called from the side.

Tom turned toward her, and Deirdre caught her breath. His face was gaunt, dark shadows beneath his eyes. She wondered if he'd slept at all last night. "We're not opening for lunch, Clem, accept it. It'll probably take a couple of days."

Clem's chin rose imperiously. "You get some tables set up, and I can cook. We can open."

Tom gestured toward the boarded-up front window. "There's no light. It would be like eating in a cave. I'd rather not open than open and have people see the place like this and not want to come back here again."

Clem folded her arms across her chest. "We could serve in the beer garden."

"The beer garden's in worse shape than the main room. I don't think any of the tables are in one piece out there."

Deirdre took a breath. "I've got those three tables for the shop. And some chairs. They could go in the garden."

Tom glanced at her, his lips becoming a taut line. "I'll think about it."

Clem snorted and went back to sweeping.

Light was a problem, Deirdre realized. One of the hanging fixtures over the pool table had been smashed, while the other was missing half its shade. The boarded-up window cut off all the sunlight from the street. The dim overheads made it hard to see the floor, but she swept as much as she could. Wood splinters, broken glasses and bottles, overturned ashtrays. Hard to believe a twenty-minute fight could produce this much chaos.

"How's Chico?" she asked Tom the next time she emptied her dustpan into the plastic garbage bin in the middle of the room.

He shrugged. "Concussion mostly. Some scrapes and bruises, just like the rest of us. The doctor said they might let him go this evening if he doesn't have any other symptoms." He turned back to the table he was working on.

Deirdre thought about apologizing again, but decided not to. All the apologies in the world wouldn't make up for this.

The front door swung open, sending a shard of sunlight flashing through the darkness. A large shape was silhouetted against the light. "My, my, my," a deep voice said. "What a freakin' mess."

Tom sighed again. "Morning, Chief."

Erik Toleffson picked up a barstool, placing it upright beside the bar as he stared around the room. "Somebody really did a number on you, Ames."

"That they did." Tom wiped his hands against his jeans, then walked toward the chief.

"Any idea who?"

Tom shook his head. "Nando grabbed one of them. He said you'd question him."

"We did." Erik gave him a dry smile. "Or that is, Nando did. I was at that resort outside Marble Falls with my wife. Delayed honeymoon. Nando called me up there, and we came back a couple of days early."

Deirdre felt like wincing. She knew Erik and Morgan hadn't

been married long, and she had a sneaking suspicion he wouldn't have enjoyed getting a call about a fight at the Faro when he was supposed to be relaxing with his new wife.

"Sorry to interrupt your time off, Chief." Tom's smile twisted slightly. "I didn't exactly enjoy it myself, to tell you the truth."

"Yeah, I can see how you wouldn't. Any place we can talk?"

"Sure." Tom nodded toward the beer garden. "Maybe we can find a couple of chairs out there that aren't in pieces."

Deirdre watched the two men walk through the door to the beer garden, her chest suddenly hollow. She swallowed hard. Craig Dempsey was going to be one sorry SOB when she finally found him, but her father was going to be a lot sorrier if she had anything to say about it.

Tom did a quick survey of the beer garden. Leon was sweeping up trash on the far side. The heavy umbrella tables were still standing, but a lot of the smaller, wood-topped café tables were splintered. And, of course, they'd wrecked the bar. Thank god the bandstand was metal and concrete—not much they could do to bring it down, although it looked like they'd tried.

Toleffson narrowed his eyes as he checked out the damage. "Looks like somebody has a real hard-on for you, Ames. You need to tell me who."

He pulled out one of the few chairs that was still in one piece and sat, studying Tom from beneath the rim of his Stetson.

Tom pulled out another chair. At least he had two that were still in one piece. "I'll take care of it myself."

Toleffson's eyes narrowed. "I don't like the sound of that. I'm the one who's supposed to take care of things around here, not you. And I sure as hell don't want you causing more trouble than you've already got."

Tom gave Toleffson his most impassive look. He didn't figure the chief would be an easy man to stare down, but maybe he'd give it a try. "I thought you had a couple of the guys from last night down at the station. Can't they tell you who was behind it?"

Toleffson shrugged. "They gave me somebody, guy named Pat Hardesty. You know him?"

Tom shook his head. "Never heard of him."

"That's what I figured. As it happens, I know Hardesty—he's a small-time crook who'd like to be big but doesn't have that kind of brains. So he didn't come up with this on his own. No way for him to profit from it."

Tom managed to look uninterested in Pat Hardesty and his plans for moving up.

Toleffson peered back at the bandstand again. "Anyway, I'm betting Hardesty didn't set this up, but I've passed his name on to Sheriff Friesenhahn so we can try to find him. Now I need to know who's actually bankrolling Hardesty and his buddies so I can figure out how much trouble we've got on our hands. I'm asking you again, Ames, who's behind this?"

Tom stared down at his feet, trying to figure a way to give Toleffson nothing without ending up in the slammer himself.

He heard the door from the bar swoosh closed and glanced up. Deirdre was staring at them both with eyes the color of slate. All of a sudden, Tom had the feeling she'd be harder to stare down than either of them.

"The man who most probably hired these thugs is named Craig Dempsey, Chief Toleffson. But the man who hired Craig Dempsey is my father, John Brandenburg. He's out of the country right now, but I'm trying to reach him. I'm also trying to find Craig. Either of them could put a stop to this, and once I locate them, I'll make sure that they do."

Toleffson blinked at her. Tom had a feeling he wasn't accustomed to being caught totally flat-footed. "Why would your father want to put Ames out of business, Ms. Brandenburg?"

"He doesn't. He's just trying to bully Tom into cancelling my lease on the shop next door and firing me from my waitress job. He figures that will make me come home." Her lips curved up in a remarkably cold smile. "It won't do that, but he doesn't understand that it won't. Tom here is caught in the middle, and he shouldn't be."

"You have proof of this?"

"No, but Tom does." Deirdre turned those slate-cold eyes on him again. "Craig threatened him when he wouldn't promise to fire me. And he told Tom my father would pay him off if he cancelled my lease."

Toleffson went on staring at her for a few moments, then sighed. "Well, it's good to know nobody else in town is going to be hit by this wrecking crew. Your father doesn't have his sights on anybody else, does he?"

She shook her head. "Not unless I go to work for them."

"Any idea where I can find this Craig Dempsey?" He narrowed his eyes. "I need to have a talk with him. The sooner the better."

She shook her head again. "I'm looking for him too, Chief. I don't think he's staying here in town anymore."

"Where was he staying before this?"

"I don't know for sure, but I'd guess the Woodrose Inn." Deirdre's lips spread in a humorless smile. "He'd want to stay in the most expensive place in Konigsburg."

Toleffson pushed himself to his feet. "If you hear from him..."

"I'll let you know," she finished.

"And don't try to do anything with him yourself, okay?"

She frowned. "I want to talk to him, Chief, so I can't promise that I won't do that. But I won't do anything else, although I can think of a few things I'd like to do to him."

Toleffson didn't look like he was too happy with that idea, but he let it go. "Okay, Ames, anything else happens around here, you call me."

"Yes sir, I'll do that." They both knew he probably wouldn't, but Tom figured there was no harm in a congenial lie now and then.

He watched Toleffson step back through the door. Deirdre stayed where she was, staring at him, her gaze defiant.

He managed to keep his voice level, a considerable feat given how pissed he felt at the moment. "You shouldn't have told him all that, Deirdre."

"Why? So you and he could go on playing John Wayne with each other? That code of the west crap? Why keep it a secret? I figure the more help we have in finding Craig, the sooner he'll stop."

And the less chance I have to wring his friggin' neck before anybody else does. Tom took another in a series of deep breaths. "It won't do any good. Even if Toleffson finds Dempsey, he'll just deny it. It'll be my word against his. Nobody else heard him."

"Maybe Hardesty will say it was Craig."

"My guess is Hardesty is long gone. And even if he isn't, he's been paid to keep his mouth shut. I wouldn't put much money on him as a witness against Craig."

"I still don't see why you think it's a bad idea to tell the chief about what's really going on."

"Well, first of all because, like I say, it won't work. There's nothing Toleffson can do about Craig Dempsey without more proof than I've got."

"And second?"

Tom pinched the bridge of his nose. "Because it sounds like I can't take care of you or my own damn place. Bad enough that I can't. I don't want to talk about it with Toleffson. The Faro belongs to me, not him."

Deirdre stared at him for a long moment, her mouth firming to a thin line, then turned on her heel, stalking away from him. She pushed open the door to the main room, then turned back to look at him again. "You, you...*guy*," she snapped.

Tom sat watching the doorway where she'd been standing as the door swung shut behind her. For the life of him, he couldn't figure out why that sounded like an insult.

Deirdre spent the rest of the day cleaning up and avoiding Tom. She wasn't sure exactly why she was so angry at him—in fact, she suspected that she was really angry at herself for being the cause of so much misery.

Clem kept trying to convince Tom to open for lunch, and Tom kept telling her no. After a while he escaped to the beer garden to avoid her. A few of their regulars stopped in to check things out. Deirdre was momentarily amazed that they actually had regulars. Rhonda Ruckelshaus stood in the doorway for a few moments shaking her head. "I guess y'all aren't serving today."

"No." Deirdre managed a slightly flat smile. "Check back with us tomorrow or the day after, though. We should be doing lunches again by then."

Rhonda grimaced as she surveyed the room. "If you say so."

Clem emptied a load of glass into the dumpster. "Goddamn it all to hell! I could have put something together. BLTs or gazpacho or grilled cheese. Something simple. We could have opened. It would have shown everybody they couldn't kick us down."

"We don't have a bar, Clem. There's no way to serve beer. And without beer, there's no Faro."

Clem's mouth was a thin line. "So? We serve beer out of a wash tub full of ice. We don't let them beat us. Ever!" She turned on her heel and stalked back into the kitchen.

Deirdre stood leaning on her broom, staring at the kitchen door. *We don't let them beat us. Ever!* Behind her she heard the main door open again.

"No lunch?" someone asked.

She turned to see Elsa Carmichael, the owner of a weaving shop several blocks down Main.

She didn't think she'd ever seen Elsa in the Faro before, but maybe she just hadn't been on the right side of the room. "Not today. But we'll be open tomorrow or the next day for sure." This time her smile felt more genuine than it had before.

Elsa nodded. "Well, good. I've been hearing lots of nice things about your lunch menu. Figured today would be a good day to try it out." She gazed quickly around the room, the muscles of her jaw firming slightly. "And I'll be back whenever you open. You can count on it."

Deirdre's chest tightened, her throat clenching. "Thank you," she managed.

Elsa gave her another smile, then stepped back into the street. Deirdre turned back to sweeping with a sudden burst of energy. There was a lot more to be done before they opened the place that evening.

Chapter Twenty-One

Tom was never exactly sure how it happened. He knew for a fact he'd still been resisting Clem and her efforts to push him into opening for lunch. Then the insurance adjuster had arrived and he lost track of what was going on around him other than the clicking of the keys on the man's BlackBerry. At least the adjustor had promised him a check, although Tom was fairly certain it wouldn't cover all the damage and his rates would now go into the stratosphere.

He figured he'd get the window replaced tomorrow. Then he could maybe reopen the day after that. Maybe.

When he got back to the main room, Deirdre was directing Leon as he hauled in a large galvanized tin tub from parts unknown. Tom watched, frowning, as Leon loaded it with ice and then as Deirdre began jamming in bottles of beer. Behind the bar, Harry lined up the few bottles of liquor that hadn't been smashed, along with a selection of water glasses to replace the highball glasses that had gone down with the bottles. Miraculously enough, the frozen margarita machine appeared to be intact and loaded with mix.

Tom leaned back against the bar, feeling tension snake across his shoulders. "What's going on?"

Deirdre shrugged. "We're getting ready to open."

He gazed around the room. The debris had been removed. There were fewer tables but enough for a moderate-sized crowd. Leon dragged in two more chairs from the beer garden as he watched—each table looked to have at least three.

"We've got no lights," he snapped.

"It's a bar. It's supposed to be dark. Besides, we got the lights over the pool table fixed. All we had to do was replace the bulbs, although we're going to need new shades."

Tom glanced toward the table. The two dangling bulbs made it look a little like an operating room in a very dubious hospital. On the other hand, that end of the room would be well-lit, probably to the point of glaring in the eyes of half the customers. At least the felt on the tables wasn't too scarred.

He sighed. "I can have some new shades for those by tomorrow. Plus the insurance guy was going to send over somebody to fix the window tomorrow afternoon. I'll be in better shape to open tomorrow night, assuming I can get the cooler fixed."

"That's good." Deirdre took off the apron she'd been wearing, folding it into a neat triangle. "But we're still opening tonight."

Tom raised an eyebrow. "We are? Who is this *we*? I own the place, and as I recall, I told you no."

"*We* are me and Harry and Leon and Marilyn and Clem. And we have decided we will be goddamned before we let a blithering moron like Craig Dempsey put us out of business. We've all decided to go for it. And we figure you'll thank us when you've had a chance to think about it."

She firmed her jaw, raising her chin. She looked a little like General Patton rallying the troops. Leon and Marilyn rested on their brooms behind her, while Harry leaned his elbows on the bar, all of them waiting for him to cave.

He chest tightened. *His* bar, *his* place. He made decisions like this, not his employees. And he'd already refused.

"Tom," Deirdre said softly, "it's okay. Let us help. We want to."

He took a breath, ready to give them a list of the reasons they obviously couldn't open tonight, then stopped. All of a sudden, he couldn't remember any of them.

Deirdre still watched him with that conqueror-of-nations look.

He took one more quick survey of the room. It looked like shit. If they were lucky, they might pull in two or three near-sighted customers, not enough to pay for the overhead. Of course, staying closed didn't exactly cover the overhead either. Still, he shouldn't need Deirdre and the others to get things going. He should be able to do that himself. He rubbed his eyes.

If he weren't so freakin' tired all of a sudden.

The front door swung open and the Steinbruners swaggered through. Denny had a butterfly bandage over one eyebrow. Harold looked slightly lumpy around the jaw. Billy Ray had a few bruises on the side of his face that were turning the color of eggplant.

"Hey," Denny nodded at him, then caught sight of the pool table. "Cool lights. Now we can see the balls better. Just what the place needed." He headed toward the far end of the room, grabbing one of the undamaged cues from the wall rack.

"Hey, that's my cue," Harold called after him. "Yours is that one with the blue mark on the side."

Billy Ray paused to collect three bottles of Corona from the washtub. "Nice set-up," he muttered. "Easier to get to the beers." He flipped a five and a one onto the bar, then turned back to join his brothers.

Marilyn and Deirdre stood watching Tom. He took another deep breath, then shrugged. "Okay, boys and girls, looks like we're back in business. Sort of."

That business wasn't exactly brisk, but it wasn't as bad as Tom had been afraid it might be. After a while, he stopped bracing himself every time the door opened. Most of the people who came in were familiar, and the few first-timers were obviously tourists. The first-timers tended to leave fairly quickly, but the regulars stuck it out. Deirdre and Marilyn kept the tables stocked with beers and the occasional margarita. After a half hour or so, Clem emerged from the kitchen with some plates of shrimp nachos and chipotle chicken quesadillas that she placed on the bar for the customers. Tom had a feeling she'd have gone on giving them away if no one had ordered them, but a couple of the larger tables put in orders and she spent the rest of the evening in the kitchen.

Around seven, Sylvia stepped through the door, followed a moment later by Chico. He was limping, and bruises covered one side of his face. His expression was even surlier than usual.

Tom felt like kissing him. Which would, of course, have meant instant death.

Chico nodded, a little painfully. "Hey."

"Hey yourself. How do you feel?"

"How do you think I feel? Like somebody used my head for

football practice."

"Why don't you go home, then, get some rest." Tom shrugged. "I can handle this."

Chico surveyed the room with narrowed eyes, then shook his head slowly, as if the motion hurt. "Fuck that. I'm working."

He placed his stool beside the beer garden door, then sat, leaning his back against the wall. For a while, Sylvia fluttered beside him until he growled something that made her stomp off toward the kitchen. She returned with her tray and spent the rest of the evening ignoring him, which seemed to have little effect on Chico's general outlook on life.

Nando appeared around eleven. "Didn't think you'd open tonight."

Tom shrugged. "Bills to pay. More of them now than before, in fact. You any further along finding the guy who hired them?"

"Dempsey?" Nando shook his head. "We've got some reports that Hardesty's still around. The sheriff's got some guys on his trail. If we pick him up, he may be able to lead us to Dempsey."

Tom nodded absently. Chico looked like he was dozing on his stool. He should probably send him home. On the other hand, he had a feeling Chico wouldn't go quietly.

"Any problems tonight?"

Tom checked the room again. Nobody but locals, most of whom, he realized, were regulars. Somehow he'd failed to notice how many regulars they had until now. "Nah. Real quiet."

"Right. I don't figure they'll be back since we've got a couple of them in jail and cops looking for the others. Takes all the fun out of it when some of them get arrested and start squealing on their buddies."

Tom blew out a breath. "Well, that's something. Of course, Dempsey may find another bunch of guys."

"If he does, Toleffson's going to be really pissed. Which means Dempsey's ass will be grass when he finds him."

Not if I find him first. Tom managed not to say it out loud, but it was close.

"You check your mail today?"

Tom glanced at him. "No. I had other things to worry about."

"You might want to look it over. Could be something interesting there."

Tom frowned. Nando didn't sound like *interesting* meant *good*. He reached behind the bar for the pile of mail he'd tossed there earlier. Mostly bills—about what he'd expected. Toward the bottom of the stack he found an official-looking envelope with the address of the Texas Alcoholic Beverage Commission in the upper left corner. A drip of ice water coursed down his spine.

Nando watched as he slit the envelope with his pocket knife and unfolded the letter inside. Tom licked his lips. "Notice of a hearing on my liquor license. They've received a citizen complaint. Fuck."

Nando nodded. "Margaret Hastings, like I said. She launched the complaint after the first fight. Now she'll use this one to show the Faro's back to its bad old ways, a menace to the neighborhood."

"Hell, Margaret Hastings isn't even *in* this neighborhood. Her store's at least ten blocks away and she lives at the other end of town."

"She's probably found somebody who does live around here to be the person whose name is on the complaint. Margaret's pretty thorough. And she's been after the Faro for a while."

"Shit, Nando, I don't even know her. Why the hell is she doing this to me?"

Nando shrugged. "Not you, exactly. She'd do it to the Silver Spur, too, if she could get away with it. And the Dew Drop. She'd like the whole town to go dry, but she knows how likely that is. So her strategy is to harass anybody who looks vulnerable."

Tom blew out a breath. "Well, vulnerable is pretty accurate right now as far as the Faro's concerned."

"You probably need yourself a lawyer, *vato*. You got one handy?"

"Nope." *Terrific.* Another expense on top of paying for the bar.

Deirdre slipped by them, heading for the beer tub. Harry had managed to keep it stocked with bottles throughout the night, along with mixing the occasional drink. Nando watched her go, smiling in a way that made Tom grit his teeth.

"Any idea why her father would put out a hit on you?"

Tom shrugged. "Wants his baby to come home, I guess.

Never met the man myself."

"If he or Dempsey shows up here, you'll give us a call, right?" Nando was smiling, but his eyes had that same anthracite look that Toleffson's had had.

"Sure thing." And he would. Right after he pounded Dempsey into paste himself. He wasn't sure what he'd do to Deirdre's father, but he had definite plans for Craig Dempsey. And they didn't involve a 911 call.

Deirdre tried her father's cell several more times during the course of the day. After a while, she stopped leaving messages. It was always possible he hadn't taken his personal phone with him on a business trip. She was one of the few people who called that number, and she had the feeling her father didn't really want to talk to her. Late in the afternoon, she called his office again and got Alanis.

"I'm sorry, Ms. Brandenburg. He's extended his stay in Slovenia for another few days. Apparently, the negotiations require him to be there."

Deirdre managed not to grind her teeth in frustration. "Did you give him my message?"

"Yes, ma'am."

She couldn't tell anything from Alanis's voice, but clearly her father wasn't giving her top priority at the moment.

"Thank you, Alanis. Please let him know I'm still trying to reach him."

"Yes, ma'am, I will."

If she couldn't contact her father, Deirdre figured Craig would be the next best thing. She called several of the plusher bed and breakfasts around town, but, predictably, they weren't eager to tell her if a man named Craig Dempsey was staying with them. Tomorrow she'd try to get Docia involved—she might be able to call in a few favors and stir up more information than Deirdre had been able to so far. But for the moment, she was stuck.

She watched Tom talking with Nando Avrogado. He seemed to have aged six or seven years overnight. She could always apologize again, but it wouldn't help nearly as much as finding Craig. And she had a feeling she needed to find him before Tom did if she wanted to save her boss from assault charges.

The evening was winding down. The Steinbruners were on their last game, judging from the amount of loud commentary they were throwing out. Around a third of the tables were still occupied, but most of them had already passed on another round. Deirdre gathered up bottles from the empty tables as she watched Nando stroll across the room to check on Chico. She wandered back to the bar and began sliding the bottles into an empty case.

Clem leaned on the bar beside her. "How'd we do?"

Deirdre shrugged. "Okay, I think. Most of the tables were full."

"Tom still pissed at us about opening?"

Deirdre glanced at him. He didn't look mad. All she saw was exhaustion. "I don't think so."

"Damned hard-headed man," Clem muttered. "When is he going to figure out we're all in this together?"

She blew out a breath. "Soon, I think."

Three more men walked out the door. The Steinbruners were putting their cues back into the rack, arguing. She let the sound of their voices wash over her. Background noise at the Faro.

After a moment, she stepped next to Tom. "Walk me home?"

"Sure. Always."

"Stay with me?"

His eyes narrowed as he checked the room. All the customers were gone. Marilyn and Sylvia were gathering up bottles. Chico pushed himself slowly off his stool. Behind the bar, Harry shut down the margarita machine and began to empty the tanks into the plastic tubs for the freezer.

"Please?" Deirdre felt like kicking herself. The last thing he needed right now was a whining female. "I'll make you some supper."

His smile was an echo of the one he'd had before Craig Dempsey had darkened his door, but at least it was still there. "What I want doesn't require any cooking, babe."

She closed her eyes for a moment. Maybe the world was back on track after all. "Well, all right. I can do that too."

She grabbed some glasses from the nearest table, her heart

suddenly considerably lighter than it had been a few moments earlier. In the kitchen, Leon was getting ready for one last load in the dishwasher. He stood, pushing one hand into his pocket. "This yours?"

Deirdre stared at the envelope in his hand. Her name was scrawled across the front. "I've never seen it. Where did it come from?"

"Found it on the floor a minute ago. Over by the door. Maybe somebody pushed it underneath."

The hairs on the back of her neck seemed to do a quick dance. "Was the door locked?"

Leon nodded. "Figured we better keep it locked from now on. Don't want nobody getting in here and doing stuff."

"No," she agreed. "We definitely don't."

Leon picked up a tray and headed back into the main room as she walked toward the door. Through the glass at the top she could see the blank darkness of the back yard. She tore open the envelope.

I have some information you want. If you're interested, meet me out back at midnight. Come alone. I'll wait five minutes, no more.

A friend

Deirdre swallowed. The hairs on her neck did an encore. All day long she'd been asking around town for Craig Dempsey. Maybe somebody knew where he was. They probably wanted money for the information. She had what was left from buying the tables. She could pay, assuming they didn't want too much.

She checked her watch. Eleven fifty-eight. Her pulse pounded in her ears. *Come alone.* But Tom and Chico and Nando would be on the other side of the door. She wouldn't really be alone in the back yard. She dropped the note on the prep table beside her and turned the latch on the door.

It took her only a moment to decide going out there was probably a really bad idea. The warm night air caressed her face. From somewhere on Main she heard the sounds of music, and she could smell night-blooming jasmine. It didn't matter—everything in the yard felt wrong.

She stepped away from the door, straightening her spine. *Come on, Deirdre. You can do this.* "Hello?" she called. "Is anyone there?"

Nothing moved in the darkness around her, but she had the sense of someone else nearby. Or her imagination was working overtime. She stepped farther into the yard. "Hello?"

She sensed rather than heard the movement beside her. A hand grabbed her shoulder, yanking her back against a bony chest. Then another hand clamped across her nose and mouth as she struggled to pull free. She smelled something sharp, acrid, cold against her nose. And then the darkness seemed to coalesce in front of her.

By twelve fifteen, the main room was clean. The customers hadn't done much to dirty it up, and the place had already been thoroughly scrubbed by the time they'd opened for the evening. Tom sent Marilyn and Harry home after a quick twenty minutes of clearing the tables and stacking bottles. Leon unloaded a tray full of clean glasses behind the bar.

Sylvia stood in front of Chico, hands on her hips. "Are you ready to go home, or are you going to be an asshole?"

Chico humphed at her, his arms folded across his chest, his eyes half-closed. Nando leaned back against the bar, clearly enjoying the show.

Tom checked around the room. "Where's Deirdre?"

Leon shrugged. "Kitchen, last I saw."

Tom stepped through the door into the kitchen. "Deirdre?" He stepped farther into the room, half-expecting to see her bending over the dishwasher. The room was thoroughly empty.

The door swung open behind him, and Leon put the empty tray on the counter.

"How long ago did you see her?" Tom asked.

Leon shrugged. "A few minutes. She got a note from somebody."

"A note."

"Yeah. Pushed under the door or something."

Tom walked toward the door to the back yard, his chest clenching tight. He pulled it open and looked out. Darkness. Silence. No Deirdre.

He leaned back into the kitchen. "When did she get this note?"

"I found it on the floor by the door. Gave it to her when she came in."

"Did she say she was going somewhere?"

Leon shook his head. "Didn't say nothing to me. Just told me to keep the door locked."

Tom stared at the door. "It's not locked now."

"Was when I went back to the main room." Leon narrowed his eyes. "I didn't open it."

Tom glanced desperately around the kitchen again. A piece of paper and an envelope lay on one of the prep tables. He picked it up, scanning it quickly, then closed his eyes.

"Shit," he muttered. "Shit, shit, shit. Go get Nando."

Chapter Twenty-Two

Deirdre woke slowly, smelling dust and old grease, aware of a scratchy wool blanket beneath her cheek and an overwhelming desire to vomit. She could hear angry male voices nearby and thought about telling them she needed a bathroom, fast. Then suddenly she remembered—the note, the backyard, the...kidnapping? *What the hell?*

"You used ether?" one of the men was saying. "Sweet Jesus, you could have killed her."

"I knew exactly what I was doing, she wasn't in danger, and you know how I feel about taking the name of the lord in vain. You watch your language around me, Seifert, or else get out."

The voice sounded lethally calm, also faintly familiar. Deirdre wracked her brain, but it seemed immersed in mush. Who was that anyway?

"So when are they supposed to send the ransom?" Man number one, Seifert, sounded slightly subdued. Apparently Mr. Lethal Calm commanded a certain amount of respect.

"Once they find the note and follow the directions, we can set up delivery."

"Set it up?" Seifert's voice had taken on that critical edge again. "You didn't just tell them where to put it?"

"So we could sit there and wait? Use your brain, Seifert. It'll take some time to pull a million bucks together. Even for Brandenburg."

Deirdre's stomach lurched again. She breathed quickly through her nose. *Well, crap.* They wouldn't be happy when they found out her father wasn't around to pull a million bucks together, even if he were so inclined. Which he might not be, given recent events.

"Of course, it could be he'll be open to another solution. One that would be better for us."

"What solution? I thought we were going for the million bucks." Seifert was definitely moving back into dangerous territory again. "A million bucks can buy a lot of ammunition."

"He could join us." The other man's voice had a slight tremor, as if the emotion was getting to him. "He could become our most powerful ally. He could help us achieve freedom for Texas."

Deirdre closed her eyes. All of a sudden she knew exactly who Mr. Lethal Calm was, unfortunately. Her stomach heaved again and she groaned softly.

A footstep sounded behind her and she opened her eyes. Milam Broadus's spectrally tall form was silhouetted in the doorway. He regarded her with an unpleasant smile, showing the full range of his picket fence teeth. "Well, Miss Brandenburg. I see you're finally awake."

Deirdre gave up and vomited on his shoes.

Nando stared down at the note, then the envelope. "Don't suppose you recognize the handwriting."

Tom shook his head, staring around the back yard as if that would tell him something he didn't already know. She was gone. Someone had lured her outside and then taken her away somewhere. While he was inside stacking beer bottles.

He stepped further into the yard, as Nando shone his flashlight around the fence. Deirdre's three café tables and chairs sat where they'd left them. Tom's chest clenched tighter. He'd been going to put them out in the beer garden. Tomorrow. He closed his eyes trying to fight back the red tide of fury and frustration he felt building in his chest. Another thing he should have taken care of and hadn't.

"What the hell is going on here?" Clem stepped through the doorway behind Nando. "It's not enough for him to wreck the place? Now that asshole kidnaps Deirdre too?"

Nando sighed. "Dempsey's a suspect, but we don't know for sure it was him."

"Who else could it have been? Nobody in town has anything against Deirdre. Hell, she's Docia's cousin. Kidnapping her gets the whole Toleffson family on your back."

"Thanks for reminding me. I better call the chief." Nando turned back into the kitchen, pulling his cell from his pocket.

Clem stepped beside Tom. "Damn. Damn, damn, goddamn!" she growled.

He nodded. "Got that right." The evening breeze blew gently through the thin grass of the back yard. Something fluttered at the edge of his vision. He turned and walked to the fence. An envelope was stuck between the boards.

"What is it?" Clem peered over his shoulder.

"Don't know. Go get Nando again. I don't want to touch it until he's here."

Clem disappeared into the kitchen, then reappeared a moment later, towing a disgruntled Nando in her wake. He glanced at the envelope and sighed. "Shit. I don't have my crime scene kit with me. We'll have to wait for the chief so we can get some gloves."

"Screw that." Clem darted back into the kitchen and reappeared with a pair of disposable gloves still in their package. "Dishwashing gloves. Unused. If you won't take it off that fence, Nando, I swear I will."

Nando grimaced, then clicked a quick picture of the envelope with his cell phone. He pulled on the gloves and picked up the envelope.

"Let's go back inside where there's better light." Tom herded Nando and Clem toward the open kitchen door.

Nando borrowed one of Clem's boning knives and carefully pried the envelope open, then slowly unfolded the note inside. Tom peered over his shoulder.

If you want to see Deirdre Brandenburg alive, have one million dollars in non-sequential bills ready in a briefcase by six tomorrow evening. Directions for delivery will follow.

"Oh for Christ's sake," he blurted. "A million bucks? In unmarked, non-sequential bills? Directions to follow? Does this asshole have any idea how many bills he asking for? In a freakin' briefcase?"

"That's not his problem, it's ours. I'll tell the chief. Somebody's going to have to notify her father. And the Feds. Probably won't let him pay the ransom, but he should know what's going on."

"Shit." Tom rubbed his suddenly stinging eyes. "Her father is out of the country. She told me where once, someplace in Eastern Europe. I don't even know if you *can* notify him."

Nando shrugged. "Got to try anyway." He headed for the main room, tucking the note back into its envelope.

"You think Dempsey did this?" Clem asked.

Tom stared down at the prep table. The red tide was rising again. "I don't know. None of this makes any sense."

Clem shrugged. "What doesn't make sense? SOB wants a million. I could use a million myself."

"By kidnapping Deirdre? Hell, Dempsey works for her father. And it's not like he can get away with it—we already know he was behind what happened to the bar. If it's him, the only way he can do this is to grab the money and run fast." He paused, swallowing hard.

"And he'll have to get rid of Deirdre," Clem finished softly. "Because she knows him."

Tom slammed his fist into the dishwasher tray, sending it flying across the counter. "Goddamn it! No. Nobody's going to 'get rid of' Deirdre. I'm not going to let that happen."

"Works for me." Clem nodded. "How do you plan to go about stopping him?"

Tom rested his hands on the counter, bowing his head. Hitting things wouldn't get them anywhere. Besides, it hurt. "It's not Dempsey. It can't be."

"Okay, I'll bite. Why isn't it Dempsey?" Nando leaned against the doorway, watching him. "Chief's heading back into town, by the way. And he'll be calling the sheriff and the Feds, in that order. Kidnapping goes to the FBI. Plus you can expect the Toleffson family to be showing up on your doorstep within the next few hours."

Tom closed his eyes. He had a feeling this might be the last chance he'd have to figure out what was going on before everything spun into chaos. "It's not Dempsey because he'd want more than a million if he decided to do this. He'd lose his job with Brandenburg. He'd have to leave the country. And if he hurt Deirdre..." He paused, drawing in a breath. "If he hurt Deirdre, he'd have a lot of people after him, including me. A million's not enough to take that kind of heat. Besides, the bastard probably already has a million or so of his own. He used to play for the Cowboys."

Nando nodded slowly. "Okay. Doesn't exactly rule him out, but it's worth talking about. If it's not Dempsey, who is it?"

"It has to be somebody who knows who Deirdre is." Clem folded her arms across her chest, considering. "I mean, most people around here just think of her as Deirdre the barmaid. They don't even know her last name. And even the ones who know her last name don't know her daddy's rich. After all, why would she be working here if she had any money?"

Tom shot her a dry look, but Clem shrugged. He knew she was right, unfortunately. "How famous is her father? If people in town knew her name was Brandenburg and she was related to Docia Toleffson, could they put two and two together?"

"Maybe, but it's a stretch." Nando shifted to his other shoulder in the doorway. "I mean Brandenburg's a famous name in Texas because they had part of the OK Ranch out west, that big spread on the Goodnight-Loving Trail. But just because her name was Brandenburg, that wouldn't mean she was part of the famous Brandenburgs. And Docia Toleffson was Docia Kent before she got married, not Docia Brandenburg. Not many people would know Deirdre came from money just from the name alone."

"So who could figure it out?" Clem mused. "Maybe somebody who knew Texas history."

"Somebody could have figured she'd have to have money to be able to open her shop," Nando said. "Maybe somebody she talked to, ordered stuff from. Maybe she told them she'd get money from her father."

Tom shook his head. "No. She's made a point of not getting money from her father, and not saying she was going to. She didn't want anyone to know about him since he walked out of her life. Besides, her biggest investment has been in the shop, and I'm her landlord."

"What about the paint? Cleaning supplies, stuff like that."

"I paid for that. She's improving my property."

"She was going to buy a coffee roaster," Clem cut in. "Those things aren't cheap."

"That wouldn't be from around here," Nando said. "She'd have to order it from someplace like Austin, and people from outside Konigsburg probably wouldn't know what the situation was here—that she was working as a barmaid at the Faro."

"Besides, I don't think she's ordered it yet. She hasn't bought much of anything." Tom felt a prickle at the back of his neck like a small electric shock. "Except..." His hands tightened into fists, almost involuntarily.

"Except?" Nando prompted.

"Except for three café tables and some chairs from that maniac asshole Milam Broadus."

Nando straightened slowly, so did Clem. "Broadus would know all about the Brandenburgs. The SOB acts like he's got Texas history tattooed on his eyelids."

"But would he know Deirdre is one of those Brandenburgs?" Clem shook her head. "I mean, it's not obvious."

"He might know she was Docia's cousin. Deirdre's used her name as a reference sometimes. Since he's such a fanatic about Texas for Texans, he might know the family trees of people in Konigsburg. All the Texans, that is. Those of us from Outside don't count." Tom's chest was suddenly so tight he had trouble drawing in a breath. He figured that pressure would ease when he had his hands around Broadus's throat.

"Okay, hold it." Nando squared his shoulders, suddenly looking a lot more like a cop than he had before. "Maybe it's Broadus and maybe it's not. But this is the end of the investigation as far as you're concerned. From now on it's up to us. There'll be more cops on this than ticks on a buck, local and Federal. You need to keep out of it, Ames."

Tom stared at him, his hands flexing.

"I'm serious. Let us handle this. If you go after Broadus, I swear I'll pick you up and throw you in a cell."

Tom took a breath, forcing his lungs to open. "You're going over to Broadus's place now?"

"Yeah, I'm going over to Broadus's place now. And I'll call the chief and tell him what's up. Stay here, Ames."

Clem put her hand on his arm. "It's okay, Tom. She'll be all right."

Tom wished to god he could believe her. He sank down into one of the kitchen chairs. "Okay. You'll call when you find him?"

"I'll call." Nando jerked his phone from his belt as he

headed for the front door. He was moving quickly, but not as quickly as Tom would have liked.

"Milam Broadus," he growled as soon as Nando had gone, "is a dead man."

Clem nodded. "One way or another. Of course, Deirdre may kill him before you can get there."

Deirdre wasn't sure how a kidnapping was supposed to proceed, but she was pretty sure Broadus's way wasn't standard. For one thing, he hadn't tied her up or blindfolded her. Not that she wasn't grateful, but that might not bode particularly well for her future if Seifert had anything to say about it.

On the other hand, Broadus didn't seem to be considering things like ending up in prison for the rest of his life with her as the star witness against him. Maybe he was counting on Stockholm Syndrome to make her a willing accomplice. *Fat chance.*

He followed Seifert into the room after sunrise when he brought her a tray with a bowl of Rice Krispies and a glass of orange juice that she suspected was actually Tang. "I apologize for taking you hostage, Miss Brandenburg. It was necessary."

"Hostage?" Deirdre took a bite of Rice Krispies. The milk tasted like nothing she'd ever had before. She managed not to choke.

"The thing is, we've had a hard time spreading the word. If real Texans knew about the Texas Secession Initiative, we'd be swamped with recruits. But the Lamestream Media won't get the news out if it hasn't been approved by the usurpers in Austin and Washington. Once we have the money from your father, we can get our manifesto published without their censorship. In fact, that's part of the delivery instructions—our manifesto goes on the front page of the *Dallas Morning News.*"

Deirdre licked her lips. "So you kidnapped me for publicity?"

Broadus frowned. "We took you hostage to make sure our message gets out. That's not 'publicity'. That's a public service."

"But aren't you also asking my father for money?" Deirdre gave him her most guileless look, the one that usually worked on accountants whose figures were suspect.

"We need money. Your father can give it to us. Your friend told me so. And after he understands our cause, could be he'll join us too. The Brandenburgs have a big part in Texas history. Now's the time for Texas patriots to join together."

Deirdre thought of all the Federal contracts currently being run by Brandenburg, Inc. She really doubted her father would be interested in seceding from the United States. But Broadus had said something interesting. "What friend of mine did you speak to?"

Broadus shrugged. "Don't know his name. Big fella. Well dressed. Looked like a football player. Saw you and Ames together and said your father would put a stop to that. You know who I mean?"

Okay, Craig Dempsey was definitely going to be suffering grievous bodily injuries if Deirdre had anything to say about it. "That's my friend from Dallas. He once played for the Cowboys. He might be someone you could recruit to your cause." She fluttered her eyelashes at Broadus, then glanced at Seifert. *Oops.*

Seifert clearly wasn't up for being charmed. His beefy arms were folded across his considerable belly and he regarded her through narrowed eyes. "She oughta have a blindfold, at least," he snarled. "So she can't say it's us. And you oughta tie her to that chair so she can't get loose."

Broadus's mouth became a thin line. "Seifert, we're citizens of the Republic of Texas. We treat ladies with respect. We don't need a blindfold or ropes." He turned back to Deirdre. "Will you give me your word of honor not to abuse my hospitality?"

"Of course." She gave him a tiny smile, wishing she could cross her fingers behind her back. "Word of honor."

Seifert shot her a narrow look. "You believe in secession, Missy? You on our side?"

"Oh, I'm not political at all," she said quickly. She pushed the abominable cereal away and sipped the Tang.

"A true lady lets her menfolk do the heavy thinking," Broadus agreed. "Although I'll give you some of our literature. You can read it over, and then I can explain all the things you don't understand."

Deirdre nodded. "Yes, thank you—that probably would be

the best way to do it."

"Still seems like she oughta be blindfolded," Seifert muttered. "And tied up."

"Seifert, I've told you. We do not tie up ladies."

Seifert muttered something that sounded like "work in a bar".

Broadus scowled at him. "What was that?"

"I said I don't know no ladies that work in a bar. 'Specially not a bar like the Faro. What kind of lady serves beer to drunks?"

Broadus turned toward her, raising an eyebrow. "He's got a point, Miss Brandenburg. What were you doing there?"

Think fast, Deirdre! "My father wanted me to experience...real life. Before I settled down and got married, that is. So I'd learn to appreciate money. And the working man. And how tough it can be to make a living. Before the government takes it all away in taxes." She knew she was babbling, but she was trying to find the right buzzwords. For a moment a totally incongruous picture of Tom floated through her mind, naked from the waist up, pale golden hair glowing in the lamp light. A working man, who'd had a tough life. *And now these morons are making it tougher.*

Broadus frowned. "Well, it's a good thing your father was trying to teach you about freedom and true Americans, but why did he want you to work in a bar?"

Deirdre shook her head quickly. "Oh he didn't choose my job. I chose it myself. I guess I was a little...naïve. I thought it was like being a waitress."

Broadus gave her an indulgent smile that made her skin crawl. "Well then your daddy shouldn't have let you go to Konigsburg by yourself. He should have come down and helped you find a job in the right kind of place. You could have worked for us, for example. We know how to treat ladies."

Deirdre blew out a breath. "Yes. That might have been better all around." She put her glass back on the tray.

Seifert picked the tray up again, watching her with cold gray eyes. "So we're just gonna leave her here? Like this?"

Broadus shrugged. "Yes we are. I'm going to lock the door, Miss Brandenburg. And you're on the second floor with quite a drop to the ground. I wouldn't try going out the window if I was you. Probably break a leg if you do. And then I'd have to tie you up, like Seifert says." He gave her another indulgent smile.

Deirdre suddenly felt like kicking him. She wondered how much damage her sneakers could do. If only she were wearing the high heels she wore when she worked at Brandenburg, Inc.

Broadus nodded toward the door, and his minion carried the tray outside. He paused in the doorway, still smiling. "You take care now, Miss Brandenburg. I'll bring you those leaflets in a little while."

"Yes, you do that," Deirdre said between her teeth. She listened to the sound of the key turning in the door. There was no latch on the inside. At least Broadus had managed to think ahead that far.

She walked to the window, noting the chamber pot under the bed and the pitcher and basin on the dresser. All the comforts of the nineteenth century home. Unfortunately, it looked like Broadus was being accurate. The ground was a good twenty feet away and the bed had only a single thin wool blanket—not nearly enough for an effective escape ladder.

She gritted her teeth, folding her arms across her chest. At least in a battle of wits, she clearly had the edge over those two doofuses. Now if she could only figure out how to use it.

Chapter Twenty-Three

Waiting for Nando's call made Tom's shoulders itch. He sent Clem home, over her protests, then sat alone at the bar, nursing a bottle of Shiner. It occurred to him that he'd been doing exactly the same thing the night before, only he'd also been watching Deirdre sweep up glass. And then, like a moron, he'd refused to stay with her.

He wanted a do-over. Hell, he wanted a do-over for the whole week.

Ham Linklatter, the dumbest of the Konigsburg cops, arrived at some point to examine the yard. He took away several plastic evidence bags full of stuff Tom was reasonably sure had nothing to do with Deirdre or her kidnapper.

He stepped outside to watch the sun inch up over the horizon, casting Main in pale light. Then he went back to his seat and dozed for maybe an hour, before giving up and dialing Nando's number.

"What?" he snapped after five rings.

"Did you find her?"

"No. Broadus's store is locked up tight. No sign of anybody around."

"What about his house?"

"He lives over his store. Nobody's home."

"But..."

"Look, Broadus is still up there on the suspect list. So is Dempsey. We're also checking for outsiders, maybe from Houston. Anybody suspicious. The Feds are trying to locate her father. If anything else happens, I'll let you know."

The sound of the disconnect in his ear was like a pistol

shot. Tom stared down at the phone, ordering himself not to throw it against the wall. After a short period of deep breathing and extreme obscenities, he headed into the kitchen to see if Clem had any coffee lying around.

Coffee. If Deirdre opened her shop, they'd have good coffee around all day. *When* Deirdre opened her shop...

Goddamn son of a bitch. He poured coffee grounds into a filter, then put in water and turned the pot on. As he headed back to the main room, he heard the front door open as Chico walked in. At least he wasn't limping. Much.

"Why the fuck didn't you call me?" he growled.

Tom decided not to pretend he didn't know what he was talking about. Chico didn't look like he'd appreciate it. "Nothing you could do. Nothing any of us can do. Broadus has taken off and nobody knows where he is."

"You sure it's Broadus who's got her?"

Tom nodded slowly. "I am. Nando isn't. Or anyway, he says he isn't. But I've got a gut feeling about this. It's definitely Broadus."

"So let's go get the asshole."

"If I knew where he was, I would. Nando said the cops raided his store and the place where he lives upstairs, but he wasn't there."

Chico shrugged. "So-and-so must have some place around here to meet with that bunch of crackers he hangs out with. Find out where it is."

"You know any of them?"

Chico frowned. Tom didn't figure he and Broadus's friends hung out together, judging from Broadus's oft-stated intention to send anybody with a Mexican-sounding name back to Mexico, whether or not they came from there. "We could check out the Dew Drop or the Silver Spur, see if anybody knows Broadus's friends."

Tom shook his head. "We wouldn't exactly be welcome in either place. And I don't figure they'd talk to us. Plus they'd probably just turn us in to Nando." He rubbed a hand across the back of his neck, frowning. He and Chico wouldn't be welcome, but that didn't go for other people. He flipped open his phone and dialed.

Docia picked up on the second ring. "Tom. Have you heard

from her?"

He closed his eyes. "No. Not yet. Look I need your help. Well, maybe more like Cal's help. Or Lars. If they can do it without letting the chief know, and maybe not the county attorney either."

There was a pause on the other end of the line. "Okay, you've got my attention. What are you planning?"

Tom laid out the case against Broadus quickly, managing not to use too many obscenities as he did. On the other hand, Docia didn't seem to be much upset about an obscenity or three.

"Holy shit! That asshole Broadus is behind this? I'll skin him alive when I find him."

"You'll have to get in line," Tom said dryly. "And we have to find him first. Could Cal and Lars ask around in the Dew Drop and the Silver Spur? And maybe some of the other places around town? See if they can find out who Broadus hangs out with? If we know who his buddies are, maybe they can tell us where their secret clubhouse is." With the right persuasion, of course, which he and Chico would be pleased to provide.

Docia sighed. "The brothers may not want to do it if it means not telling Erik or Pete, but that doesn't mean I can't do it myself. And I know some people who'll help and who won't tell Pete or Erik. He's a great chief of police, but he'd want us to butt out."

"Yeah, I got that impression." Tom rubbed his eyes. "Thanks Docia."

"No problem. Just make sure you keep in touch."

"You too."

"So?" Chico narrowed his eyes.

"They'll work on it."

Clem pushed the front door open so hard that it almost crashed back against the wall. "Anything?"

"Not yet."

"Shit."

"Why are you here, Clemencia? There's nothing you can do."

Clem put her hands on her hips. "Yes there is. I can make lunch. If we could open last night, we can open for lunch today. Particularly if the guy shows up to fix the window."

Tom gazed around the room. He'd almost forgotten about opening the Faro and cleaning up after the riot. Other things were suddenly more important.

"We can't just stop because of this, Tom," she said gently. "Let's get the place fixed up and running before she comes back."

After a moment, he nodded. "Yeah. Let's do that."

The glass repairman showed up an hour later and spent the rest of the morning reinstalling the front window. The air conditioning had to be turned off, but the light made things inside more pleasant. Bobby Sue and Leon shuffled in an hour or so after Clem, then had several whispered consultations with Chico. Tom figured they were getting the news about Deirdre. Bobby Sue looked shocked, or as shocked as someone who was normally expressionless could look. Leon just went back to sweeping.

The lunch crowd was small, but at least they had one. Tom took up the slack for Deirdre, serving iced tea and coffee along with the occasional beer, and bringing Bobby Sue's orders out from the kitchen.

Around one thirty, the door opened and Tom watched three striking women walk into his bar—a statuesque redhead, a slender blonde with hair like tarnished gold, and a pixyish brunette. Docia and her sisters-in-law, Jess and Janie Toleffson. None of them were smiling. Tom did a mental head slap. These were the people Docia had used to try to trace Broadus?

Docia shook her head. "Don't worry. We didn't tell the guys what we were doing. We didn't even tell Morgan since she might have divided loyalties on this one. They'll all find out, of course, but by then we'll have found her. Knock wood." She rapped her knuckles on the bar.

Jess Toleffson pulled up a bar stool and sat down, pushing her wispy golden hair out of her eyes. "Unfortunately, we didn't have much luck," she said. "I took the Silver Spur lunch crowd, and Docia tried the Dew Drop, but nobody in there knew anything about Broadus. Except he's a jerk, which we knew already."

Janie leaned against the bar experimentally, resting one foot on the brass rail. "From what I heard he's pretty much a Puritan. Doesn't drink or smoke or take up with wild women."

She grimaced. "Not that Deirdre would qualify. But he probably wouldn't show up at the Dew Drop or the Silver Spur."

Tom drummed his fingers against the bar as he thought. "Restaurants, then. Particularly ones that don't serve booze. Only probably not the Coffee Corral, since Al Brosius keeps that signed picture of Obama next to the cash register."

"He might have gone to Allie's, but given Broadus's views on Latinas, maybe not." Docia rolled her eyes. "And my guess is he's even less sympathetic to gays, which means he'd avoid Lee and Ken at Brenner's."

"I talked to a few of the people at the franchise places on the highway, not that I can picture Broadus in McDonald's either," Janie said. "But none of them have seen him. I also checked some of the local places like Floyd's and the barbeque out on Highway 16, but no luck."

Tom smacked his hand flat in frustration. "Jesus, where else is there? Where the hell would the man hang out?"

Across the room, he saw Bobby Sue pause, staring at them. Her eyes widened. He wondered if she was upset by all the cussing.

Docia sighed. "I'll call Allie. Even if she doesn't know anything about Broadus herself, she might be able to think of somebody who does. If she comes up with anyone, I'll check them out and get back to you."

Tom nodded. "Okay. As soon as we're finished here, I'll hit the street myself and see if I can stir anything up."

"Right." Jess pushed herself upright again. "We'll check around at a few of the used furniture stores too. Maybe Broadus's competitors know something about him."

He sighed. "Thanks. Good hunting."

"You too."

Tom glanced at Bobby Sue again, but she was back to serving her tables.

By two, the room was empty. Leon moved across the floor, sweeping up and collecting dirty dishes. Bobby Sue walked across to the bar, leaning forward so that Tom could hear her soft voice. "Y'all lookin' for that Milam Broadus fella?"

Tom's pulse accelerated slightly. He told himself to cool it. "Yeah. He's not at his store, and we need to find him."

"You think he's the one took Deirdre away last night?"

Tom nodded again. "Looks like it."

Bobby Sue's jaw squared and she turned back toward the room, looking for her son. "Leon? Get over here."

Leon stared at her for a moment, then leaned his push broom against the nearest table. "What's up, Ma?"

Bobby Sue suddenly looked like a woman who specialized in taking no prisoners. For the first time, Tom believed she wasn't exactly a pushover for Leon and his schemes. "You know where that miserable son of a bitch Milam Broadus holes up out in the country, don't you? You tell Tom where he is right now."

Leon gave Tom a hunted look, then dropped his gaze to the floor. "I don't hang out with them no more."

"But you did." Bobby Sue's voice was relentless. "Once upon a time, you did. And it wasn't that long ago, neither."

"But..."

Tom grasped the edge of the bar to keep from grabbing him by the throat.

Chico didn't restrain himself. He took hold of the back of Leon's shirt, hoisting him in the air until his toes were dangling. "Where the hell is Broadus, Leon? You tell us now, and I don't punch you in the face."

Leon whimpered, and Chico shook him gently, like a dog shaking a puppy.

"I didn't have nothin' to do with this, so help me," Leon whined. "I wouldn't hurt Deirdre. I ain't talked to Broadus for a couple months."

"So just tell us where you used to meet him. No skin off your nose. And we can go find out if Deirdre's there." Tom nodded at Chico, who dropped Leon back on the floor.

"Up in the hills," he panted. "Back beyond Powell's ranch. He's got an old house up there. Used to belong to his family."

Tom leaned forward. "How do we get there, Leon? What road?"

"I don't know exactly. They'd blindfold us before we went up there—Broadus's got this thing about keeping the place secret. Thinks the Feds'll come after him."

"So how do you know it was beyond Powell's place?" Chico rumbled, his face dark.

"Wasn't much of a blindfold, tell you the truth. I could see under it if I tipped my head. You go up on that road that runs by Powell's pasture for a couple miles or so, then you turn off on a road to the house. Don't know what it's called or nothin', but there's a big bunch of prickly pear and an old pump right where you turn."

Tom threw down his bar towel and headed for the door, Chico at his heels.

"Wait a minute," Clem called, "I'm coming with you."

Tom turned, stepping to the side so Chico didn't run into him. "No."

Clem narrowed her eyes, her chin rising mutinously. She balled up her apron and tossed in on a chair. "Yes."

"No, Clem. I need you to stay here and be the contact person. Also to make sure Dempsey doesn't show up, or if he does to call the cops."

Clem grimaced, then shrugged. "Hell. Okay."

"Give us twenty minutes," Tom said. "Then call Nando. Tell him where we're going and that I hope he'll head up there too."

Clem's lips spread in a dry grin. "You think that's going to keep him from throwing you in the slammer?"

"Maybe. At this point, I don't really give a shit."

Chico hit the door, and the two of them trotted for Tom's truck.

In the few hours Deirdre had spent at Broadus's hideout, she'd learned two things. First, that Broadus was just as loopy as everyone thought he was. He'd dropped more than a few hints about what he'd do with the million dollars from her father, most involving the establishment of the Republic of Texas with Broadus himself at the head. He was so optimistic about the future of his own little nation-state that Deirdre almost felt sorry for him. Not that she wouldn't have pushed him out the window anyway if she'd had half a chance.

The second thing she'd learned was that Seifert was a complete loss as a minion. And that he was considerably more dangerous than Broadus.

Broadus left the house around noon, claiming he was going to leave instructions for the delivery of the million dollars. Deirdre wasn't sure where he was going to leave them or for whom since her father was nowhere near Konigsburg, but she didn't argue.

She'd checked the room out thoroughly by then and hadn't found much that could help her get away from the house. She'd decided she needed to get downstairs somehow. Maybe there she'd find a few more opportunities for escape.

Unlike Broadus, Seifert didn't leave her alone in her room. He paced back and forth from the window to the door while Broadus walked out to his truck and drove away, glancing in her direction every few moments. Deirdre considered asking him to take her downstairs for a bathroom break, but he didn't look like he'd be all that accommodating.

He paced to the window one more time and turned, staring at her with narrowed eyes. "You," he said. "Up."

"What?"

"Stand up?"

"Why?"

It seemed like a reasonable question to Deirdre, but apparently not to Seifert. He stomped toward her, balling his hands in fists. "Because I said so, bitch. Now get up."

Deirdre considered reminding him of Broadus's opinions on the treatment of ladies, but she had a feeling Seifert didn't share them. And he was bigger and stronger than she was. She stood up, and let him shove her through the door, then herd her down the stairs.

They paused at the bottom as she got her first view of the rest of the house. Not that there was much to see—living room, dining room, kitchen, all of them without any visible charm.

Seifert pushed her into the living room, toward a couch upholstered in faded plaid. The walls were papered in pale stripes of what might once have been flowers but now looked more like inkblots. A fireplace with built-in bookcases filled one wall.

Broadus had loaded the shelves with more dusty antiques. Deirdre did a quick survey, hoping for some guns or at least a bayonet, but all she saw were ancient cloudy bottles, a few buttons and coins, and some round things that looked like rocks but probably weren't.

"Broadus may think it's okay to let you run around loose, but if I was kidnapped and I had a chance to walk out, no word of honor would keep me from doing it." Seifert nodded at an ancient rocker in the corner. "Sit down there."

Deirdre took a quick breath. "My father will pay you if you let me go. Whatever Broadus has promised you, my father will pay you more."

Seifert gave her an unpleasant grin. Apparently, dental hygiene was not one of his strong points any more than it was with Broadus. "Broadus is paying me a million. Only he don't know it yet. Course he won't be around to watch neither."

Terrific. Crazy as Broadus was, Deirdre had a feeling he was preferable to Seifert. "My father will give you more."

Seifert's grin turned to a grimace. "No he won't. All he'll give me is a quick trip to Huntsville. Now sit down, Missy. I got stuff to do, and I don't want you wandering around the house while I do it."

His gaze slid down her body, leaving a track of invisible slime, and Deirdre's nerves went on high alert. Being tied up around Seifert suddenly seemed like a very dangerous proposition.

She edged toward the fireplace. "Why can't I just go back upstairs? You can lock the door again. I can't get out."

Seifert's face darkened. "You don't hear so good. I told you to sit down." He stepped toward her, reaching for her shoulder.

Deirdre dodged away from him, moving sideways.

Seifert growled and grabbed again, one hand grazing her shoulder. "C'mere bitch. I got some plans for you."

Deirdre jerked to the side, trying to pull away from him as his fingers fastened on the back of her neck, yanking her forward. And then Seifert jammed his mouth against hers, his teeth grinding against her lips.

She fought the wave of nausea that hit her along with Seifert's breath, although vomiting in his face had a certain appeal. His fingers dug into her buttocks, jamming her pelvis against his as he tried to stick his tongue in her mouth.

Deirdre fumbled frantically along the fireplace shelves behind her, knocking over bottles and buttons before fastening onto one of the round rocks. It was surprisingly heavy. She brought it up swiftly and slammed it into the side of Seifert's head.

He staggered back staring at her with furious eyes. She

struck him again on the temple, as hard as she could. The rock cracked open in her hand and she realized it was hollow. Hollow or not, however, it seemed to be solid enough to do the job. Seifert's knees buckled beneath him, and he collapsed slowly to the floor.

Deirdre closed her eyes for a moment, catching her breath. Her stomach was still roiling, but she ignored it as she tossed the remains of the rock to the floor beside Seifert. No time to be sick—time to get out of there.

Behind her, the front door crashed open. She turned to see the elongated figure of Milam Broadus standing in the doorway like one of the aliens in *Close Encounters*. "Woman," he roared, "what have you done?"

Chapter Twenty-Four

Broadus pointed to the remains of the rock Deirdre had used on Seifert. "That," he intoned, "was a cast iron cannon ball fired at the Battle of the Alamo. You just destroyed a priceless historic artifact."

"Wasn't much of a cannon ball if it fell apart when it hit something," Deirdre snapped, edging back toward the shelves again. "And it was better that than being raped by your buddy."

Broadus sucked in a breath. "That's a lie. Seifert is a citizen of the Republic of Texas. He would never dishonor a lady. Of course—" his mouth contracted to a sneer, "—you're obviously no lady."

"Obviously." She glanced back at the shelves, keeping Seifert's body between Broadus and herself. "What else have you got here, Mr. Broadus?" She slid her hand along another shelf. "Any other priceless historic artifacts?"

Broadus's face paled. "Get away from there!"

Her fingers closed on a piece of china and she darted to the side when he took a step toward her. "Looks like a plate. No name on the back, but I guess not all antique plates have them, right? Blue willow ware, I'd say. Gee, is that a picture of the Alamo?"

"Put that down," he snarled.

"Not right now. I promise I'll put it down fifty yards from your house, provided you step aside and let me out the front door. Otherwise, I might have to throw it against that wall."

Broadus's face transformed from pale to the color of eggplant in a matter of seconds. "You're a fifth-generation Texan. How can you destroy your own heritage?"

"I'm a fifth-generation Texan who wants to get the fuck out of this house. Now what's it gonna be, Mr. Broadus, me or this plate?"

Seifert moaned, and Broadus glanced at him. "Boone? Are you awake?"

"Seifert won't be waking up for a while yet," Deirdre said, hoping devoutly that she was telling the truth. "No help there. Now get away from the door."

Broadus balanced on his tiptoes, clearly trying to decide whether the plate meant more to him than his potential million dollars. She tightened her grip on the plate's edge, ready to let it fly if he took a step closer.

Suddenly Broadus himself flew through the air in front of her. For one odd moment, she wondered if he was a lot more physically fit than she'd thought. Taking a leap like that was really something for a man his age.

And then Tom was charging through the door after Broadus, planting one knee in the middle of his chest and clenching his hands around his throat. "Give me one good reason not to push your nose through to the other side of your head," he growled.

Chico stepped into the room behind him, staring down at the prone figure of Seifert. He turned back to Deirdre. "You do this?"

She nodded, carefully replacing the plate on the shelf.

Chico's smile reminded her of a proud parent regarding his offspring's latest accomplishment. "Good work."

Broadus had begun to squeak under Tom's squeezing hands. His words were largely incoherent, but Deirdre thought she heard "stop", "murder", and "outrage" in no particular order. His face was back to eggplant again. She stepped forward and placed a hand on Tom's shoulder. "Maybe you should loosen your grip."

"Not a chance," Tom growled.

Outside there was the sound of squealing brakes, followed by heavy footsteps on the porch. Chief Toleffson appeared in the doorway, with Nando close behind him.

"Let him go, Ames." The chief's voice sounded deceptively calm. Deirdre watched a muscle dance in his jaw.

Tom glanced up at him, then down at Broadus again. He

stood slowly, only releasing the man's throat at the last moment. Then he turned to Deirdre. "Are you all right?"

Deirdre licked her lips. She wanted to be civilized, sophisticated, blasé. After all, it was only a small, unsuccessful kidnapping.

Then Tom opened his arms, and she threw herself against him. At least she managed not to sniffle. His arms closed tight around her, pulling her in against the hard muscles of his chest. She felt the whisper of his lips brushing her forehead. "It's okay," he murmured. "You're okay now."

Toleffson sighed. "Okay, let's gather up these two miserable excuses for criminals and get them back to town. Whole lot of law enforcement types want to talk to them, once they figure out who's got jurisdiction."

Broadus sat up, his eyes regaining some of their old snap. "I am a citizen of the Republic of Texas. I recognize no law but theirs."

"I'm sure the Rangers will be delighted to hear that, seeing as how they're currently fighting with the Feds over who gets to nail you to the wall." Nando jerked Broadus to his feet, fastening his hands behind him.

Seifert groaned again, and Toleffson glanced down at him. "Who's this? And who's responsible for putting him out of commission?"

"I am," Deirdre mumbled against Tom's chest. "His name's Seifert. He tried to...get familiar with me."

She felt Tom's chest muscles stiffen beneath her cheek. She put a hand on his arm. "It's okay. I took care of it. I hit him with a cannonball."

He stared down at her, his forehead furrowed. He looked as if he might like to check her for concussion.

Nando kicked a piece of crumpled metal on the floor next to Seifert's prone body, grinning. "Oh man. He's going to have a hell of a time living this down. Very nicely done, Ms. Brandenburg."

"Put him in the car with Broadus," the chief rumbled. "He'll probably need a stop at the hospital—we can call ahead so Friesenhahn has a deputy waiting to keep him in custody. We'll get all of this sorted out when we get back in town."

He turned back to Tom and Deirdre. "Okay, Ames, given

the way this turned out, I'm not going to haul you in, although I ought to throw you in a cell for obstructing my investigation. Now go back to Konigsburg and see if you can stay out of my sight for the rest of the week."

Deirdre heard Tom sigh as he rubbed his cheek against her hair. "Okay, babe, let's head back down. Clem's waiting to hear that you're okay, along with everybody else at the Faro."

"I said you could go back to the Faro, Ames, not Ms. Brandenburg." The chief's voice had an undercurrent of steel.

Deirdre glanced up at him. "Are you arresting me?"

For a moment, the chief looked like he was on the verge of a grin, then he shook his head. "No ma'am, I'd say Seifert got just what was coming to him. But you're the one at the center of this thing. We need you to tell a whole bunch of people what happened so they can sort out what to do with that sorry pair of assholes. Then you can go work the dinner shift at the Faro if you want to, although I'd advise you to go home and get some rest."

"I'll drive her," Tom said in a clipped voice. The pressure of his arms around her shoulders was almost painful.

The chief turned toward him, unsmiling. "No, you won't. She'll ride down with us."

"In the same car with Broadus and his buddy? I don't think so. Better she rides with me and Chico."

"She can ride in front."

Deirdre licked her lips. "I'd really like to ride with Tom, Chief, if that's all right with you."

Tom and the chief stared at each other for another moment. Then Toleffson shrugged. "You can follow us. But no stops along the way. She comes straight to the station."

Tom peered down at her. "Okay with you?"

"Okay. I'm not sure I'll be awake when we get there, though." Deirdre blew out a breath. Suddenly, she felt so tired she would have slumped if Tom hadn't kept his arms around her.

Tom glanced up at the chief again. "Do you have to have her now?"

Toleffson sighed. "Yes, Ames, I have to have her now. But I'll let her go as soon as I can. Now everybody get a move on so we can get this production underway."

In the end, Tom sat in the parking lot at the police station. Toleffson wouldn't let him inside, but he wouldn't leave without Deirdre. In fact, he couldn't leave without her—something inside wouldn't let him. Harry and Chico opened the bar for the evening, with some help from Clem. According to Clem's texts, Sylvia was being a pain in the ass, but Tom didn't figure that was anything new. He slid down in his seat and closed his eyes for a few minutes that turned into a couple of hours. Finally, he woke when somebody knocked on his window.

Nando stood outside, grinning. "You ready to take her home, Ames?"

He'd been ready since he'd seen her standing across from Broadus, holding a plate in her hand like a Frisbee. He'd never been so close to killing somebody before—Broadus's throat had felt like a toothpick. One good squeeze, and he'd have been history. It was only Deirdre's soft hand on his shoulder that had stopped him from doing it.

Tom blew out a breath and pushed his door open.

Deirdre looked like she was one step away from being dead on her feet. Her eyes were at half-mast, and her skin was the color of library paste. Tom put his arm around her shoulders. "C'mon. We'll go to my place. Doris is pining for you again."

She winced slightly. "How can you tell?"

"Her beady little eyes take on a reminiscent gleam every time your name is mentioned."

"Probably hunger."

"Maybe. I can take care of that too—in your case, anyway. Clem said she sent over some quesadillas."

Deirdre yawned. "Good, I'm starving. But I think I want to take a shower before I do anything else. I can still smell Broadus's house on my clothes. Maybe we should stop at my place first so I can change."

Tom had no intention of taking her anywhere but to his house. "Don't worry. I'll get you something while you shower."

Tom called Docia while Deirdre took the longest shower in history. Or maybe it just seemed that way.

"Erik told us what happened. Is she okay?"

"Tired. Shaken up. But okay overall."

"Do you need anything?"

He hesitated. "She'll need some clothes. I brought her to my house and all she's got are the ones she was wearing when Broadus...took her away."

"I'll be there in twenty minutes," Docia said firmly.

Actually, it was more like fifteen. Docia handed him a pair of jeans and a blouse along with some underwear. "They're mine from pre-baby days, but she should be able to wear them for tonight if she rolls the pants up. Thanks, Tom. For everything."

He sighed. "It was my pleasure, believe me."

The clothes might have been from Docia's pre-baby days, but they were still big enough to give Deirdre lots of room. She rolled up the cuffs of the jeans and the sleeves of the blouse, then sat at his kitchen table. He watched her eat three of Clem's quesadillas along with a glass of iced tea. He himself had never felt less hungry in his life. He figured it was the adrenaline, which would probably wear off sometime in the middle of the night. Except, of course, it was already the middle of the night, or close to it.

"Did anything else happen at the Faro?" Deirdre raised an eyebrow.

"Anything else...?"

"With Craig, I mean."

Tom sighed. Amazingly enough, he'd forgotten all about Craig Dempsey. Maybe that was one thing he could thank Broadus for. "No. It's been quiet. Well, not quiet exactly. We were all worried about you."

"How did you find me anyway?"

Tom rubbed his eyes and told her about Clem and how they'd figured out it couldn't be Craig who'd kidnapped her and about Bobby Sue and Leon.

Deirdre's brow furrowed. "Leon's one of Broadus's supporters?"

"Not anymore, he says. He and some other guys around town used to hang out with him, but Leon says he scared them off when he, and I quote, 'went nutsy on us'."

She sighed. "Thank god for his lousy blindfold."

"I'd have found you anyway. One way or another, I'd have found you."

Deirdre's lips trembled. "It's really strange. I wasn't scared while it was happening. I kept thinking I'd been kidnapped by F-Troop. The weird thing is I'm scared now. Thinking back. About the way things could have turned out." She rubbed a hand across her mouth, eyes bright. "Stupid, I know."

Tom reached for her, pulling her into his lap. "Not stupid. Hell, it still scares me when I think about what could have happened."

Deirdre pulled back slightly, staring up into his eyes. "Let's go see Doris."

"Right." He grinned. "We can see her on the way."

"On the way where?"

"Where do you think?"

Tom's bedroom was dark except for the reflected light from the lamp shining in Doris's cage in the living room. When Deirdre reached for the light switch, he caught her hand.

"Leave it. For tonight, I want it dark."

She wrapped her arms around his neck pulling herself against his body again, his warmth, his arousal. He slid his lips along the edge of her throat, nipping the delicate skin at the base, and she sighed against him. *What if it had all gone wrong? What if I'd never had the chance to touch him again?* She drew a shuddering breath. *What if...?*

"I would have found you," he whispered against her hair. "Wherever they took you, I would have found you. So help me, Deirdre. I would have brought you back."

She slid her hands to his waist, feeling the slight indentation of his hip bones beneath her palms. Then she raised her gaze to his ice blue eyes, dim in the evening light. "I believe you. You're the most reliable man I know, Tom Ames."

His breath puffed against her cheek, and then he took her mouth, his tongue sliding deep as he buried his fingers in her hair.

He moved her toward the bed, his hands busy unbuttoning and sliding inside her clothes. Clothes she suddenly didn't want to be wearing. She felt the mattress against the back of her legs as Tom jerked her blouse over her head. And then they were down, side-by-side.

She pulled at his denim shirt, her fingers suddenly clumsy with the buttons. "Damn it, damn it, damn it!"

"It's okay." He chuckled softly. "I'll get it."

She watched him pull off his shirt and pants in the moonlight, his dusky figure almost dreamlike. A pain started somewhere low in her belly, the pull of wanting him. The pain of what had almost happened. She reached her arms toward him, and he moved into her embrace, reaching down to pull off her jeans, leaving only the bikini panties she'd gotten from Docia. She reached for them, then found herself bunching the sides in her hands and yanking. The sound of ripping silk seemed unnaturally loud, but the tearing cloth seemed to release something inside her.

Tom reached down, taking the remnants of silk from her hands and tossing them over the side of the bed. "Sorry. That's all the underwear she brought."

"I'll go commando."

His teeth flashed white in the darkness. "Works for me."

He cupped her breasts in his hands, his lips brushing along the top in light, whispering kisses. Then he was sliding down her body, lips and tongue leaving a burning line from her collarbone to her abdomen. Deirdre arched her back, rubbing herself against him. He parted her folds, then leaned over her, warm breath, warm tongue against her center, sending arrows of pleasure that was almost pain.

She twisted on the bed, reaching for him, but he brought his mouth down again, sucking hard against her. She cried out, her voice raw in her throat, as the waves swept over her. He traveled up her body again, tongue sliding around her navel and up, lips fastening on one nipple, while his fingers pinched hard against the other.

"Please," she gasped. "Oh, please. Now."

She slid her fingers into his hair, pulling his mouth to hers, plunging her tongue deep. *Please, please, please* seemed to thump along with her pulse.

Another moment and he was fumbling to sheathe himself, then sliding inside her. She wrapped her legs around his waist, pushing him hard, trying to drive him deeper. His breath rattled in her ear, as he thrust harder against her, touching deep inside.

Deirdre heard herself make a sound she was pretty sure she'd never made before in her life as the wave of heat and light washed over her. Above her, Tom cried out too, burying his face in the crook of her shoulder, his teeth nipping on the fine skin at the base of her throat.

She wrapped her arms around his shoulders, holding him tight against her, as the small shocks still coursed through her body.

I might have missed this. I might never have felt this again.

She ran her hand along the back of his head, feeling the slight prickle of his hair against her palm. She might have missed it all. But she hadn't. And she was tired of feeling like a damsel in distress.

"Did I remember to thank you?" she murmured.

"For...?"

"Showing up when you did. You and Chico riding to the rescue."

Tom's grin flashed again in the darkness. "We didn't do all that much. You did a pretty good job of rescuing yourself."

Deirdre folded her arms above her head, closing her eyes. "I did, didn't I? That was sort of cool."

"That was very cool." Tom leaned down to kiss her breast, running his tongue across her nipple.

"You know, I don't think I could have done that when I first got to Konigsburg." She slid a fingertip down the slope of his nose. "And that's definitely something I have to thank you for."

He rolled onto his back, pulling her over on top of him. "Glad to oblige."

"Now we just need to take care of Craig and my father and everything will be fine."

A shadow seemed to pass across his face. "One problem at a time, Deirdre."

"Don't tell me something else happened?"

Tom closed his eyes. "Could we go back to what we were doing? Much more enjoyable."

She ran her tongue down his chest, pausing to dip into his navel. "My turn to be glad to oblige. Believe me. Very glad."

Above her his lips spread into a slow smile and she drew a line of kisses down his body.

Chapter Twenty-Five

Tom hated to admit it, but Deirdre's kidnapping had provided an almost-welcome distraction from his problems at the Faro. When they got there the next day, however, he realized distraction time was over. The window had been repaired, but the beer garden was still a shambles. And they had a band coming in for the weekend. Deirdre's café tables provided some seating, and he and Chico were able to cobble together a few more tables, using spare parts from some of the ones that were beyond repair. They still had the heavy picnic tables with umbrellas around the perimeter that hadn't been damaged. But they were short of chairs, and they'd have to rig up a bar.

And he was on the verge of losing his liquor license. Tom tightened his grip on the clamp he was using to fix another patio table. He wondered if talking to Margaret Hastings would do any good. He'd only seen her a few times at Merchants Association meetings, and she'd reminded him of the psycho prairie wife on *Big Love*. Somehow he didn't think she'd be interested in hearing his point of view.

He also figured Craig Dempsey wasn't through yet. Dempsey struck him as the kind of jerk who wouldn't back off until he'd beaten his opponent into the ground. Or gotten beaten into the ground himself. Of the two, Tom favored the latter possibility, but he didn't know how likely it was.

Nobody else seemed as concerned as he was. Clem and Marilyn had both hugged Deirdre as soon as she'd walked into the bar. Bobby Sue had shed some tears and apologized profusely for Leon, even though he hadn't had anything to do with Milam Broadus for several months. Even Sylvia had given her a slightly limp squeeze on the shoulder.

The Steinbruners showed up at five, nodded at Deirdre and Tom, and took up their places at the pool table. Chico stationed himself on his stool, far enough away from the door to the beer garden to discourage anyone from trying another sneak attack. The washtub of beer and ice remained beside the bar even thought the cooler was functioning again since Harry and Sylvia both claimed it made things easier. As the tables filled up, Tom told himself they were back to normal and tried his best to believe it.

He failed miserably, spending the evening with his stomach in knots as he watched customers come and go.

That night he went home with Deirdre at midnight. They hadn't talked about it. She hadn't invited him. They just did it, more or less automatically.

She snuggled against his body in the darkness of her barren bedroom, resting her head on his chest. "What's wrong? Are you worried about Craig?"

Tom blew out a breath. "Do we have to talk about it?"

She propped her chin on one hand. "Yes, as a matter of fact, we do. I need to know what's going on."

He sighed. He'd really rather avoid the whole discussion, but he had a feeling she wouldn't let him. And besides, she deserved to know. They all did, since they were all on the verge of losing their jobs if the Faro closed down.

Deirdre listened to his quick description of the upcoming license hearing and Margaret Hastings' complaints. "Why is she so down on you? You're not the only one in town serving liquor."

"But I'm the only one who had to close down because of a riot. Nando says she goes after any bar that's having trouble. And that's me right now."

"But why? What's in it for her?"

Tom shrugged. "From what I hear, her father was an alcoholic. She's very anti-booze, wants to dry up Konigsburg one bar at a time."

"But if the TABC knew the truth, that you'd been targeted, that the Faro isn't really a problem bar, they wouldn't take your license away."

"I can try telling them that, but it sounds like a stretch

even to me."

"I could come with you and testify. I'll tell them about Craig and my father."

Tom's stomach tied another knot. "No."

"Why not?"

"Because it's not your problem. It's mine. I'll take care of it. I don't want you involved."

Deirdre propped her chin in her hand again, staring down at him with troubled eyes. "Why is it so hard for you to take my help, Tom Ames? Or Clem's help? Or Chico's?"

Tom closed his eyes rather than watch her frown. "The Faro is my club. I take the profits. I pay the bills. When we get in trouble, I take the heat. I appreciate all of you, but that's the way it is. I'm not dragging anybody down with me on this."

"It doesn't have to be that way."

Tom blew out a breath. "That's the way it is," he repeated.

Deirdre looked like she wanted to say more, but after a moment she rubbed her face against his chest. "Damn Craig Dempsey! We need to settle this."

Tom felt a quick spike of heat to his groin. "Deirdre, believe me, Craig Dempsey is the last person I want to talk about right now."

Judging from the way she slid down his body, and the level of ecstasy she managed to produce over the next half hour, he decided she must feel the same way.

Deirdre didn't go back to the Faro when Tom left the next morning. She told him she'd decided to spend the morning pricing roasters online, and she did do a couple of quick searches, just to keep herself on the near side of honest.

Then she spread out her Texas map on the dining room table and opened her hotel and motel guide beside it. She'd checked all the lodging within a twenty-mile radius of Konigsburg when she'd searched for Craig the first time. Now she widened her radius to fifty miles.

She was still mildly shocked when the resort hotel in Marble Falls connected her to Craig's room. By then, she'd become accustomed to hearing the desk clerk say, "We have no guest named Craig Dempsey."

Craig's "Yeah?" sounded both fuzzy and pissed. Deirdre figured she'd managed to wake him. *Good.*

"Craig, this is Deirdre Brandenburg. You know, 'Dee-Dee'." She put as much venom as she could into the name.

"Yeah?" He sounded more awake now, but also wary.

"Yeah. I thought we might talk about that little riot you arranged at the Faro a few nights ago. I was there, by the way. Did you figure I would be?"

There was a tiny pause on the other end of the line. "I don't know what you're talking about."

"Oh, bite me. You know exactly what I'm talking about. The cops grabbed two of the rioters, and they told them the whole story. They're tracking down Hardesty as we speak. You're busted, Craig."

She heard his quick inhale. "Bullshit."

"I don't care if you believe me or not. I just wanted to ask if you also had a hand in the kidnapping."

"What the hell are you talking about?" This time he sounded honestly confused.

"Your buddy, Milam Broadus. Owns a used furniture store in Konigsburg. He and a friend of his kidnapped me a couple of days ago. Fortunately, Tom and the cops were able to find me before anything too bad happened. But before they did, Broadus happened to mention that you'd told him Daddy would ransom me. So I just thought I'd ask—did you plan the whole thing, or were you just an advisor?"

"No! Jesus, what are you... Why would I kidnap you?" He sounded panicky now. Probably he was telling the truth. Not that it mattered.

"I don't know exactly. I haven't told the police about what Broadus said yet. Of course, if they ask him, knowing Broadus, he'll tell them all about it. At least enough to get you some fairly nasty publicity."

He sighed. "What do you want, anyway?"

Deirdre flattened her voice to ultimatum tone. "You need to come to the Faro tonight after midnight."

The pause this time was long enough to make her believe he was actually thinking for once. "Why would I do that?"

"To keep yourself from being dragged into this whole kidnapping mess. If you come, I won't tell the police about you

257

and Broadus. Besides, it's time we settled this thing. Once and for all. Do we have a deal, Craig?" Deirdre held her breath.

Finally, Craig sighed again. "Yeah, goddamn it, we have a deal."

Craig tossed his suitcase in the back of his rental SUV, chewing down another antacid. No matter what Dee-Dee thought she had on him, she couldn't tie him to that lunatic at the furniture store. It wasn't his fault that old fart had twisted his words—he hadn't told him to kidnap anybody.

The problem was that chief of police they had in Konigsburg who was blowing a bar fight into some kind of felony. Hardesty had managed to give him a call on his way out of state, and he hadn't been encouraging. Still, Craig figured most people in town would recognize the cop's campaign for the exaggeration it was. Hell, from what Craig had heard, that bar had a reputation for being broken up. He'd just helped things along a little. He figured Big John could take care of it with a few well-placed lawyers and some pointed references to lawsuits for wrongful arrest if worse came to worst. And Craig could always supply a couple of autographed game balls to sooth any hurt feelings among the police force.

Of course, Big John would only help him out if he brought Dee-Dee back to Houston. If he came up empty-handed again, there was always the chance that the big man would cut him loose. The acid in Craig's stomach felt like a tidal wave. Without Big John's support, Craig wouldn't have the money to pay off the bookies who kept leaving nasty messages on his voice mail. And not paying his bookies could have all kinds of unpleasant results, results he really didn't want to contemplate just now.

He turned onto Highway 281 heading toward Konigsburg. All of this could be taken care of easily enough. Dee-Dee had to see reason. She had to leave Konigsburg and go back to Houston. When she did, she'd realize that Craig was actually the man she was supposed to end up with, the only man who actually made sense. She was Dee-Dee Brandenburg, for Christ's sake, daughter of one of the richest men in Texas, a freakin' millionaire in her own right. How could she even consider some asshole nobody in a dead-end tourist trap?

Craig blew out a breath, pushing the accelerator down to

pass a couple of semis. Dee-Dee just had to get her head screwed on straight and all of this would go away.

Of course, if Dee-Dee had her head screwed on straight, none of this would have happened in the first place. And no way was he losing out to a goddamn bartender.

Nando showed up at the Faro just after lunch. "Where's Deirdre? I thought she'd like to know what happened with Broadus and Seifert."

"She's off pricing coffee roasters on her computer." At least that's what Tom thought she'd said. Right now he and Chico were trying to set up a makeshift bar out of whiskey barrels and an old door, so he wasn't exactly thinking about it.

"Oh. Well, tell her the powers that be still can't decide who gets to try those idiots, but they all agreed it wouldn't be us. Anyway, they're on their way to Austin. Eventually, she'll have to testify, but my guess is it won't be for a while. And if Broadus's lawyer has any sense they'll plead him out."

"Broadus has a lawyer?"

"Appointed by the court. Ol' Milam's still refusing to talk to anybody who isn't ready to secede. Sounds like a great basis for an insanity plea."

Tom sighed. "Tell that to the governor."

Nando leaned back against the doorway to the beer garden, surveying the few remaining lunch customers in the main room. "Heard anything more from Dempsey?"

Tom shook his head. "Maybe the kidnapping scared him off." *But probably not.*

"Right. Well, Toleffson's still looking for him. If he shows up, give us a call."

"Will do." *Right after I convert him into a lawn ornament.*

Deirdre arrived just before the evening rush while he was tapping a new keg, so he didn't get a chance to pass on Nando's news. He figured it was just as well. She seemed to have gotten over Broadus and Seifert, and he didn't particularly want to bring them up again.

The evening wasn't that busy. He sent Harry home early since he'd been working extra hours, then he sent Marilyn off at eleven. Sylvia took Chico home at eleven-thirty after she and

Deirdre had finished serving the last remaining customers.

Tom wiped down the bar and stacked some empties in the kitchen as Deirdre cleaned the tables. "Quiet night," he said.

"So far." She bit her lip.

Tom narrowed his eyes. "So far? What do you know that I don't? Should I call Chico back?"

Deirdre shook her head. "No. You won't need him."

Behind her, the door swung open and Craig Dempsey walked into the Faro.

Tom grabbed his sawed-off pool cue, flipping up the gate at the end of the bar to let himself out. Dempsey braced himself, grinning.

"C'mon, bartender," he growled. "You think you can take me? Let's do it."

Deirdre stepped in front of him. "Stop it. Both of you. There's nobody here but me and I'm not impressed." She turned to Tom. "I told him to come here."

Tom stared at her, trying to sort out all the questions that suddenly flooded his brain. "You knew where he was?"

"No, I called all the luxury hotels within a fifty-mile radius. He was staying at a resort in Marble Falls."

Dempsey smirked. "A lot more comfortable than Podunk Center here, believe me."

Tom gripped the pool cue so tightly his hand ached. "And why exactly is he here?"

Deirdre rested her hands on her hips. "He's here because I have a proposition for the two of you. A way to settle this thing now."

Dempsey's smirk hadn't altered, but his eyes became watchful. "The only way to settle this thing is for you to come back to Houston. I told you that."

"That's one possibility."

Dempsey narrowed his eyes. "There isn't any other possibility."

"Yes, there is. You go back to Houston yourself. Only before you do, you write out a quick statement for the TABC, telling them you were behind the riot here so they don't take Tom's liquor license away."

"And why would I do that?" Dempsey said between gritted teeth.

Deirdre shrugged. "Because you lost the game."

Tom stared at her. "What game?"

"The game the two of you are going to play tonight. Poker. Blackjack. Best two out of three. I'll deal."

Dempsey gave her an incredulous look. "Let me get this straight. We play poker. If he wins, I have to write out a statement for the TABC and head back home. What do I get if I win?"

She took a deep breath. "I go back to Houston with you. And I go to work for my father again."

Tom felt as if his spine had turned to ice. "You go..."

She nodded. "If he wins."

Tom stared at her, a cacophony of voices roaring in his head. *I don't want you to go. I won't let you go. How can you go?*

"Tom?" She licked her lips. "If he wins. Only if he wins."

Tom blinked. She expected him to win it? He hadn't looked at a poker hand in three years. And who knew how good Dempsey was?

Dempsey's smirk spread into a faintly nasty grin. "What's the matter, Ames? Don't like poker? Maybe we could play Old Maid instead."

Tom studied him for a moment. Behind that smirk, his eyes had a familiar avid brightness. A gambler. And maybe not a good one. But he only had three games to find out.

Deirdre was watching him, her shoulders tense. She knew Dempsey better than he did. He met her gaze.

Trust me. Please.

Tom blew out a breath. "Okay, Dempsey. But no blackjack. Five card draw. And two out of three isn't enough. We go three out of five."

As he said it, the words of an old David Bromberg song floated through his mind. *A man should never gamble more than he can stand to lose.*

Deirdre took the deck out of the box, then shuffled the cards, trying very hard not to drop them. She hadn't thought she'd be this nervous when they actually sat down to play. She'd even told herself there was nothing to be nervous about. Tom was a professional gambler, or at least he had been. Craig was an amateur who had an inflated opinion of his skills. She knew for a fact he'd dropped thousands playing poker in Vegas.

But he'd won sometimes too. Even Craig wasn't dumb enough to go on playing if he always lost.

Deirdre didn't play poker herself, although she knew the basics. She'd been counting on them playing blackjack until Tom had refused. She watched the two men stack the chips she'd given them, shuffling again. Craig pushed his chair in beside her on the left. Tom regarded him stonily. Deirdre didn't know exactly what he'd done, but she figured he was being an asshole again. Her stomach clenched.

Craig tossed a chip into the pot. So did Tom. Deirdre dealt each man five cards.

Tom's face was resolutely blank. The corners of Craig's mouth edged up into the same smirk he'd been wearing all evening. He tossed three chips into the pot. Tom added three of his own.

Craig tossed a card into the discard, then turned to Deirdre. "Give me one."

Deirdre picked up the deck and started to deal.

"Discard the burn," Craig snapped.

She stared at him.

"Throw the top card into the discard, then give him one," Tom explained. His voice was as expressionless as his face. Deirdre did what he told her to do.

Tom tossed three cards into the discard. She gave him three new ones. After a moment, Craig tossed five chips into the pot. Tom threw in five of his own.

"Four sixes." Craig laid down his hand, still smirking.

Tom studied it, then shrugged. "Pair of queens."

His face showed nothing. Deirdre's stomach felt like she was wearing a corset tightened to Scarlett-at-the-barbeque level.

Craig gathered in the chips, his grin so wide that Deirdre felt like kicking him. "One thing you'll find, Ames. I don't bluff."

Tom straightened the stack of chips in front of him. "Usually what a man says right before he bluffs the next hand." He tossed his ante into the pot after Craig.

Deirdre shuffled again, her palms sweating, then dealt five more cards to each of them.

Craig studied his cards, then tossed in five chips. Tom tossed in his own five.

Craig's grin almost split his face. He discarded a single card. Deirdre dealt him another.

Tom tossed two. Deirdre's heart hammered against her ribs as she dealt him two more.

Craig tossed in another five chips. Tom matched him again. "Call," he said flatly. Craig checked his cards again, then laid them down on the table. "Three eights."

Tom shrugged. "Beats my sixes." He shoveled the cards back to Deirdre.

The pressure around her heart was almost painful. She took a deep breath as she shuffled, trying to remember everything she knew, everything she'd read over the past day, about poker. This game seemed to be going much more quickly than it should be. Shouldn't they be using more strategy here? Shouldn't she?

She dealt five more cards to each man, then wiped her hands on her thighs. One more win for Craig and she was back in Houston wearing a suit. And Tom was in Konigsburg running the Faro without her. Deirdre bit her lip. What if he thought that was a good deal? Was that why he was hurrying through the game?

Craig was still grinning. She'd never noticed how annoying his grin was before. Did he really think if she went back to Houston, she'd go back to him? Did Tom? She glanced at him but his face was still blank.

Craig tossed five more chips into the pot. Tom tossed seven. Deirdre's heart hammered again. Craig threw in two more.

Craig discarded a single card. Tom discarded two. Deirdre dealt with shaking fingers.

Craig threw in seven chips. Tom threw in nine. Craig stared at him for a long moment, then threw in two more chips. "Call."

He lay down his hand. "Flush," he said. "Ten high." Deirdre studied his cards—a ten, nine, six, four, and three of hearts.

Tom smiled slowly. "Interesting. Me, too." He laid down his cards slowly—ten, nine, seven, five, and two of spades. He pulled the chips toward him.

Craig's smile dimmed. "You took a hell of a chance."

"Just lucky I guess."

Deirdre dealt again, the tightness in her chest easing fractionally.

Craig glanced at his cards, unsmiling. Tom's expression didn't change. Craig tossed in his usual five. Tom matched him.

Craig looked at his hand again, then shook his head. "No cards."

Tom regarded him impassively, then tossed one card into the discard stack. Deirdre picked up the deck again and dealt him one.

Craig tossed nine chips into the pot. Tom tossed ten. Craig scowled at him. "Big spender."

Tom shrugged.

Craig threw in another chip, then five more. Tom matched him, and added another.

Deirdre could hear the slight whistle of Craig's inhale. She sat very still, biting her lip. *Houston and suits. Konigsburg and T-shirts.*

Craig threw in another chip. He sat holding his cards for a moment, then lay them down on the table in front of him. "Pair of tens."

Tom smiled slowly, then flipped his own cards face-up. "Three eights."

Deirdre wiped her hands on her thighs again. One more hand, and it would all be over.

Behind her the door opened and she heard the sound of boot heels on the planked pine floor. "Evening, Ames," Erik Toleffson said.

Deirdre closed her eyes. *Or not.*

Well, crap. Tom pushed the cards in Deirdre's direction. There was probably a city ordinance against gambling in a bar, but he could maybe slip by it given that the bar was closed and they weren't playing for money.

No money. Just Deirdre.

"Evening, Chief," he said easily.

Dempsey stiffened, licking his lips, which was perceptive of him. In his position, Tom wouldn't much like meeting the chief of police himself.

He glanced up at Toleffson again. "What can we do for

you?"

Toleffson settled on a barstool, leaning his elbows back on the bar as he studied the table. "Who's ahead?"

"Even at the moment."

Toleffson nodded absently, then turned to Dempsey. "Don't believe I know you. I'm Erik Toleffson, chief of police here in Konigsburg."

Tom was suddenly certain that the chief knew exactly who Dempsey was, but he figured he'd let Dempsey play it his way.

"Dorsey," he croaked. "Cary Dorsey. From Amarillo."

Deirdre bit her lips, maybe to keep from snickering. Tom could see her point. As an alias, Cary Dorsey struck him as one step up from I.P. Freely.

Toleffson didn't blink "Just visiting, Mr. Dorsey?"

Dempsey nodded. "Yeah. Passing through."

"With enough time for a little poker."

Dempsey nodded again. "Friendly game. No money involved."

Deirdre cleared her throat. "Actually, we were just changing the game, Chief. Four hands of poker is enough for me."

Tom stared at her. *What the hell?*

She shuffled the cards briskly. "Fan Tan, gentlemen."

Dempsey stared at her. "Huh?"

"You mean sevens? You want to play seven-up?" Tom frowned.

She nodded. "Right. Only in this version, you throw in a chip every time you can't play a card. And I'm dealing myself in because you can't play with only two people." She glanced up at Toleffson. "Want to play, Chief?"

Toleffson shook his head slowly. His lips moved into a faint grin. "I'll just watch. How does it work?"

"Very simple." Deirdre ruffled the cards. "Deal out all the cards and then you play in order. Sevens go down first, with sixes on one side and eights on the other. Play up on the eights and down on the sixes. If you have a card that plays, you have to play it, but other than that, you choose the order to play your cards in. If you can't play a card, you pass and throw in a chip. First one to play all their cards wins."

"Sevens?" Dempsey sounded outraged. "Jesus, that's a kid game."

"Dealer's choice." She smiled at him sweetly. "Would you like me to explain the rules in more detail?"

"I don't need to hear the rules," Dempsey snarled. "I know the freakin' rules. You sure you don't want to play Old Maid?"

She shook her head. "Seven-up is fine." She dealt quickly, throwing the last card to Dempsey. "And by the way, this game counts."

Tom stared at her, dumbstruck. So did Dempsey. Deirdre smiled at them both, then picked up her hand.

"Like hell," Dempsey blurted.

She turned toward him, raising an eyebrow.

"Is there a problem Mr....Dorsey?" Toleffson's voice rumbled from behind them.

Dempsey paled slightly, licking his lips. "No. No problem." He arranged his cards in his hand.

"You start, Cr...Cary." Deirdre gave him a smile that could have caused sugar shock.

Dempsey stared at his hand for a long moment, then threw down the seven of hearts. Tom added the seven of diamonds.

Deirdre gave them all another saccharine smile. "Oh good, we're all being nice." She placed her seven of spades in the row above Tom's card.

Dempsey stared at his hand again. "Shit," he muttered and played the eight of diamonds.

Tom dropped the six of spades.

Deirdre glanced at him, her eyes dancing, then played the six of diamonds. "You are naughty," she murmured. "You're holding that last seven, aren't you?"

Dempsey stared at him for a long moment, then threw the nine of diamonds on the eight. For the first time since they'd sat down at the card table that night, Tom's shoulders began to loosen up.

Judging from the muttered obscenities from Dempsey's side of the table, he didn't have much of a hand. Tom, on the other hand, had a very good one. Amazingly good, in fact. Only one ace and no kings, several short runs, and a seven protected by a six and a nine. He used the seven to squeeze out most of the cards he needed to fill out the runs, while Dempsey fumed and occasionally passed.

Deirdre's hand wasn't bad either, judging from the fact that she passed less than Dempsey did.

Tom's ace was the sticker, as he'd guessed it might be. He played all his other cards, then sat holding his ace, watching the number of cards in Dempsey's hand diminish, while Dempsey's shit-eating grin returned.

Tom glanced at Deirdre, and did a double-take. She had only two cards left to Dempsey's five and his one. Tom narrowed his eyes as Dempsey muttered again and threw out a chip. He'd be willing to bet one of her cards was the other missing ace. If she had that and the two of clubs, she'd win since she played before he did. All she had to do was play her ace, then she could get rid of the two before Tom could play his own ace.

And then they'd have to play another hand of poker, once Toleffson left. Good thing he was used to staying up until two.

Deirdre glanced at him, and then back to her cards. And then she played the two of clubs.

Tom stared at her, half-tempted to call her on it. Once upon a time, he would have refused to be helped. Once upon a time, he'd have insisted on doing everything on his own. His bar, his problems, all his.

Once upon a time, he'd been an idiot.

Dempsey snarled and flipped the jack of spades.

Tom flipped his ace of clubs on the table, and leaned back in his chair. "I'm out."

Dempsey stared at him blankly, then threw his remaining cards on the table. "This is bullshit! You hear me? Total bullshit!"

Tom shrugged. "You lost the game Dem...Dorsey. That's the way it goes."

Dempsey pointed at Deirdre. "She cheated."

"No I didn't." Deirdre smiled. "I made a choice. One of several. This one happened to work out."

"Goddamn it," Dempsey began.

"Could I see some ID, Mr. Dorsey?" Toleffson's voice was quiet, but it brought Dempsey to an immediate halt.

"Why?" he asked warily.

"You're making a bit of a disturbance here. Plus I like to know who's passing through my town. Just routine. You do have, ID, don't you Dorsey?" Toleffson stood up. He was taller than Dempsey by several inches, although Dempsey looked like he had him on weight.

"I…it's in the glove compartment in my car. I'll go get it." Dempsey started for the door, but Deirdre stepped into his path.

"Not quite yet, Cary. You were going to sign a statement for me, remember?"

Toleffson folded his arms across his chest. "What statement would that be?"

"Oh, it turns out Cary here has some information about the riot that broke up the Faro. He's going to sign a statement about it that we can give to the TABC at the licensure hearing. Actually, this is a great coincidence, Chief. You can witness his signature."

She ducked behind the bar and emerged with a printed sheet. "Here, you go, Cary. Just put your signature at the bottom. Your real signature, that is." Her jaw squared as she looked at him.

Dempsey swallowed hard, then glanced at Toleffson. "I sign this, and you'll let me go out to my car to…ah…get my ID?"

Toleffson glanced from Deirdre to Dempsey, and then to Tom. "You have any opinion here, Ames?"

Tom smiled. "I think ol' Cary's statement would be a good thing to have. And I'm damn sure Deirdre wrote it out just right for the TABC. She's a very good businesswoman."

Toleffson's mouth narrowed to a thin line as he looked back and forth between them. Then he shrugged. "Read it and sign, Dempsey. Then you can get out of here."

Craig grabbed the pen from Deirdre's hand and scrawled his signature at the bottom of the page. For a moment, his gaze locked with hers. "I know you cheated," he growled. "I didn't lose."

She sighed. "Whatever. Have a safe trip back to Houston."

Dempsey gave her one more burning look, then stalked out the door.

Deirdre shook her head. "You'd think he'd have learned by now not to sign anything without reading it first. Sort of fits with his other business decisions, though. Now if you could just sign here as a witness, Chief." She pointed to the bottom of the page.

Toleffson sighed, pulling out a ballpoint. "Do you know for

a fact he won't be back here to break up the place again?"

"Let's say I'm ninety-nine percent sure he won't. Of course, with somebody like Craig you can never be entirely sure. Still, given that you're likely to arrest him if he shows up again, I'm guessing not." She looked up at Toleffson from beneath her lashes. "You *are* likely to arrest him if he shows up again, aren't you?"

"Oh yes, ma'am, I'm more than likely." Toleffson signed, then replaced his Stetson carefully on his head. "In fact, if he delays at all in getting his ass out of town tonight, I might reconsider and throw him in the slammer right now, just on general principles."

Deirdre gave him a sunny smile. "I'm sure he's aware of that, Chief. Nice doing business with you."

Toleffson grinned back. "Yes, ma'am. You take care now."

Tom watched him walk out the front door. A few moments later, he heard someone whistling "The Eyes of Texas Are Upon You" as he walked down the street.

Chapter Twenty-Six

Deirdre went back with Tom to his place once they'd closed down the Faro again. By now, she had a couple of T-shirts, a pair of jeans, and some underwear tucked into his bureau. She figured eventually Tom might develop the *cojones* to ask her to move in. Or she'd ask him to move in with her, although that made less sense since she was living in Docia's apartment with no furniture and Tom had his own house. But she knew they'd do one or the other. She was fairly sure she was in love with him. She just had to wait for him to wake up to the fact that he loved her.

Not that he looked very awake right then, just tired.

Deirdre yawned, rubbing a hand across the back of her neck as they walked up the steps to his front door. "Well, that was interesting."

He nodded, turning the key in the lock. "That's one way of putting it."

"We should probably get some sleep." She followed him through the living room. "We've got a lot to do tomorrow."

"Got that right." He stepped into the dining room and froze in the doorway. She heard his quick intake of breath.

"What?" she said, moving beside him.

Craig Dempsey sat in one of the dining room chairs. A bottle of tequila was open on the table in front of him. He was holding a large black handgun pointed at the center of Tom's chest.

Tom took hold of her arm, jerking her behind him. "What do you want, Dempsey?"

"We're gonna play that last hand," Craig snarled. "No way

am I losing to you, shithead. And no way is this settled. Seven-up. Jesus."

"Okay, we'll play. Let Deirdre go."

Dempsey shook his head. "And have her head straight for that chief of police? I don't think so. Besides, she's gonna be the dealer. I'm not trusting you."

Tom started to object again. Behind him, Deirdre squeezed his hand. She wasn't going anywhere anyway.

"Okay," he said. "If we're playing, let's go into the living room. The light's better." He moved slowly back into the other room, keeping Deirdre behind him.

Craig lurched to his feet, grabbing the neck of the tequila bottle in his other hand. Judging from the way he was walking, he'd already had more than a few samples. But he still held the gun steady, and it still pointed straight at Tom.

"How are you going to hold your cards, Dempsey?" Tom drawled. "In your teeth?"

"Don't worry about it," Craig snapped. He motioned toward the couch with the gun. "Siddown." He placed the tequila bottle on the coffee table, then narrowed his eyes at Deirdre. "Go get some cards. And no funny stuff or your boyfriend buys the farm."

Deirdre decided he'd probably been watching too much Spike TV. She went to Tom's bookcase.

"Top shelf," he called after her. "On the left."

She found the deck of cards and brought them back, regarding Craig with narrowed eyes. He was still looming at the side of the table. "Are you going to sit down? Or do I have to toss you the cards?"

Craig thumped down into a chair across from her, his gun jumping slightly. Deirdre swallowed. Guns and drunken idiots were never a good combination.

"Just out of curiosity, how did you get in here, Dempsey?" Tom asked.

"You ought to lock your windows, Ames." Craig's lips spread in another insolent grin. Obviously, he was pleased with himself. "Course if you had, I'd have had to break it, so I guess you had no way of winning here."

"And the gun?" She raised an eyebrow. "I never knew you were a gun nut, Craig."

"I got a permit," he snarled. "I'm legal."

Also shit-faced, she figured. She ruffled the cards, then set them in front of Craig. "Cut."

Craig shook his head, nudging the gun in Tom's direction. "Let him." He leaned back in his chair, dangling the hand that wasn't holding the gun off the armrest.

Deirdre slid the cards in Tom's direction. He divided them neatly in half and passed them back across the table to her.

"How exactly are you going to take me back to Houston if you win?" Deirdre kept her voice casual. "Because you know I won't come willingly. You're forcing me to play at gunpoint, after all. Do you think this is what my father wanted?"

Craig narrowed his eyes. "Told me to use my judgment. This is my judgment."

Got that right. Her hands stilled. "So he didn't actually tell you to break up the Faro?" she said slowly.

"Used my judgment," Craig repeated. "Best way to get you out."

She flipped him a card, wishing it was a poison dart. "Did you ever tell him what you did?"

Craig shrugged. "Don't need to. He wants results. I got 'em."

Her teeth were gritted so tightly they ached. "Oh yeah. You definitely got 'em." She flipped Tom a card as she heard a familiar scratching sound.

"What's that?" Craig's glance darted around the room.

"Doris." Deirdre tapped the deck on the table.

"Who's Doris?"

Tom's mouth moved up into a faint grin. "That's Doris," he said, nodding toward the floor next to Craig's chair.

Doris stared up at him, her beady black eyes bright.

Several things happened so quickly that it took Deirdre a while to sort them all out. Craig leaped to his feet, yelling. As he yanked his hand upward, Doris fastened onto the flesh at the side, sinking her teeth deep. Craig waved the hand frantically. Doris, no doubt thoroughly terrified, hung on for dear life.

Craig brought his gun hand around, pointing the weapon in the general direction of Doris's head. Tom picked up the bottle and brought it down on Craig's wrist, splashing tequila across the table as the gun went flying. Deirdre went flying after it.

"Get it off me," Craig screamed. "Shoot it! Kill it! Get it off me!"

"Oh for the love of Mike," Deirdre muttered as she walked back, the gun dangling from her hand. "It's just an iguana."

Craig babbled something, and then his knees began to fold.

She watched, fascinated, as his body slid slowly, almost gracefully to the floor. "He fainted," she said when he was stretched out full length. "The big sissy fainted."

Tom shrugged. "Passed out, more likely. Too much tequila and adrenaline aren't a healthy combination." He pulled his cell off his belt, punching in 911. "This is Tom Ames again, Toleffson. We've got a home invasion here." He listened for a moment, then shrugged. "Nah. It's just Dempsey, and he's out cold. But we need somebody to come collect him."

Erik's voice on the phone was loud enough for Deirdre to hear, although she couldn't make out the words. She figured that was just as well, given the volume.

She knelt beside Craig's prostrate form. "Is the chief coming?"

"Yeah, he said he's on his way." He knelt beside her. "We probably need to detach Doris. I don't want them taking her along with him." He stood up again, and walked toward the kitchen.

"How did she get out anyway?"

He returned, carrying a pair of grilling gauntlets. "I opened the cage as we walked by. I figured she might provide a distraction."

"Some distraction. She might have gotten hurt."

"Yeah. I didn't think she'd go this far."

Doris was still clamped tight to Craig's hand. Deirdre thought she could see blood seeping around the wound. "Is her bite dangerous?"

"She not venomous, but she's got some teeth on her." Tom pulled on the gauntlets, then knelt on the other side of Craig. "And I'd just as soon she didn't sink them into me instead of Dempsey. Get that tequila, please."

"You want a drink? Now?"

"Nope, but Doris might. Take one of those tissues and soak it. I'm going to flip her upside down. You wave the tissue in front of her nostrils so she gets the fumes."

Deirdre thought of several things she needed to ask, most importantly exactly where Doris's nostrils were, but she decided to ignore them. She saturated the tissue in the tequila, then watched Tom flip Doris upside down, pulling gently on her dewlap as he did. Deirdre waved the tissue in the general vicinity of where she thought the nostrils might be, hoping that Doris didn't decide to go from Craig's hand to hers.

After a moment, Doris opened her mouth. Tom flipped her right side up and delivered her speedily to her cage. Deirdre stared down at the neat circle of bloody indentations on Craig's hand. It looked like he might need stitches.

Or at least she really hoped so.

Tom was still awake at three a.m. Not that it was by choice. After turning Craig over to Toleffson and promising to show up in the morning to sign a statement, he and Deirdre had had a thoroughly enjoyable victory celebration in his bed. Deirdre had promptly dropped into the sleep of the just. Tom hadn't. Now he lay there, feeling her soft weight in his arms, and wondering when the other shoe was going to drop.

It couldn't be over now. Could it?

Deirdre moved in his arms, snuffling. "Go to sleep," she muttered.

He kissed her forehead. "Don't worry about it."

She raised her head, yawning. "What's up?"

"Nothing. Go back to sleep."

"Not without you. Now tell me what's bothering you."

He took a breath and blew it out. "I know what you did."

She raised a questioning eyebrow.

"Come on, Deirdre, I made my living playing poker for a few years. I know the feel of a shaved deck. I wasn't sure until we played seven-up."

She shrugged. "Docia showed me how years ago, when I was a kid. She gave me a shaved deck for magic tricks, and then she showed me how to play cards with it. I tried it a couple of times—never for money, though. I thought I could help you if you played blackjack. But I don't know poker very well. When you switched to five card draw, I couldn't do much. Does it matter?"

"Yep."

"Why?"

"I wanted to beat the SOB on my own. Besides, it's hard to throw somebody the right cards on five-card draw. You were just as likely to screw things up. I was afraid you'd try."

"I thought about it. You scared me to death when you lost those first two hands."

He shook his head. "It takes a hand or so to learn how to read somebody. Between trying to figure Dempsey and trying to keep you from messing up the game, it took me a couple of hands. But that's why I said three out of five."

She grimaced. "I should just have given Craig lousy cards. It would have been more effective."

"You made up for it in seven-up."

She grinned. "I did, didn't I? Good thing I gave myself the deuce, though."

Tom stared down at her, unsmiling. Part of him wanted to yell. He'd never used a crooked deck in his life.

Deirdre's grin curdled slightly. "Don't you dare get all holy with me about being an honest player, Tom Ames. Not with Craig Dempsey. Not after what he did to the Faro. If I could have tackled him and forced him to sign the damn statement, I would have, but he outweighs me by a ton. So I used guile."

Tom blew out a breath. "Still..."

"No." She shook her head. "You need to learn to let other people help when they want to. Like Clem and her dinner menus. And Bobby Sue with Leon. And me. We care about you."

He shook his head. "I don't expect that. People work for me. They're not obligated to give a damn."

"They care about you," she repeated. "They're the closest thing we've got to a family. Both of us."

"Your father..."

"Is maybe not as bad as I thought, but right now I'd still trust my Faro family farther than I'd trust him."

"Your 'Faro family'?" He raised an eyebrow. "Seriously?"

"Seriously. Sue me."

Tom sighed. "I'd rather shag you." He slid his hand down to her hip, feeling the slight jut of the bone against his palm.

"Good," she said, "that's what I had in mind too." She ran

her tongue along the edge of his collarbone, then dipped down, sliding tongue and teeth in a line across his chest and stomach.

He closed his eyes. Wherever she ended up was okay with him.

She placed her hands on his thighs, then arched herself over him to slide her tongue around the tip of his cock. He gasped in a quick breath as she leaned forward, taking him deeper. Her hands reached beneath to cup him, one fingernail scratching along the underside until he gasped again.

He looked down at her, at her dark head moving against his body. As he watched she opened her eyes, gazing up at him, smiling.

"Jesus," he croaked. "Come here." He pulled her up, settling her in his lap, his cock jutting against her. She adjusted herself to take him in, pulling him into her dampness and heat, then she placed her hands on his shoulders, staring down at him, eyes wide, and began to rock against him.

Tom kept his gaze on hers as he felt heat flowing from the depths of her, as his own body began to strain. He placed his hands on her hips, moving her in time to his own rhythm, joining her, joining them to the beat of his pulse, the rhythm of his body. Deirdre's hands tightened on his shoulders, and she moaned, moving against him more desperately.

Her breath came in small sobs, her body stiffening in his hands. "Tom," she panted, "I can't...I need..."

"Yes," he whispered. "Yes, you can. Now."

She convulsed against him, her body pulling him deep, setting off a series of shocks through his spine, heat rushing upward like an electric charge. And then he was plunging into her, stabbing deep, his voice ringing in his own ears as he shouted.

Deirdre collapsed against his chest, sliding her arms around his neck, her breath hot against him. After a long moment, she raised her head slightly. "You're the nicest thing that's ever happened to me, Tom Ames. You and the Faro. I wonder what I did to deserve you."

For one of the few times in his life, he couldn't think of a single coherent thing to say. "Likewise," he muttered finally.

From the living room he heard a scrabbling of claws against glass. "Doris doesn't approve," Deirdre murmured.

"Doris is probably jealous."

Tom didn't blame her a bit. He pulled Deirdre close again, still buried deep inside her, not even trying to pull loose. His eyelids finally drooped, and he rested his cheek against her hair. *The nicest thing that's every happened to me.* That sounded about right.

As he drifted off, he wondered if he could locate a male iguana somewhere. Why shouldn't Doris have a chance to feel this good too?

Chapter Twenty-Seven

By Saturday afternoon, with Chico and Leon's help, Tom had managed to get the beer garden into minimal shape for the show. He was glad for once that Junior Bonner didn't draw the same crowds as Frankie Belasco. They'd probably be able to handle a medium-sized turnout, and if Junior suddenly got popular, they could always pull some tables and chairs out from the main room.

He'd located another washtub for the beer and he and Chico had dragged a keg out to the space behind the makeshift bar. He was still trying to decide whether to leave the frozen margarita machine inside or bring it outside when he heard somebody yelling in the main room.

He ran back through the door just before Chico did, grabbing Leon's push broom out of his hands in case he had to persuade somebody to shut the hell up and get out of his bar.

Depressing how routine that request was becoming.

The man who was doing the yelling looked too old to be one of Dempsey's minions. Also too well-dressed. He wore a silver-gray suit with a subdued tie, accompanied by a cream-colored Stetson and what looked to be hand-tooled cowboy boots. If he was a thug, Tom decided there was more money in thuggery than he'd ever realized.

"Where's the goddamn owner of this goddamn dive?" the man yelled. "And where's my goddamn daughter?"

Tom stepped in front of him, doing a quick size assessment. The yeller was maybe an inch shorter, and definitely soft. Also, he appeared to be in his early sixties. Tom figured him for a one-punch wonder, but that one punch would probably be good. "I'm the owner here," he said. "What can I do for you?"

The man turned furious eyes in his direction. Furious and oddly familiar. "You the asshole who kidnapped my baby?" he bellowed.

Tom heard a sigh, and suddenly noticed Nando standing at the end of the bar, well out of reach. "Mr. Brandenburg, I've already told you. Your daughter is safe. Tom here is the one who rescued her. The kidnappers are in Austin being arraigned. Chief Toleffson is out on a call, but when he returns, he can..."

Brandenburg ignored him. "You," he snarled at Tom. "You take me to my daughter. Now."

Tom shrugged. Right offhand he couldn't see any reason not to. "Last time I talked to her she was next door. We can go over and see if she's still there."

Deirdre took one more quick look around the shop. She'd managed to push most of the junk into the back room so that the main room looked neat, at least. And, of course, the walls and shelves had all been painted. She hadn't really had a chance to put down the rich brown acid stain she wanted to use on the floor yet. Still, the shop looked acceptable. Neat, professional, and ready for her father.

She'd heard him yelling at least a half block away, and she figured he'd head to the bar first. After all, she didn't even have a sign up yet, and she didn't know whether Craig had told him about the shop. In fact, that was one of many things she was hoping to find out.

She ran her hands over her hair to smooth it a little, and pulled down her T-shirt. At least it was for Fat Jack's Pizza. If she'd known her dad was coming, she'd have dug out the one for Rustler's Roost.

The yelling next door reached a crescendo and then stopped. Deirdre took a deep breath. Show time.

Tom pushed open the door, his expression blank. "Someone to see you, Deirdre." He stepped aside and Deirdre was face to face with her father for the first time in over a month.

He looks old. It was the first thought that popped into her head. Either her father had aged a decade or so since she'd last seen him or she hadn't realized just how old he'd looked before.

"Hi, Dad," she said softly.

Her father took a long shuddering breath. "Dee-Dee," he said and then stopped for another breath. "I got a note at the office. Said you were kidnapped. A million dollars. And then some asshole from the FBI showed up. And you left all those phone messages. I thought..." He closed his eyes for a moment, then seemed to pull himself together. "I don't know what I thought. Are you all right?"

"Yes, Dad. I was kidnapped, but it didn't last very long. Tom rescued me." She smiled at him, then caught sight of Nando leaning in the doorway with Chico and Clem. "Along with the police. Everybody helped. So everything's okay now."

Her father stared at her blankly. He looked a little like a man who'd just stepped off a particularly steep roller coaster. After a moment, he shook his head. "Who's this Tom who rescued you?"

"That would be me." Tom leaned easily against the counter behind her. Deirdre resisted the urge to join him. "Tom Ames. I own the Faro next door."

Her father looked at him, then nodded. "Thank you, then. For saving my daughter."

"My pleasure."

Her father started to say something else, but Deirdre cut him off. "You owe him more than that, Daddy."

"I owe him?" His eyes began to take on some of their old spark again. She felt a little like smiling.

"Craig Dempsey hired men to break up Tom's bar after you sent him down here to force me back home. You need to pay him for the damages."

Her father stared at her for several moments, open-mouthed. "What?" he said finally.

She waved an impatient hand. "Craig followed me down here like you told him to do. When he found out I was leasing this shop and working for Tom, he tried to bribe him to fire me and break my lease. Tom wouldn't do it, and Craig decided the best way to force me back to Houston was to drive Tom out of business. Since Tom's business was hurt because of your orders, you need to make it up to him." She folded her arms across her chest.

Her father closed his mouth for a moment, and then opened it again to bellow. "Goddamn it! I never gave that pissant Dempsey orders to do anything except find you and offer you your job back. I sure as hell didn't tell him to hire anybody to break up a bar. If I ever see that SOB again, I'll hang his scalp on my desk."

"I may be able to help you there, Mr. Brandenburg." Nando grinned. "Mr. Dempsey is currently in residence in one of our jail cells, after being picked up last night for invading Mr. Ames's home and threatening him and your daughter with a gun. Of course, if you want to scalp him, you may have to get in line behind my boss."

Her father stared at him blankly, his mouth open. "Home invasion?" he choked out finally. "Gun? On Dee-Dee? I'll kill that bastard!"

Deirdre shrugged. "No you won't. Now sit down." She pushed chair toward him. Her father collapsed into it almost gratefully.

"Whether you ordered him or not, Craig damaged the Faro because he thought that was what you wanted." She raised her chin. "You need to pay Tom for his trouble."

Her father narrowed his eyes in a slightly crafty expression. "That can be negotiated."

"Negotiated? For what?"

He darted a quick glance at Nando, Chico and Clem in the doorway. "Let me take you to lunch."

"We can do lunch right here. Clem does one of the best lunches in town."

"*The* best lunch," Clem snapped, then shrugged. "Except possibly for Allie Maldonado. I'll send Leon over with a couple of plates." She turned back toward the Faro, jerking Nando and Chico along with her.

Tom pushed off from the counter. "Speaking of that, I need to go get set up for the lunch crowd."

"I'll be there in a little while." Deirdre squeezed his arm as he passed her.

Tom smiled. "You can take noon off today. It's been a big week."

She leaned back against the counter, studying her father again. He still looked older than she remembered, but he'd picked up more color in his cheeks. She recognized that expression. He was into Dealing Mode.

"Okay, why won't you just pay Tom what you owe him? Craig was down here as your representative even if he did overstep his orders."

He shrugged. "I don't mind paying for the damages. But I always like to get something for my money. You know that."

Deirdre gave him her driest smile. "And moral satisfaction isn't enough?"

"Nope."

"What would be enough?"

"I need you back in Houston."

She shook her head. "Not negotiable. I like it here. I've got friends and family. And I've got my coffee roaster, or I'll have it in a month or so."

Her father leaned back in his chair, studying her. "Suppose you came back part-time. Just a couple of days a week?"

She shook her head again. "Wouldn't work. I know the company, remember? You can't get by with a part-time executive."

Her father pushed a hand through his hair, grimacing. "Okay, here's the thing, Dee-Dee. You remember Kaltenberg? The accountant?"

Deirdre nodded, warily.

"His work turned out to be as screwed up as you said it was. And now I need somebody to straighten it out. And you already know what the problems were so you've already got a head start. Anyway—" he sighed, "—what would you take to come back to work? As a consultant, say, or a contractor? Until we get this all taken care of?"

She grinned, feeling warmth spread down to her toes. "That might work. I can come back part-time as a consultant until my shop is ready to go, which I estimate will be around a month. In return, you will pay for all the repairs Tom needs in the Faro, and you will unfreeze my accounts to give me access to my own money. Which, by the way, was a really lousy thing to do since that money was mine to begin with."

Her father shook his head, looking sheepish. "Sorry. I forgot all about that. Lost my temper, I guess."

"I guess." She narrowed her eyes. "And you will stay for

dinner tonight to say hello to Docia and Aunt Reba, along with the rest of the family. And you will get to know Tom, who will make a much better son-in-law than Craig Dempsey in my humble opinion. And, of course, my opinion is the one that counts."

Her father's mouth dropped open again. "Son-in-law?" he croaked. "The bartender?"

"The bartender. The man I love. The best son-in-law you're ever going to have."

"You got that right." Clem pushed through the front door, carrying a tray with two covered plates. "Sooner rather than later would be my guess. Of course, this will all be news to Tom, but he catches on fast."

She placed the tray on the counter. "Tortilla soup, with gulf shrimp nachos. I would have brought wine, but Tom still hasn't talked to the distributor, so you'll have to make do with Shiner. Enjoy." She grinned at Deirdre, winked at her father, and walked back out the door.

Her father stared after her blankly. "Who *are* these people?"

"My friends and co-workers." *My Faro family.* Deirdre took the cover off the plates. The soup smelled of cumin and cilantro. Fat pink shrimp coated in shreds of melted cheese spilled over the edges of the corn tortillas. "Which reminds me, I need to get back to work. Bobby Sue can't handle the lunch crowd we're pulling in these days, no matter what Tom says. Eat up."

She placed his plate in front of him, then twisted the top off the beer. When she looked up, her father was chewing on a nacho, his expression blissful. "Hot damn, Dee-Dee. Whoever that woman is, she sure can cook."

Deirdre grimaced, gathering a nacho off her own plate. "Okay, that's one more demand. My name is Deirdre, not Dee-Dee. If I'm going to be your hired gun, you need to at least use a name that doesn't make people snicker."

Her father was busily slurping up tortilla soup. "Anything you say, sweetheart," he murmured. "Anything you say."

Tom surveyed the beer garden, listening to Junior Bonner tune up. It seemed he'd seriously underestimated Junior's following. Along with the tables they'd managed to rig up in the morning, they'd ended up dragging another half dozen from the main room to the outside. And people still stood around the edges.

The Steinbruners had given up the chairs around the pool table, acknowledging that they didn't sit down that much anyway. Some of the drinkers had moved to the bar, and a lot of the usual customers from inside had moved outside. Grumpily maybe, but they'd moved nonetheless.

The Toleffsons took up an entire side of the garden. Cal and Docia sat with Deirdre's father and a platinum-haired woman who had to be Docia's mother. Considering the way the two of them muttered at each other all night long, she and Deirdre's father were obviously sister and brother. Pete and Janie sat with Lars and Jess. They hadn't brought any of the kids, but Tom could see it happening sometime in the future. Kids running around the beer garden while the band played had a nice feel to it. Maybe they could put in a sandbox in the corner.

Around nine, Erik Toleffson walked in with Morgan. Even out of uniform, he looked like a cop. Probably a real advantage in his line of work, although it did put a damper on a table of college kids down from Austin. Tom had already checked their IDs, but they still looked faintly nervous when Erik glanced their way.

Deirdre was working, although he'd told her to take the night off so that she could sit with her family. She'd ignored him quite pointedly. Every once in a while, he'd catch her father watching her, looking totally confused. Tom didn't blame him. He found himself feeling the same way a lot around Deirdre these days.

Once Bonner started to play, almost everybody moved outside, so he and Chico transferred the remaining tables to the edge of the garden, while Harry served beer and mixed drinks at the outside bar.

Although calling it a bar was a stretch, given that it lacked everything most bars had, including a sink. He planned to call around about repairs on Monday, but Deirdre told him not to worry about it because the new bar would be even better than the old one. He'd asked her what she meant exactly, but she just shook her head and went back to grabbing beers out of the washtub. Tom figured he'd find out in time—he frequently seemed to be the last one to find stuff out these days. Right now he just enjoyed the view.

The Toleffsons were dancing around the edge of the bricked area on the far side of the garden. They took up a lot of room, but they seemed to be having a great time. Deirdre's father had apparently invited his sister to dance at one point, but she'd given him a look that would have turned a lesser man to stone.

Deirdre dodged around them all, delivering beers and margaritas. Her father said something and she tossed him a look that was very similar to the one her aunt had given him earlier. Tom wondered how long they'd keep the man in the doghouse—not that he really cared.

Around eleven, the band swung into a tune that sounded vaguely familiar. Deirdre appeared in front of him, dropping her tray on the bar. "C'mon," she said. "Dance with me."

Tom wondered for a moment what he would have said a few weeks ago if she'd made a similar demand. Probably *Not right now*. But then again, maybe not. Maybe he'd always been ready to dance with her, from the first time he'd seen her in the doorway, with her terrible clothes and her absolute determination. He tossed his towel on the bar and took her into his arms.

Behind them the band swung into a slow waltz that he now recognized as "Midnight on the Water", one of Bonner's specialties. It wasn't the kind of tune you usually did any crotch grinding to, but Tom didn't mind. He rested his cheek against Deirdre's hair, moving her slowly around the area beside the bar.

"I have a question," he said finally.

"Mmmm?" She didn't bother to open her eyes.

"If Dempsey had won the card game, would you have gone back to Houston?"

She opened her eyes a fraction, studying him. "Of course."

Tom's chest clenched tight again.

"But then I would have turned around the next day and come back. After I'd read my father the riot act."

Tom grimaced. "Thanks for just taking another five years off my life expectancy."

She grinned up at him. "I do need to go off to Houston for a few days over the next couple of weeks to save my father's behind, but no way am I staying anywhere but here. After all,

I've got a coffee roaster to open. And drinks to serve. And dinners to plan. We are going to have a dinner menu aren't we? Clem's raring to go."

Tom gave her another quick turn around their corner of the garden. Things seemed to be happening very fast. Not that it bothered him all that much. Now that he'd given up being the Lone Ranger. "A dinner menu sounds like a plan."

"And wine. We need to talk to Morgan. Maybe we can work a deal with Cedar Creek Winery to feature their varietals. Only they're sort of expensive, so we may need to bring in some others, too. There's a Wine and Food Festival in October so we can do some comparison shopping."

"Right." Tom detoured around a couple of senior citizens who were doing a pretty good job of whirling around the picnic tables.

Deirdre put her hands on his shoulders, smiling. "Face it, ace, you're stuck with me. I'm not leaving. I'm in it for the long haul."

Tom slid his arms around her waist, pulling her close. "I wouldn't have it any other way, believe me. You're mine, Dee-Dee. As long as you want to be."

"I want to be yours. I just don't want to be Dee-Dee."

"Okay, Deirdre," he took a deep breath. *Go for it.* "I love you. How's that?"

Her smile lit up the garden. "Perfect. And convenient since I love you too."

Behind him he heard some raucous shouts from the general direction of the Toleffsons. They might have been directed at him and Deirdre, but maybe not. He didn't bother to find out. He spun her around one more time, reveling in the warm night air, the rapidly improving band, and the sweet smell of beer from his very own bar. He shifted her slightly closer to his body, closing his eyes as he touched his cheek to her hair. She smelled even sweeter.

"I think you've got yourself a bartender, ma'am. Pretty much permanently."

"Good." She smiled up into his eyes. "Now let's dance."

About the Author

Meg Benjamin is the author of the Konigsburg series for Samhain Publishing: *Venus In Blue Jeans, Wedding Bell Blues, Be My Baby, Long Time Gone,* and now *Brand New Me.* Meg lives in Colorado with her DH and two rather large Maine coon kitties (well, partly Maine coon anyway). Her Web site is www.MegBenjamin.com. You can follow her on Facebook (www.facebook.com/meg.benjamin1), and Twitter (http://twitter.com/megbenj1). Meg loves to hear from readers—contact her at meg@megbenjamin.com.

GREAT
CHEAP
FUN

Discover eBooks!